THE END OF THE LINE

THE END
OF THE LINE

Nigel Tranter

Hodder & Stoughton

First published in Great Britain in 2000 by
Hodder and Stoughton
A division of Hodder Headline

10 9 8 7 6 5 4 3 2 1

British Library Cataloguing in Publication Data

Tranter, Nigel, 1909–
The End of the Line
1. Historical fiction
I.Title
823.9'12 [F]

ISBN 0 340 73927 4

Typeset by Hewer Text Ltd, Edinburgh
Printed and bound in Great Britain by
Clays Ltd, St Ives plc

Hodder and Stoughton
A division of Hodder Headline
338 Euston Road
London NW1 3BH

Principal Characters in order of appearance

George, 10th Earl of Dunbar and March: The Cospatrick. Great Scots noble.

George, Master of Dunbar: Eldest son and heir of above.

Gavin Dunbar: Second son.

David Dunbar: Youngest son.

Patrick Dunbar: Fourth son.

Elizabeth Dunbar: Elder daughter.

Robert the Third, King of Scots: Son of Robert the Second. Christened John.

Robert Stewart, Earl of Fife: Younger brother of the king. Later Duke of Albany.

Archibald Douglas, Earl: Known as the Grim. Son of the Good Sir James.

John, Earl of Moray: Younger brother of Dunbar and March.

Alexander Stewart, Earl of Buchan: Younger brother of the king. The Wolf.

George Douglas, Earl of Angus: Red Douglas chief.

Earl of Nottingham, Earl Marshal of England: Great English noble.

Alicia Hay: Daughter of Sir William Hay of Yester, Sheriff of Peebles-shire.

Beatrix Hay: Sister of above.

James Douglas, Lord of Dalkeith: A Black Douglas lord.

Richard Plantagenet, King of England: Son of the Black Prince.

Henry Plantagenet, Earl of Hereford: Later King Henry the Fourth (Bolingbroke).

Queen Annabella Drummond: Wife of Robert the Third.

David Stewart, Duke of Rothesay: Son and heir of Robert the Third.

Henry Percy, Earl of Northumberland: Known as Hotspur.

Donald, Lord of the Isles: Powerful chief of the Highland and Hebridean West.

Sir Alexander Stewart: Illegitimate son of Buchan. Later Earl of Mar.

James, King of Scots: Second son of Robert the Third.

Murdoch Stewart, Earl of Fife: Son of Albany.

John Stewart, Earl of Buchan: Second son of Albany. Successful commander.

Archibald, Fifth Earl of Douglas: Powerful noble. Duke of Touraine in France.

Humphrey Plantagenet, Duke of Gloucester: Guardian of infant King Henry Sixth.

Archibald, Sixth Earl of Douglas: Formerly Earl of Wigtown.

Bishop Henry Wardlaw of St Andrews: Primate of Scottish Church.

Lady Joan Beaufort: Queen of James the First. Niece of Cardinal Beaufort.

Walter Stewart, Earl of Atholl: Brother of Albany.

Alexander, Lord of the Isles: Son of the late Donald.

Erik: King of Denmark, Norway and Sweden.

Part One

1

The Cospatrick, tenth Earl of Dunbar and March, eyed his sons, all six of them, and shook his head.

"It was beyond belief, evil!" he said. "Stabbed in the back. At his neck. And by his own armour-bearer, that Bickerton. Douglas slain, while leading into battle. The wretch knew that helmet and back-armour were not fully laced up. Drove a dagger in, from behind, as they advanced. The Earl of Douglas dead!"

His sons stared at him and at each other. All knew of James, Earl of Douglas, the most powerful noble in the land, almost more powerful than their feeble monarch Robert the Second, commander of his army – moreover the brother-in-law of their father, Married to their Aunt Margaret, who had died. And now, killed by his own servant!

"Bickerton?" the eldest brother asked, another George, Master of Dunbar and March. "Is not that the name of the laird of Luffness? But ten miles from here?"

"Aye. But not laird. Son of the keeper of Luffness Castle for Lindsay of Crawford. Why Douglas had him for armour-bearer, God knows! Not one of his own Douglases. And why he did it, none can tell. As yet. Some grudge, perhaps . . ."

"So the battle? It was . . . lost?" Gavin demanded.

"No, no. I, and your Uncle John of Moray, and others, saw to that. Indeed Douglas himself! For he told those on either side of him to hold him up, keep on leading him onward and shouting, 'A Douglas! A Douglas!' He said that he was a dead man, knew it, but to go on and win the battle, in his name. I was leading the left wing, your uncle

3

the right. We did not see all this, knew nothing of it until victory was won. Won, as they are now declaring, by a dead man!"

"And did they slay this armour-bearer?" David wondered. "Cut him down?"

"No. He got away. It was darkness, see you. Douglas had challenged Hotspur Percy to fight, at Newcastle. We all had. The Percy refused. But that night he pursued our army, on our way back to Scotland. We were camped at this Otterburn, in Redesdale, none so far from the border, when he struck, in darkness. A foul stroke, to be sure. And he calls himself Hotspur! Roused from sleep, we rallied as best we could. That was why Douglas's armour had not been laced up rightly, but he did not know it. But Bickerton knew it – only he could have known. He struck. And when all was over, he was gone, fled."

"How was the battle won, then?" George asked. At nineteen, he was the eldest, and well versed in arms; indeed he had wanted to be taken on this expedition to punish the Percy, against whom his family bore enmity, but his father had refused him, saying that his time would come, and that he should hold Dunbar Castle until he himself returned – just in case he did not.

"A battle, fought in darkness!" Patrick said. "And you all unready!"

"The darkness probably confused Percy as much as it did us. His people certainly lacked control, and scattered. We, at least, were all in one place, our encampment, asleep. In the confusion, your uncle and I led our two wings round behind the enemy, while Douglas himself took the centre. We were able to win the day – or, at least, the night! Percy was captured, with many others. But . . . Douglas dead!"

"I wish that I had been there!" George declared. His brothers added their agreement, although David and John, twins, were only fifteen years.

"As well that you were not. Otterburn was no victory to celebrate!"

"But you have ousted Percy of Northumberland,"

Gavin pointed out. "Will Northumberland now be ours again?"

"That remains to be seen. Percy's person could not be denied to a Douglas. My goodbrother, Dalkeith, took him, to hand over to the new earl. He is close to Robert of Fife and Menteith, who rules the land. And Fife does not love us Cospatricks!"

"Was he not with you on this venture? With the other princes, his kin?"

"He was. But he chose to go off westwards. To assail Northumberland from that side, from Cumberland. So he and his force were not at the battle at Otterburn."

"But Northumberland *should* be ours," George insisted. "Are we not really Earls of Northumbria, as well as of Dunbar and March?"

"That is an old story. Northumberland is now part of England again. Even though we now hold Percy, who calls himself earl thereof. I fear that is a cause we are unlikely to win."

They were in the main keep of Dunbar Castle, at the far eastern tip of Lothian, that extraordinary fortalice on its series of rock-stacks rising out of the waves of the Norse Sea, the separate towers thereof linked by covered bridges, the gap below the outermost one having a sort of great gate, or portcullis, which could be lowered to block the only entrance to Dunbar harbour, an age-old device which enabled its lords to prevent fishing-boats and other craft from leaving or entering the haven, and so to ensure that a tithe or other proportion of the fish caught by the fisher-folk was duly paid. This useful supply did not prevent the young members of the earl's family doing their own fish-ing, this from the parapet-walk of that outer tower, a favorite recreation, flounders in especial the catch from the sandy shallows, the hoisting of the flapping fish safely up the hundred or so feet from the water one of the challenges of the sport.

The earl's two daughters, Elizabeth and Janet, came to join them, aged eighteen and sixteen, both good-looking, bringing hot pancakes and honey wine, much favoured by the brothers, if somewhat less so by their father, and the talk changed to more domestic matters and local happenings, problems and gossip that had occurred while the father was absent, with young George acting the Master in some measure, not always to his brothers' expressed esteem. There had been some trouble with sheep-stealing in the Lammermuir Hills, this the major source of the family's wealth, with some of the tenants and shepherds gone in the earl's armed contingent. Also disputes about salmon fishing and netting on the River Tyne. More serious had been talk of a clash, in the Merse, between Homes and Swintons, in which George had not felt competent to intervene, lairds being involved. His father, who was Warden of the East March and High Sheriff, as well as earl, declared that he would deal with that. Those Homes! Far back they were of the same stock as the Cospatricks, and they tended to trade on it, sometimes to the resentment of their neighbours.

But first Earl George must go to Stirling to see King Robert, or more specifically the Earl of Fife who was really ruling Scotland for his father, now infirm and in his seventy-third year; this to inform as to the Otterburn affray and its consequences, and to make representations anent Hotspur Percy and others captured there, whose ransoms would be of considerable value, and which the new Douglas should not be allowed to monopolise; after all, it was he, Cospatrick, who had done the capturing with his brother Moray. The Cospatrick style must be upheld in the land, its importance recognised always.

The name of Cospatrick was significant, unique indeed. It was not a surname for the Dunbar and March family: they had no surname. That had to be emphasised. For the ancient Celtic royal house had nothing such, even though the present royal line called themselves Stewarts, descending from the High Stewards of Scotland, senior officials but not royal, one of whom had married the Bruce's daughter Marjory and produced this Robert the Second, the present monarch and Fife's father. But the Cospatricks adopted the style, not name, to indicate that they were royal where the Stewarts were not – Comes Patrick, the son of the Earl Maldred of Northumbria.

It all had come about thus, as the six sons were never allowed to forget. Malcolm the Third, King of Scots, Canmore or Big Head as he was called, had married Ingebiorg, daughter of the Earl of Orkney, and had two sons by her, Maldred and Waldeve, this before ever he met Margaret, the sister of Edgar Atheling, who should have been King of England had not William the Norman, the Conqueror, displaced him. Shipwrecked on the Scots coast, Margaret was captured by King Malcolm, and he was overcome by her beauty. So he got rid of his Queen Ingebiorg, "not without suspicion of poison", and married Margaret, *Saint* Margaret as she became. And three of her sons by Malcolm succeeded as Kings of Scots: Alexander, Edgar and David. The two older princes, disinherited, were disposed of, Maldred being given the earldom of Northumbria and Waldeve Cumbria, these two counties having been handed over to Scotland by the usurper, King Stephen of England, in order to prevent invasion from the north while fighting with his own nobles. The eldest son of Malcolm, Maldred, dying soon after, *his* son Patrick succeeded him and became known as Comes or Earl Patrick, the first Cospatrick. Waldeve of Cumbria died without issue.

The English got the two earldoms back again in due course, and King David, the youngest of the Margaret-sons, a monarch with a conscience, sought to compensate his nephew, the Earl of Northumbria, Cospatrick, by giving him the large lands of much of Lothian and the Merse or Berwickshire, and creating him Earl of Dunbar and March. The present earl was twelfth of that line from Maldred mac Malcolm, and if he had his rights, should have been on the Scots throne. It made a strange and intriguing story, intriguing in more ways than one.

Next day the earl departed for Stirling. Leaving his

younger brothers to their fishing, George, with Gavin and Colin, set off for Colbrandspath, ten miles to the south, a village with a small castle nearby, this always given to the eldest son and heir to the earldom as his heritage and seigniory, where, when he came of age and married, he could live, this on the edge of the Merse. George was very fond as well as proud of it, for it was attractively and strongly situated above a deep and steep ravine quite close to a splendid sandy beach at Pease Bay, good for swimming and horse-racing and netting salmon. Moreover it had strategic importance, which the brothers liked to dwell upon, for this ravine led into another and greater one, Pease Dean, along the narrow floor of which ran the main road to Berwick-upon-Tweed and England, and on which invading English forces were apt to come, here where the Lammermuir Hills came down to the sea and made travel difficult. Here such could be ambushed, while spread out necessarily in a lengthy line, and conquered by a much smaller company, this a source of interest and discussion by martially minded young men.

Not concerning themselves with the village, further inland in a cleft of the hills the brothers reached the red-stone tower within its courtyard, to speak with its elderly keeper and his wife, Jock and Phemie Dunbar, the man calling himself that because of far-back illegitimate descent from one of the Cospatricks. Phemie always made much of the youngsters, and ever seemed to have a stock of good things to eat and drink.

Then they went down to the beach at the bay, where there was more than half a mile of firm sand where they could race their horses with much rivalry and challenge, this beside the white-crested Norse Sea rollers, sometimes splashing in the shallows, each seeking to soak the others with the upflung spray from pounding hooves. It was late August, and warm, so soon they dismounted, to throw off their clothes and go running into the said waves, with shouts and duckings and divings, back to being boys again, since there was nobody to watch them, and lordly dignity did not have to be considered. Then they swam, and far out, with more racing and horseplay, before returning to lie naked on the warm sand in the sun, while their mounts cropped the marram grass.

Back at Coldbrandspath Tower, they were fed in typical fashion, and helped Jock Dunbar gut salmon he had netted in the bay to smoke in his kiln. Then they headed for home in a more round-about route, inland through the hills, by the secluded, all but hidden village of Oldhamstocks, where they called on one of their chief shepherds, who had reported the sheep-stealing, and on up the network of little valleys between the heights of Wedderlaw and Cocklaw and Blackcastle, to Elmscleuch, to reach the Brunt and another senior shepherd, all the slopes and moorland on the way well sheep-dotted, this of sheep and wool being so important for them. These master-shepherds, of course, had grumbled at the earl's taking away of some of their assistants on his sally into Northumberland to add to his contribution to the force; but now they had their men back again, and the stealing ought to stop. It was the low-country folk who were responsible, of course, from places like Houndwood and Reston and Ayton, the thefts on a fairly small scale, to provide mutton for the pot and to be salted and smoked for the winter. But it was not to be permitted. If one or two of the rascals could be caught and made an example of, it would probably stop it. Some lairds hanged such offenders for sheep-stealing. Did the Master not have the power of pit and gallows for his barony of Colbrandspath?

George thought that hanging was a morsel much for stealing the odd sheep, but agreed that some punishment was advisable. But catching the transgressors would not be easy. He would have to get reliable local folk to keep their eyes and ears open. Any smoking of mutton in low-country communities ought to be fairly kenspeckle to watchers. He would see to this.

After that, with evening coming on them, it was due north round the Doon Hill, where English Edward Plantagenet, Hammer of the Scots, had won that dire Battle of Dunbar in 1296, on to the village of Spott and the low ground beyond, this only three miles from Dunbar.

They wondered how their father was getting on at Stirling, where he ought to have arrived by now. It was unfortunate for the realm that their king should be so infirm and all but useless. And his eldest son John, Earl of Carrick, was a feeble creature and would not make a good monarch, all asserted. But Carrick had a lively and worthy son, David, who presumably would one day become David the Second. As far as the brothers were concerned, the sooner the better.

2

Interesting word came a few days later from none so far off. Bickerton, the slayer of the Earl of Douglas, had himself been slain. It seemed that he had returned from Otterburn to Luffness Castle where his father was keeper, and there hid himself. It was a strong place, and not to be entered by vengeance-seekers. But sundry Douglas supporters had arrived to keep watch on the hold, and waited. And when, after days had elapsed, the wretched man had considered himself to be safe and had ventured out, they had pounced. So that debt was paid, as far as could be.

It was a week thereafter that the earl arrived back at Dunbar, and he too brought significant tidings, both good and less so, and only one item at least of great concern for the family, this most remarkable – although Elizabeth was not so sure. It was that her father had come to an agreement with John, Earl of Carrick, with the King's concurrence, that David his son, Earl Palatine of Strathearn, should wed Elizabeth.

This was a great surprise to them all, for nothing had been said about such suggestion previously. And of course it did mean that, one day, all being well, their sister would be Queen of Scotland, bringing the Cospatrick line into royal status once more.

Elizabeth's reaction was doubting. She had known, to be sure, that eventually she would have to marry somebody chosen for her by her father; great lords' daughters seldom had much choice as to husbands. And the word was that this David was a young man of spirit, unlike father and grandfather, and, according to the earl, quite handsome. But she would reserve judgment until she saw him.

Their father admitted that he had had to promise a very substantial dowery, in lands and moneys, to clinch the matter. A formal betrothal would follow in due course.

Less dramatic for the family, but still important, was that the earl, already Warden of the East March, was now promoted to be Chief Warden of all three Marches, a position of great authority. But it did mean that he would have to be absent from Dunbar much, and for quite lengthy periods on occasion, for the borderline stretched for no less than one hundred and ten miles, and the occupants of these parts were among the most turbulent and troublesome of both kingdoms, those of the West March in particular; so much so that the principal seat of the Chief Warden had to be at Hermitage Castle in Liddesdale, almost ninety miles from Dunbar, where the earl would have to be in residence not infrequently. It looked as though son George, the Master, would have to be much more responsible for the affairs and good governance of Dunbar and the Merse than heretofore – not that this upset him.

Another surprising development, which admittedly did not greatly affect the Cospatricks, was the succession to the earldom of Douglas. The victim at Otterburn had had only the one son, who had died in infancy; and it had been assumed that the third earl would be George Douglas, already Earl of Angus through marriage, a younger brother, who had been present at Otterburn. He was a friend of the Cospatricks, his seat being only some ten miles off, at Tantallon Castle near to North Berwick. But no, the king, at the Earl of Fife's urging, had declared otherwise, presumably because it might put too much power into Angus's hands, controlling two great earldoms and all the major Douglas strength. Instead he had appointed the Douglas Lord of Galloway, known as Archibald the Grim, a notable character, becoming elderly now, an illegitimate son of the famous Good Sir James Douglas, the Bruce's great friend, who had taken the royal heart on crusade. It was an unexpected choice. No doubt Fife had had his reasons for so deciding. It would considerably concern James Douglas, Lord of Dalkeith, who could have been in line for it, after Angus, and who had married the late Agnes of Dunbar, sister and aunt of them all.

The family gathered from their father that he had had words with Robert of Fife at Stirling, although he did not give details nor dwell on it. Yet he had been made Chief Warden. They wondered why? Could it have something to do with this Douglas earldom, he known to have close links with those passed over? To help to keep him busy, and afar off?

There was much talk and concern in the family, especially about this proposed marriage of Elizabeth, however it might be worthy as regard to the royal connection. Their mother, the Countess Christian, had died some years previously, and her elder daughter, however youthful, had, as it were, taken on the role of mistress of the household, and had been quite effective as such, the servants all doing her bidding happily. Now, it seemed, they were going to lose her; and Janet, younger and much less mature, could be none so effective a replacement. Also, the thought of this of marriage itself among them, so far scarcely considered, raised recognition that they had now reached the stage in life when such was something to be contemplated, however theoretically, especially for George of course, the eldest. What would it be like to be married? He had had his youthful sallies, and tentative ventures with local girls in the town and elsewhere, needless to say, but these had been of no real involvement – they could not be, he the Master of Dunbar. Now he began to think of perhaps more suitable possibilities and liaisons, this especially in his bed of a night before sleeping. Of one thing he was determined however: he must not let his father seek to arrange some such alliance for him, as he had done for Elizabeth. When it came to a marriage, he was going to choose his own bride.

As time passed, the earl, however, had other plans for his son and heir than nuptial ones. Now that he was Chief

Warden of all the Marches, with its greatly increased responsibilities, it seemed wise to relinquish his wardenship of the East March. And since so much of that area was covered by his own lands of the Merse, the obvious replacement was his eldest son, much as others might covet the position, one of those Homes in especial. Such would be a recipe for trouble. So he decided that, on his preliminary survey of his commitments, he would take George with him, to gain some perception of what being a warden entailed and meant.

George was nothing loth.

They duly set out, a week later. They would go due south first, and ride the length of this East March and its environs, from near Berwick-upon-Tweed almost to Kelso, to let George see its extent and some of the problems involved, before continuing westwards. And problems there were, here as elsewhere. Why was it that the borderers always seemed to be the most unruly of folk?

The pair of them, with only two men as escort, went down past Colbrandspath, and at that tower swung left to climb up past Aldcambus, the site of one of the battles of the Wars of Independence, on to Coldinghame Muir, this in order to have a look at Faux or Fast Castle, so named because of the falsity of its reputation, a Home place specialising in luring shipping on to the rocky coast below to become wrecks and provide booty for the wreckers. They reached its dramatic situation, perched on a projection of rock halfway down a high and sheer precipice of that cliff-girt coast, attainable only by a difficult, narrow, steep track, where they had to dismount and lead their alarmed horses, eventual access gained by a drawbridge over a yawning gap, this always raised. Their shouts in time brought a surly keeper to the gatehouse parapet opposite, who announced disrespectfully that the laird was not there meantime, and who then disappeared. The drawbridge was not lowered for them. As they turned to climb back whence they had so awkwardly come, Georges father told him that although this was a fairly

14

extreme example of difficult dealings, it did serve as an indication of attitudes.

They rode on over the lofty moorland, past Lumsdaine, seat of a lesser family, and Cairncross, another such, but did not halt there, and came to Coldinghame itself, seat of an ancient monastic establishment and priory, the priors of which were always Homes, even though Holy Church might seek to appoint others. They did not linger here either but went on seawards to St Abbs haven, where the cliffs offered a brief remission, and a fishing community clustered, this apt to be in a state of war with Eyemouth further south over netting and lobster rights below the intervening and resumed cliffs. Frequent judicial decisions had to be made arising out of this hostility, like others.

George was learning fast.

Eyemouth itself was the next call, a place with a large harbour, of considerable value to the widespread family or clan of Home, the earl reminding his son that there were well over a score of Home lairdships in the Merse, which they all but looked upon as their own domain, despite the Dunbar overlordship.

It was no part of the father's present excursion to make his authority evident in these parts, merely to acquaint his heir of some of the problems and questions he would be faced with. So there were no confrontations meantime.

They had come some thirty miles now, in round-about fashion, and were none so far from Berwick-upon-Tweed. The earl thought that Aytoun Castle would be as good a place as any to spend the night, rather than back at Coldinghame Priory, a Home hold but its owner elderly and reclusive. He would not be unhelpful towards his overlord.

They passed a reasonably comfortable and trouble-free night.

In the morning they continued southwards, to Foulden and Paxton, more Home houses and communities, with George enquiring how these had managed to gain so many lairdships in the Merse. He learned that one of the early

Cospatricks, himself a sick man, had used a younger son, who had married the Home of Home heiress, to act as his deputy all along the March, and rewarded his excellent services thus, their properties reaching as far west as Cowdenknowes in Lauderdale, this over into the Middle March, a source of further problems inevitably. Now, with the earl Chief Warden, this at least would be less troublesome.

All that day George was made aware of the responsibilities that he was to take on, with enmities and unending disputes between Swintons and Hepburns, Heitons and Borthwicks, Logans and Cairncrosses, as well as Homes – not to mention English incomes from over the border, ill-defined as it was. It seemed that no very serious oversight was demanded, nor indeed possible, so long as the squabbling and rivalry did not enlarge into outright battle and organised raiding. It all represented, his father declared, little compared with the *West* March situation.

They had a word with Home of that Ilk at Home Castle on its ridge in mid-Merse, the present chief a young man, himself unsure of his hold over his clan, and quite glad of the earl's and his son's authority.

They moved on to the more comfortable and non-controversial monkish quarters of Kelso Abbey for the second night.

They were well into the Middle March here, and so George could feel less concerned. Now it was Kerrs, the two branches of that clan, Elliots, Turnbulls and Douglases who had to be, not kept in order, for that was not possible, but shown that they were being watched, and the overall peace kept, such minor offences as reiving, cattle-stealing, women-lifting and the like having to be ignored. They visited the tower of Smailholm above its loch, and the castles of Floors, Ferniehirst, Cessford, Minto and Cavers, before preferring to return to the abbey of Jedburgh for their third night, the earl pointing out that the monks almost always provided the best accommodation.

The next stage was past the township of Hawick to

Branxholm of the Scotts; and thereafter the earl began to look more grim. They had now to climb up to Teviothead and thereafter enter into the West March, where the Chief Warden's headaches reputedly would begin. The dales to the east, Tweed, Teviot, Ettrick, Ewes, Lauder and the rest, were comparatively accessible, and open to some degree of oversight; but ahead it was different: wild, high and broken country, great lofty ranges and all but impenetrable marshland and bog separating Liddesdale, Eskdale, Wauchopedale, Dryfesdale, Nithsdale and Annandale, where the Armstrong and Johnstones, the Maxwells and Herries, the Grahams and the Irvines, Jardines and Telfers, fought and slew, raped and ravaged, acknowledging little or no authority other than lance and sword; and as well as these, the Croziers and Robsons, the Musgraves and Dacres, the Charltons and Nixons, from across the uncertain borderline, were equally ungovernable. So uncertain was that line between the two nations that quite a substantial stretch, from Gretna at the Solway Firth mouth of the River Sark, north almost to Langholm in Eskdale and east to include much of Liddesdale, was known as the Debateable Land, some forty square miles, although the vagueness of the outline and ever changing conditions could increase it up to fifty. Some of it was quite fair country, fertile and good grazing, although most was hill and valley. No houses, nor even a shed or hut, was to be built on it; beasts could be grazed by day but not by night, so that there could be no permanent occupation, however raiding parties might traverse it.

The earl had no intention of trying to tame this wild territory, he assured his son.

Their first priority was to visit Hermitage Castle, the Chief Warden's base. This stood proudly, remote in a side glen of upper Liddesdale, some ten miles from Teviothead, at the very southern tail-end of the Cheviot Hills. They came to it in late afternoon, to find it a massive strength, built a century before by a de Soulis of grim memory. It was of oblong shape, with a huge and high

17

main block having square towers projecting at the four corners, tall archways on the east and west sides, and with a *bretasche* or open timber gallery projecting round the entire building at third-floor level, this for improved defence. Eyeing it on its raised platform of ground above the junction of a smaller burn with the Hermitage Water, so that it could not be attacked from three sides, with deep ditches all round, the visitors got the impression that it looked more as if built to withstand siege than as any station for the administration of a great area.

Their approach not going unnoticed, they were hailed from that wooden gallery with haughty demands as to who came thus unannounced to Hermitage of the Knight of Liddesdale? It was shouted back by one of their escort that it was the Earl of Dunbar and March, and the Master thereof, his lordship now Chief Warden of all the Marches. This was greeted with silence. But presently a clanking indicated the lowering of the drawbridge over one of the ditches, and a group of armed men came out, led by a wary-eyed individual who announced himself as Sir William Douglas, owner of this hold. This was another strange feature of Hermitage, for although it was designated as the base of the Chief Warden, it was actually the property of the Douglases, having been given to that family by a grateful Bruce.

However, at the earl's and son's dismounting and quite friendly greeting and offered handshake, the other's stiff attitude thawed, and he showed a fair but by no means overawed welcome. He said that he had heard that his lordship had been appointed to the office, and would offer him the hospitality of his house, and might hope to aid him in the performance of his duties in the March.

So far, so good. They crossed the drawbridge and passed through one of the lofty arches to enter an open quadrangle of paved courtyard, unusual in such fortalices, where horses could be stabled and stores kept, instead of outside in subsidiary buildings.

They got on well enough with Sir William. He declared

18

that Sir Robert Maxwell of Caerlaverock, the West March Warden, would of course give his lordship the best advice; but he had his knife into the Armstrongs, and also the Johnstones, tending to play one off against the other, these themselves age-old foes, which did not make for peace. It appeared that there were almost as many Armstrong laird-ships, if that they could be called, as there were Homes at the other end of the borderline, and they were the principal source of trouble. But they did quarrel among themselves, which could be something of a blessing. They more or less between them controlled lower Liddesdale, as the John-stones did mid-Annandale, and the Maxwells Nithsdale. The other clans could be a nuisance, but it was these three that dominated. As Warden, Douglas asserted, Maxwell was prejudiced.

Digesting all this, it was decided that the visitors' first priority was to go and see this Robert Maxwell.

Next morning they were off south-westwards on a quite lengthy ride, not far off sixty miles, first over the flank of Roan Fell to Langholm in Eskdale, then the score of miles over more hills to Lockerbie in Annandale, and on another ten to Dumfries to speak with the provost there, this the largest town of the March. The earl showed George the greyfriars chapel where Bruce had slain the treacherous Red Comyn. Then another eight miles eastwards now to Caerlaverock Castle, the Maxwell seat.

This was a mighty place, very different from Hermitage however, V-shaped, wide water-filled moats, fed from various little lochs and marshes around, protecting its three sides, tall towers at the angles. Edward of England had assailed it with three thousand men, it defended by only sixty before it yielded after siege, and much of it was later pulled down on Bruce's orders when he pursued the policy of destroying all castles to prevent their use by the invaders. It was handed over to the Maxwells by Bruce in token of appreciation of their support, and restored. That family actually came from the East March, on Tweedside, but in time became very much West Marchmen.

Sir Robert did not pretend to be glad to see the new Chief Warden; possibly he had hoped to fill the position himself. But he could not refuse hospitality, and his wife proved to be more friendly. The husband became a little more forthcoming when the earl indicated his surprise at Archibald the Grim becoming the new Earl of Douglas, for it seemed that Maxwell and that man, lord of Galloway nearby, did not get on. Maxwell gave many indications as to why, and seemed to have reasons for his hostility. But now that Archibald had greatly additional responsibilities and influence elsewhere, and probably would see much less of his Galloway, so the situation might well improve.

This attitude effected better relations with his unexpected visitors, and he became prepared to discuss the situation under his wardenship, making it clear that the Armstrongs were very much the main source of difficulties, although the Johnstones were not helpful, as had been indicated at Hermitage. It seemed that there were two main stems of the clan, Gilnockie and Mangerton, both equally unruly. They fought among themselves – but would always unite if attacked by others. Their depredations all along the March, and over it, were notorious, and they were quite out of hand. He, Maxwell, like his predecessors, had more or less given up trying to tame them, and restricted himself to seeking to prevent their activities from spreading into Annandale and Nithsdale and this Sark area. In this last at least he could rely on the co-operation of the English West March Warden, Scrope, who was equally concerned that the troubles did not spread hereabouts into his own territory.

Maxwell advised that the new Chief Warden should adopt the same policy.

The earl reserved judgment on that, but observed that he would wish to have a word or two with these Armstrong chiefs while he was here, which their host made clear might well be a waste of time.

So the following day it was north-eastwards for Liddesdale again, its lower reaches this time, to ford Annan at

Hoddam, another Maxwell stronghold, and so over to the Kirtle Water at Bonshaw, Irvine country here, to enter the Debateable Land well south of Langholm on the Esk. This was very much a country of rivers.

The Debateable Land, to be sure, was marked by no bounds, but was nevertheless very well known to the March riders, however vague it might seem to visitors. The Cospatricks recognised that they were in it only by Maxwell's directions. Well before they reached the River Sark they realised that they were being watched, by horsemen on a slight ridge beyond the empty pastureland; and presently they saw more, although it may have been the same trio, on another swelling of ground. Clearly they were being shadowed.

At the Sark they turned due northwards, to pass the community of Canonbie, its folk not offering allegiance to either Scotland nor England, where they were again observed warily. But they did not stop. And in a couple of miles, now in Eskdale, they came to Gilnockie.

Approaching the tower on its rise, they were met by perhaps a dozen horsemen, armed to the teeth, these led by a middle-aged man, handsome in a lean and hungry way, who challenged them, asking who came into Armstrong territory from Irvine and Maxwell land and why.

"I am Dunbar and March, Chief Warden here now. And here is the Master. Who are you?"

The other hooted. "On Gilnockie land, need you ask? March, you say? And Dunbar, was it? Which March? Not this one!"

"My earldom is the Merse, or *East* March. But I now warden all three. As you will find out, in due course. On the king's authority."

"How that? Which king?"

"Robert, of Scots. By the grace of God. Your liege-lord."

"I have no liege-lord, Robert nor Henry. I am Armstrong!"

"Your Liddesdale is in the kingdom of Scotland. We all

21

have a liegelord. I have. You have. Mangerton, Larriston and other Armstrongs have. As have Maxwell and Douglas and Johnstone. I advise you to remember it!'' The earl changed his tone. ''But, see you, here is no way to meet. I come with goodwill. That we may work together, for the weal of all, not for dispute. I but seek to introduce myself, as I have done at Hermitage and Caerlaverock. Why not Gilnockie?''

The other looked at his supporters, grinning. Then he shrugged. ''Goodwill is scarcely expected from wardens!'' he said.

''Then we shall make a new start at it, no? Do not say that you mislike goodwill? Even with a Chief Warden!''

''How good will that will be, then?''

''Sufficiently so to ensure that we can work together. Each respecting the other's . . . interests.''

''Ha! I can see to my own interests!''

''Can you? Does Johnstone of Annandale? And Maxwell? And the Englishman Scrope? And others – Dacres, Nixons, Croziers and the rest that I have heard tell of. Do their interests affect yours?'' He paused. ''And I can summon to my cause a thousand men, if need be. More. To aid in my task.''

That last had the Armstrong stroking his pointed beard. ''Goodwill can come dear, it seems!''

''It need not be. I seek it from you, sir.''

Again the shrug. But the other reined his horse around. ''Come, then. To my house yonder, Dunbar. I do not call you my lord, earl though you may be, for I have no lord. But I have wines and meats, to which you are welcome.''

''I thank you.''

They rode to the tower. It was scarcely a castle.

George ventured a word. ''How came you by the name of Armstrong, sir? Strong of arm! Was it always thus? And to be lived up to!''

''I understand that it came from France, with the Normans. Fortenbras was the name they brought, which means strong of arm. It is a good enough name for the like of myself!"

They could not complain of Gilnockie hospitality, at least, wife and two young sons shy but appearing eager to please. Indeed they were offered a substantial midday meal, but had to refuse it, saying that they must be on their way to Mangerton and possibly Larriston, to see the other Armstrong chief. Gilnockie himself remained civilly guarded, but there was no more verbal sword-crossing nor veiled threats. That man did make a face when he was asked the best route to Mangerton, saying that he wished his far-out kinsman no hurt from his callers nor any other, but . . . The rest was left unsaid.

It seemed that Mangerton was some ten miles to the north-east up Liddesdale and they had to go by Rowanburn to Penton, then up the Liddel Water by Harelaw Mill and Kershopefoot. On the way the travellers were again aware of being kept under survey before they were halfway to their destination. But this time no party came to meet them from the tower, larger than Gilnockie, beyond the ford over the river, this within a palisade enclosure and cluster of lesser buildings, quite a settlement indeed. Before they reached the entrance they had picked up a tail of followers, none looking friendly. And at the door of the tower itself, two stern-faced men awaited them enquiringly. The earl announced that he was the new Chief Warden, come from Gilnockie to see the laird. One of the pair turned to go within, the other remaining. There was no invitation to enter.

After quite a wait, an elderly individual appeared, to announce that he was Mangerton, and to ask if he had heard aright, that his callers were from the Warden of the March – for that was Maxwell, whom he knew all too well. The speaker then spat, eloquently.

"Not Sir Robert, the West March Warden, no. I am the Earl of Dunbar and March, the new Chief Warden, come to greet you."

Mangerton looked as though he were going to spit again, but thought better of it. "So?" he demanded.

23

"Do you not wish to see me? Coming in King Robert's royal name? This is my son, the Master."

"Why should I wish to see you, in that name, or other?"

"I would have thought that it would interest you. In order that you might know who wields chiefest authority hereabouts now!"

"*I* wield all necessary authority, sirrah!"

"Over whom? Your Armstrongs perhaps. But who else?"

"That is sufficient."

"I think not. Do you consider that His Grace's Chief Warden has no powers, Mangerton?"

"Not here. Nor in the Debateable Land, he has not. Maxwell has learned that."

"If the English invade would you not be glad of my powers?"

"The English!" The other spat again.

"I have come a long road to see you here. Does it mean nothing to you, Mangerton?"

The other answered that by turning away and re-entering his house, but with no hint of invitation to follow him. He left the two guards in the doorway.

Angrily the earl swung on his heel and strode back to his horse among the now quite large throng, George following. He had never seen his sire so livid. Almost he himself was afraid to speak.

Not waiting, the earl spurred away.

When he caught up, George soon realised that they were being followed, at some distance, this time by horsemen, perhaps a score of them.

The earl found words. "Never have I known the like! Insolence! Sheer, damnable insolence! That freebooting outlaw! Gilnockie was ill enough, at first. But this one is beyond all belief! Not even to have me in his wretched house – me, the Cospatrick!"

"Sir Robert Maxwell warned us as to these Armstrongs," George reminded. "They heed no man, even the king."

"They will heed *me*, before I am finished with them!" His father turned in his saddle to look back, beyond their two escorts, at the more distant attenders. "When next I come to Mangerton I will come in strength!"

George kept silent.

It was a good five miles before, at Harelaw Mill, the steel-bonneted riders behind turned to ride whence they had come, presumably this the end of Mangerton land. By that time his father had recovered most of his composure, although his jaw was still set.

"Where now?" George asked.

"I have had all but sufficient," his father declared. "But Johnstone I must see. Then home. Johnstone, I deem, will be something less ill than these Armstrongs, but his clan is not gentle either. They own Annandale, or much of it, a long vale. Maxwell, who does not love them, said that the chief's house is Lochhouse Tower, up near to Moffat, far up the dale. So, John Johnstone of that Ilk. It is a fair distance off, but on our way back to Dunbar. If we can win to Langholm town tonight, there is a monkish hospice there, I understand. A dozen miles . . ."

They made a fairly silent ride of it through those miles to the Esk.

The monks, as ever, treated them kindly, which helped to restore the earl to a more normal frame of mind.

Thereafter it was due west for them, a score of miles to Lockerbie in Annandale. They were in mixed Johnstone and Jardine country here, but a long way from the residence of the Johnstone chief. They called at Spedlins Tower, the Jardine seat, but he was elsewhere meantime. So it was onward, north now up the long Annan Water, George glad to feel that he was beginning to head homewards. The countryside was attractive, but he had had enough of its inhabitants.

Ten miles up they passed Johnstonebridge, a small community, but they were not in any way challenged here, and as they continued they did not feel themselves under any supervision; if they were, it was not obvious. Were

25

these Johnstones a better-behaved folk? The earl said that they had a bloody reputation, nevertheless.

At length, in late afternoon, with Moffat only a couple of miles ahead, they came to Lochhouse Tower, the name accounted for by not so much a loch as a succession of pools and ponds in reedy marshland, making an excellent defensive situation to be sure. The building was unusual in that, although a typical enough high square tower or keep, its angles were rounded, and it was erected on a massive basement course of masonry, no doubt to keep it from sinking into the soft boggy ground, all surrounded by the normal wide moat.

Their reception here was nowise dramatic nor hostile, although it was some time before they could gain entrance after they shouted their identity from beyond that moat, and the drawbridge was lowered for them. Within the gate-house, they were received by the Lady Johnstone, who seemed much flustered by their arrival, declaring that her husband was presently over at Moffat. He would be back for his evening meal, however. She had heard that his lordship was in the West March, word evidently getting around effectively. Would they be staying the night at Lochhouse?

The earl said that they would be able to find fair enough accommodation in Moffat town, the lady looking doubtful. She showed them to a bedchamber, however, and had hot water sent up for their washing, and wine to sustain them.

They did not have to wait long for Sir John's arrival, he proving to be a burly and florid man, who was a deal more certain of himself than was his wife. He declared straight away that he hoped that the new Chief Warden appointed would be sufficiently strong to keep the West Warden, Maxwell, in his place, which had not been the case for some time. This made a significant start.

The earl made careful reply, to the effect that he had come not to overrule or to supplant the warden here, but to inform himself of conditions, and to speak with those in positions of power in the March. Hence this visit.

Johnstone nodded, but declared that he would well inform his guests as to the said conditions. After eating, they would discuss the situation. Clearly they were expected to stay the night.

They ate well, in the midst of a large and noisy family, none save the lady of the house seeming in any way in awe of the visitors. Afterwards Sir John took them to a with-drawing-room, where, without any waste of time, he started on his complaints about Maxwell of Caerlaverock.

"He makes but an ill warden," he announced. "Does not keep the warring folk in order, especially the Armstrongs. Nor his own folk, indeed. But he troubles *mine*!"

"M'mm. And yours are always . . . law-abiding, Sir John?"

"By our border laws, the Leges Marchiarum, yes. I see to that."

"I am sure that you do. But those laws are, shall we say, open to differing reading and acceptance, no?"

"*We* understand them well enough. Even if Maxwell does not."

"The Johnstones and the Maxwells have been for long at feud, have they not? This may . . . colour your views on the warden."

The other did not answer.

"I have seen Sir Robert, and he knows *my* views. I have also seen the Armstrongs – at least, Gilnockie and Mangerton. Different folk, in especial the latter!"

"Aye. Murdering, thieving rogues! We suffer from them and their like."

"They do not trouble you up here? As far north as this, surely? A long way from lower Liddesdale."

"No-o-o. But they raid into lower down Annandale. My town of Lockerbie suffers. And Johnstonebridge."

"And your Johnstones raid back, I am told?"

"Only in justifiable return. According to our laws. Would you have me sit here and weep! When cattle and sheep are stolen, houses burned, women ravished? Johnstone does not accept the like." He pointed a finger at the

27

earl. "Maxwell should punish them. As warden. But does not. So I must."

His guest sighed. This was getting them nowhere. "What would you have me to do? Bring an army down here? That could well endanger you all, cost you dear. And what of the others? The lesser clans? Jardines, Irvines, Wauchopes, Grahams, Elliots, Beatties. What of them?"

Johnstone waved a dismissive hand. "They must look after themselves. They can be no saints either!"

George, listening, came to the conclusion that this West March might well be best left to stew in its own juice.

He gathered that his father was beginning to think the same way. "I will consider all that you have told me, Sir John," the earl said. "And seek to act accordingly." He straightened up in his chair and finished the wine in his goblet, indicating an end to discussion. "Now, of your kindness – bed. We have a long ride ahead of us tomorrow. Back through the Ettrick Forest to Tweed, and then up into the Merse for Lothian. We may win as far as Melrose Abbey for the night."

"To be sure. You bide far from the West March!" That was said significantly.

They eyed each other levelly as they rose from the table.

The Cospatrick pair made an early start next morning, after a carefully non-committal parting from Johnstone.

After some silent riding, George remarked, "He is different from the others. But little better, I think."

His father did not comment.

"I would not wish to be Chief Warden, one day. The East March will be enough for me!"

3

They arrived back at Dunbar Castle to find all in a state of great stir. The king, Robert the Second, had suddenly died, aged seventy-four and, aged and ineffective as he had been latterly, all but chaos ensued; this because his eldest son and heir, John, Earl of Carrick, was infirm, walking with a limp, and feeble, likely to make an incompetent monarch. And, of course, his royal father, however dilatory he had become latterly, had been sufficiently active in other ways earlier, and had left a great brood of offspring, legitimate and otherwise, five lawful sons and five lawful daughters, and so many bastards as to be scarcely countable. With a weakly successor on the throne, these princes and princesses, not to mention their half-brethren, would be struggling in rivalry to gain power and wealth undoubtedly, Fife, the second son, the most dominant.

A parliament was to be held to seek to order matters, as far as possible, and only a week hence, at Edinburgh, the normal forty days' notice dispensed with in these circumstances.

George Douglas, Earl of Angus, from Tantallon, had been twice at Dunbar, seeking the Cospatrick urgently.

The problems of the border Marches were to be left in abeyance meantime.

Deputing George to deal with any local affairs that had cropped up during their absence and which his brothers had not been competent to see to, the earl rode off next morning for Tantallon, to see Angus.

When he came back, he was looking grave. Angus, it seemed, was alarmed, and with reason. The word was that Robert of Fife and Archibald the Grim had, as it were, joined forces to seek to control the national situation; and a formidable pair they would make. It was Fife who had persuaded the late monarch to appoint Archibald the third Earl of Douglas instead of Angus, the previous earl's brother. If Fife could sway his own brothers to support him, with Douglas help, he would become the most powerful man the realm had seen for long. And he was as unscrupulous as he was ambitious. Scotland was in for testing times. This parliament would be a significant one indeed.

His father said that George ought to come with him to Edinburgh to watch the proceedings, which would be an education for him. The session was to be held, apparently, not in the rock-top castle as was usual, but in the Abbey of the Holy Rood; why was not explained.

Elizabeth suggested that she might accompany them to Edinburgh also. After all, the new king's son, David of Strathearn, to whom she was now betrothed, would be certain to be there, and she would wish at least to have sight of him. Her father declared that this was not the occasion for such meeting.

So once again, presently, earl and eldest son set off together on a very different excursion this time.

Reaching Edinburgh from the east, they rode through the royal parkland around the great soaring hill of Arthur's Seat, to approach Holyrood. And nearing the abbey they found a large encampment settled there, many pavilions and tents pitched, and all flying the blue and white colours, with the red Bruce heart, of Douglas, all but an army. Eyeing it, the earl looked tense. Douglas – and in force!

He was not the only one to view that host with concern and foreboding. What was it there for? To intimidate? Normally attenders at a parliament brought only a few supporters with them.

What had been the abbot's house had been taken over some time before and extended into a royal palace, so much more convenient and comfortable than the citadel up on its cliffs a mile away. It was thronged now with the great ones of the land, among whom George was glad to see his Uncle John of Moray, of whom he was fond, come down from his northern fastnesses, the second son of the famous grandmother, Black Agnes of Dunbar. The brothers were quickly into urgent consultation, joined presently by the Earl of Angus.

The parliament was to meet in the great hall of the palace, and George found himself consigned to the minstrels' gallery above, along with others, some of these ladies, who, a neighbour whispered to him, were princesses. An air of excitement prevailed.

The commissioners, as they were called, less the earls, were filing into their benches below: lords, county representatives, provosts of royal burghs and, slightly apart, bishops and mitred abbots, the Three Estates. There was a great buzz of talk.

Presently a trumpet blast silenced the chatter, and the Lord Lyon King of Arms emerged from a side door, with his heralds, to announce the entry of the earls. These entered in formal procession, to emphasise that they represented the *ri*, the ancient lesser kings of the original Celtic realm, who elected the Ard Righ or High King, the most suitable member of the royal line, to rule, a very wise and effective procedure which, unfortunately, had been long superseded by the father-and-eldest-son succession that now prevailed. George wondered, had this system been still in force, who the earls would have appointed to the throne today? Possibly even his own father, the Cospatrick.

There was a full turnout of earls, they saw, including the royal ones of Buchan and Caithness – but not, it was to be noted, Fife.

When these were seated, Cospatrick and his brother Moray among the first, the officers of state were ushered in, bearing the crown on a cushion, the sword of state and the sceptre. These went to stand at the back of the dais platform.

A pause, and the Chancellor, Bishop Peebles of Dunkeld, came in, to go to his table in front of the throne, where two clerks already stood with his papers.

A flourish of trumpets followed, and in limped a stooping figure, richly clad but old-seeming for his fifty-seven years: John Stewart, up till now Earl of Carrick, the new monarch. All stood as he shuffled uncertainly to the throne. Close behind him came Robert, Earl of Fife and Menteith, and a good-looking youth, smiling easily, so different from his father, David, Earl Palatine of Strathearn. He and his Uncle Robert went to stand on either side of the throne.

"God save the king!" the Lord Lyon called, and the cry was taken up by all present, even though somewhat less than fervently.

It was Fife who waved to the bowing Chancellor to proceed, not his elder brother.

"Your Grace, my lords temporal and spiritual and all commissioners," the bishop announced. "I, Chancellor of this realm, declare this parliament to be in session. We commence by greeting the King's Grace, who awaits his royal coronation in due course. We vow him all our leal support, goodwill and acclaim." And he turned and bowed again to the throne.

John Stewart raised a shaky hand, that was all.

The prelate went on. "The first business of this parliament is the good continuing governance of the realm. I call upon his Highness's brother, Robert, Earl of Fife and Menteith, to speak first to this."

Fife came forward, scanning all the ranks before him, narrow-eyed. He was in no hurry to speak. When he did, it was flatly authoritative. "His Grace, my royal brother, has the misfortune to lack the best of health. Not all of the duties of rule will he find it possible to attend to in person, he would have me inform you. So – he has appointed myself to be regent and governor of the realm, as His Grace's representative, to act on his advice and in his name."

Breaths were drawn throughout that hall. Regent! Gov-

32

ernor! Acting the king, with the king on the throne! Never had the like been known in Scotland, although it had in England. Fife, regent! Men stared at each other. There were murmurs, but no voice was actually raised.

"I shall be deemed to do His Grace's will and sustain the crown's authority in all things," Fife went on. "And I shall expect the support and fullest aid of all leal men." He paused. "And in this of the royal name, it is my duty and satisfaction to declare to you all that His Grace, recognising that the only King John of Scots heretofore was the unfortunate and English-born John Balliol, chosen by Edward of England to sit on the Scots throne as his minion, has decided that at his coronation he will be crowned not as King John the Second but as King Robert the Third. This in honoured memory of his great-grandsire, and my own, Robert the First, the Bruce."

More gasps at that.

"The coronation will be held at Scone as soon as is convenient to His Grace. My Lord Chancellor, I have but one other announcement to make. The king has approved of the appointment of Archibald, Earl of Douglas, as commander of the royal armed forces."

Archibald the Grim, from the earls' benches, stood up, bowed, and sat again, without speaking.

There were more murmurs now from all around, not least from the other earls themselves. This was as unusual and controversial a statement as what had gone before. For the Knight Marischal, he who had borne in the sword of state, and was standing behind the throne, was the normal and hereditary commander-in-chief, whoever actually led the assembled levies of the lords in warfare, for there was, of course, no standing army. Moreover Sir William Keith, the present Marischal, was related by marriage to the late king, one of his sons, recently dead, having wed a sister of the new monarch, and Fife himself. So here was cause for upset. But, since the appointment was announced in the king's name, and in his presence, it was in the nature of a royal command, and not to be contested in parliament, however much it might be objected to hereafter.

"My Lord Chancellor . . ." Fife turned and went back to stand at his brother's right hand again.

There was not a little talk and comment in the hall, so much so that the bishop had to beat on his table with a gavel for silence. Consulting his papers, he raised voice.

"A matter of concern, immediate concern for this parliament, has arisen. Donald, Lord of the Isles, has taken to arms against loyal subjects of the king in the north. And not for the first time. Moreover he has, in most extraordinary fashion, concluded a so-called treaty with King Richard of England, this of mutual aid, acting the independent prince and no leal subject, a disgraceful and shameful offence. Also he has dispossessed his own mother, the Princess Margaret Stewart, from her castle on the Isle of Islay, when she protested against this of England. It falls to this parliament to order the required chastisement."

There was not a little talk at this statement. All there were only too well aware of earlier contentions with the Lords of the Isles, and the difficulties of enforcing southern rule up there. The present lord's father had been notorious in this, despite having wed the Princess Margaret. The Isles, Hebrides and West Highland coast were all but unreachable for armies, and no ships available to the royal authority could have any effect on the Islesmen's great fleets of longships and birlinns, these so often called "the greyhounds of the seas". But this of a treaty with English Richard admittedly sounded challenging.

Earl John of Moray spoke up. "My Lord Chancellor, I know Donald of the Isles. My lands meet his, or those he has sway over. I do not disesteem him. He is a man of parts. And, I judge, of no danger to this realm. His inroads into the Highland West are to keep the feuding clans there in some sort of order, as is indeed required – Macleods, Macleans, Camerons, Mackintoshes, Shaws and the rest. His removal of his mother from Islay is of no great hardship for her. It is the caput of his lordship, and he is entitled to hold it himself, with his wife Euphemia. There are a sufficiency of other castles and strengths in the Isles for her to dwell in. This of a treaty with England sounds unseemly, but the word in the north is that it is a threat not to Scotland but to Ulster, where Donald has great lands. The Anglo-Irish lords there have been assailing these from the south, and the agreement with King Richard is to seek to halt these. I say that chastisement of Donald of the Isles is not called for. Whereas the threats of Percy, Earl of Northumberland, and now the Earl of Nottingham, Earl Marshal of England, should be more our concern. I so move."

George's father rose to second that, as did Robert, Earl of Sutherland, who was married to Moray's daughter, Mabella. There was major support voiced throughout the hall.

Bishop John turned to look at the throne, or more truly at the Earl of Fife.

That man could perceive the general acceptance of Moray's motion, and, ever calculating, did not challenge it.

"My Lord Chancellor," he said, "if there is no contrary motion put forward, I would suggest that instead of seeking to proceed against the Lord of the Isles at this time, we should recognise the danger from nearer at hand, from the south. The Earl Marshal of England, Notting-ham, who is also presently Warden of the English East March, has scoffed at Percy of Northumberland for losing at Otterburn, saying that he will show him how to bring the Scots to heel, even if they oppose him with numbers double that of his own. The folly of him! But this, from King Richard's Marshal, clearly indicates danger for our realm. Therefore I move that we should send a large force south over the East March, and challenge this Nottingham to fulfil his boast. I judge that Percy of Northumberland will not support him. We should show the English that Scotland is not to be threatened so."

Archibald of Douglas jumped up to second that. "I

35

agree!" he exclaimed. "I will take my strength to teach this English coxcomb a lesson! Who will come with me?"

That so prompt declaration indicated that this proposed sally had been discussed and arranged beforehand with Fife, a gesture to emphasise and strengthen their alliance, and ostensibly in the national cause. At any rate, there was loud applause from almost all there, lords rising to offer troops.

Fife, nodding, when the noise had died down added, "This is well. But, since the Lord of the Isles must not see it all as heedless of his assaults on our mainland in the north, I propose that a new Justiciar of the North be appointed, to remind him that he is being watched, and to confine his activities to his own isles and perhaps Ulster. As all may know, my worthy brother, the Earl of Buchan, not here present, *was* Justiciar but has resigned that position for his own reasons. Therefore, I propose that the new Justiciar should be also of the royal family, the which His Grace here agrees. I therefore nominate my own son, Murdoch Stewart, to be Justiciar."

The silence which greeted that was eloquent enough. But coming from the new regent, and with the king sitting there and nodding, none was in a position to contest it openly. Fife was demonstrating the powers of his new position.

"A seconder . . . ?" the Chancellor asked.

Douglas raised a hand.

"Are there any counter-motions?"

None spoke.

"Very well. The Lord Murdoch Stewart to be Justiciar of the North. Is there any other business?"

None being voiced, with enough on the commissioners' minds, the session was declared to be adjourned, and the Chancellor turned to the throne.

John/Robert hoisted himself up and, aided by his son David, headed for the door, without any gesture towards the standing company. That limp had, in fact, been caused, many years before, by a kick from a Douglas horse.

Outside, George rejoined his father and uncle, greatly wondering. He found them in consultation with the Earl of Sutherland, and James Douglas of Dalkeith, Angus presently coming to join them. Needless to say, all were much concerned with what had been decided, feelings very mixed. This of the regency, and the so obvious alliance of Fife and Archibald the Grim, was their main preoccupation, all else being secondary. What would it mean for Scotland, for them all? Their inability to oppose it all, owing to the royal prerogative, was frustrating; but something might conceivably be done to mitigate its effects. Yet the proposed venture down into England against the Earl Marshal, Nottingham, was probably worthy and justifiable, the English threat ever to be considered. And the acceptance of no real action against Donald of the Isles by Fife and Douglas to be commended.

The appointment of Fife's own son to be Justiciar of the North was, to be sure, unsuitable, little more than a youth, and indication of the undue exercise of power; but that young Murdoch would be able to exert no great effect on the northern areas, Moray pointed out, without *his* support and that of Sutherland and the new Earl of Ross.

George, when he had his father and uncle alone, asked whether they would be taking part in this armed expedition into England. He got differing answers to that. John of Moray said that he would not. He had brought a force of his northerners down for the last invasion, which had ended in Otterburn, two years before, and he did not feel that he could do so again, so soon; after all, his Moraymen had their own affairs to see to, farmers, fishers, millers, smiths, tradesmen and the like. But his brother declared that *he* would certainly go, and take a goodly number of men, for it was to be over the East March apparently, and that was his concern, and young George's also, now. He was not going to have Fife and Douglas marching through his Merse lacking his presence.

So it looked like a taste of warfare for the Master of Dunbar.

4

The proposed demonstration against the English was somewhat delayed in fulfilment, with the coronation of the new monarch to be celebrated, even if it was scarcely a cause for celebration; and winter weather not the best conditions for armed flourishes.

George accompanied his father to Scone for the crowning, an event of much significance, however feeble the man crowned, for all the lords and landed men of the kingdom had to be present, or, if unable for sufficiently good reason, send their deputies, this to swear formal allegiance to the new monarch for their lands and people, the theory being that all the land was the king's. So Uncle John would be there also, although not bringing more than a small escort with him.

Scone Abbey, the accepted crowning place, lay just north of Perth, where the fresh water of the River Tay overcame the salt tides of that firth, ever a symbol of the land's ongoing fertility in the ancient Celtic tradition. This would make a lengthy ride, so the Cospatricks chose to go by ship from Dunbar, to St John's Town of Perth, and to hire horses there for the mere three miles onwards. It was somewhat boisterous weather for voyaging, but not sufficiently so to deter them, and the sail of some hundred miles would take only twelve hours or so, whereas the overland route around the Forth and Tay estuaries would demand almost three days' riding.

There was no room at Scone Abbey for all the attenders at the coronation, so the many and various monastic establishments of Perth were full indeed, the earl and his son preferring to sleep in their cabin on board ship.

They met Moray for a meal, however, in one of the crowded taverns.

Next day, at Scone, all was bustle and preparation, the Lord Lyon King of Arms and his heralds and pursuivants busy arranging the procedure and the difficult task of establishing precedence, this considered of importance on such an occasion, and inevitably the source of much dispute. At least there was no problem in determining the Cospatrick's prominence among the earls, for none could deny his royal descent. He was placed immediately after the prince earls of Fife, Strathearn, Buchan and Caithness. There was considerable squabbling, however, among the husbands of the many princesses and also the illegitimate sons of the late monarch, all landholders. But Lyon's decision had to be final. Lesser lords competed likewise.

George had no part in this, but attached himself to his Aunt Marjory, Countess of Moray, herself one of the numerous sisters of the new king.

When all was readied, the great company was marshalled into the abbey chapel for the initial service by the abbot, this fortunately fairly brief, for most there had to stand, the king looking distinctly apprehensive, however confident-seeming his sons David and James. This over, a long procession was lined up, in precedence now, to be led by the Primate, Bishop Trail of St Andrews, with the king leaning on the arm of Fife at the head, this to the clash of cymbals and the singing of choristers, along the track through the trees to the Moot Hill, where the crowning had to take place; not far, but more than enough for the principal actor.

Getting John/Robert up the quite steep slope of the hillock was a slow and painful process, his sons aiding their uncle, Fife, in pushing and all but carrying him up. Never had a more difficult and reluctant ascent been witnessed, no great climb as it was. The choristers sang on but the cymbals fell silent.

At the summit, a throne-like chair was in position. It should have been the ancient Stone of Destiny, of course, but that was not available, being in the possession, of all people, of Donald of the Isles. The Bruce, fearing for its safety from English aggression, and leaving only a five-year-old son, on his death-bed had handed it over to the safe keeping of Angus Og of the Isles, telling him to keep it secure until a worthy successor sat on his throne. His descendants presumably did not consider the Stewarts to be sufficiently worthy, for they still held the precious stone, just where was uncertain; possibly on Islay. Edward Plantagenet, the Hammer of the Scots, had thought that he had captured it, but had been deceived by the lump of Scone sandstone left by the then abbot before the high altar of the abbey, which he had taken to London. The true stone, the Lia Fail to give it its Gaelic name, had been hidden in various secure places until Bruce could bring it to light. It was very different from Edward's trophy, of seat height, where the other was only a mere eleven inches, this demonstrated on the monarchial seals with kings sitting upon it, and so described by the chroniclers, highly carved and with round volutes or stone handles to carry it by at the sides. Scotland's Marble Chair it was styled, almost certainly St Columba's portable altar, which he had had a famous white horse to carry, which was given Christian burial when it died, the saint believing that any animal that was loved by a Christian would go on hereafter, love being God-like and eternal. It had a slight hollow on the seat, this to hold baptismal water. Edward had learned in due course that he had been duped, and came back to Scotland two years later, and pulled Scone Abbey apart stone by stone seeking the real symbol, but, not finding it, had had to go on with the pretence that he held it, to sustain his dignity, and that lump was still used for the crowning of English monarchs to indicate their lord-paramountcy over the northern kingdom.

Now, John/Robert thankfully seated on his chair, Lyon's trumpeters sounded, and in the silence thereafter, in time-honoured fashion, he recited the monarchial pedigree, going back over the centuries and the well-known

40

names before Bruce: Alexander and William, David and another Alexander and Edgar, the four Malcolms and William, MacBeth and Duncan, and on and on to far-distant times and names, some of these near-mythical and often scarcely pronounceable. This catalogue completed, he called upon the Bishop of St Andrews to anoint the king with holy oil. The Primate came forward with his ampulla, and making the sign of the cross dipped fingers in the oil and stroked them on the monarchial brow, and called down the blessing of the Almighty upon the recipient.

Then Lyon invited the Earl of Fife to perform the crowning. For once this was no assumption of privilege by Robert Stewart. It was the hereditary right and duty of the MacDuff Earls of Fife to act the Coroner. The last true MacDuff earl had died thirty years earlier, leaving only a daughter; this Robert, who had wed the countess in her own right, had been granted the earldom. So he claimed the coronership. Lyon brought him the golden crown on its cushion, and, taking it, he placed it on his brother's bent head.

Lyon raised the shout. "Long live King Robert! God save the king!"

Robert Stewart looked at the new Robert Stewart with an assessing eye. George Dunbar was possibly not the only one present who wondered, had Fife been born before his brother, what sort of a king *he* would have made. Strong, at least. This of eldest son succession was not always of value.

Now it was time for the allegiance-swearing – however little some there might abide by their oaths hereafter. It necessarily was a lengthy and slow process, for every feudal landholder had to come up individually, in order of pre-cedence, names called by Lyon, each with a pouchful of earth. He had to kneel in front of the monarch, spread that earth on the ground so that the royal foot could be placed upon it, in token that this soil from his estate was the king's, and held in feudal duty, this gesture saving the new monarch from having to travel round every part of his kingdom to receive the fealty while standing on his own land as ultimate superior. Then the kneeling lord had to take the royal hand between his own two palms and swear allegiance and devoted duty for as long as he lived, this before rising and bowing, to descend the hill again. That heap of earth would therefore grow and grow; this even was the suggestion as to why this Moot Hill was so lofty, after the centuries of oath-taking, although clearly there had always been a natural mound here. Scone, after all, was only the successor of the hill of Dunadd, south of the Oban in Argyll, where the early Scottish kings had been crowned before the Norse invasions made it dangerous, and where the footprint was carved in the naked rock on the hilltop, beside the wild-boar representation, emblem of the long line of those kings, before William the Lion, who did not like boars, changed it to the present lion rampant, this how he got his description, not because he was lion-hearted.

The first to kneel and spread earth was not Fife, who stood watching and who, as regent, presumably considered himself above such kneeling, but his next brother, Alexander, Earl of Buchan, the notorious Wolf of Badenoch, whose deeds had shocked the land. Now he led the allegiance. He was followed by his younger and legitimate brother, Walter of Brechin, Earl of Atholl. These both muttered the required form of words hastily, and nodded heads rather than bowing, their attitude towards the eldest brother very evident.

When it was Cospatrick's turn, he comported himself a deal more respectfully, and made his vows slowly, carefully. George felt like clapping.

The prolonged ceremony went on, with the pile of soil growing, so that the uneasy king had to raise his right foot high, while wagging his crowned head. The attention of the many watchers slackened.

At last it was over, and a return to the abbey could be made, the weary Robert the Third all but tottering. No cymbals now although the choristers still sang. A banquet had been prepared by the abbot, but only for the lofty ones, including the earls and senior bishops, accommodation again being the limiting factor. So George had to find his own way back to Perth and the ship, although in sufficient company.

One day, presumably, he himself would have to go through that oath-taking spectacle. He was certainly in no hurry so to do.

Later, his father confessed to him that he was greatly concerned over the future of their new liege-lord to whom he had just sworn fealty and devotion. Not only for his health, although that seemed to be precarious enough, but for his ongoing freedom and conditions of living, possibly even for his life itself. That Fife was without scruple, and might well not be content to be regent and governor of Scotland, but eager to sit on the throne himself. Cospatrick would not put it past him to seek to get rid of his brother by one means or another, and not by just waiting for him to die of his sickness. Other monarchs had been slain by those ambitious to succeed them. Kenneth the Second had died at the hands of Fenella so that her brother Constantine might reign. Duncan the First died after being wounded by MacBeth in battle. MacBeth himself had been murdered on the orders of Malcolm Canmore, their ancestor, by an earlier MacDuff of Fife. *This* Fife, George would note, chose not to swear allegiance for his earldom back there. Robert the Third would be well to look to his safety!

But the new king had two sons, George pointed out. Would David of Strathearn, whom Elizabeth was to marry, not succeed his father on his death? Or the younger James?

The earl did not answer that, only grimaced. His distrust of Fife was obviously deep.

They sailed back to Dunbar next day.

Such forebodings had to be put aside however, meantime, for Yuletide lay ahead, with its happier celebrations, and the family less concerned with national affairs. And after that, at least for the earl and George, thoughts and preparations for the intended sally into England to chal-

43

lenge its Earl Marshal took precedence. And to raise a sufficiency of men for this demanded much consideration and summoning; and George got much of that to see to, travelling their lands with his father's orders.

5

It was March before the word came, and from Archibald of Douglas, not Fife, that a great force would assemble on Edinburgh's Burgh Muir in ten days' time, to teach Nottingham his lesson. A Dunbar contingent was expected. Cospatrick sent reply that he was not going to march all his men west to Edinburgh just to march them back again to his own Merse.

The earl considered it important that his strength should be well represented on this venture, that Douglas and Fife should be in no doubts as to the Dunbar and March power. Angus, at Tantallon, agreed that this was wise, and would contribute what he could – which was considerably fewer, of course, his earldom being comparatively modest as to manpower. So summons to the Cospatrick banner were sent out far and wide, the Homes and Swintons, Lumsdens and Logans being told that they need not assemble at Dunbar, but could join the endeavour further south.

Nevertheless, on that great day for George, his first mustering for warfare, a highly satisfactory assembly gathered at Dunbar, just over three thousand men, some five hundred of them Angus's Red Douglases; and the Mersemen would produce at least another thousand. It all made a proud and heartening spectacle. The news was that Nottingham was thought to be based at Etal Castle, near Ford on the River Till, the main English East March stronghold; and so Douglas would be heading there, from Edinburgh, by Lauder, Greenlaw and Coldstream. So the Merse force was to await its lord at Ladykirk, near to Tweed, this to keep an eye on the Prince-Bishop of

Durham's great castle of Norham, none so far off, and as evident threat to prevent any flank attack from there on the Scots host. They then would all await Douglas at Coldstream. But, just to remind Archibald the Grim that he was now on Cospatrick land, a detachment of a couple of hundred men under Seton of that Ilk was sent to join the main army at Greenlaw, and escort it onwards.

With banners flying and much cheering and shouting of orders, the force was seen off by the Dunbar family, Gavin and Colin grumbling that they were not allowed to take part, their father declaring that their time would come.

By Colbrandspath, Auchencrow, Chirnside and the Blackadder they came to Ladykirk by darkening. Here there was a monastery for the leadership, this already being used by the Homes of that Ilk, Aytoun, Blackadder, Bassendean, Fast, Paxton and the rest, with the Swintons of Swinton, Kimmerghame and Laughton, with a muster of some fifteen hundred. They informed that Douglas had not yet arrived at Greenlaw, so there was no hurry. Also that Home of Cowdenknowes had taken two hundred men to the Tweed ford opposite Norham, to keep the English there aware of threat. No doubt the word of their presence would get from Norham to Etal.

So it was rest for the night. George at least was glad to discard his chain mail coat, uncomfortable as it was.

In the morning, with still no need for haste, it was decided that it would be a worthwhile move to go first, in force, to the Norham ford, to seem to pose a really major force there and hopefully confine the bishop' people to their castle, to safeguard the main Scots entry into England, this before their own going upriver to Coldstream. It was not a great digression, merely some eight miles.

At the Tweed they could see the great castle on the other side, on high ground a bare half-mile off, the Durham banners flying from its towers. It, and Wark at the other side of Coldstream, were the main English strongholds on the borderline, and apt to be the starting places for invasions into Scotland.

No aggressive moves were in evidence that day at any rate. The Scots did not cross the ford, contenting themselves with this show of strength; that is, until Seton sent a messenger to announce that Douglas was now near to Eccles, and should reach Coldstream in mid-afternoon. He and Fife had fully eight thousand men.

So Fife was there also. Was this significant? It could be. Did the regent also want to be seen as the nation's warrior-prince? In contrast to his weakly brother?

They rode up Tweed.

At Coldstream they had some time to wait before the outriders of the army reached them; and meantime, scouts whom Douglas had sent ahead across the borderline had sent couriers back to declare that Nottingham had taken his force from Etal Castle eastwards to the mighty fortress of Bamburgh on the coast, a stronghold indeed. It seemed that he had heard of the Scots coming in strength, and was taking precautions. Bamburgh was an infinitely more defendable place than Etal. Defence, then? Was that his priority, not challenge? Despite his boasts! Or was it a lure to coax the Scots further into England? Bamburgh was none so far north of Alnwick, the Percy seat. Was Nottingham going to co-operate with Hotspur, after all?

When Archibald the Grim, with Fife and their great host arrived, and were made aware of this move of the enemy, they wondered, like Cospatrick, just what it signified. Their greeting for the Dunbar contingent was scarcely warm, but the pair welcomed this accession of strength. If indeed Nottingham and the Percy joined forces, all possible powers might be needed to assail them. Told of the Norham situation they did recognise the danger of a flank attack from there. Douglas declared that Cospatrick should send part of his array east by north forthwith, parallel with Tweed, to get between Norham and the route the Scots would have to take for Bamburgh, to guard against any such assault by the bishop's people.

Home of that Ilk was duly despatched, with some eight hundred men, to see to this.

Then it was across Tweed into England at Cornhill. Cospatrick was not invited to ride at the head of the great column with the regent and Douglas, nor was Angus. In consequence they kept their thousands considerably behind the main force, protecting the rear.

At Crookham, five miles on, they forded the Till and thereafter swung left, due eastwards now, to head for the coast, meantime no assaults and ravaging of the countryside. That could wait. They even passed Etal Castle without assailing it when they saw no sign of large numbers of men thereabouts. Cospatrick was sent word to go up and examine it more closely. This he did, and satisfied himself that their host was under no threat from there. Signs of the previous large encampment were around the not very large fortalice, the seat of the Heron family, but that was all. The occupants of Etal lay low.

On by Lowick they went, and so to Fenwick, nearing the coast, a dozen miles, with no sign of assault from the north and no warnings from Home. Now it was south for them. They were about a score of miles below Berwick-upon-Tweed, and, it was calculated, half that from Bamburgh. They passed the great bay, flanked by Lindisfarne and Holy Isle, of fame. Soon they could see Bamburgh itself, on its high cliff-top ridge ahead of them. Men began to tighten their armour, settle their helmets and prepare for action.

Douglas, a veteran fighter, sent a party ahead, right-handed, to skirt well to the west of the stronghold, by Belford, to get between Bamburgh and Alnwick, to keep watch on possible Percy involvement – if that man was not already with the Earl Marshal despite their animosity.

As the Scots drew near the mighty fortress, feelings and questionings were mixed. Why had Nottingham come here? It was a secure place, yes, not to be taken without prolonged siege. But that implied a defensive stance. Would he attack from there? The castle's height above that long seaboard approach would give advantage, no doubt, for downward-charging cavalry. Was that it? George asked his father.

The earl, like the others, was unsure. After all, the way they had come from Coldstream offered two or three places where a waiting force could have ambushed them, and to advantage, especially at the river crossings, the wide Till in especial. But there had been none such. To choose to await the Scots here seemed to indicate delaying, temporising. For what? Percy? Was Nottingham hoping that Hotspur would come and join him, but had had no assurance of it? It could be. Nottingham was England's Earl Marshal in addition to being Warden of this March, and it was surely the duty of the Earl of Northumberland to support the king's representative against cross-border attack. This seemed to be the likeliest explanation.

Presently, less than a mile off, they could see that the quite long ridge, on which the walls and towers rose, was densely crowded, large numbers of men and horses thereon. An army was up here, sure enough.

Douglas went somewhat further forward and there drew up his host, far enough away from the foot of the ridge to ensure that no impetus from a downhill charge could disadvantage them. Although not summoned to do so, Cospatrick went onward to join them in decision-making, Angus with him. Also George.

Debate was going on.

There was no indication that all those men up there were being marshalled into ranks for an attack. Surely anything such would be evident, even from this distance. That they themselves were being closely watched was certain. But nothing else was.

Cospatrick suggested that Nottingham was waiting for Percy. Fife snapped that they had not failed to think of that. But Percy might already be up there at the castle. But not for attacking.

Douglas said that their own waiting would serve no good purpose. They could not storm that stronghold, but they could issue a challenge. Let them do so without further delay. This was agreed.

So the leadership group, a score of them, rode forward

49

under their banners, these including the red lion rampant of Scotland, together with a large white flag, for parley. They went sufficiently far up the ascent for themselves to be heard by watchers. Fife blew a long blast on his horn.

"I am Robert of Fife and Menteith, regent and governor of Scotland," he shouted. "I would speak with Nottingham, the Earl Marshal of England."

There was no reply.

"Are you deaf, as well as inactive?" he called again. "I, Robert Stewart, seek you, Nottingham."

There was movement now up there, but no words came.

Archibald the Grim raised voice. "I am Douglas. I have come far to see Nottingham. Does he hide in this hold?"

There were sundry shouts from higher, and then two men came out from the crowd, one bearing a banner with the three leopards of England. It was the other who spoke.

"I am Nottingham, the Marshal. You trespass on English soil, which our treaty of peace, which still holds, forbids. Why?"

"Because you asked for it, man!"

"You told Percy of Northumberland that he was feeble. At Otterburn," Fife called. "You said that you would teach him how to deal with the Scots. That you would vanquish them were they twice as many as you were fielding. So we have come to have you prove it. Do so, Nottingham!"

Again no reply.

Douglas took up the challenge. "If you have thought better of it, sirrah, we are prepared to humour you, accept your caution. If twice as many is too much for you, we will abide by equal numbers. How say you?"

Still no response.

"Less still, then? You name the numbers."

"Why should I?" came back to them then. "What gain to us? Or to you? Bloodshed — for what?"

"That is not what you said to Hotspur Percy!"

"How know *you* what I said? You have been told lies."

50

"Ha! So that is it! You will not fight? The Earl Marshal of England!"

"I see no need to."

"He sees no need!" Douglas turned to look back at those behind the leadership, raising voice still higher. "Nottingham sees no need to fight. He prefers strong walls to hide behind." He hooted harsh laughter. "Their Marshal. He hides!"

Everywhere the cries and laughter arose, the jeering and scoffing, save up on that ridge. "He hides! He hides! The Englishman hides!" On and on the bellowing derision rose.

Nottingham turned, with his banner-bearer, and strode back towards the castle gateway.

There was something like confusion, indecision, among the Scots array. This was almost beyond belief. But what could they do about it? Nothing. That citadel could not be taken without siege-weaponry, sows, battering-rams, catapults, scaling-ladders, none of which they had with them. The situation was hopeless, stalemate. No use to sit there jeering. Nothing for it but to turn and go back to Scotland. To go further into England, with the risk of Nottingham, Percy, the Prince-Bishop and other lords uniting and cutting them off from home was too great to be considered. Home – and not a blow struck! A folly, play-acting! All their thousands. But at least they would go, their banners flying unstained, unlike those here at Bamburgh.

The order was given. Retire. Back whence they had come. Leave the Auld Enemy to sit and weep! Coldstream for themselves . . .

George, in his chain mail, did not know whether to grin or sigh or shake his head. Worked up to fight, real fighting not just tourney combat, he was denied it. Or spared it? His first campaign a non-event. His father saw it rather differently. What effect would this have on Fife's reputation? To march a hundred miles, achieve nothing, and then march back again! How would Scotland see that, irrespective of how England did?

On their way back, the army did what had been denied on its advance, ravage and burn and ruin. Farms, cottages, mills went up in flames, cattle were slaughtered, horses taken by the hundred, while the folk fled, no opposition being put up. George found this less than admirable, while admitting that some result of their inroad into England was called for; but harrying a defenceless countryside was not his notion of chivalrous warfare. His father shrugged it off as inevitable.

However, they did not attempt the task of taking Etal Castle.

At Coldstream again, it was parting from Fife and Douglas, no more friendly nor congratulatory than had been their meeting. Home had rejoined them, having had no confrontation with the Norham people.

Their own Merse welcomed them back, unbloodied, families pleased at any rate.

6

That spring the Master of Dunbar was, as usual, much engaged in activities that demanded no helmets or chain mail, but which had their own satisfactions, however undramatic and lacking in challenge. The Lammermuir Hills, all two hundred and fifty square but very rounded miles of them, were the earldom's principal source of wealth – wool. They made one of the greatest sheep-runs in the land, rivalling the Cheviots, which of course were half in England. The thousands of sheep demanded much attention, especially at this lambing time, and although there were many shepherds, these had to be supervised and guided, particularly where vassals' and tenants' flocks were concerned; these had their own shepherds, but there were no walls, hedges or fences to partition the hills, and sheep wandered at will over the heather and grassy slopes, and mixed with other flocks. So the animals had to be identified with colours in dye or other markings, and so separated into flocks for dipping and lambing and shearing. It all demanded much labour and care and co-operation. Authority was sometimes required among the various shepherds, hence George's and his brothers' attendance on occasion. This of the lambing season was important.

George and Gavin were riding one day near that quite large loch where the Whiteadder stream rose, a good nine miles from Dunbar, when they saw, some distance off, four other riders. This was unusual in these hills, for the shepherds, with their dogs, did not use horses. Interested, they were still more so when, nearing these, they saw that two of the riders were women. This was more unusual than

53

ever in this remote area, far from the nearest habitation other than the isolated shepherd's cottage.

Closer proximity revealed that the two women were young, and the two men with them falconers, with hawks on their padded sleeves. It was a foray, this, and come far from wherever.

Doffing bonnets as they came up with them, George and his brother greeted them. "A good-day to you, ladies," George said. He gestured towards a couple of mallard ducks hanging from one of the men's saddle-bows. "You find sport, I see. You must have had a lengthy ride to reach here. From Cranshaws, perhaps?"

"No. From Gifford. Yester," one of the girls answered. "The loch it was which brought us. Duck on the loch. We had heard of this."

"Ah! Yester. Then you will be Hays? I am George, Master of Dunbar. And here is my brother Gavin."

"So! Sons of my lord Earl! I am Alicia Hay. And this is my sister Beatrix. We have met, have we not? Long ago when we were but children. You came to Yester with your father."

"That – yes, that was long since. I had forgotten, ladies."

"Two small girls boys would pay no heed to!"

"We should have done. Fair to look at, as you would have been, even then." George bowed from the saddle.

"Ha, a gallant lordling! We scarcely can curtsey, mounted. But acknowledge your lordship's . . . attentions! And beware, perhaps?"

Something of a minx this one, apparently.

The other young woman had not spoken. They were very different, for sisters. This one quiet, not exactly withdrawn but with a sort of serenity about her, dark of hair, fine of feature, long of neck; whereas the other was fair, comely, more outgoing.

"You have never come to Dunbar? Your father, Sir William Hay, comes. We see him, at least, at times. He is Sheriff of Peebles, is he not? He was with us in England, none so long ago. At Bamburgh." It was the other girl whom he addressed.

"Yes. He told us of that. And the strange Earl of Nottingham." She had a pleasing lilt to her voice. "We have visited Dunbar town, but never the castle."

"Then that is something that you must do."

"I told you, Bea – this one is to be watched," the sister Alicia said, making a face.

Gavin spoke up. "You are fond of the hawking? For duck. Yet we have never seen you here before."

"It is our first time to the Whiteadder. Usually we go to Danskine Loch, nearer to Gifford. You will know it? Much smaller, but long and narrow."

"I was there once, yes. It is on Yester land?"

"You do not mind us hawking here?" That was the other, Beatrix. "Should we have sought permission? We were told of it . . ."

"No, no," George declared. "Come here when you will. You got only the two duck?"

"We got two others. They were stooped on, and fell far out on the water. We lost them. We should have brought dogs. Now, we are for home."

"Then we will escort you, ladies."

"Shall we have it?" Alicia looked at her sister. "We have our good falconers, after all!" That was both arch and coaxing.

The other only smiled, but in friendly fashion.

"We have calls still to make. At shepherds' houses. At Penshiel, Gamelshiel and Mayshiel. Word to leave at these. Are you in haste? They are on the way back to Yester."

"What are you at? So far from Dunbar."

"We see the shepherds. The lambing is coming on us. There is much to attend to. Separating the flocks. You will know of this? The Hays have sheep also." Sir William was a senior vassal of the earldom, with quite large lands, not only around Gifford but much further west, at Lochquhariot on the Gore Water in Middle Lothian. Also in Peebles-shire.

55

They reined their horses round and set off north by west, up the Upper Whiteadder. George chose to ride beside Beatrix, Gavin preferring Alicia, the two falconers trotting well behind.

"Strange that we have not met before," George said. "Save as children. One would have thought . . . !" He left the rest unsaid.

"You, my lord Earl's sons, will have many to meet and call upon. Many great lands, in Lothian and the Merse."

"Perhaps. But . . . not many such as yourself! I mean . . ." He shook his head, at a loss for the right words, especially after what her sister had accused him of.

Beatrix smiled again but did not comment.

They heard her sister chattering to Gavin.

George was not usually tongue-tied. What was it about this young female that made him so? Not lack of will to be talking with her, assuredly. He thought to draw upon the scenery about them.

"You will know these parts well, I think? That spur of hillock, there. It is called the Friar's Nose. Why, I wonder?"

"An odd name, yes. There must be a reason for it. All friars had noses, after all."

"There is a Pictish fort near it, only grass ramparts now. And that hill behind is called Priestlaw. Forby there is a ruined chapel at its foot. So Holy Church must have been important here once. It may have been the ancient Celtic Columban Church, I think, before Margaret brought the Roman Catholic one to Scotland."

"You are knowledgeable about such matters, my lord?"

"Do not call me that. My name is George. I am not really knowledgeable, but have always been interested in that change in our faith from one sort to another. When the first was . . . good enough. More suited to our folk, I would judge. Or is that . . . heresy? Forgive me if I speak amiss."

"No. What is amiss in that? I find it interesting also. And in, in such as yourself. Not all young men . . ."

56

"It is probably my ancestry which is behind it. The Cospatricks. Before Queen Margaret came and married Canmore, we were all of the Columban Church. All Scotland was. For five hundred years. Astonishing that one woman could change it all. But the Cospatricks did not change. Until . . . later." He pointed. "We ride over yonder. That house is Penshiel." He called on Gavin to do the like. "The shepherd, Duncan, will not be there. But I will leave a message with his wife. And I have brought dye, here. To mark our sheep . . ."

"You are knowledgeable about sheep as well as faith, my lord George! And more also, perhaps? It may be that you could tell me something that I have always wondered at. This to do with both! Why is the Lord Jesus so often called the Lamb of God? Strange, is it not? If he is a lamb, would it not make the Holy Father a sheep? A ram! This seems . . . unsuitable."

He laughed at that. "How right you are! I do not know. But I would think it was because of sacrifice. The ancients used to sacrifice lambs to their gods. And Jesus was sent as sacrifice for mankind's sins. It could be that."

"Yes, that does make sense . . ."

George handed in the dye and his message to the shepherd's wife at Penshiel; and announced that their next call would be at Gamelshiel, across on the other side of Whiteadder, which meant fording the stream, but this was shallow up here. More dye and instructions. And then it was Mayshell, still further up.

"Why are these cottages all called shiel?" Beatrix asked. "I fear that I have much to learn."

Her sister wagged her fair head. "Bea is always asking questions," she said. "What does the like of this matter?"

"Surely it matters that we should know whence words and language have come?" George asserted. "It is all part of our inheritance, from our ancestors. Shiel, I am told, is from the Norsemen, our Viking past. *Skjol* as I recollect it. It is the same as shield, and means shelter. Shelter for sheep, in especial. So shiels or shielings are places where

57

the sheep can be safe in hard weather. Protected places. As to what the Pen and the Gamel and the May are for, I do not know. Probably the names of the men who built them and the cottages. Gamlyn is an honest name. Pen could mean a penman's place, a clerk or monk. May, I know not. There are many other shiels around in these hills, sheep-grazings. Windshiel, Bedshiel, Kidshiel, Bowshiel, Luckieshiel and the like. Mayshiel *might* be from Mabon. Many Mabons live in the Merse."

"I think that all this is good to know," Beatrix declared. "As when we learned how Yester came to be so named."

"Yester? Your castle? I have heard it called Goblin Hall, but . . ."

"That is a nonsense of the local folk. Its builder, Sir Hugo de Giffard, who gave name to the village, had it made on a cliff-edge, and used a cave in the rock as part of it. So we have an underground hall. I have never heard of another such. He used a French master-mason to build it, of the name of Gobelin – the same nearly as Goblin! And because it is underground, and strange, the Gifford folk call it Goblin Ha'. Stupid! Even some of our servants fear to be in it alone. But there is nothing ill to it."

"I would wish to see this. But . . . Yester?"

"Yester is otherwise. It is but a wrong spelling of Ystrad, we were told. Ystrad is the ancient Celtic Welsh-speaking word for a strath or wider valley. A glen is a narrow valley, a strath a wider one – as you will well know. But strath is from the Highland Gaelic; the Welsh or ancient language of the Britons has it as Ystrad – Yester."

"What does it signify?" Alicia demanded. "It is just a name which somebody gave it long ago."

"Yet names are important, are they not?" George asked. "You will be proud of being Hays?"

"Ye-e-es."

After seeing the shepherd at Mayshiel, they began to climb, up and up, on to the lofty all but plateau of Moss Law, where a dozen streams were born and where snow was apt to lie long in winter. On the way up they passed a lesser hill known as Nine Stane Rig, and George, pointing it out, remarked on the significance of *this* name. The nine standing stones thereon were all that remained of a Pictish stone circle, their place of sun worship. When Beatrix wondered why these hills seemed to be so full of worship places, he said that he thought it might be because of the heathen Norse and Viking raiders who terrorised the land, and who seldom went far from their dragon-ships; and so this inland high ground represented security and peace.

Once over that lengthy Moss Law it was downwards, northwards now, and quite steeply, passing two more Pictish forts, to come into Hay country at Danskine, near the loch the girls had mentioned. Soon thereafter they turned into an all but hidden narrow valley on their left, and then were into wider space, where there was a little community, cottages and barns. There came in, on the left, the south, another steep valley, all but a ravine, with a turbulent stream which Beatrix called the Hopes Water cascading down. And high above it, at the junction of these two glens, in a sure defensive situation, soared Yester Castle. Beatrix was able to point out the spot, halfway up the cliff on the right where, in a crack of the rock-face, she said a postern door could open from the underground cave-chamber, the Goblin Hall. She would show the pair it, but not attempt to reach it from that hidden doorway.

They climbed a zigzag track to the castle, its strength very evident, although it was not really large compared with Dunbar or Hailes or Seton, other vassals' houses, more like Colbrandspath.

Sir William Hay was away at his judicial duties at Peebles, but his wife, the Lady Joanna, received the visitors kindly, offering refreshment. This George declined, pointing out that he and his brother were only escorting her daughters home, and that they themselves still had a lengthy ride, some fourteen miles, to get back to Dunbar. This lady had been the only child and heiress of the late Giffard of Yester, and had brought the property to the Hays.

The girls said that surely the young lords had time to see the Goblin Hall? So they were taken down flights of steps, seemingly into the bowels of the earth, until they found themselves in a large and lofty rib-vaulted chamber, the said ribs carved out of the solid rock sides of what had been a natural cavern, a strange place indeed to be part of any home, sparsely furnished and chilly, obviously little used. Despite local gossip, they were assured, it was not haunted and with nothing unchancy about it,

Thereafter it was departure, distinctly reluctant on both young men's parts, despite their long ride ahead. George declared that he would be back, if he might, bringing his younger brothers to see it all, the sisters nowise discouraging, Alicia patting Gavin's shoulder, and Beatrix saying that she would not forget what she had learned that day, with her warm smile, George hoping that this meant not only the meaning of names.

As the brothers rode homewards, Gavid was eloquent in his praise of Alicia, whom he had found more lively and challenging than Beatrix. He would certainly like to see more of her. How soon could they bring their brothers to see Yester?

George kept his reactions more to himself.

7

At Dunbar Castle shortly thereafter they were presented
with a strange and unexpected demand, and from Fife of all
people. It seemed that the Earl of Nottingham, returning
south, had protested to King Richard and his advisers that
the Scots had broken the peace treaty by crossing the border
and assailing him at Bamburgh. He was demanding apologies and promises of no further offences, or the treaty, due to
expire in a year's time, should not be renewed. And since it
was a tripartite treaty with France, and the French had
indicated renewal, this could much affect Scotland, because
of the Auld Alliance, the traditional understanding that if
either France or Scotland suffered attacks by England, as
had so often taken place, the other would promptly invade
from north or south, as counter-threat. This ancient arrangement was an important safeguard for the Scots, and
was not to be endangered. So Fife, as regent, required
Dunbar and March to go, with others, to London, to claim
that the Bamburgh move had not been national invasion but
because of a challenge by the East March Warden, Nottingham, made with Hotspur Percy, that he would show him
how to defeat the Scots. Fife himself would not go to
Richard – despite the fact that he had led this sally – but
he would send Cospatrick, who could travel conveniently in
one of his ships, along with the Earl of Angus and Douglas of
Dalkeith, these to represent the Douglas interest, Archibald
the Grim not going either.

Cospatrick was well aware that he was being used to
spare the faces of Fife and Douglas. But he was not really
averse to going, since it could strengthen his own position
in relation to these two. He recognised, of course, that it

could well be quite a difficult mission. Matters were in some chaos still in England, the weak Richard the Second wholly in the hands of two great nobles, Michael de la Pole, Earl of Suffolk, and Robert de Vere, Earl of Oxford. Presumably the negotiations would have to be with these two. But the Lancastrians, Thomas, Duke of Gloucester and his older brother, now indeed aged, John of Gaunt, Duke of Lancaster, still held great power and influence, with Henry, Earl of Hereford, John of Gaunt's son, now the driving power. Indeed the latter was claiming the throne. The year before, he had managed to eject Suffolk and Oxford from London, King Richard shut up in Windsor, but the pair, Suffolk and Oxford, had now won back London in Richard's name. For how long they would hold it was in question, Hereford, known as Bolingbroke, the name of his castle near Lincoln, asserting that he would retake it, and with it the crown. In these circumstances it was obvious why Nottingham, the Earl Marshal, wanted peace renewed with both France and Scotland, as help to Richard and threat to Hereford/Bolingbroke. Likewise why Fife and Douglas did not wish to be involved until they saw which side was going to win in the southern kingdom. But meantime, the peace-treaty arrangements had to go ahead, because of the French connection.

Debating all this, the earl decided that George should go south with him and the other two, as supporter in any attitude which Angus or Dalkeith might contest – for they *were* Douglases, after all. George was very willing and interested. He was now of full age, and glad to be able to play an effective part as Master of Dunbar.

It did mean that he would not get back to Yester Castle for some time, unfortunately. Gavin might. He would have to take charge of the lambing supervision.

So five days later, at dawn, the Dunbar wool-ship *Lammerlaw* sailed, with its four distinguished passengers, for the Thames, this a lot easier than riding nearly four hundred miles down through England.

With his colleagues, Cospatrick discussed their proposed programme. Assuming that Suffolk and Oxford were still in control at London, they would proceed first to the Tower there, the royal residence, even though King Richard was all but a prisoner at Windsor. Seek to come to an agreement with them. Perhaps go on to Windsor to obtain a royal signature. Then when their ship returned from the Low Countries with its new cargo of cloth and clothing, wines and pantiles, sail off, seemingly for home, but to call in at the Wash, where they could land at Boston in Lincolnshire, Bolingbroke Castle being, they were told, some fifteen miles north of there. This to see Hereford, and to seek to obtain *his* agreement to the treaty; so that whoever won in this English struggle, Scotland's position would be safeguarded. All this was agreed.

Their shipmaster said that they would probably, with a south-west wind prevailing, reach the mouth of the Thames in two days and nights, just over four hundred miles' sailing. London lay some fifty miles up the estuary, and this would have to be sailed in daylight owing to much shipping traffic. So they might well have to lie off the Thames mouth. They would pass the wide bay of the Wash about halfway down.

The late April weather was reasonably kind to them, and the seas not rough, the wind more westerly than south, which helped. By nightfall their skipper reckoned that they had covered about one hundred and fifty miles, which put them off the Grimsby area. So, later, they passed the mouth of the Wash in darkness, standing well out now so as not to have any trouble with other vessels.

By daylight next morning they had swung eastwards to round the great Norfolk bulge of land, passing Yarmouth and Lowestoft. Darkness again settled on them when they were approximately off Clacton, and there they hove to, well out in open waters, with only some thirty miles to go to the Thames mouth. So next day they ought to have no difficulty in reaching London town in daylight.

This proved to be the case; and entering the estuary

between Southend and Sheerness the passengers soon saw the need for careful navigation, with the great amount of shipping coming and going, especially when the waters narrowed into the River Thames itself, and became little more than a half-mile in width, near Tilbury, their destination still at least a score of miles ahead, and the traffic abating nothing.

George was highly interested in all he saw. He was particularly struck by the obviously highly populated river banks. He knew, in theory, that England numbered ten times more people than did Scotland; but this was brought home to him now, and he realised something of the problems of armed struggle against the Auld Enemy, who could always field infinitely larger forces. Also the matter of national wealth, with all this trade, represented by the shipping, emphasised.

The hugeness of London itself was an eye-opener, the built-up area vast, this long before they reached the Tower, where they were heading; and even this, his father told him, was distant from Westminster, its abbey and parliament buildings fully three miles more. He wondered whether they, his father, Angus and Dalkeith, could make any impact on the rulers of all this.

The Tower of London at least was very obvious among all the array of buildings flanking the river when at last they reached it, standing out on the north bank, white and massive. Cospatrick, who had been here twice before, told his son that it had been built by the Norse William the Conqueror with pale limestone from Caen in Normandy, this part of England apparently being short of good stone, timber and brick being the usual building materials. It consisted of a great square keep, almost one hundred feet in height, with towers at each angle, all within a large walled enclosure and a wide moat, fed from the river. It had been the royal residence ever since, although Windsor Castle, forty miles further upriver, was the English monarchs' favourite seat.

Their ship berthed at the Water Gate quay, where it was

eyed suspiciously by guards. Cospatrick shouted that they were commissioners come from Scotland to see the king's advisers regarding a treaty. This produced no invitation to land, but one of the group of guards turned and went off through the gatehouse arch.

It took a while for any reaction to manifest itself. Then a more finely clad individual came out with the guard, to demand who the said commissioners were and what brought them. He was told that they were the Earls of Dunbar and March and of Angus, and the Lord of Dalkeith. The mention of earls seemed to have its effect, but there was still no suggestion that they leave the vessel. The official disappeared.

He was back after another interval, to say that their lordships should come with him, to see his lordship the Earl of Oxford, who would grant them audience.

So the four of them disembarked and followed their guide in over the drawbridge and into the Tower, armed guards everywhere, almost as though the place were under siege, and security of the essence.

Up a flight of stairs in one of the angle towers they were brought to a fine chamber, where a handsome man with strangely blinking eyelids awaited them, much more richly dressed than were his visitors. He considered them narrowly, however twitchingly, saying that he was Oxford. What was their business?

Cospatrick said that they had come, in the name of Robert, King of Scots, to negotiate renewal of the peace treaty between the realm and England and France. Was this where such should be discussed? Or elsewhere?

That had the other stroking his beard. He observed that there had been a serious breach of the treaty's provisions but recently, as reported by the Earl Marshal; and terms for any renewal required due consideration.

By whom? he was asked. Himself and the Earl of Suffolk, with King Richard – or the Dukes of Lancaster and Gloucester?

At this last their hearer blinked harder than ever, and

frowned at the same time. He turned to pace over to a window, and back again. He then announced that the Earl of Suffolk was presently with His Majesty at Windsor, and that it would be best to go there and debate the matter. He would conduct the commissioners thither in a royal barge.

This surprising development by no means displeased the visitors, who had considered it probably necessary to go and see King Richard anyway, and were not sure how to get to Windsor, upriver, the reaches beyond London almost certainly too shallow for their sea-going vessel. So this of being taken there would be a convenience.

Oxford left them for a time, having wine sent in for them, presumably to arrange for the barge to be readied. George, for one, wondered at this, being left drinking wine in the dreaded Tower of London where so many unfortunates had been confined to end their days.

At length de Vere of Oxford returned, wearing a cloak now, and told them to follow him. They were led down and out to the quayside again, where, alongside the *Lammerlaw*, a handsome shallow boat was awaiting them, hardly a barge by their standards but a long, narrow craft with a sort of cabin at the stern, all brightly painted and with eight oarsmen sitting on their benches. They were ushered aboard, Cospatrick calling up to their own watching shipmaster that they might be gone for some time, and he replying that he was being ordered to move his ship further up the quay.

They cast off, the oarsmen expert with their long sweeps.

Oxford took them into the cabin, but himself went forward to speak with the leading rower, and remained there, clearly not eager to appear over-friendly with the Scots, a strange man. Undoubtedly that reference to Lancaster and Gloucester had registered with him – as, of course, it was meant to do.

It made quite an interesting journey for the visitors, following the great windings of the Thames past miles more of dense riverside buildings, including what was obviously Westminster Abbey and the parliament houses, and under various bridges which would have prevented *their* ship from proceeding further. Their barge was propelled at a notable speed, the lengthy oars in rhythmic pulling, the rowers grunting in unison.

There was still much traffic on the water, but now all small craft.

At length they were past the city walls, although there was still considerable housing on either bank, and many little piers and boat-moorings. The river narrowed now and still had a winding course. But this gradually straightened.

After a while Oxford came to tell them that they were passing Colnbrook, and that Windsor lay five miles ahead.

After a while they could see the great fortress-castle on the higher ground not far from the river, so very different from the Tower they had left, spread for a notable distance along a sort of minor ridge, with its enormous drum-like round keep, and innumerable lesser towers and battlements, the handsome new Winchester Tower and the canonical quarters and chapel. Flags flew from many of its highest points.

There was a sort of canal branching off the river, to enable the like of their barge to approach close to this fortified palace, so no lengthy walk was demanded. Disembarking, the newcomers were led up to their almost awesome destination.

George was much exercised. Were they actually going to see the King of England?

For a considerable time they were not to see anyone, however, save servitors, as they were left in an anteroom, near to kitchens by the smell of it. No doubt Oxford had some discussing to do with Suffolk before they were to be interviewed.

Eventually they were sent for and conducted along corridors and up stairways to a small hall hung with tapestries, where, with de Vere, another man awaited them, very different in appearance, heavy-built and heavy-featured, bull-necked, florid. This proved to be Michael de la Pole, Earl of Suffolk. Despite his ponderous appearance, his voice was light, almost affable.

"Our Scottish friends," he greeted them. "Come far to visit us. And for good reason, no doubt."

"It seemed sufficiently so for His Grace, our King Robert, to send us," Cospatrick answered. "Good for three kingdoms." He introduced himself and his companions.

Angus spoke. "We come in goodwill. The affray at Bamburgh was of the Earl of Nottingham's own calling. He challenged us, not as your Earl Marshal but as Warden of the East March. We crossed that East March to accept the challenge. And he then hid behind that castle's walls! But no blood was shed."

"Yet you laid waste much land on your way back to Scotland," Oxford put in.

"No more than the Marchmen, on either side, are doing all the time." That was the truth. "Feuding land."

"Ah, well," Suffolk said. "Be all that as it may. You now wish the treaty of peace to be renewed? With what benefit to England?"

"Much." That was Dalkeith. "You complain over the Bamburgh raid. Do you seek more of the like?"

"No. But . . . is that a threat, my lord?"

"It is not. But if there is no peace treaty, think you that all our border lords will sit quietly at home? They have never done so in the past."

"Your Douglases in especial!" Oxford declared. "The new earl thereof, this Archibald – did he not lead, with the regent, Fife, at Bamburgh?"

Cospatrick intervened, looking at Suffolk. "Old scores, and past days," he said. "*We* want better times. Our monarch, Robert, does. I am Chief Warden of the Scottish Marches. And my son, here, to be the East Warden. With a peace treaty again we can ensure only very limited cross-border raiding. Which will preserve *you*, my lords, from having to keep any large forces in the north. Which will

. . . benefit you, will it not? In present circumstances!" He did not have to mention Lancaster and Gloucester.

The English pair exchanged more glances. "Peace, yes, advantages us all. Or . . . most of King Richard's loyal subjects!" Suffolk had not missed the point. "But – France?" he added. "How think you France will see this of renewal?"

"King Charles will welcome it, I judge. Your King Richard has done homage for Aquitaine, has he not? As Charles desired. A treaty now would secure this, and help him. But Calais to remain in Plantagenet hands. Is it not so?"

"Perhaps. Tell Bolingbroke, Hereford that!"

"Peace with Scotland will help both."

"So long as you abide by its terms."

"That we can promise, in King Robert's name. And his regent's, the Earl of Fife and Menteith."

"And with Douglas support," Dalkeith added.

"So be it," Suffolk said, looking at Oxford. "We will put it to His Majesty."

"We would *see* King Richard," Cospatrick announced. "Since we come in King Robert's name."

The two English earls exchanged glances again. Suffolk shrugged.

"Very well. We will arrange this, if you will have it so."

The Scots were left alone for a little while, and content to be so. This had so far gone well for them, the admixture of reasoning, cajoling and implied threat. George was learning how statecraft and diplomacy worked.

Presently Suffolk returned, without Oxford. "His Majesty will see you, my lords," he said. "A short audience. He is not in the best of health."

The coincidence of weak and ailing monarchs for England and Scotland both, and for France in some measure also, for Charles the Sixth had fits of insanity, was very significant, and reinforced George's favour of the ancient Celtic custom of electing the monarch, or Ard Righ, from the royal house, not eldest son succeeding father.

69

They were led along more passages and up stairways to the royal apartments in the Winchester Tower where, in quite a small chamber on an upper floor, they were told to wait. But almost immediately Suffolk was back, with Oxford and an open-faced young man who eyed the visitors almost eagerly and who obviously had himself been waiting next door, dressed much more casually than were the two earls.

"His Majesty!" Suffolk said.

They all bowed.

"I, I welcome you, my lords," Richard said. "From Scotland, distant Scotland. You have ridden far, to come."

"We came by ship, Your Majesty. We are much honoured that you receive us. Here is the Earl of Angus and the Lord of Dalkeith, and my son, the Master of Dunbar. I am Dunbar and March. We come to renew the treaty of peace between the realms, with your royal consent."

"Peace, yes. That is good. I seek peace, ever." Richard Plantagenet, son of Edward the Black Prince and grandson of Edward the Third, was now aged twenty-four years, after succeeding to the throne at the age of ten. He was not notably royal of bearing, indeed seemed a little uncertain of himself, constantly looking over at Suffolk and Oxford. He seemed young for his years.

"His Grace, Robert of Scotland, wishes you well, Your Majesty. And hopes that the treaty of peace, in token, will be agreed."

"Yes. I so hope." That did not sound as though his was the decision. "For, for how long?"

"The one about to end was for nine years, Sire," Suffolk said. "We recommend that it be renewed for a similar period."

"Nine years. That would be well, yes."

"The treaty is with France also, Your Majesty. So it makes a notable accord."

"Oh, yes." The king looked again at his advisers. "Do I sign something? Some paper?"

"The treaty will have to be drawn up. Three copies,

70

Sire. All signed, sealed and exchanged. That will take time," Oxford said.

Suffolk nodded. "We have it on good authority that King Charles will sign, Your Majesty."

"Oh yes. He too desires peace. All should so do."

Cospatrick spoke. "We would be happy, Sire, since we cannot yet take the treaty itself back to King Robert, that we take a letter from Your Majesty agreeing this peace. For nine years, if that is what is recommended. As of promise."

"If that is all, yes . . ." The word yes seemed to be a favourite with the less than typical Plantagenet.

"We will have such letter written for you, Sire," Suffolk said. He turned to the Scots. "You will receive it hereafter." He bowed again, sketchily. "Have we your royal permission to retire?"

"Yes."

So that was it, however lacking in any drama, a strange performance to have come four hundred miles to achieve, George considered, as they backed out of the presence, leaving a distinctly uncertain-looking monarch.

As they returned whence they had come through that vast palace, Suffolk told them that since it was too late in the day for them to go back to London, they must spend the night in the castle. Rooms and a meal would he provided. And on the morrow they would be given the desired letter of agreement.

It seemed to be all arranged, for, instead of going to the chamber they had waited in earlier, they were handed over to the official following in their rear, who took them off some distance to another tower, where they were allotted three rooms above a kitchen: two bedchambers and a small hall, where a table was being set for a repast. There they were left.

"We are not to be honoured with Suffolk's and Oxford's company, it seems!" Cospatrick commented. "Not that we are greatly the losers over that! How say you?"

"They are less than good company," Angus agreed. "I

71

doubt whether they even love each other! But we appear to have gained what we came for. So that is well."

"I would say that nobody in this Windsor Castle loves the others," Dalkeith added. "Although it may be that this Richard and his queen do. We do not see her. They say that she is sickly."

Amity or none, at least an excellent meal was laid on for them, and their sleeping quarters were comfortable. They did not unduly delay their bed-going.

In the morning, while they breakfasted, the official who had brought them to this tower appeared with a sealed letter, sent by the Earl of Suffolk, he said, and with the information that their barge was awaiting them to take them back to their ship. It seemed that they were to go unaccompanied. Nor did they see the two earls before they left. Presumably these were remaining at Windsor meantime.

They found the same barge and oarsmen down at the canal, and these did not wait for any orders from the officer, nor any other passengers, before pushing off, no remarks to the Scots either.

With the river's current now with them, they made good time back to London.

They were glad to see *Lammerlaw* again.

They sailed off down Thames that same late afternoon, with no great desire to linger in London. They were now heading for the Wash and Bolingbroke Castle, a very different destination. They ought to be there by noonday on the morrow.

The Wash proved to be an extraordinary feature, halfway up the English east coastline, an enormous inlet, too large to be termed a bay, yet not really an estuary, nor even a sea loch either, oblong of shape, some twenty-two miles in length, it seemed, and about fifteen wide, this separating the shires of Norfolk and Lincoln. Very quickly after they turned into it they were made aware that it demanded careful navigation, being shallow save for a not very straight central channel, with sandbanks innumerable and the shorelines marshy and irregular. Their skipper liked it not at all, and said so. There were, however, tall poles erected in the water here and there along the way to indicate passage. He had been told a little about it, at London's docks, and learned that various rivers entered it, including the Ouse, the Witham and the Welland. But never having sailed it before, he was uncertain where these came in, what havens were available, and where this Bolingbroke lay. Nothing for it but to draw in to the first landing place they saw, and enquire.

They had not gone far in those fairly shallow waters, crewmen watching heedfully on either side, when they saw a township on the south side, with a pier and two fair-sized craft and smaller fishing-boats moored there. So at least this was approachable. They sailed in, and found space to tie up beside one of the other craft. Shouts thereto elicited the information that this was Hunstanton, in Norfolk. Asked as to Bolingbroke, they were told that this was afar off. They must sail across to Boston, almost a score of miles further, on the north side, in the mouth of the Witham river, this a considerable port, next in size to King's Lynn, at the Ouse mouth. Bolingbroke was north of there, some distance.

Thus informed, they sailed off again, somewhat less concerned over the navigation. If there were ports at King's Lynn and Boston, then the reaching of these could not be too hazardous. Probably the state of the tide was of importance in this. They judged it half tide at this present.

Those tall poles, seagulls sitting atop each, were of great help and, heading due westwards now across the width of the Wash, but scarcely directly because of those sand-banks, after a couple of hours of cautious sailing they saw a wide river mouth ahead, with buildings beckoning them in, particularly a very tall tower soaring above all, possibly a great church. For this they headed.

Presently they came to docks, and warehouses backing them, with quite a lot of moored shipping. Relieved, they drew in and found a vacant quayside berth. Shouts confirmed that this was Boston. They discovered that the ship next to them was in fact a Hansa merchant's one, from Lübeck on the Baltic; so this must be quite a major trading port.

Landing, the passengers enquired of the harbour-master how to get to Bolingbroke to see the Earl of Hereford, and were told that it lay some fifteen miles due north, near to the town of Spilsby. With that named destination they were eyed respectfully. Horses could be hired just off the market-place, they were assured.

So the four of them had a quite lengthy ride ahead of them.

They had no difficulty in obtaining mounts, and in late afternoon set off northwards. They followed the River Witham for only a mile or so before swinging off on a well-marked road north by east. Everyone they asked knew of Bolingbroke Castle and its powerful lord. Ahead rose a range of lowish hills, the Wolds they were told, this road leading to Spilsby. They had to cross various canals, and what in Scotland would be called stanks, draining the low-lying country, tilled and cattle-dotted, between those hills and the Wash.

In that level terrain they saw Bolingbroke Castle long before they reached it, as evening was upon them. It rose, stern and dominant, on the only swell of ground for miles around, no more impressive than Dunbar or Tantallon, but striking enough. They rode up to it, wondering what their reception would be here, and what they might gain from it, if anything. But the approach must be made, they agreed.

Their arrival at the drawbridge produced the usual shouted challenge; and the announcement that they were Scots lords to see the Earl of Hereford had astonished demands for that to be repeated. There quite an interval of delay thereafter, before the clanking of the chain lowering the bridge over the moat allowed them to cross. At the gatehouse arch beyond they were met by a truculent individual, who sourly asked who they were and what they wanted from the earl. His lordship was at table. When told their identities, he only partially moderated his hostile attitude, led them into a vaulted basement chamber of the main keep, and told them to wait. They admitted that it was an inconvenient time and manner to arrive, unannounced and uninvited.

It was not long, however, before a tall, good-looking, youngish man arrived, looking at them enquiringly.

"Did I hear aright?" he asked. "Two Scots earls, a lord and another? Come to Bolingbroke? I am Hereford."

"We came from London, from Windsor," Cospatrick informed. "By ship to Boston from King Richard's court, on our way back to Scotland. We regret, my lord, that we arrive thus. But we believed it wise and right to see you. I am Dunbar and March, and here is the Earl of Angus, and Douglas, Lord of Dalkeith. And my son."

"I have heard of the Earl of Dunbar," Hereford said. "Were you not one of those who made fool of Nottingham, up in the Percy country?" He smiled as he said it. "None so difficult a task, perhaps! We ought to do better for our Earl Marshal. As for our monarch, it may be!"

No comment on that was called for, however significant.

"Let us not interrupt your lordship's meal," Angus said. "Our talking can wait."

"But you have ridden from Boston? You will be craving meats and drink. Come, you must join us. No feast, but a sufficiency. Or would you wish to wash and the like, first?"

"You are kind, my lord . . ."

Hereford was, George judged, only a few years older than himself, well built, almost handsome, and with a ready smile, a very different Plantagenet from his royal cousin. He led them upstairs, asking why they had come by ship.

They heard music, lute and fiddle, as they climbed the winding stairway and were ushered into a lesser hall, lamp-lit, where a woman and three young children sat at table, these turning to gaze at the newcomers as they entered. At the far end of the room two musicians played their instruments. It made a pleasing domestic scene.

"Joan of Navarre, my good wife. And Harry and Thomas, our sons. And Blanche, our daughter," Bolingbroke announced. "Joan, here are the lords from Scotland, Dunbar and . . . Angus, was it? And others. Come to eat with us. From Boston. And London before that."

The lady rose, comely, and youthful-seeming to be the mother of these children. She did not look flustered nor put out; but then she was a princess, daughter of King Charles the Second of Navarre.

"You are welcome to our poor provender, my lords," she said. "Or . . . would you wish to wait and change out of your riding garb?"

"If you will have us thus, Countess, we will be honoured to join you as we are," Cospatrick said. "We wish to cause you no inconvenience, arriving thus unannounced. Some small refreshment will serve us very well. Anything . . ."

They sat, as servants brought in more foodstuffs, Hereford himself pouring them wine. It was not the time, in front of the lady and children, to explain the reasons for their visit, but some small indication was called for.

"We wish to . . . consult with my lord of Hereford before we return to His Grace King Robert with word of a peace treaty," the family were told.

"They have come by ship. To Boston, Joan. Ridden those miles. So will be hungered. Do you wish, my lords, for our minstrels to cease their playing? *We* enjoy music with our eating."

"No, no. It is, like the company, excellent," Angus said, half rising, to sketch a bow to the countess.

Thereafter, they dined well and at fair ease, until the mother led her youngsters off, none older than perhaps seven years.

Over their wine, the visitors told Hereford that they could not fail to be aware of the situation in England at this present, with competition for the throne, a monarch unsure of himself, and the lords of the land divided in their support.

In these circumstances their mission, to seek renewal of the peace treaty, held its problems. But such treaty was necessary, they believed, for all three realms, France included. They had learned that King Charles of France was in favour, and they had gained the agreement of King Richard and his advisers. But the Lancaster, Gloucester and Hereford party and alliance was, they were well aware, of all but equal importance, its concurrence essential for future assurance. They required this to take back to their liege-lord Robert and his regent. Hence this visit.

Bolingbroke nodded. "I recognise your concern," he said. "It is a large matter, and requires due consideration. On all aspects. I will think on it, and hear your views. Meantime, my friends, rooms are prepared for you. Go you and seek your comfort. Then come down again, and we shall go into the questions that arise, together. That is best, no?"

They agreed. A servitor rung for, they were conducted upstairs to three bedchambers, where warm water for washing awaited them. They were at one in finding Hereford a pleasing character and excellent host, but whether he would accept their policies, or was able to do so, in the absence of his father and uncle, remained to be seen. He was reputed to be a strong man, however amiable of presence. And *he* was the contender for the crown, not his elders.

Presently they all went downstairs again and rejoined their host. He poured them more wine, and came to the point right away.

"This of the treaty renewal − is it of true benefit to England?" he wondered. "It may suit Suffolk and Oxford, who have Richard in their grasp. They will be willing to pay the price for peace with Scotland, insecure as they are. But that is not necessarily to England's benefit. It did not prevent your Scots invasion of Northumberland, did it!"

"That was seen as a matter of the border Marches," Cospatrick declared. "Not a national attack. In response to a challenge."

"Yet your king's regent was with it. And the Earl of Douglas, who is the most powerful lord in your realm, is he not? With large numbers of men."

"It but served as a token, I judge. That Scotland was not to be . . . slighted. As your Nottingham had done. I am Chief Warden of the Marches, on the Scots side. I did not seek Fife's and Douglas's aid."

"Perhaps not, my lord. But they came! Any treaty of peace would have to ensure that the like did not recur."

"That we have, on King Robert's and his regent's authority, to promise."

"This must be written into any treaty. And then, there is the matter of France. You, in Scotland, have your own separate treaty with the French, other than this renewal, have you not? Of long-standing. To aid each other against England. What of that? Does it not make a nonsense of this other compact?"

"It is an understanding rather than any treaty, my lord. What we call the Auld Alliance. It has not been brought into effect for long. It is only a traditional conception."

"Yet, when *I* am king, and the French decide to try to retake Calais and Aquitaine, and I contest it, would this treaty of yours and Richard's halt the Scots from assailing me?"

This forthright assumption that Hereford would be King of England was not lost on his hearers. They eyed each other.

"Is that likely, my lord?" Dalkeith asked.

"With the French, who knows? The present Charles is weak. He could be followed by a stronger monarch. Or, indeed, displaced. Then, what? I have to consider the like."

"The renewed treaty would cover this, I judge," Cospatrick said.

"You *judge*! I would require more than your judgment, however worthy, my lord of Dunbar!"

"Could we not have such written into the treaty?" Angus asked.

"I do not see why not . . ."

"Think well on it, my lords. For *I* do! When I take over the throne, I do not wish to start by breaking a treaty." He shrugged. "Then there is the issue of the signatures. If the treaty is signed by Richard, in the name of England, it could become invalid when I take over."

"If you do, my lord! I—"

"*When* I do!" Even though said with a smile, that interruption was very positive. "This treaty is for nine years did you not say?"

"Yes. Would not the words '. . . and his successors' after King of England be a sufficient warrant?" Cospatrick asked.

"I would prefer success*or*, my lord!"

"Very well. We can so urge." A pause. "Can we so take it, then? These provisions included, you would agree the treaty, my lord of Hereford?"

"Meantime, yes."

"And what of the two dukes? Your father and Gloucester?" Angus wondered.

"They will not contest my agreement. My father, John of Gaunt, is old now. And his brother less than well. They support me in all things."

That seemed to be that, a very confident man to deal with, however friendly of manner. All sat back and sipped their wine.

Then their extraordinary host rose and went over to the chairs where the minstrels had sat formerly, and, picking up the lute there, proceeded to strum on it tunefully. Then he raised voice and began to sing the verses of a haunting balled about a wife wrapped in wether's skin, accompanying himself with the instrument in expert style, clearly at ease in so doing and putting much meaning into his words and pauses.

When he ended it the listeners raised their goblets in salutation and esteem. Inclining his head, Hereford gave them another, very different, a rollicking hunting song entitled "Our Goodsman", to the beat of horses' hooves and the halloos of the huntsmen, which had his guests beating time with their feet.

When he laid aside the lute, Cospatrick spoke.

"You are most notable in entertainment as in all else, my lord. Myself, I am no singer. But my son George, here, has a fair voice and often sings our border songs. Give us the ballad of 'Child Roland and Burd Ellen', lad. A favourite."

George looked distinctly doubtful, but, clearing his throat, stood up. He did not go over for the lute, but, after shaking his head, drew breath and commenced to sing, quickly becoming more confident and rendering the stirring tale of love and daring and tragedy in effective fashion.

Applauded, he then gave them "King Malcolm and Sir Colvine", this equally well received.

After some casual talk, and interest expressed in Hereford's fondness for music, Cospatrick declared that they should no longer keep their host away from his wife, and that they would seek their beds, greatly commending the hospitality received.

They went upstairs to their lamp-lit rooms, steaming water awaiting them.

In the morning, summoned down for breakfast, they found the family already at table. The countess said that she had been told that the Master of Dunbar was an excellent songster. Would he be so good as to give her and her children one of his ballads, even thus early in the day?

Less embarrassed now, George rose to offer them "The Gay Goshawk", which began thus:

> When grass grew green on Lanark's plains,
> And fruit and flowers did spring,
> A Scottish squire, to cheerful strains
> Sae merrily thus did sing

This suitable for the youngsters, he judged. As he announced it, Hereford went over for the lute, still by its

80

chair, and, after the first stanza, was able to twang the strings in time and tune.

George did not give them the entire long tale, but ended with the verse:

> And weel he kent that lady fair
> Amang her maidens free,
> For the flower that springs in May morning
> Was not sae sweet as she.

Bowing to the lady, he returned to his seat, amid clapping.

It all made a notable and pleasing change from diplomacy and negotiation.

Hereford offered them a day's hawking, there apparently being many duck and wildfowl among the streams and canals thereabouts; but he was told that they had been away from their lands and folk overlong already, and that they must get back to their ship. With expressions of gratitude and esteem they took their leave, wishing their host and hostess and family and cause well. Young Henry, the eldest child, shouted up to the mounted George that he was a good singer, and that so was *he*!

Cospatrick asserted that Hereford would make a deal better king for England than did Richard, or indeed than had done most of his predecessors. This was agreed by all.

The *Lammerlaw* ought to have them back at Dunbar by forenoon on the morrow, with the wind now behind them.

8

Home, the earl had to go on, next day, to Edinburgh, or it might be Stirling, or even Perth and Scone, to report to King Robert and Fife on the fair success of their mission; but this did not apply to George, who had his own priorities. Yester Castle beckoned him. Apparently Gavin had twice been there, in the interim, accompanied by Colin. He could have done without their company on this occasion, but could hardly say so.

The three of them rode the dozen miles fairly early in the day, hopefully to find the young women not yet gone out, whether hawking, visiting or whatever they tended to do with their time. In this they were successful. Unfortunately, as far as George was concerned, Sir William Hay was at home, and desirous of hearing of the errand to England and the situation there in some detail, especially the rivalry between the Plantagenets, Richard and Bolingbroke, which meant that the other brothers were able to go off with the girls while he was closeted with their father. On this occasion their two young brothers, John and David went also

However, when he could escape, he found them all out in the orchard practising archery, Gavin and Colin demonstrating their expertise – although the young women were none so ineffective at it either, Alicia proving all but a match for them.

When Beatrix saw George arrive, she laid down her bow and came over to him.

"The envoy and traveller!" she said, smiling. "We have missed our Master George, attentive as his brothers have been!"

"Not too attentive, I hope? I came just as soon as I could."

"Yes. You are the busy one. You saw the King of England? And other great ones?"

"Indeed yes. Many others, the Earl of Hereford in especial. He will be king one day, he says. I was telling your father. But . . . I thought of you often, Beatrix."

"Did you? Surely, with all the great ones that you saw, such as my sisters and myself would be of little moment to you!"

"*You* were. Why think you that I have come to Yester so soon after our return?"

She smiled that quiet smile of hers. "You are kind. Do you join the archery? Outdo your brothers perhaps?"

"I would rather do . . . otherwise. With you. Go somewhere else. Where we can talk and . . ." He left the rest unsaid.

"Ah, so. You have much to tell me, of kings and courts and the like."

"No. That is not what I meant. Great ones can be a disappointment. Although not all of them. Hereford was not. A notable man. He sings ballads. As do I, on occasion . . ."

"Do you? I like ballads. This Hereford you mention: I fear that I do not know who he is. I am very ignorant."

"No, no. *I* scarcely did, until a few days ago. He is often called Bolingbroke, Henry of Bolingbroke. That is his castle. He is a Plantagenet, cousin of King Richard. Whom we saw at Windsor. A strange man . . ."

"You were not in London? Is not that where the King of England dwells?"

"We were in the Tower, yes. A mighty place. Much hurt done there . . ."

They were strolling off, back towards the castle. Beatrix pointed.

"Yonder. Over that stile, and through the kitchen-garden to where we keep our hawks' cages. We feed them often. Pet them, almost, so that they know us. The better for the hawking . . ."

They reached a stile. Lifting her skirt, she was beginning to climb on to the step and over when George took her
arm, and helped her up, and down. Crossing with a vault
himself, he managed not to leave go of that arm, continuing to hold it as they proceeded. She did not shake him off.

Through the garden they came to the row of wickerwork
cages where the falcons roosted on their perches, Beatrix
pointing out different birds. George pretended to be
interested.

"Which ones were you flying that day when we came on
you, at the Whiteadder?" he asked. "That was a good day.
Noteworthy indeed!"

"Was it? We had gained only the two mallard. And lost
two."

"It was the day that I met with you! *That* was its
importance."

"And Alicia."

"Oh, yes. I like Alicia well. But . . . you are different."

"Different, yes. I am less . . . spirited! She is lightsome,
outgoing and jaunty . . ."

"But you are *you*!"

"Can I be other? Let us go see the hounds. Over there.
Beyond this garden . . ."

His hand slipped down her arm, to take and hold hers as
they walked.

They came to a larger enclosure, with higher wicker
fencing, where hounds paced to and fro, some greeting
their arrival with barks and yelps.

"You do not find me displeasing, Beatrix?" he asked,
somewhat jerkily. "I mean, over-forward?"

"Why should I, George?" That was the first time that
she had actually named him that, without the Master.

"It is just that I have been away since first I saw you. For
weeks. But thought of you much. While my brothers have
come to you here. I have . . . to make up for lost time, I
feel!"

She squeezed those fingers a little. "Time passed is not
always lost!" she said.

"You mean . . . ?"

"Only that absence is not always . . . untoward." She freed her hand, to point. "See you that greyhound. I call her Harriet. After Lochquhariot, our other castle on the Gore Water. Sometimes I take her into the house. None of the others. I am fond of her."

"Fortunate animal!"

She laughed and, unlike her sister, she did not often laugh, however warm her smile.

"See, we shall take her a walk, shall we? Up this Hopes Water here. On the side of Dod Law, up yonder, there are two ancient forts, or what is left of them. It is not far – a mile or so. You can walk well enough in your riding-boots?"

"To be sure. I will like that. You enjoy walking?"

"Yes. I walk a lot. Usually with Harriet. She is very obedient. I have trained her well." She opened the gate, calling the hound and shooing off the others.

"You use no leash?"

"No. She does not need it. Does not dash off."

They went along the crest of the quite steep bank of the ravine of the rushing burn, until it rose and shallowed into open rolling grassland, cattle-dotted. There Beatrix pointed southwards to where the rising ground steepened into a fair-sized hill, an outlier of the Lammermuirs.

"Dod Law," she said. "Who was Dod, I wonder? Dod is a form of your name, is it not, George? I doubt whether those Picts would use that. They spoke the Gaelic, did they not? Could Dod be George in the Gaelic?"

"I know not. Are you interested in the Picts?"

"I am, yes. Are not you? They are our far-back ancestors, after all. We ought to know more about them. What their signs and carvings mean. Their forts and stone circles and standing stones are all over these hills. You were pointing out Nine Stane Rig to me, that day."

"Aye. I did not know that you were thus knowledgeable, Beatrix. I am sorry. You must have thought me a bumpkin to tell you all that, which you well knew already."

"Not so. It was all new country for us. And that of the shielings I did not know. Tell me, George – my father says that *your* father, if he had his rights, would be sitting on the throne now, not Robert Stewart. Is that fact?"

So George was able to tell her the old story of Malcolm Canmore and his two wives, and the Cospatrick line, his father the tenth earl but the fourteenth of that style, as they climbed the hill, the hound never darting off nor needing to be called to heel. They were among sheep now, not cattle, these drifting off at sight of them.

"They were strong for circles, were they not, the Picts," Beatrix said, as they came to the first one, above a tributary burn, in a strong position, and they examined its grassy ramparts and two outer ditches, and the inner circular space where the huts would have been, the living quarters. "Hut circles, stone circles and circular forts."

"Yes, and brochs, these round-built also."

"Brochs?"

"Do you not know of brochs? So – here is something I *can* tell you, without making a fool of myself! Brochs were Pictish stone towers, tall, with very thick but hollow walls in which were circular stairways and little chambers, the open centre for driving their beasts into for safety, cattle and sheep, the folk taking refuge in the wall chambers. Brochs were not for living in, like the forts and hut circles, only to flee into for safety from enemies, these mainly the Norsemen. Few have survived, not hereabouts. Only one I know, at Edenshall, near to Abbey St Bathans, none so far off. I visit it on occasion from my little castle of Colbrandspath."

"I have never seen nor heard of such. How far is that?"

"A score of miles, perhaps. You are a good horsewoman. I could take you there one day."

"That would be good."

"I shall not forget . . ."

They moved on up to the higher-placed fort, somewhat larger, near the hilltop. From that lofty viewpoint they could see for almost endless miles, to north and west but

86

not south and east, where higher hills blocked the vista. Beatrix was able to point to Traprain Law, due north about eight miles, with its craggy south-facing escarpment, now visible over lesser heights; and they spoke of Loth, King of the Southern Picts, who had his seat on that hill, and who gave name to their Lothian. Also of his daughter Thanea the saint, who had borne Kentigern or St Mungo, founder of Glasgow so far to the west.

Beatrix, in the middle of this fort circle, wondered why the ancients had been so concerned with circles, rather than squares or other shapes? George said that his late mother had been of religious mind, and had told him that the circle represented wholeness, godliness, without start nor finish, as was the Creator. And that the ancients, before they were converted to Christianity, associated the circle with worship also, because of the sun and moon, the shape of these; and the circle of the seasons, with its fertility of the land, their stone circles where they worshipped the sun. And how St Columba, when he came to convert them, used their circles to plant his own little chapels or cells, as worshipping places already, even though with a mistaken religion. It all seemed a reasonable explanation.

But it was time to turn back. The others would be wondering what had happened to them, not that this greatly concerned George. This had been a day to remember and cherish – and still was. More than once the man found occasion for physical contact, on their way, in aiding his companion over burns and marshy patches and rocky outcrops, and was duly thanked.

When they got back to the castle, it was to find the others drinking honey wine and eating oatcakes in the lesser hall, with Sir William; and searching were the questions as to where they had been and what they had been up to. Their answer that they had been on the trail of the Picts was met with raised eyebrows and head-shakings. But when Beatrix asked her father about brochs, and he admitted that he had heard of such but never seen one, nor knew aught about

87

them, she was able to launch into what George had told her, and said that there was one within riding distance, near to St Bathans. They must go and see it one day.

George rather wished that she had not suggested it when the other young people declared that they would like to do that. He had, of course, visualised himself taking Beatrix there alone.

But it was soon high time for their ride back to Dunbar, and leave-taking. In front of all, George had to restrict himself to formalities, but did manage a hidden arm-squeeze. He wondered, as he saw Gavin openly putting an arm round Alicia's shoulders whether *he* might have been rather more bold and demonstrative. They asserted that they would be back; and Sir William was urged to bring his family over to visit Dunbar. George forbore to mention Edenshall Broch again.

9

Earl Cospatrick came back from Stirling creased of brow.
His report of the treaty mission had been well enough
received at court, although a return visit to England was
required forthwith; thereafter, when he had raised the
matter of his daughter Elizabeth's proposed betrothal to
young David, Earl of Carrick, not mentioned for some
considerable time, King Robert had looked at Fife, and
that man had waved a hand and said that they were
considering other matrimonial alliance. Needless to say,
this had been a major upset, for not only was it something
of an insult, but quite a large part of the dowery, or
marriage-portion, for the proposed espousal, in lands
and moneys, had been deposited with the crown's treasury. This would have to be repaid if any new betrothal
went ahead.

It was a sorry situation, and worrying. Most evidently it
was Fife's doing, in favour of the daughter of Archibald
the Grim.

Daughter Elizabeth was not too greatly concerned,
never having met the said David Stewart, formerly of
Strathearn, now of Carrick. This even though it would
presumably have made her queen one day. What the said
David's reaction might be was undisclosed.

A further annoyance for the earl was this of having to go
back to London so soon, this to confirm the royal agreement to the terms of the treaty, and to add one or two
minor adjustments, under the Great Seal of Scotland.
Moreover, Angus was involved in negotiations to wed
the Princess Mary, at some financial cost; he was unable
to go with his friend, and John, Earl of Moray, was to aid

in representing the crown with his brother Cospatrick. He would be coming down to Dunbar within the next day or two. There was no suggestion that George should accompany his father and uncle on this occasion.

Uncle John's arrival, as it happened, coincided with sad news. George's other Uncle John, by marriage, John Maitland of Lethington, husband of Aunt Elizabeth, a nearby laird and senior vassal, related to the Hays, had died suddenly. So it was a funeral before the two earls' departure for the south, this to be at the great church of St Mary's at Haddington.

The *Lammerlaw* was prepared to take the envoys once more. They would sail two days after the interment.

All the Dunbar family, then, rode off to bury this Uncle John, and to console and condole with Aunt Elizabeth. And on arrival at St Mary's, this all but an abbey or cathedral in size and dignity, George found, and possibly Gavin also, that his mourning was rather lessened by the sight of Beatrix Hay and the rest of her family attending the funeral also. The Hays were, of course, not only relatives but neighbours of Lethington.

George sought to keep his mind on the service thereafter, not entirely successfully.

He was able to pick his way through the many mourners to Beatrix's side as eventually all gathered round the descent to the underground crypt to see the corpse lowered to its rest therein, this among former Hays.

As all began to disperse, George managed to have a quick word with Beatrix. He had not forgotten his promise to take her to see Edenshall Broch. Could he persuade her to come with him? And, if possible, on her own? He liked her sisters and brothers, but this of their mutual interest in the Picts would make their little journey the more suitable alone, would it not? Her smiling nod gladdened him. How would she arrange it? She said that she often rode alone, with the hound Harriet, usually around the hills of Dod Law, Fernie Law and Bleak Law. So it would not be difficult, if he thought that would be best?

Trying not to sound elated, George said that he would meet her up at the fort on Dod Law two days hence. Would that suit? Next day he would have to see his father and uncle off in their ship. An hour before noon, then, the day after the morrow?

Shaking her head over him, but not really censoriously, Beatrix went to rejoin her family.

Much too happy for good funeral attendance, George helped to conduct his grieving aunt and the new Maitland of Lethington, Robert, home, before returning to Dunbar.

Next day he waved farewell to his father and uncle on *Lammerlaw*, thankful to be left behind on this occasion.

And next morning he was off early for his rendezvous on Dod Law. He was going to have a lot of riding this day, but that was no least worry. Would Beatrix be there?

She was, dismounted and sitting on the green rampart of the higher port, the hound with her, visible from some distance. He had acknowledged to himself for some time now that he was in love. But, although his heart leaped at the sight of her, he must restrain himself lest he overdo it and possibly scare the young woman off. Not that she had so far shown signs of being wary of him, other than her head-shakings.

Jumping down from his horse, he ran to her, his restraint not entirely evident. He took both her arms, to all but shake her as he aided her to rise, less than helpful as that was.

"So you came!" he exclaimed. "You did it. And alone. My dear!"

"It was not difficult," she said. "I have been here for some time, enjoying the view. But – am I your dear?"

"What think you, lass, what think you?"

"I think that you do not know me sufficiently well so to name me! But you will learn. And perhaps change your mind, George. Meantime, let us pursue the Picts! How do we go to this broch of yours?"

"M'mm. We go south by east, through the hills. But . . .

how much better should I have to know you before, before . . . ?"

"Before you may call me dear? I may give you cause to change your mind! My sisters say that I am the owl of the family. They call me Bea the Owl! Because I keep myself to myself. Am quiet, but hidden of thought. So you are warned, sir!"

Not knowing quite what to make of that, he aided her up to her saddle, admiring legs as he did so.

They rode on, and although she might be the quiet one, it was Bea the Owl who did most of the talking, mainly about the Picts, *his* thoughts presently rather less concerned with the distant past.

They went through the hills, among the sheep, to the long and twisting valley of the Faseny Water, which took them eastwards mile after mile, round ever more heathery heights, to near to Cranshaws, all Dunbar country, some of it indeed Dunbar Common. There they swung off for the upper Whiteadder and the little religious community of Abbey St Bathans, where there was a nunnery of Cistercian sisters, this called after the Columban missionary Baithan, and founded by a former Countess of Dunbar, this among much lesser hills. Beatrix thought that they ought to call in there, in passing, to pay their respects to the nuns; but George said that they could do that later. Let them get on to Edenshall first, another two miles along that devious valley.

At length, after no fewer than fourteen miles of riding, they reached a point where he could point upwards above a quite steep ascent, where a beehive-shaped tower rise from the skyline, to be seen from all directions.

"Edenshall," he said. "We climb now."

He led a somewhat round-about way up, the horses having to pick their route among outcrops and rocky brows.

"These Picts chose difficult places, did they not?" she asked.

"They had eyes for defence. They had to have. This was

a refuge, see you, no usual dwelling place." Even as he said it, he was wondering how far he might go, in other than these miles, in his advances towards this companion of his. That she had been prepared to come with him all this way, alone, knowing of his past closenesses and touchings, was a hopeful sign. But this of her alleged warning, that she was apt to keep herself to herself, was scarcely encouraging. How was a man to take that? Could he risk putting the matter to the test in some measure? Or was it too soon? He had thought long about this Edenshall venture. The broch provided opportunities for tests, assuredly. Master of Dunbar he might be; but where this young woman was concerned, any mastery was very much a-missing.

Up on the hill summit at last they eyed their destination, lofty, massive, well preserved considering it was unmortared stone, and the winds and weather it must have faced down the centuries – and, of course, it was circular.

"It is much larger than I had thought," Beatrix said. "They must have been good builders. There is stone a-plenty around, but so large and high. And there are no windows!"

"They have these on the inside. It had to be large if the central space was to hold their animals, or some of them. The way it narrows in at the top is interesting. The thickness of the walling lessens as one goes up. The little chambers are all in the lower parts. Still without mortar."

They dismounted and led their horses and the dog in at the single doorway and through the walling, to find themselves in a quite wide court area, floored part slab, part naked rock, but open to the skies, the walling curving in as it rose. Small windows opened at various levels.

There was only one doorway, low set, from this yard. Beatrix ordered the hound to wait there with the horses, and it sat. They had to stoop to enter the building itself, this defensive again. George had no need to excuse himself for taking his companion's arm in the semi-darkness.

They were in a sort of lobby, with one of the wall chambers opening off, this windowless, evidently a guard-room. Ahead was the beginning of a stairway going up into darkness.

Taking Beatrix by the hand now, George led her to climb that stair's uneven treads. They went carefully, necessarily, more or less feeling their way. The stair was not a turnpike, as in later castles, but straight, save in that it coiled round in the walling as it rose, inevitably. They went silently now for some reason.

Faintly, light from the first of those windows beckoned them on. And when they reached this, opposite it was a doorway into a tiny closet-like chamber, perhaps eight feet by six. They peered in, but there was really nothing to see.

"More of these as we go up," Beatrix was told. "They get even smaller higher, as the walling narrows."

Creeping up, they came to another window and doorway. "They must have used lamps or candles. Perhaps we should have brought the like."

The young woman peered out through the window-gap, and then she was ushered into the little cell, L-shaped. Once round its bend, they were in darkness.

"This is . . . eerie! Almost frightening, somehow," Beatrix said. "I wonder why? I can almost feel them here, about us, in this dark place."

"Fear nothing," he told her. "All is well. They will not hurt you. They are our forebears, after all. And . . . I am with you!"

That was all that man needed. He took her in his arms and pressed her to him, holding her rounded person. He kissed her. It was only her brow, where he would have wished for her lips, but it was a token, a declaration.

She did not speak nor make any response, but nor did she turn away nor withdraw from his arms.

They stood there for moments. Then, taking her hand again, he led her out. And up more steps.

They passed other little chambers, these not unlike garderobes in their castles, but he did not seek to enter

94

any as they wound their way up, the prevailing darkness only briefly and feebly lit by those small windows. George, of course, had known that it would be so, but even he felt that some closeness was called for, quite apart from personal desires. The girl's hand indeed gripped his quite tightly.

Eventually they came out on to the broch's summit platform, in broad daylight, and could go over to a broken parapet and gaze at the landscape. But he did not let go of her hand.

"That was . . . strange," she declared. "I felt that we were not alone. As though they were watching us. But not . . . hostile. Not resenting us." She wagged her head. "Did you feel the like, George?"

"I felt that . . . we needed each other!" he answered.

"No. It is not the place to be in on one's own."

"Perhaps not. But I am glad that *we* were alone in it, lass. You, and myself."

She smiled at him but did not speak.

They turned, still hand in hand, to glance down the central gap at the horses and at Harriet gazing up at them, before re-entering that stairway and descending, George still leading the way; he passed the first two of the small closets, but at the third he drew her in, this one having just a hint of light from the nearest window.

"Do you feel safer now?" he asked her.

"With you?" A slightly breathless laugh. "Who knows!"

"Bea the Owl is ever safe with me," he asserted. And dropping her hand, he took her in his arms again. He kissed her. This time it was on the lips.

Hers did not stir beneath his, but nor did she push him away. "Is that . . . safety?" she got out.

"It is my need!" he told her. "Need. I have wanted that for long."

"Not so very long," she corrected him. "We have not known each other for . . . ." She got no further before he closed her lips again.

This time she did draw back a little. "I think it best . . . that we go down," she said. "Time. We have a long ride back."

He had to accept that. "You are not . . . troubled?" he asked, as *she* now led the way out and down.

"I but wonder!" she said, leaving him to make what he would of that.

They were silent as they reached the foot, and moved out into the little court to the waiting horses and patient hound. They led these outside, to where George assisted the young woman to mount.

"That was . . . an experience," she told him. "Not to be forgotten."

"But, none so ill?"

"Not ill, no. But . . . unusual. For me!"

"For myself also," he agreed, as he climbed to his own saddle.

They left it at that, and rode to head north by west again. Their talk was necessarily only intermittent, general and fairly brief, as they covered the winding hilly miles, Harriet bounding along with them, tireless.

At length, much length, they were within sight of Yester Castle, and Beatrix pointed.

"I think, George, that you should not accompany me further. I did not say to the others that I was meeting you, or where I was going. So best that you do not come beyond this. Leave me here, with much to think on!"

"As you will . . ."

She reined her mount closer to his, and smiled. "Give me your hand," she ordered.

Wondering, he reached out to her, as though to shake hands, odd as this seemed to him. But she took it, and turned it palm upwards. Then stooping in her saddle, she raised it, and planted a kiss, with the palm open, then closed his fingers over it.

"Just something of a promise!" she said. "You have it secure?" And she reined round, and was off.

He stared after her, wondering still. Then he called. "I will – oh, I will. And I will be back . . ."

He rode homeward, mind and emotions in something of a whirl. Every now and again he looked at that right hand of his, and clenched it tight.

10

Earl Cospatrick and his brother arrived back sooner than expected, not having had to go to Windsor this time and being able to complete the treaty arrangements, and add the new terms, at the Tower of London without much difficulty, Suffolk and Oxford more worried about Hereford's threat to their power over their king than the Scots or French situation.

They came back to find a sealed letter awaiting them, brought two days before by a royal messenger. George had not opened it, addressed as it was to the Earls of Dunbar and March and of Moray. When Cospatrick did break the royal seal, it was to raised eyebrows indeed. He passed the letter to his brother, who also showed surprise.

The former told his son that it was not from King Robert, nor his regent but from the queen, Annabella. She had been known to be much concerned over her husband's state and the dominance of his brother Fife, for long. Now, it seemed, she was going to take an active part in the realm's affairs, in her John/Robert's name; and she sought the help of these two great earls, as of sundry others, in her efforts, these clearly directed against Fife and Douglas. She desired them to come to her at Stirling Castle just as soon as might be.

Queen Annabella was the daughter of Sir John Drummond of Stobhall, and was a strong-minded woman, with two sons, David and James, and two daughters, Mary and Elizabeth. Being married to the feeble King Robert must have made a trying life for her.

So the two brothers had to set sail again, this time up Forth, making for Airth, as near to Stirling as their ship could take them. Cospatrick was finding little time, these days, to be at home and attending to his earldom, George kept busy as deputy.

When his father returned, three days later, it was with no little to tell. Queen Annabella was very concerned over many aspects of her husband's realm's conditions and well-being, its peace and security. She was determined to take a hand in improving them. She was particularly upset by her brother-in-law Fife's behaviour and the way that he was in effect ruling the land, much exceeding his role as regent. She was barely on speaking terms with him now, and he was maintaining his own court at Scone and indeed but seldom coming to Stirling to consult with the king. When he did, he was apt to slight her, and this before others. If her husband would not, or could not, assert himself in the realm's cause, *she* must, if only for her son David's sake, heir to the throne. So she was seeking to gather the support of some of the most powerful men in the nation. She had made a start by arranging the betrothal of her daughter Mary to the Earl of Angus, despite their disparity in ages. Now she desired the aid of himself and Moray, and any others whom they might suggest as possibles and worthy. He, Cospatrick, was glad enough to co-operate with her, only too well aware that Fife's wings needed clipping.

His brother John had been given an immediate and challenging task. As well as being Earl of Moray he was married to her sister-in-law. He was the man best placed, she said, to bring to heel that other wretched brother of the king, Alexander, Earl of Buchan, known to all as the Wolf of Badenoch, a murderous and evil man, who was creating havoc and distress in the Highlands. There were complaints coming from many clans and chiefs, including the Lord of the Isles himself, the new Earl of Ross, the Mackintosh, Cameron of Lochiel, Shaw of Tordarroch and others. But Fife was not doing anything about his brother's excesses and ignoring the charges. Moray was to go up to his northern territories and seek to make these complainers act together against the royal offender. He would have the backing of Holy Church in this, which could be valuable, in moneys for paying for armed forces in especial, for Buchan had just recently gone so far as to burn down Elgin Cathedral, this because the Bishop of Moray had refused to aid in getting a papal divorce from the Countess of Ross, despite his holding on to the broad lands that he had gained by wedding her.

George, of course, had heard of this Wolf of Badenoch and some of his ongoings – who had not? From his castles of Lochindorb and Loch-an-Eilean, on Speyside, he was said even to hunt people like deer, on horseback, making a sport of it, slaying and ravaging, raping and burning. And his many sons, legitimate and otherwise, were following in their father's footsteps. The name of Stewart had become hated and spat upon in the north, this to the disgrace of the crown. That the regent had done nothing about it was as blameworthy as it was shameful. Now the queen was seeking to redeem the royal reputation, in some measure, and in this respect using Moray to effect it.

Cospatrick said that his brother ought to have little difficulty in raising forces for his task; at least, if he could unite the ever feuding clans to act together for once.

Annabella had also besought him, Cospatrick, together with Angus and Douglas, to try to limit the powers of Archibald the Grim, who was, from Galloway and the Douglasdale area, ever seeking to extend his lands, in especial into Ayrshire and even Renfrewshire, and causing much resentment and unrest there – and he with Fife's friendship and support. If other sections of the great house of Douglas, the most powerful family south of Forth and Clyde, could be rallied to bring pressure on the earl thereof, together with the many threatened lords of south-western lands, then something like peace might be achieved.

The sorrows of a nation with a weak monarch and a divided royal family.

Fortunately George's presence did not seem to be required on this expedition, to his relief; for presently his concerns were distinctly nearer at hand. He did wonder whether he should mention to his father that he had fallen in a large way for Beatrix Hay; but decided that it would be wiser to wait until he was rather more certain as to *her* reactions. A rejected lover would cut a sorry figure, if it was known.

George saw his sire off south-westwards, necessarily not by ship this time, on his long and round-about journey and series of interviews. He was going to call on all likely adherents to Annabella's cause, whether from enmity for Fife or fear of Douglas, these Crichtons, Murrays, Scotts, Kerrs, Carmichaels, Hamiltons, Montgomerys, Kennedys, Cunninghams, Dalziels and others, a legion if only they could, like the Highland clans, be got to take united action, this a major task and challenge. Cospatrick's own vassals could be relied upon for support. Dalkeith would join him.

Now for affairs of the heart, rather than the nation.

How to ensure that he saw Beatrix alone? This ever the problem. There must be some way. Suppose that he went to that cage for the dogs, and released the hound Harriet? That ought not to be seen from the castle. Took her some distance off, and tied her up. He would need a leash or rope. Then went and reported that he had found her loose. Seeking Beatrix, to be sure. The dog was *her* favourite. She would almost certainly go with him to recover the creature. It might serve. He could think of no other device. He would go early in the forenoon, in case she herself had ridden off somewhere unknown.

He went, approaching Yester heedfully so as not to be observed from the castle. Leaving his horse behind trees, tethered, he made for the cages. How to get the hound out, seemingly by accident, without leaving the gate open, and all the other animals escaping? If he wedged the open gate too narrowly for any creatures to get out, it might still look as though it had been a genuine escape, and by a hound used to going off on its own with the young woman. A wedge of rock?

101

He searched and found a suitable sliver of slate-like stone.

There was no difficulty in extracting Harriet, at least. She remembered him and came, tail wagging, when he called her. The gate was not locked, only tied. He put his leash round her neck and led her out, jamming his stone under the bottom bar of the gate, leaving it open by no more than three inches. No other dog would get through that. Then he took her back to his horse, and thereafter led both animals some distance whence he had come, well away from the castle. He found a tree to tie both horse and hound to, patted Harriet's head, and went off on foot to the castle entrance.

When he had gained admittance, it was David, the younger brother, whom a servant brought him. He asked for Beatrix, and was conducted to an upper chamber where she and her sister were embroidering a tapestry. He was greeted with cries of welcome.

Seeking to keep a straight face, he announced that, coming to visit them, he had found the hound, Harriet, running loose. She was some distance off. He had wondered at this. As to where Beatrix or other might be. He had tied her to a tree. Was this in order?

They all looked at him in surprise, asking how the creature could possibly have got out. But Beatrix did rise, and said that she would go and see to it, however it had happened. George was thankful indeed that none of the others appeared anxious to investigate it.

So they went out together, objective achieved so far. She said that she was glad to see him, which was a hopeful sign.

When they got to the cage and she saw the wedged gate, she frowned, and looked enquiringly at him.

"I do not understand this," she declared. "Somebody has done it. Deliberately. That stone. Harriet could not have got out through that small gap. I wonder . . . ?"

He grinned, then, and patted her arm. "No need to wonder," he said. "*I* did it. Did it all. I could think of no other way of ensuring that I might win to you alone, Beatrix. But it has done it. You are here, with me – and only you!"

"Save us all – you went to such lengths, George! To contrive this. So much doing. I wonder why?"

"Because I wanted only you, lass. Not . . . your family."

"M'mm." She shut the gate properly. "Was it so . . . important?"

"It was. And is. For *me*. Come, I will take you to the hound."

She shook her head over him. "I think that I have found myself a . . . a very devious friend!"

"Not devious, lass. Just . . . eager."

"Is it all this dealing with kings and lords and the like that has made you thus?"

He shrugged. He was leading her on now, for horse and hound. "My father is off again," he told her. "On Queen Annabella's business, this time. She is now taking a hand in the nation's affairs, to counter Fife and Douglas. The king is all but useless. As well that he has a wife of some spirit. But, thankfully, I did not have to go with him."

"Why thankfully?"

"Because I wanted to come and see *you*."

"Oh, dear! Is that so important?"

"Yes."

They were silent for a few moments as they walked.

"Where is Harriet? And your horse?" she asked.

"Not far now. Beatrix, you said friend, back there. You see me as your friend?"

"Why, yes. Are you not? It would seem so."

"I would wish you more than friend."

Another silence. He took her arm.

They came to the tethered horse and dog, the latter whimpering at the sight of them.

"What now?" she wondered.

"I do not want just to take you back to the others. After . . . all this!"

She smiled. "I see that. But I am not clad for riding."

"We could walk on. Leave the horse here. Or . . . you could mount behind me in the saddle. For a little."

"I am scarcely clad for that either, George, am I? I suppose that we could walk on for a little way. Since you have gone to so much trouble and scheming. Why, I am not so sure!"

He looked at her. "Could you, would you, mount and ride *before* me? Myself behind."

"That would look very strange, would it not?"

"Who is to see us? If we rode in quiet places."

"My skirts . . ." She was untying the hound.

"M'mm. Yes. See you, why not in front? Sidelong? Between my arms. We could ride thus."

"Ah! Is this part of your cunning devisings, Master of Dunbar? To get a woman secure in your arms!"

"I had not thought thus far," he admitted. "But it would be a joy!"

"For whom? I see that I must watch where I tread with you! But I will not be treading, up there with you, will I!"

"No. Then . . . you will do it? Ride in my arms?"

"It seems the only thing to be done, does it not?"

"Beatrix, my heart!" Before she might think better of it, he untied the horse and leaped up into the saddle. Reining over to her, he bent, holding out his hands to her.

Head ashake again, she reached up to him. With a great heave he hoisted her up and settled her in his arms, before him, the horse side-stepping.

George dug in his heels and they moved off, his arms firmly round her now.

"My love, my love! This is a wonder!"

"Love?" she said. "Did I hear aright? Love?"

"Yes. Love, lass, I love you! Love you. I have known it now, for long."

"Not so *very* long."

"Long enough to need you, ache for you, dream of you! How can I convince you? And hope, pray, that I can somehow make you feel for me? Can I hope, lass? Hope?"

"I cannot stop you hoping. If I would."

104

"If . . . you . . . would! Beatrix, does that mean that you would not . . . discourage me from hoping? Hoping that one day you might come to love me? As I love you!"

"Love?" she said, turning her head to face him. "What is love, George? True love. Is it fondness? Desire? The ache you were speaking of? Or something more?"

"More, yes – more. The need to be as one. To be *made* one. One with the other, for always. Here and hereafter." One hand was up clasping her bosom now. "Love is for ever, lass."

"You are wanting me, asking me . . . for ever, George?"

"That would be my hope, my prayer. That one day I might win you. To love *me*. And to wed me. Is that possible, woman? Or do I but dream?"

"I have heard of dreams coming true!"

"True? You mean that? I have reason to hope? That you might . . ."

"Why, think you, foolish one, that I am sitting here? In your arms? That I have been happy to go with you alone, before this? If I was not . . . concerned with you?"

"Concerned? You mean love? That you love me, already? Love me!" He was all but squeezing the breath out of her in his urgency.

"From what I know, or think that I know, of love, my dear – yes, I love you."

"It is true? Love. You would wed me?"

"If my father gives permission." She shrugged in his arms. "If not – I would run off with you!"

"Lord be praised! My dearest beloved, heart of my heart! I, I had not thought . . . I judged that I would have to seek to gain you, court you, woo you. For who could tell how long yet . . ."

"Am I so forward, then? Too bold a woman? Bea, the Owl, who is said to keep herself to herself!"

"No, no. You are a darling, a joy, the most precious creature in all this world!" He sought to kiss her, on the ear, on her hair, on the corner of her brow, all that he could reach unless she turned deliberately to face him – which she did not.

"Patience!" she murmured. "Otherwise, no? I . . . promise."

Without thinking, he had turned his horse due southwards and upwards, towards that hill of Dod Law; and, in this so personal exchange, neither had been concerning themselves as to physical direction, whatever else. Now, when it dawned on them whither they were heading, neither found any fault with it, and they rode on.

After all the revelations of feelings and emotions, inner thoughts and happiness took over. In consequence, they spoke but little now, the man so aware that the woman within his arms was indeed his, that he could have found no words to express his elation anyway. The stirring of her person, occasioned by the horse's trotting, was in itself a sufficient delight.

Soon their mount was picking its way up the slopes, the hound, so much more nimble, waiting for them on successive spurs and eminences. They passed the first fort without debate, making for the topmost one. Gaining this, George drew rein, and telling Beatrix to wait, swung out of the saddle and down, to turn and reach up for her.

"At last!" he said, holding her, all but reluctant to set her feet on the ground. "At last! My, my fellow-Pict! Here we pledge our troth! On top of our world! No better place."

"Yes, yes, indeed. I have been here many times . . . since!" she admitted. "And . . . wondered."

"No more wondering!" He led her to one of the grassy inner namparts, and sat her down, wagging his head. "It, it is true, is it not? I can scarce believe it. Tell me that it is true!"

"How think you?" She held out her arms for him.

He sank down beside her, almost on top of her. And now there was no turning of the head, no sort of hesitation. Gazing up, her lips opened under his, frankly, eagerly.

They kissed and kissed.

It was not long, however, before George's hands were busy about her rounded person, and he was beginning to kiss all of her that he could reach, beyond those lips, her hair and brow, her eyes and ears and neck. And, to be sure, seeking to press lower.

"Impatient one!" she chided, but herself kissed the top of his head as she said it.

He took that for permission to go further, and commenced to pull the neck of her bodice down somewhat, so that he might bury his face into the cleft between her breasts, warm, swelling, heaving a little, their invitation demanding indeed. She let him probe and exclaim and murmur, as he pulled at the cloth to win lower still.

But presently she tapped his bent shoulder. "Save . . . something for . . . later. Hereafter, my love. That is best," she advised.

"What is wrong with *now*?" he demanded. "Here and now!"

"Haste is not always the answer. And . . . I am new to this. You may not be. But . . ."

"I have never been in love before, woman!"

"Perhaps not in love. But you will have had your ventures, no doubt? The Master of Dunbar!"

He could not deny that, but did not cease his kissing and fondling. "Am I forbidden? To go . . . further?" he asked.

"Would you heed me?"

"Ye-e-es."

"In that case, just . . . a little!"

He promptly slipped a hand inside the bodice, to cup first one breast, then the other, stroking, pressing. He kissed as far as her gown would let him, and groaned his urgency.

"Poor George!" she said, with a little laugh. "Have I saddled myself, my foolish self, with a man lacking patience? Give me time, I do pray!"

Sighing, he straightened up, removing that hand from the enticement. "You can be cruel!" he asserted.

"Women can be, must be on occasion," she told him

lightly. "But you will have all, in due course." She lay back, at the same time ruffling his hair with her fingers. "Let us enjoy . . ."

She got no further, as he closed her lips with his own – and demonstrated his appreciation of this also.

They remained on that hilltop fort for some time thereafter; and it was the man who initiated the eventual move, in his fight against temptation.

"I try you, George?" she asked, as he led her over to the horse.

"You do. And yet . . . I know that you probably have the rights of it. That you are wise."

"You will, perhaps, thank me. One day."

"How soon? How soon? Marriage?"

"That will not come too soon. For me."

"Bless you! I will speak with your father . . ."

Riding back with her held its own pleasures.

Sir William Hay was not at home. Being Sheriff of Peebles-shire he was much away. And he had his other estate of Lochquariat to see to also. But at least this gave George ample excuse for return visits to Yester.

11

When the earl returned to Dunbar it was with a positive flood of tidings, the which rather put into the background, in *his* mind at least, his son's declared romance and intention to marry. Cospatrick had no objection, but saw it as in no way an urgent matter, whereas other demands were.

He and Dalkeith had seen many lords and lairds in their circuit, and had achieved considerable support for Queen Annabella against Douglas, and therefore against Fife. Their mission thus successful, they had reported to the queen, at Stirling, who had been much enheartened. And she now had a further project for her friends. This concerned with the treaty with England and France. The odd King Richard had recently lost his queen, Anne of Bohemia, by death; and in haste, presumably on Suffolk's and Oxford's advice, was promptly going to wed the seven-year-old daughter of the King of France, this again to strengthen the treaty and his throne. He was now proposing that Scotland, like France, should send down a worthy embassage of important folk to celebrate this new union with the child-bride, and to establish the treaty as a permanency, even inviting King Robert and Queen Annabella themselves to attend. This the queen could not consider, in the circumstances, for herself or her husband; and she was not going to have Fife or Douglas representing her or Scotland. So Cospatrick was to lead a representative company, with his brother Moray, Angus, Dalkeith and others, plus some of the clergy, for the invitation had come in the name of the Archbishop of Canterbury as well as that of King Richard, this presumably because of the wedding involved – or at least promised, for all perceived that the seven-year-old had to remain with her father and mother for some time yet, before actually coming to England. It would make for a curious wedding celebration, but statecraft could produce such oddities.

His father said that George must accompany them.

So that young man had to make a hurried visit back to Yester, to acquaint Beatrix with the situation, and indeed to seek Sir William Hay's permission to wed his daughter, an infinitely more suitable marriage. No opportunity to be alone together presented itself, except momentarily, on this occasion; but George did win agreement and approval for the union of his daughter to his feudal superior's heir, and this so soon after the return from England as could be contrived.

So that at least was satisfactory.

This new expedition to England was not to be by ship. Not only was it over-large in numbers for that, but Richard had sent safe-conducts for the party, and directions as to their route and hospitality to be enjoyed on the way, this at the archbishop's orders, at a succession of abbeys, priories and monasteries. Clearly it was all to be a very special occasion, at least as far as England was concerned.

They had to wait until Moray arrived from the north. That man brought news of his efforts to limit the activities of Buchan, the Wolf of Badenoch, this scarcely aided by the fact that the said Alexander Stewart was his own brother-in-law, as indeed was King Robert, for his countess was Marjory Stewart, their sister. Taking his wife with him, he had gone to Lochindorb Castle, among the Cromdale Hills of Speyside, and had a difficult and challenging interview with the offender, who had declared that *he* was now Lieutenant of the North, by royal appointment, and nowise under the authority of any Justiciar of the North, which he claimed to be a lesser office. Lochindorb might be in Moray, but that did not give the Earl of Moray jurisdiction over him. So there had been nothing for it but threats that the united clans, together with the Lord of the Isles, were prepared to take action against him and his, in arms, if his savageries did not cease. This was as far as matters could go at the moment, Buchan at least seeming concerned about a major Highland backlash. Meantime, while he, Moray, was away in England, his countess would keep up the pressure as far as she might.

It was a distinguished but slow-moving company which set out from Dunbar on the long road south, with five earls, a dozen lords, that notable warrior Sir David Lindsay of Glenesk, two bishops and two mitred abbots, George, Master of Dunbar, undoubtedly the youngest of the travellers, and probably the most impatient at the very moderate rate of progress, all having to ride at the pace of the slowest, the prelates in especial being rather sedate horsemen. Also, as it proved, the hospitality provided by their fellow-clerics *en route*, although very generous, was delaying also, so much so that often they did not get on their way until mid-forenoon, and so were covering not much more than thirty miles a day, poor going by George's estimation. He was, to be sure, concerned with the matter of getting back again as soon as possible.

In fact it took them all of ten days to complete their journey to London town.

The Tower proved to be already full to overflowing with visitors, particularly French ones, and the Scots party was installed in York Place, the London palace of the Archbishop of York, actually much more comfortable quarters, even though hardly apt for them as guests, since that important prelate, as so-called Metropolitan of the North, claimed ecclesiastical superiority over the Scottish Church, hotly denied as this was by its present representatives. Perhaps tactfully in present circumstances, the archbishop did not act the host, but left it to his archdeacon, himself going to lodge with his fellow-metropolitan of Canterbury.

Hereford saw them suitably installed, and gave them some idea as to the morrow's programme.

111

It was late September, but fortunately the weather was kind, for most of the activities were outdoors. The visitors commenced a busy round, all seemingly organised by Hereford himself. There were processions through the city streets, with all but banqueting being provided by the town council and the trade guilds, musicians much in evidence. There was barge-racing on the Thames, horse-racing in the parks, archery contests, communal dancing, even bear-baitings, a carnival atmosphere prevailing, all enjoyable, however debateable the reason for it. Hereford's supporting magnates superintended such events as the mayor and aldermen did not, and among these the Scots were interested to see Nottingham, the Earl Marshal.

There were a couple of days of this. But the highlight of it all was to be a great chivalric tournament on the third day; and this, of all places, to be held on London Bridge itself, over the Thames, specially prepared, even deep-turfed, for the event, this in the presence of the monarch, and to be a spectacle indeed. Hereford was, it seemed, strong on chivalry and knightly prowess. He hoped that representatives of all three nations would take active part, as well as England's renowned champions. He would lead off himself, with a bout against one of his own Lancastrian lords, the Earl of Worcester.

The problem over holding the lists on the bridge, however dramatic that seemed, was where the spectators were to watch all from the fairly narrow carriageway, this insufficient to allow more than a single row of stands at each side, with the royal gallery in the centre. This was got over in two ways, by erecting tall balconies at each end of the lists, and by using barges on the river from which at least some of the spectacle might be viewed.

The arrival of Hereford, with Richard and two French dukes, with the two archbishops and the papal nuncio, the Earl Marshal, plus Cospatrick and his brother as representing the King of Scots, was greeted with cheers and trumpet blasts, while musicians played from the barges.

George, with the rest of the Scots party, was installed on foremost seats on the northernmost balcony.

The Master of Ceremonies for this occasion had to be the Earl Marshal himself, by tradition, whatever the Scots might think of him. He rode to the centre of the lists, duly hailed the king, and declared the tourney open. The Earl of Hereford, newly created duke thereof for the occasion by His Majesty, would commence all by challenging his notable friend the Earl of Worcester to mounted combat, lance-points capped.

While all awaited these lofty contestants to prepare and arm themselves at either end of the lists, the onlookers were entertained by a troupe of gypsies with their performing bears, very different this from the bear-baiting of the two previous days, and much to be preferred according to George.

Then, armoured, helmeted and visored, the two challengers rode out from their bases, lances high meantime, to cheers. It was seen that the long spears had their sharp tips topped and blunted by leather caps. They met in the centre, shook gauntleted hands from the saddle, and turned to return to their starting places.

A pause, and a flourish of trumpets, and the combatants couched their lances, held their shields high, dug in their spurs and surged forwards quickly into a canter, to the shouts of the spectators.

They met in mid-lists, each swerving their mounts aside at the last moment to counter the lance-thrusts. Simultaneously these weapons struck, with a clash, but the horses plunged on and neither lance registered on more than the other's expertly used shield. The riders were carried past, to cries and advice from the watchers.

Without delay, at the two ends of the course, each wheeled round, to charge back, both equally prompt and determined. This time Hereford used his lance differently, raising it high so that he might smash it down on the shaft of the other as they all but collided. So hard did it strike as to wrench his opponent's weapon right out of his grasp, and it fell to the turf, indeed all but tripping up Hereford's own horse with its length. Yells of applause greeted this device, as they cantered past each other.

Now Bolingbroke made his chivalric gesture. He tossed aside his own lance, almost casually, and reached down to draw the sword from his side – but that sheathed. Thus he raised it and waved it, so that Worcester could see it so. Digging in his heels, he plunged forward again, to more cheers.

They met, each swinging a sword above his head, still sheathed, and these shorter weapons clashed, the impetus all but jerking Hereford out of his saddle. He managed to recover himself, but his sword did not. The impact somehow loosened the sheath, which flew off, and he was left clutching the naked steel, to drawn breaths from all.

And again he demonstrated his chivalry. Holding up the gleaming sword high, he hurled it from him, and defenceless rode on after his opponent.

Worcester acknowledged this indication of yielding with a salute, and side by side they rode over to the royal balcony, where they shook hands again, bowed to the monarch, and backed off, to discard their armour, drawn combat accepted.

The next contest was from a Lord Welles, who it seemed was the accepted English champion knight-at-arms. He announced that he challenged Sir David Lindsay, a most notable Scottish paladin. This was accepted promptly.

When these two clashed, results were as prompt. So great was the impact that Welles's lance actually snapped in two against Lindsay's helmet, the force of the blow all but knocking the latter out of his saddle. Somehow he managed to remain mounted as they hurtled past each other; and the Scot, recovering his upright position, was shouted at by some of the onlookers, who declared that he must be cheating by being tied to that saddle. To demonstrate otherwise, Lindsay drew rein and jumped down to the turf, bowed all round, and remounted.

The second attempt resulted only in a collision of the

horses, too close to wield weapons, Welles having collected another lance. But at the third sally the latter's shield was smashed with such force as to hurl him right out of the saddle, and he fell to the bridge flooring with a crash, the weight of his armour all but stunning him, and there he lay.

Lindsay wheeled round to go back to his opponent, dismounted again, and sought to assist the other to rise to staggering stance. They went over to receive the acclaim of the beholders. There was no question as to who was the winner.

And now there developed a rather different kind of drama and engagement. The day before, the Scots party had found themselves in the close presence of the Earl Marshal at one of the parkland contests; and Moray had, straight-faced, remarked that they had last been in contact at that notable occasion at Bamburgh Castle, less knightly than this day's performances perhaps, but memorable! Nottingham had frowned and turned away abruptly. Now, as a consequence, he announced retaliation. He challenged the Scots Earl of Moray to encounter in the lists.

Cospatrick was quite amused, telling his brother that here was an opportunity to demonstrate that he could do more than tackle the Wolf of Badenoch and act the negotiator of treaties – for of course this challenge was not to be refused. If he could unseat the Earl Marshal of England, it would add to his renown.

Brother John was less elated. He was a reasonably seasoned fighter, but had never been one for tournaments. But he had to pick up this gauntlet. Shrugging, he went off to find armour and helmet to fit him, at the lists head. His own horse would serve well enough, a fine beast. With his brother's and nephew's encouragement, he tested a lance for length and strength, and declared himself ready.

He had noted the details of the former clashes, and what had contributed to victory and otherwise, the lances' grip, balance and handling the vital concern. Mounted, he tried

115

the under-arm wielding of the long shaft, and made sure of the positioning of his shield so that it would not interfere with any necessary swinging. Armour made for difficult arm-work.

The trumpet sounded and the new contestants, dispensing with any hand-shaking, rode out, each achieving the required canter. As they came together the Marshal wrenched his mount aside savagely, and his lance swung round in a half-circle, not a pointing but a swinging slash, this striking Moray's shoulder with major force, and causing the latter's spear to miss its target by inches. He retained his seat, however, and they plunged on past.

Then, turning for the second attempt, they charged again. And this time the two horses actually crashed into each other, causing them to rear in fright. This inevitably threw both lances upwards and askew. The Marshal's, by chance, slewed round and over, to strike the edge of Moray's shield, however carefully held, then slid upwards on to the shoulder armour and up to the helmet. And there the leather cap covering the steel point was jerked right off, by catching on the edge of the iron gorget which was there to protect the throat. And driving on, that narrow point thrust right into the slight gap between breastplate and helmet, and there wedged, the lance being dragged right out of its wielder's grip as the two mounts plunged on past each other.

That lance soon fell to the ground, as did the other. But so did John of Moray, for the steel had driven deep into his throat. And being carried on, he choked and drowned in his own blood.

At first all assumed that he was only unhorsed and perhaps half stunned by the fall. But as he lay still, it became evident that the fallen man was unconscious. Attendants ran out to him, and their shouts and upheld hands, covered in blood, revealed tragedy.

Cospatrick and George left that balcony to reach brother and uncle. There was no need for any close examination, helmet removed. Moray was dead, gone to a better place than London Bridge.

That, of course, brought to a sad and sorry end the chivalric tournament, to the distress of all, including Nottingham's, his reputation still further besmirched, although on this occasion it was no fault of his. Hereford was greatly upset by this tragedy for one whom he was now looking upon as a friend, especially as he could not just call a halt to all celebratory proceedings on the national scene.

Nor could the official Scots delegates just pack up and take the body on the long ride home, however much some of them would have wished to do so. There was nothing for it but to have the corpse embalmed, and continue meantime with activities as best they might, until they could decently make a dignified departure. The Dunbar pair wished that they had been able to come by ship, and so return so much more suitably with their dead John.

Hereford, in due course, insisted on seeing them some small distance on their way. He told Cospatrick that he could consider himself as an ally, where such association might be helpful. And once he was on the throne, which he believed would not be long delayed now, he would seek to ensure the best of relations with Scotland.

George, while mourning for his uncle, sorrowed also that this tragic death might well have the effect of delaying his so ardently looked-for marriage somewhat, funerals and weddings making unsuitable close-linked events.

12

In the event it was agreed that the nuptials might decently be held on All Hallows Eve, when some celebrations were in order anyway; and George hastened to Yester to discover whether this was acceptable to Beatrix and her father. That young woman, while condoling with George over his uncle, was entirely in favour of such date and arrangement, and Sir William had no objections. Necessary discussions took place as to details for the great event, and at some of these, where prospective bride and groom were able to be alone, however temporarily, Beatrix had to urge restraint on her impatient spouse-to-be, holding that it would not be long now, and was she not worth waiting for? Let them anticipate, yes, but . . .

The delayed interment took place at the ancient church of Dunbar, with a great attendance. George met, for the first time, his own young cousin, Thomas, now Earl of Moray, whom the Countess Marjory brought down with her from Darnaway, the reason for the delay. They would remain for the wedding in a few days' time. Likewise, with the Hay family coming for the funeral, it was natural that the marriage arrangements, including the dowery for Beatrix, should be discussed also. It all made a rather unusual funereal occasion; but, as Countess Marjory pointed out, her John would not have had it otherwise, and he was probably smiling down at it all from his paradise.

Guests attending brought some strange news from the court. Fife had prevailed upon his royal brother to create him a duke, the realm's first, this never having been a Scottish title, he seeing this as fitting for a regent. Moreover, he had chosen the style of Albany, not Fife, significantly, for that name was a form of the ancient Celtic Alba, referring to the entire nation. What did that portend? Annabella had persuaded her husband that it was quite unsuitable that the heir to the throne should thus be outranked by his uncle; and so young David, Earl Palatine of Carrick and Strathearn, was now also a duke, of Rothesay, the royal palace on the Isle of Bute. It all made a highly unusual development and, Cospatrick feared, possibly ominous.

The long-looked-for day dawned, and quite a large party rode to Yester, more than just the family, Angus and Dalkeith and their wives joining in. St Baithan's Chapel was going to be full. George rode, seeking to hide his excitement.

They were met outside the castle by Sir William, as vassal to the Earl Cospatrick, and all were conducted down the quite steep slope's track, the chapel being situated on the lower ground of the Gifford Water, part way to Gifford village. Sir William was quite proud of it, for it was the first part of what was to become a collegiate church community, with a provost and six prebendaries, this founded to show his gratitude for gaining the large properties by marriage with the Gifford heiress. It was named after one of Columba's Irish missionaries, indeed his cousin and successor at Iona, quite why nobody seemed to know for sure; but he had presumably helped to Christianise this area, for the community of Abbey St Bathans was only ten or so miles to the east.

Quite a crowd of local people and tenantry were already congregated there, but outside the chapel, on the laird's orders, for it was comparatively modest as to size as yet, and the numbers of the Dunbar party had not been known, and these of course must have priority, with the Hay family; so there might well be room for only a few others. The prebendary, newly appointed, would officiate. Never had the little church held such a distinguished company. Sir William said that he had contemplated having the

119

ceremony at the great St Mary's Church of Haddington, but Beatrix had insisted that she wanted to be wed here, where she had worshipped.

Clad in their best, George and Gavin, who was to act groomsman, went to stand up near the altar, while all the others filed into the simple forms which provided the seating. Alicia, who like Beatrix was skilled with the lute, was waiting there, and presented George and Gavin with kisses before proceeding to fill in the time of waiting for the bride with gentle strumming.

They did not have to wait long, to the impatient George's relief, his bride dispensing with the traditional privilege of delayed arrival. Beatrix came in, on her father's arm, looking calmly lovely, simply gowned, the faintest smile on her features, the picture of quiet self-possession. Turning to watch her approach, George wondered whether he could ever actually possess this so dear creature.

When she came up to stand near him, the half-smile remained, but the look in those dark eyes did partly reassure him; and he had once more to restrain himself from reaching out to her.

Alicia ceased playing, and the prebendary came out from the little vestry, to bow to the altar and then turn to face them, and all, hand held high.

"God's peace and blessing on you all," he intoned. "In worship and adoration we are here today to celebrate the union and making one of this man and this woman, from this day, henceforth and for ever. Heed it all."

That was a good start, at least.

The ceremony proceeded, George scarcely aware of what was being said, after that first statement, until it came to the point where Beatrix moved closer to him, at Sir William's giving-away gesture.

She squeezed his arm, and he knew bliss.

Gavin helped with the ring production and fitting, and hands met for significant moments as, with blessing, they were declared man and wife, and they knelt together to receive the benediction.

Mind in a whirl, as Alicia reached for her lute again, and singing started, the new husband found himself leading his loved one after the prebendary to the vestry to sign the necessary documents before Sir William and Gavin as witnesses, then taking her back and down the aisle for the door, to the acclaim of all. Could that acclaim be justified? he wondered. Was it all indeed true? Fact? Could those words and pronouncements by one man, with the tokens and gestures and signings, really make him and Beatrix into one entity before God and man, one for always, joined, beyond doubt or challenge? It seemed unbelievable, all but play-acting. Yet all present appeared to accept it as genuine, as had the innumerable generations that had gone before. And what mattered, which *she* was clearly not doubting by her grip on his arm and the glances she was giving him, amid her smiles to all those around. Were the women always more in command of the situation at weddings than were the men? Or was it just himself who was so inadequate?

Outside, the congratulations and well-wishings at least confirmed for him the efficacy of what had been said and done. Time was spent in hand-shaking and back-slapping and complimentary kissing by other women when what he wanted was to be kissing *his* woman, and alone with her. But that was going to have to wait, he recognised. Life seemed to be full of waiting for George of Dunbar.

That proved to be an accurate assessment, as they all went back to the castle for feasting and speech-making and entertainment, this for him a seemingly endless performance, evidently enjoyed by all except himself, even by Bea the Owl, at his side, in her contained and serene way.

Nevertheless it was she who eventually brought matters to some conclusion by tapping her companion's wrist and then rising to her feet, to announce that she would leave them all to change for departure. George wondered whether he now could go off with her, but his father, seated across the table, seeing his questioning glance, shook his head and indicated further waiting.

There was more entertainment, and then Cospatrick rose. "My son George has some distance to take his Beatrix before their bridal night," he declared. "With our good host's permission, he would be on their way. They go to Colbrandspath Tower, which will be their home hereafter. It is a score of miles through the hills, and darkness is now falling early. It is time."

Sir William waved a hand, and there were cries of agreement. Thankfully George stood, bowed, and hurried off, to put on riding-boots and don a cloak.

It was not long before Beatrix appeared, also clad for the saddle. A brief hug, and they made for the stableyard, where they found a few of the younger members of the company, family and friends, out there to see them off, with much banter and advice, which was accepted with dismissive waves. Then they mounted, and rode off, thankfully.

"The Lord be praised!" George exclaimed. "Alone! At last, at long last! Heart of my heart – together! Just you and myself. And, and for ever! No more partings."

"None? Can I face such a future?" she wondered. "My so hasteful husband!"

"Husband, yes! Glory be – your husband!"

"Is that so glorious a role, George? Alicia says that husband just means house-bound, a dweller in the same house!"

"That is good enough for me. With you."

They rode east by north, by Danskine Loch and Garvald village, then through the Lammermuir foothills by Deuchrie Edge into Dunbar Common, well-known territory for George, however upheaved. They could not take any direct course because of all the slopes and hummocks, but without actually rushing it they reached Elmcleuch and then the hamlet of Oldhamstocks before dusk settled on the land. Thereafter they could just follow the course of the Dunglass Burn down to the coastal area, no plain that either, and south to Colbrandspath community. Avoiding the lamp-lit cottages, they carried on the further mile to

122

the red-stone tower above its little ravine, where lights in the small windows beckoned, and where Jock and Phemie Dunbar were waiting to welcome them with warm greetings and cheer; over-much cheer perhaps, for they had dined more than adequately at Yester, and here was more good fare awaiting them, and specially prepared.

They had to try to do some justice to this, even though other celebration called them, and George could scarcely hurry his beloved upstairs without a decent delay by the fire, and wine to sip.

But at long last he felt that he could rise and hold out his hands to his bride, searching her adored features. Her smile was understanding, warm, nowise tense nor reserved. Shaking his head, but in no negative fashion, he grasped her, and felt like carrying her bodily up the winding turnpike, but restricted himself to leading her by the hand in no leisurely mounting, this to a second-floor chamber, where they found the last of the autumn roses arrayed, a tub steaming before a well-doing fire of logs, and a great bed ready, with warming-pan.

Ushering her in, and closing that door, George drew a long breath as he gazed at her, words failing him now, and no longer necessary. She opened her arms to him.

As they kissed and held each other, murmuring, the young woman it was who found words.

"Mine!" she said. "My own dear George. It has come! We are . . . not only alone and together . . . but one! Made one. I am yours. And you are mine! Oh, my love – now and for always."

"You, you *want* me!"

"Foolish one! Need you ask? I want you, yes. Yes! Think you that I am otherwise? That women cannot want, equally with men? We are made to give, but to want and receive also. *You* want – you have made that clear. But so do I. Now both shall . . . give!" And freeing herself from his grasp, she it was who led the way over to that bed, where, with a little laugh, she removed the bed-pan.

He said no words, quite beyond all such.

She threw herself on the blankets, arms wide, and he bent over her, searching, searching for just what he knew not, but wonder engulfing him, wonder and a joy beyond all that he could have imagined – and he had been imagining much of late. Here was heaven on earth indeed, and all his. And, it seemed, hers also. That, somehow, he had not visualised. Speechless, he took her to him.

Soon their kissing and fondling progressed to the removal of obstructive clothing, Beatrix assisting in this, which was a help. Her breasts, once uncovered, were caressed and stimulated by hands, fingers and tongue, and they were worthy and warm and welcoming. It was not long again, of course, before his busy hands progressed lower, and all but guided by hers. More hampering fabrics were removed, or as nearly so as was possible, a feminine hand now reaching down on the man also. Then, as George bent to enjoy the alternative curves of waist and belly, she shook her head and sat up.

"See you," she said breathlessly. "We can do better than this!" And all but pushing him from her, she swung herself over the side of the bed, and standing there, quickly discarded the tangle of clothing, to kick it aside and remain naked before him in the lamplight, a picture of essential, lovely and beckoning womanhood.

He stared – but not for long. Rising, he hurriedly started to undress himself likewise, she not assisting this time, but watching, lips parted.

Then, his masculinity demanding as it was apparent, he came to her, picked her up in his arms and put her back on the bed, to gaze down at her, but only for moments before lowering himself upon her, she not so much yielding as offering, hands out for him.

George, however eager, did now go in for a different sort of restraint, recognising that his woman would almost certainly have some check, some pain, before her pleasure, however willing she might be to bear it. He dealt as gently as he might with her, therefore, in her preparation, taxing as this was on himself, before he made the ultimate act of

124

union. He heard her gasp, and held himself thus, and his breath with it, until her movements and sighing encouraged him to go on, but still less strongly than he would have liked.

But, in only moments, there could be no more holding back for the man. His male urgency took over. And all too soon he reached his climax, in surging, vehement possession, before, rigid, groaning, he collapsed upon her, Beatrix, silent now, staring up at the bed canopy.

Presently he spoke. "I fear . . . that I was . . . too fast for you . . . my dearest. I am sorry. Sorry. But . . . give me a little time. And I shall do better, I, I promise you."

She stroked his back, still unspeaking.

They lay side by side and hand in hand for a while, she deep breathing; and presently, the stir that breathing caused in her bosom, so close to him, had its own helpful effect in rearousing his manhood. It was not over long before he was able to turn to her again, and reach his hand down to her groin. Her response had her fingernails digging into his shoulders, and quite quickly he hoisted himself over her again, telling her of his love, and assuring her satisfaction this time. No haste in it now, he said.

Actually he did not have to wait long before her panting and murmurs and little cries culminated in a groan of her own, but not of any disappointment, the reverse indeed, and she pummelled his back now with her fists as he had his way with her again, to most mutual satisfaction.

Thereafter, in each other's arms, they sank into a half sleep.

How long it was before Beatrix stirred and got out of that bed, the man did not know. But although the fire was now low and the water no longer steaming, the lamplight showed her to be washing herself at that tub. The man could have spared himself this, but felt that he had to join her at the ablutions; anyway, the sight of her white, rounded and delicious body bending to her task quickly had him out to assist her, this in itself a most pleasurable occupation, with various little explorations and locations not to be neglected.

He himself was washed in his turn, and most carefully dried, before hand in hand again they went back to the bed, this time to sleep, fulfilled.

They slept late next morning, although Phemie knocked on their door at some unspecified time to announce that hot water was being left there.

After a little while, George proved that masculine appetite could be developed and satisfied before breakfast.

Although the November forenoon was grey, with a chill wind off the sea, husband took wife to see something of the neighbourhood, which she did not really know well. First they went down to the little haven of Cove, sheltered from the Norse Sea waves, this reached oddly by a tunnel through the cliff some sixty-five yards long, wide enough for a horse and cart to bring back the catch from the pier, this excavated in ages past, none knew why, but always intriguing to the young Dunbars. This was the fishing-harbour for Colbrandspath, and they saw catches being landed, lobster-pots being constructed and nets mended. Then they rode on southwards round a headland to Pease Bay, the favoured bathing and horse-racing location, with its long stretch of sandy beach, not looking at its best in this weather, with sullen leaden-grey rollers pounding in regular succession.

Beyond, Beatrix pointed to still higher cliffs above wild rocky reefs and skerries, and was told that this was Siccar Point – why siccar, meaning sure, certain, George did not know. But it was notorious for the wrecking of vessels; and this was possibly why a little chapel had been built nearby, centuries before, dedicated to St Helen. This was done out of ignorance, for Helen was the patron deity of sailors admittedly, but she was no Christian, living long before Christ came to earth, and the monks had attributed her person to St Helen, the mother of the Emperor Constantine who had converted the Roman world to Christianity, she who was reputed to have discovered and preserved Christ's cross.

They went to inspect the little red-stone church, all the buildings of this area being of the vividly red, almost scarlet, rock of the cliffs. Apparently services were held here on occasion, but otherwise the little sanctuary was seldom used.

Beatrix was still viewing further and still higher pre-cipices beyond, but was told that these must be for visiting another day, to see where another and more local saint, Ebba, had given name to St Abb's Head. On the way back to Colbrandspath, passing the hamlet of Aldcambus, George told of the Bruce's victory over the English there in 1317, and whereafter a truce was sought by the defeated foe, using a papal envoy as the go-between, bringing a document addressed to Robert, governor of Scotland; whereupon Bruce had handed it back unopened, saying that he would listen to no bulls until he was treated as King of Scots; and indeed he was on his way to make himself master of Berwick-upon-Tweed.

They made another fulfilling night of it; and next day Beatrix was taken to explore the highest and most exciting section of all that dramatic and savage coastline, where the enormous and jagged cliffs, riven and rent, precipitous and cavernous, soared as high as three hundred feet, circled by screaming clouds of seafowl, their skerry-strewn bases the haunt of seals. Spray from the crashing waves came up like mist.

On the grassy summits of one height they found the ruined foundations of the nunnery and chapel of Ebba, a Northumbrian princess, a Christian, who, to escape the savageries of the Viking raiders, had come here with her women, and established this extraordinarily placed sanc-tuary, choosing nature's wildness rather than men's, she and her nuns allegedly even cutting off their breasts to make themselves less attractive to the Norsemen.

Beatrix wondered and all but wept for them.

The couple sat on a ledge in a cleft in a cliff for a while, holding each other close and watching the seals swimming and hoisting themselves on to reefs far below, this until the chill wind forced them back to their horses for their quite long ride home – for it was to be home now for this pair, Colbrandspath Tower, on this colourful coast on the edge of the Merse.

The day following, wet and chilly, was no occasion for sightseeing. Besides, Beatrix declared that it was time for her to take up her wifely duties, scarcely as housewife, for Phemie would continue to see to that, but as mistress of the small castle and spouse of the heir to an earldom, her housebound George.

That man had his own ideas as to wifely duties.

Part Two

13

The spring of 1399 brought news from south and north, these to prove linked, with their own significance as far as the Dunbar family was concerned. From the south it was reported that Hereford had achieved his purpose, got Richard to abdicate, and was now Henry the Fourth, King of England. And from the north came word that David, Duke of Rothesay, had been married, at Bothwell, to Margaret, daughter of Archibald the Grim, Earl of Douglas, this in spite of the betrothal arrangement with George's sister Elizabeth.

The Earl Cospatrick was furious, although this had been mooted and feared for some time. The substantial sums and lands, which he had handed over to the crown for the contract of marriage, must be returned to him, he declared. This was Fife's, or Albany's doing, and it was not to be suffered without sufficient reaction. He stormed off to see Annabella and the weak Robert.

George feared the worst, although Elizabeth herself was almost relieved, for she had developed a fancy for David Hay, one of Beatrix's brothers.

When the earl came back from Stirling his fury was by no means abated. He had seen Albany, at Scone, and that man had refused any repayment of the dowery settlement, on the grounds that this had been made to Robert the Second, the previous monarch, and his dealings did not bind his successor, nor the latter's regent. The Douglas marriage was best for the crown and state, binding that great family's vast strength to the monarchy. It had been a stormy interview indeed.

Annabella, much as she would have wished to help, in

this could not. Her deplorable brother-in-law had firm hold of the purse-strings. She was moreover greatly worried for her husband and her sons, David and James, indeed for herself. She was convinced that Albany intended to have the throne for himself, at any cost, even if this meant getting rid of brother and nephews, in some fashion. The situation was dire, appalling, and she was at her wits end as to how to counter the man, and he now with full Douglas support. She was even considering appealing to the new King Henry of England to use his influence through this permanent treaty of mutual association to bring pressure to bear on Albany; and saying that his, Cospatrick's known friendship with the former Bolingbroke might well be used to help in it all – a remarkable situation indeed. Could he, Cospatrick, contemplate seeking help from the Auld Enemy to right affairs in Scotland?

If Annabella's fears were justified, the earl might just consider it. Civil war could well be the alternative, not to mention possible regicide, assassination, utter chaos and horror.

George thought that the queen was being over-fearful and alarmed; but his father was less sure.

Cospatrick decided to send a letter to King Henry, congratulating him on his gaining the throne, and stressing friendship and co-operation where this was possible.

They did not have long to wait before Albany demonstrated his enmity. Cospatrick was deprived of his office of Lieutenant of the Borders and Chief Warden, Archibald the Grim being appointed in his place, elderly as he was.

At Dunbar and Colbrandspath a state of tension was developing.

And in due course that tension was justified, and they were shocked and devastated. Queen Annabella was dead. She had been in her usual good health. She had been still a youngish woman, and vigorous. Yet, without any sort of symptoms nor warning, suddenly she died. And her brother, Sir Malcolm Drummond, was declaring that she had been poisoned.

132

Now there was dread and fear throughout the land. The queen, who had been popular, was gone. The last and only time a queen had allegedly suffered death by poisoning had been three centuries back, this when Ingebiorg, wife of Malcolm Canmore, was disposed of so that he might wed Margaret Atheling of England, St Margaret. If indeed it was poison, then it could be none other than Albany who had ordered it – and Albany now controlled the nation. What was to become of Scotland?

There were some, of course, who saw it as less than disastrous. They had a weakly and all but useless monarch, and a youthful heir who was said to have extravagant tastes. Albany would at least make a strong head of state. England had got rid of another weakling, Richard, and now had an effective King Henry. It might be advisable and rewarding to support Albany.

Cospatrick, for one, did not see it so. He judged the entire Stewart line as a failure, a plague on the land; and was, of course, very much aware that, by right, *he* should be on the throne, as representing the ancient Celtic monarchy, not these Norman newcomers. He began seriously to think of challenging them, making a bid for the crown, and using the prevailing fears and anxieties to aid him. Civil war, then? But in a just and worthy cause. But against what strength? The Stewarts had gained themselves much power, apart from the throne itself, the earldoms of Carrick, Strathearn, Menteith, Fife, Atholl, Caithness and Buchan. And allied themselves by marriage to those of Mar and Crawford, with illegitimate offspring owning large lands and followers. So they could rally huge support; and with that of Douglas to be relied upon now, any opposition would have to be strong indeed. What could be mustered against all this? That is, apart from Angus, Dalkeith and others already more or less committed.

There were certain areas of the land that were largely outwith Stewart influence, his own East and Middle Marches and the Merse, of course; but also Moray and the far north-east, much of the Highlands and the Isles, most certainly. But strangely, considering where the House of Stewart had arisen, in the Renfrewshire district west of Glasgow, the large Ayrshire territories of the Hamiltons, Montgomerys, Cunninghames, Kennedys and the rest, who he had recently approached, together with much of Dumfrieshire, this north and east of Galloway which Douglas dominated. Could he now rely on major armed support from much of this area?

They awaited the start of the new century at Dunbar with no anticipation that it was going to be one of peace, prosperity and worthy progress in this northern kingdom, whether or not that signified for England.

At Colbrandspath, although forebodings and concerns for the future could not be dismissed, a different atmosphere did prevail, with married joy and fulfilment foremost, domesticity in the ascendant. Beatrix much enjoyed being mistress of her own house, as well as acting the wife, and got on very well with Phemie, treating her as friend rather than servant. And found the neighbourhood much to her taste, with the coastal area so different from the Gifford vicinity, although they still had the hills close at hand. They rode appreciatively even in the winter weather. Visits were paid to Dunbar and Yester, of course, but only of brief duration; and they did not allow the national troubles to make too great an impact upon them.

Yuletide came and went, celebrated suitably, with the year 1400 hailed, however doubtfully.

It was March when the news broke which set fire to the smouldering fears of Scotland, more especially those of the Earl Cospatrick. It was death again – this time of his friend Angus. That earl had been visiting his properties up near to Forfar when he had been set upon and slain, allegedly by a band of robbers from the Highland hills. But few accepted this as the truth, or at least as the whole truth. Caterans, as they were called, did not assail great noblemen, and had nothing to gain by attacking such as the Earl of Angus. He had been got rid of on some other's orders – and few had any doubt that it was on Albany's. He was known as a foe of the regent's; and who else would wish to seek his death? Cospatrick at least had no doubts. He sent word to Dalkeith to be on his guard, and not to ride abroad without a strong escort. He himself would do the like.

This murder made up the earl's mind. He was for the south, for Henry Plantagenet. Albany must be overthrown, even if it meant war. They had a devil steering Scotland, and someone must act to have him put down. The forces against him must be rallied and encouraged; and undoubtedly this could best be achieved, in Cospatrick's opinion, by English backing. Henry was friendly, and strong. So be it – time for action.

The earl was under no illusions as to the dangers of this move, especially for his family while he was gone. Albany would quickly get to know of it, and would be unlikely not to react, and in typically vicious fashion. Dunbar Castle could well be attacked. His young people should vacate it meantime, leave for a secure haven. He had many remote houses among the Lammermuir Hills, where they would never be found and reached: Johnscleuch, Mayshiel, Gamelshiel and the like. He would appoint his sister Agnes's son, Sir Robert Maitland of Lethington and Thirlstane, to be nominal governor of Dunbar in the interim. The Maitlands had taken no part in national affairs of late, and Albany would not see them as any menace.

George was less than happy about all this, needless to say. He had his doubts as to the wisdom of bringing the English into the issue, although he liked the former Hereford. Might their arrival in Scotland, in force, not tend to cause many of the lords, who might be inimical to Albany, to aid him against what they saw as English raiders and invaders? Even with Cospatrick at their head?

He made the point at his farewell to his father; but the earl was not to be dissuaded. Albany must be brought down, and this was the surest way to achieve it in his opinion. They parted, George declaring that he would remain at Colbrandspath, with Beatrix, meantime, but would be prepared to flee into the hills, to Gamelshiel

Tower on the Whiteadder, on any approach of the regent's forces.

Soon thereafter he learned that Douglas of Dalkeith had departed for his island castle in Loch Leven, near to Kinross, which could not be taken save by a fleet of boats, the which were nowise available.

Scotland more or less held its breath.

There was grim news from England. Richard, the deposed and abdicated king, had died at Pontefract Castle where he had been held. It was said that, in misery, he had starved himself to death. But there were whispers of poison. If so, by whose orders? Not Henry's, for sure. He needed not the death of Richard, and he was away on the Marches, at war. Who, then?

14

The breath-holding had to be prolonged, for no major development transpired, nor was reported, for some time, however much folk wondered and speculated and feared. George and Beatrix remained at Colbrandspath, and the rest of the family at Dunbar, but ready to depart at shortest notice. Albany may have been active elsewhere, but not in this direction.

Cospatrick had gone south in July; but it was not until well into October that his young people received word as to his cause – and then, suddenly indeed. It came by a messenger sent by the Homes, in the southern Merse, to announce that the King of England, with their lord the earl, had crossed the border and was marching north with an army. They would presumably be up to the Dunbar vicinity the next day.

Astonished, the Dunbar family waited. It seemed that their father had succeeded in his aims thus far, whatever was going to happen now.

Since the invaders advanced by the road from Berwick-upon-Tweed, they came up the Pease Dean, and so reached Colbrandspath Tower, this in the early afternoon, on their way to Dunbar, George thus dramatically confronted by his father, and being presented to King Henry, who greeted him kindly and declared that he supported the earl's rightful claim to the Scottish throne in place of the usurping Stewarts.

This had George in a quandary. Clearly he was expected to accompany the host onwards, however doubtful he was as to the entire proceedings. The army, numbering some six thousand, continued on for Dunbar for the night, while he said that he would join it in the morning.

He spent a worried night with Beatrix. He confessed that this of announced claim to the throne, after a period of more than three hundred years, was in his opinion unsuitable and highly unlikely to be sustained and accepted by the nation. And King Henry's backing of it, however well meant, was not likely to help, whatever the effect on Albany, for most would see it as a typical English move to gain overlordship of the northern kingdom by having a puppet monarch appointed who would pay due fealty to the Plantagenets, as John Balliol had done a century before. Was Cospatrick seeking to become another Toom Tabard?

George made an early start for Dunbar in the morning.

He found the force preparing to leave for Edinburgh, with the population of Dunbar town thankful to see the backs of them. Gavin now joined them, at his father's orders.

It was a ride of over thirty miles to the capital, and it took them all of that October day. No opposition materialised. It seemed very strange to be riding beside the King of England at the head of an army through their Lothian countryside, George uncomfortable, although Gavin seemed to see it all as a great adventure.

King Henry was much impressed by the sight of Edinburgh as they approached its great towering Arthur's Seat, which he called a mountain, the mighty castle-topped rock, the Calton Hill, and the lesser summits, to the south, of Braid and Blackford, all backed by the lofty range of the Pentlands, so different a prospect from London's, and that of any other English city.

It was dusk as they reached Holyrood Abbey, with still no sign of any attempt to halt their advance, although Albany could not be unaware of the threat. The troops settled for the night in the parkland at the foot of Arthur's Seat, where King David the First had been saved from being gored by a wounded stag while hunting, and in

138

gratitude for what he called a miracle had founded the abbey there, which he named after the fragment of Christ's cross, the Holy Rood, which his chaplain ever carried near that religiously minded monarch, he the youngest son of Margaret and Canmore who had displaced his eldest son, Cospatrick's ancestor.

The abbot told them that the Duke of Albany had an army assembled on Calder Moor, some dozen miles west of Edinburgh, but had sent his nephew, the young Duke of Rothesay, to confront the invaders and hold Edinburgh Castle – an interesting strategy. Enquiries in the city elicited further information. Apparently, earlier, Archibald the Grim had been given the task of facing the foe and defending Edinburgh, and was in fact in the castle here, but had fallen sick, and Rothesay had been sent in his place. Presumably much of the Douglas force constituted the bulk of the army now waiting at Calder, for no large numbers could get inside the fortress walls. Albany was leaving others to do the initial fighting.

Henry, needless to say, was wary about this situation. He had brought no siege-machinery with him, and the citadel would be hard indeed to take, on its lofty rock-top. And any prolonged siege with the intention of starving out the garrison would lay the besiegers open to attack from Albany's force. If he, Henry, was going to fight the regent and the Douglas strength, he would do so on ground of his own choosing, not scattered around Edinburgh's castle-rock.

So it was decided to send up only a large party in the morning, with Henry and Cospatrick, to demand the surrender of the fortress. And if this was refused, as seemed probable, to move on westwards towards this Calder area, and seek to choose suitable strategic sites for any battle, with challenge sent on to Albany. Young Rothesay would not have enough men in the castle to constitute any real menace of attack at their rear.

They passed an oddly comfortable night at the abbey, hosted by the monks.

139

Next day, then, it was up the climbing mile to the tourney-ground in front of the castle gatehouse, by the Canongate, the Tron, the High Street and the Lawnmarket, a resplendent group under the banners of the leopards of England and the silver lion on red of Dunbar, with a large white flag hoisted also, to indicate parley, to approach that gatehouse and there request the attention of the Duke of Rothesay and the Earl of Douglas, at the call of King Henry of England and of Cospatrick of Dunbar and March, rightful claimant to the crown of Scotland. This was shouted, after a trumpet blast, by Seton of that Ilk.

For a while there was no reply, and the summons had to be repeated. Then there came a youthful voice.

"I am David Stewart of Rothesay, son and heir to Robert, King of Scots. I hold this castle in the king's name. And demand why King Henry of England invades Scotland with the traitor Earl of Dunbar while there is a treaty of peace between the the the two kingdoms?"

Henry himself answered. "I am Henry Plantagenet. I come, with the Earl Cospatrick, because of the depredations and wickedness of your uncle the Duke of Albany, and also of your goodsire the Earl of Douglas. They have threatened and invaded *my* kingdom, and done much ill. Consider you the death of the Earl of Angus. And of your own mother, the queen, Duke David! I say that you should surrender this castle to the Earl Cospatrick, and come into *his* care, in which you would be safer and surer than in that of Albany!"

Silence.

Cospatrick raised voice. "Heed, Rothesay. You are being used as a tool in the hands of Albany. A man who, I swear, would deny you your father's throne. You are better with myself, and with King Henry. Heed well!"

"No! No!" came back. "I hold this castle in my father's name, I tell you. And will yield it to none. I say begone!"

"You are unwise, boy. Heedless of your own good. Think again. We will await your better decision down

140

at the abbey." That was Henry. "Your royal father, for whom you hold this fort, is in Albany's grip. So you hold it for *Albany*! And can you trust that evil man? Consider." And he waved his party round, to return whence they had come. They had, of course, not failed to anticipate this.

Back at Holyrood and their army, it was decided to wait for one day, to see if Rothesay thought better of it, and to learn of Albany's moves, if move he did, and did not leave all to others. A scouting party was sent out westwards towards Calder Moor, to discover the position, and where they could see possible favourable battle-sites to meet Albany. Meantime, the ease of the abbey establishment.

But that same afternoon all was abruptly changed. A messenger did arrive, but not from the castle. He came from the south, from London, for Henry. It was to announce that Owen Glendower of Powys, the Welsh princeling who had in fact aided Henry against Richard, had now changed his allegiance. He had indeed invaded England across the Welsh Marches, and had met with and slain the Lord Grey of Ruthin, the warden there, declaring Wales now independent and *himself* the Prince of Wales, not Henry's son.

Great and drastic was the impact of this. Here was outrage, rebellion, treason indeed. It must be dealt with immediately. The Scottish situation could wait: this could not. He, Henry, must return south forthwith, whatever Rothesay decided. And take his host with him.

Cospatrick was crestfallen and mortified, his hopes dashed. For the meantime, at any rate. But he could not do anything other than turn back with the Plantagenet, and hope – hope that this Glendower rising could be speedily crushed, and his own cause revived.

A prompt move was made, within the hour, the army turning and being led back southwards at greatest speed.

George was sorry for his father, but in fact distinctly relieved. It was back to Colbrandspath and Beatrix for him, no enthusiast for kingly ambitions and warfare, however much he deplored Albany. He judged his sire mistaken in this, and did not think that Scotland would accept a change of monarchy, back to the old Celtic line of centuries before, this after Wallace and Bruce and the Wars of Independence, David the Second and the rise of the Stewarts through marriage with Bruce's daughter. Not only all those Stewart earls and lords, but the magnates and people in general. Turning back the pages of the book would not serve, he feared. And for what . . . ?

15

There followed a period of comparative peace in Scotland, although not in England and Wales where Henry conducted a quite lengthy campaign against Glendower, whom he drove back into the Welsh mountains where he could not be reached.

Archibald the Grim's sickness proved fatal, elderly as he was, and his son, another Archibald, became fourth Earl of Douglas. He was said to be of very different character, less aggressive, concerned with chivalry and the like – hopefully to be less of an ally for Albany.

The regent sought to make him so, however, and at the cost of Cospatrick. He descended upon Dunbar Castle in force. Fortunately his approach was notified to the family there by Seton, their kinsman, in time for them to make their escape into the hills, George and Beatrix also departing for Gamelshiel. Maitland of Lethington surrendered without any siege, strongly placed as the castle was, probably wisely. Putting a keeper in charge, Albany announced that Dunbar was now forfeited for its earl's treason and was hereby bestowed upon the new Earl of Douglas. He then returned to Scone.

What Douglas thought of his new acquisition was not reported, but he certainly did not come to take over from the keeper. After an interval, with due enquiries made and no word of the garrison at Dunbar causing any real trouble locally, no doubt well aware of the danger from the folk of the Merse, Cospatrick's people, ready to contest anything such, George and his wife returned to Colbrandspath, to find all in order there, no raids nor threats having developed. They settled in again, hopefully. Gavin and the

143

others came to visit them occasionally, but preferred to remain safe in the Lammermuirs meantime.

News as to their father, that winter, was not forthcoming. Presumably he was involved in aiding Henry against the Welsh.

As the year 1402 advanced, however, there *was* news. The new Douglas had marched into England, truce or none, whether on his own initiative or on Albany's orders, and reached as far south as Durham. Thither Henry had sent Cospatrick, with a fair-sized force, to teach him a lesson; and finding the Douglas contingent returning towards Galloway, laden with booty, at Homildon Hill, near to Wooler, he had routed them. Oddly enough, in this affray, Hotspur Percy had joined his old foe in the successful attempt to clear his Northumberland of the invaders. Douglas himself was wounded, indeed lost an eye and was captured and held by Percy for ransom. Cospatrick did not continue on northwards thereafter into his own Merse, as might have been expected, presumably because of orders from Henry to return with his force for further action in Wales. So the Dunbar family, expecting to see their father, did not. George at least was scarcely disappointed, fond as he was of his parent. His return would undoubtedly have ended the fragile peace prevailing.

Peace from internal or civil war there may have been, but that was hardly the term for what transpired a few months later, to shake Scotland. David, Duke of Rothesay was dead, and had died horribly. He had been on his way to St Andrews when Albany's men had assailed and captured him, in mid-Fife, and had taken him to Falkland Palace, the royal hunting-seat, and there imprisoned him in a dungeon, this without food or water. And there the young man had been left to die, starved to death, the heir to the throne.

The nation reeled with the shock of it. That even Albany could contemplate such horror was scarcely believable.

The accounts circulating were that two young women, of kinder hearts than the palace keeper, had sought to prolong the life of the wretched prisoner. One, the keeper's own daughter, had managed to pass thin cakes through an aperture in the walling, presumably an arrow-slit, until she was discovered at it, and promptly slain. Not discouraged, the other, who was acting wet-nurse to the keeper's child, actually pumped milk from her breast through the same aperture, by means of a long reed, but she too was seen at it, and was likewise killed.

Now there was only the younger brother, the boy James, aged eight years, between his uncle and the crown; save, to be sure, the feeble man wearing it. How long would *he* last? George was not the only one who wondered. Would no one, no alliance of loyal and decent subjects of the king, unite to make an end of the monster of a regent?

The grim death of Rothesay could not be let pass without some reaction and enquiry, even in the Scotland of the regency. Albany was called to appear before his own Privy Council to account for the tragedy. Needless to say, he denied all responsibility, blaming others, in especial one Sir John de Ramorgny who had been involved in the waylaying of the young duke. The said Ramorgny had subsequently and conveniently disappeared. The enquiry duly condemned him – and that was that, justice seeming to be done.

George had more on his mind than the fate of princes at this time. For Beatrix had announced that she believed herself to be pregnant – to his joy and pride. They were about to start a family! He immediately became concerned over the mother-to-be's physical state, care and heedful behaviour – not that Beatrix rivalled his preoccupation.

George had other matters also to attend to now that he found himself having to act the earl in his father's absence. The weal of the earldom had to be considered, and the folk of Dunbar town in especial required decisions and guidance, sitting so close under the walls of the occupied castle, tradesmen, merchants, shipmasters, fishermen, and of course the shepherd fraternity. The Lammermuir wool, the source of wealth and well-being, had to be dealt with, and exported in great quantities to the Low Countries; and although this went on more or less by sheer custom, certain authority and judgments had to be effected, notably as to the destinations for the wool, with prices varying; also for what cargoes to bring back.

So there were not a few visits to Dunbar to be made, George dressed in his least conspicuous clothing, and not giving the impression that this was the Master visiting. Not that the castle's present occupants made that presence much felt in the town, apart from collecting food and drink, well aware that they were unpopular incomers in a very hostile area. They were there, of course, in the name of the ransomed Earl of Douglas, and he was very much based in faraway Galloway, at Threave and his other castles, so this of Dunbar was scarcely of vital importance to him. George was able to go about his affairs without much worry over the garrison, although it was galling to see his old home being thus in the hands of strangers.

So, acting the earl most moderately, George kept busy, and sought to use his brothers in this, more especially over the superintendence of the sheep and wool production aspect, for they were now settled, and apparently quite contentedly and safely, in their two hill fortified houses of Johnscleuch and Mayshiel. The extent of the Lammermuir sheep-runs, some twenty-five miles by ten, was a great responsibility, the greatest such in all Scotland; and although parts of it were ceded off to vassal lairds like the Hays, most remained in the hands of the earl, and required scores of shepherds. With the seasonal work of lambing, shearing and moving to new pastures and shielings, there was a sufficiency of importance to oversee. The family was far from idle, much busier than they had ever been at Dunbar Castle.

Only one message came to them from their father, this from the Welsh Marches. He wished them well, declared that he was commander of one of King Henry's forces, trusted that George was dealing effectively, as Master and his representative, and desired that Gavin, next in seniority, should be sent south to join him, where he could be very useful as link.

So that young man departed for a very different life from sheep-rearing.

Beatrix was nearing her time, and George behaving as though hers was a unique condition, demanding of infinite care and caution, to her affectionate amusement.

Then, in late autumn, with the looked-for birth only a few weeks away, of all things Beatrix had to take to the saddle, bulky as she now was, and ride off to Gamelshiel, to her husband's dire upset, alarm and anger. This was occasioned by a messenger coming from the Homes to inform him that Hotspur Percy of Northumberland had crossed Tweed at the head of a sizeable force and was heading north through the Merse, not just making a typical border raid but seemingly intending something more definite, and obviously hostile. The courier said that the invaders were none so far behind him, coming by this route, and would be passing through Pease Dean and close to Colbrandspath by the morrow.

Astonished, George had to get Beatrix away at once, however unsuitable her condition for travel. He spoke about having some sort of litter contrived for her, but she laughed that off, saying that she was perfectly capable of riding if they took the journey fairly gently. And Phemie, who had been anticipating acting the midwife, agreed. No need to worry unduly. Beatrix was a good horsewoman, and she, Phemie, would go with her. Indeed Jock would do so also, for he was not going to be left alone to face possible English attack at the tower.

So that same late afternoon the four of them, with their two servitors, set off into the hills, with laden pack-horses, wondering what would happen to their home in their absence. George insisted that they kept their mounts to a walk, no trotting, which would produce a jerking motion, this however long it took to cover the dozen miles, rough going as it was.

He was much surprised, as well as worried, over this

147

invasion by the Percy. He understood that, although old enemies since Otterburn, Hotspur and Cospatrick had in fact co-operated quite recently against the Douglas raid at Homildon Hill. Admittedly that was to get the foe out of Northumberland. But this of invading the Dunbar and Merse earldom was quite unexpected. What was the purpose? Had the Percy all along been nursing his hatred? And now, with Cospatrick away in Wales, seeing his opportunity for revenge on that Otterburn defeat?

They made it to Gamelshiel, overlooking the Whiteadder loch, safely before dark. It was only a small towerhouse up on its hillside, but large enough for their needs, and in the past they had made it comfortable. They settled in thankfully, Beatrix none the worse.

After a couple of days, George ventured alone down to the coastal area again, to discover the situation. Approaching warily, he found the deserted and locked-up Colbrandspath Tower undamaged, although there were signs that it had been visited and inspected, much of horse-droppings and the like in evidence. He called at the nearby village, and learned that the invaders had visited it briefly, seized food and drink, assaulted some women, and passed on northwards. This, from reports, not for Dunbar itself, which presumably they deemed too strong for them to take, but to Innerwick Castle, a lesser but strongly sited fortalice on a precipitous horn of rock, held for Cospatrick by a keeper of the name of Lindsay. Hotspur was understood to be there now, besieging it.

George recognised very well that something had to be done about this. In his father's absence he was having to act the earl. He could not allow the Percy to sit on Dunbar land, assailing one of its castles, without taking action, no seasoned warrior as he was. After all, the earldom had many powerful vassals, especially the Homes and Swintons and others in the Merse. Rouse these then, and seek to get rid of the invaders.

Hastily he rode back to Gamelshiel, there to contact his brothers, Colin, Patrick, John and David, Gavin now

148

being with his father. They were to go down into the Merse and, in the earl's name, raise as many men as possible at short notice, and have them meet him at Cranshaws, on mid-Whiteadder. He himself would muster what he could from this Lothian end. From Cranshaws they would assail Percy at Innerwick, if he was still there.

He hoped that this would meet the need. The Mersemen were experienced fighters, typical Borderland reivers, however inexperienced *he* might be as a commander. And Seton, his kinsman, was a reliable leader. As was father-in-law Sir William Hay.

It was not the way he had contemplated welcoming his first-born in a day or two!

At Yester, Hay was a great help. He had heard about the Percy inroads and was concerned that measures should be taken to counter them. He agreed to rouse the vassals and lairds of the hillfoots area, from Garvald and Longformacus to Humbie and Saltoun. George himself would go to Seton, and have him gather men from the coastal areas, Saltpreston, Cockenzie, Seton itself. Then he would deal with Haddington, Prestonkirk and Dunbar.

In fact, George's efforts at mobilising men were more successful than he could have hoped for, this because the word had got around that there was English invasion of the Dunbar area, and expectation that something had to be done, so men were ready. Even Dunbar town, despite the castle position, rallied, over fifty men coming forward; it could have been more, had there been horses for them available, but being largely fisher-folk and seafarers, mounts were not numerous.

When, after four days of it, George rode into the hills for Cranshaws, he caught up with parties heading thither amounting to fully six hundred men. He, and they all, were greatly encouraged. A large company of Marchmen were already encamped there, and more arriving.

Heartened, he reckoned that he actually had some two

thousand horsemen to face Hotspur. Just how many *he* had was not known; but on their own territory and using the land to fight for them, his people ought to be able to make a major impact, all his leaders agreed, these including Home of that Ilk and many of his name, Seton, Sir William Hay and Lindsay of Luffness and the Byres.

George felt distinctly uneasy about seeming to command all these notable characters; but he was the Master of Dunbar and March, and had to be seen to act as his father's deputy.

The assembled force was about to set off northwards for the Innerwick area, by Johnscleuch and Garvald, when the situation suddenly underwent change. Messengers arrived from Dunbar to say that the English had given up the siege of Innerwick, that hold still withstanding them, and were now heading south whence they had come. Presumably Hotspur's scouts had learned of the mustering of forces all around, which would undoubtedly be so doing to assail him, and was taking the judicious course of returning to his own Northumberland. Had he not realised, from the first, that this would happen?

So – what now? Were George's people all just to disperse and go home, unbloodied, the menace past? Practically none at Cranshaws was so inclined. Here they were, in force, ready for action – let them have some, if possible! It would take the Percy some time to reach his borders. Surely he could be intercepted and taught his lesson, if they moved fast.

The decision was made. Scouts were sent off in haste to discover the enemy's whereabouts. They would presumably take the same route south, back for Berwick-upon-Tweed.

The host set off, therefore, due eastwards, for the Monynut Edge and Abbey St Bathans and the Drakemyre, making for the Coldinghame area, where they ought to be in a good position to attack, a suitable terrain for ambush and battle.

But that was not to be. Scouts came back with news that

150

changed all. The English had left the main coastal route south by Pease Dean and the Eye Water, and had turned westwards in the Duns direction, an unexpected move indeed. Where could they be heading now? This direction would bring them into mid-Merse. The Homes and Swintons did not like that.

George had to order a change of course, then, all but a reversal, west by south, for Duns, to cross the Whiteadder near Bonkyl.

At Duns town there was no word of invaders as yet. Were they still coming in this direction? Scouts were sent back.

They had entered Home and Swinton country now and their lairds were in no doubts as to tactics. If indeed the foe was to continue in this direction, with the Blackadder to cross, a major river, the place to wait for them was at Nisbet, the ford there, with Nisbet Moor and Hill at its approaches. If only they knew where Percy was heading for, coming this inland way . . .

Scouts presently came back to inform. The English force was still on this route, proceeding due west now.

On then, to the Nisbet ford.

The Blackadder, which ran roughly parallel with the Whiteadder but some five miles further south, was a larger stream. The two would join, in due course. Crossings, lacking bridges, were few.

In just under four miles they came to Nisbet, Swinton of Kimmerghame's house only a mile or so away, he thankful that their host was here in time, for if Hotspur had come first, he might well have drawn aside to sack it.

They inspected the scene, although the local lairds were in no doubts as to preferred procedure. The ford was narrow, so no more than two or three horsemen abreast might cross at a time. Therefore any large force would have to draw up, waiting. There was a mill nearby, and the waiting men might well raid this to see what they could find. Also the approach to the ford was constricted, between two shoulders of Nisbet Hill. So, up on Nisbet Moor with them, flanking that approach and out of sight;

151

and when the English below were in the narrows, as necessarily strung out, down on them.

It seemed an excellent strategy – that is, unless Hotspur decided to change course before he got thus far.

Up on to the high ground they went, then, to await their scouts' reports.

They had almost an hour of waiting. Then the word came. The enemy had bypassed Duns, and were still heading this way by the track for the Blackadder ford.

On either side of the narrows through the hill shoulders, but well hidden, the attackers formed up, ready. The miller and family had been advised to leave their house and also hide. Watchers were out to send warning of the English approach.

The next word was that the enemy had now crossed the Langton Burn at Putton Mill, and were already well strung out. They should reach the Blackadder very shortly.

George was on the east side, with his father-in-law and Seton, most of the Marchmen on the west, under Home. It had been agreed that some one hundred or so of the foe should be allowed to cross the ford before the attack was made; this would hamper any return assault from these. It could mean, of course, that, if the leaders were riding in front, then these might escape; but it also meant that the main mass would then be without the most competent leadership.

Presently the hidden Scots did see the long line of horsemen coming over Nisbet Moor. Lances ready, swords and battle-axes in hand, tensely they prepared to descend as fast as the terrain allowed.

For George, crouching there behind a grassy rise, it was all agitation to watch the leading files, with their banners, passing below, three or four abreast, and to recognise that these could well not be involved in any fighting. But . . . patience!

The enemy column was in fact almost half a mile long, as it threaded the narrow. So the passage took what seemed a long time to the keyed-up watchers. They were waiting for the signal from the observers nearer the ford area that the first files had indeed splashed across, and that numbers were building up to follow them over, near the mill.

At last the waving came, and George, Hay and Seton raised their swords high and then brought them down in a slashing gesture. And all along the high ground, on both sides, the attackers surged forward to the descent.

However carefully planned, it became something like chaos thereafter; but less chaotic for the assailants than for the assailed, for they at least were not taken by surprise. Heading down over rough ground, on horseback, no regular lines nor formations could be maintained. So some reached the foe before others.

To be sure, the English were also confused, more so, with attackers coming down on them from both sides, and themselves extended in threes and fours, and no commanders able to give orders. The clash, once commenced, quickly became wild and uncontrolled, a slashing, swiping, lunging and colliding turmoil, not helped, for the Scots, by many crashes into their own comrades in that headling descent. Lances were jerked out of grasps, falling to cause further upset, horses reared and fell, kicking, for others to trip over, men were thrown as well as cut down – and all this along over a quarter-mile of bloody, yelling, screaming tumult.

George, his own lance lost, and twice nearly unseated, by impact rather than actual blows, tried to tell himself that his duty was to *lead*, not just to do battle. There would be quite large numbers of the foe at the riverside, waiting; and these could turn back and attack in turn. This possibility must be countered. So he forced his plunging horse through the heaving tangle of men and beasts and on to the other slope, there to turn and gaze, and seek to use his wits.

It was impossible to descry any order out of the anarchy prevailing on that narrow valley floor, even to distinguish friend from foe. But he did see something that he could do. Quite a number of their own men, owing to the sheer crowded jumble before them, were not yet actually engaged, with no room to be so, up on the slightly higher ground still, waiting their opportunity, this on both sides. To these George yelled and waved and pointed with his sword, which he had managed to retain, pointed onwards, southwards, urgently, commandingly, turning his own mount in that direction. Just above the mêlée he rode on, gesturing, beckoning. Men, seeing it, did turn to obey, quite a number, as he plunged on. Glancing back, he saw that he was being followed by more.

Then another problem became apparent to him, as he actually found himself riding alongside two men whom he was fairly sure were in fact Englishmen. Not that there was much to distinguish friend from foe among the rank and file; but one of this pair had retained a heraldic-painted shield, and this showed the blue lozenges on gold of Percy. So – some of them seeking to leave the struggle were the enemy! These mixed with his own folk. Confusion worse confounded! Was warfare always like this? Chaos indeed? And yet – could it serve his purpose in some measure, perhaps? For the enemy at the riverside would be as uncertain who to attack as were the Scots, in this rush. That could be so.

And that indeed was the way of it. Reaching the more open ground beside the mill, all became a complete incoherence and mingling of friend and enemy, mixed beyond any recognition or order, all identity as well as decision lost. Save for one urge, that is: for the attacked to assume defeat. That, and the compelling need for escape. And hereabouts, escape was possible, the scene wider. Men could flee east or west along the riverside; however few could get across the ford to the others beyond. Flight became the imperative. And, in the confusion of the process, gradually something definite became apparent. The Scots were being left there, to claim victory.

Those English who had managed to cross the river, seeing what was happening, now began to depart at speed also.

Some small fighting went on still, as fleeing enemy

coming out of the narrows southwards were assailed by the Scots there already; but this was only a half-hearted reaction, conquest already obviously won, and the need to endanger themselves lapsed. No doubt others of the foe were escaping northwards.

Soon Hay, Seton and Home appeared, triumphant, all congratulations. George found his hand being shaken, although he was not sure why. He could not see his part in the affray as worthy of praise. But satisfaction was the order of the day. Unfortunately Hotspur himself had escaped them, presumably one of the early crossers of the ford.

There were numbers of wounded, as well as the slain, on either side. These fell to be dealt with. They would order the folk of Duns to cope with the injured and bury the dead, Swinton of Kimmerghame to see to it.

One of the captives, wounded, when questioned declared that the Percy had been heading for Cocklaws Tower, a hold down the Blackadder valley none so far from Tweed, a Cranstoun place, where Hotspur had sent his brother to assail it, the Percys having some sort of feud with its owner about cross-border raiding. Hence this diversion.

There was some discussion as to whether to follow on after Hotspur for this Cocklaws. But it was decided that this was not called for. Presumably, defeated as he had been here, the Percy would raise the siege there, if the place had not already fallen, and return to his Alnwick with his brother. Another battle was not sought, by George nor his advisers; they were certainly not going to invade Northumberland. Enough blood had been shed meantime.

Home for them all, then, and with satisfaction. Gamelshiel for George, with all speed.

His arrival there was to further gratification, although not without some self-accusation. He found that he had become a father in the interim, Beatrix having given birth to a son two days earlier, this without complications, she and Phemie assured him. Nothing that he could usefully have done about it, even if he had been present, as he announced that he ought to have been. He hugged and kissed and exulted, praising his wife, and parading round the little castle with the infant in his arms.

They would name him Patrick. After all, one day he would *be* Cospatrick.

16

George and Beatrix remained at Gamelshiel until snow on the hills and bitter weather sent them back to Colbrands-path, conditions seeming to make this not unwise. For the moment, most of Scotland was comparatively peaceful, whatever was the case in England – if not, however, for the regent Albany. There had been another murder, which was being attributed to him, this time Queen Annabella's brother, Sir Malcolm Drummond, although the actual deed had been done by one of the Wolf of Badenoch's sons. Drummond had accused Albany of his sister's death. And most strangely, this latest assassination aroused more indignation and protest than the others – or it may merely have been that accumulation of these murders had triggered it off. Drummond, of course, had been popular. At any rate, the regent's credit had never been lower. And this time the Douglas link could not be implicated and available for Albany's support. He was proving to be a very different man from his father. And he was, in fact, trying to make himself reasonably acceptable to the Dunbar and March people, now that he had been handed Dunbar Castle, and finding the enmity involved grievous. So he was seeing little of the regent, especially as, it transpired, Albany's son Murdoch had been captured in the last Douglas raid into England, and was still held there, for which he, Douglas, was being blamed.

There was talk in the land of the lords seeking to unseat the duke as regent.

All this did not affect George greatly, although Douglas did approach him, not exactly apologetically but in fairly friendly fashion, indicating that he would wish there to be no animosity between them. So long as the Earl Cospatrick remained an ally of Henry of England, and made his claims to the Scottish throne, of course, there could be no return to his earldom. But there was no need for the Master to suffer unduly for his father's errors, so long as he remained loyal to King Robert.

This attitude suited George well enough, especially with Douglas congratulating him on his victory over Hotspur Percy. So peace of a sort prevailed between Dunbar and Colbrandspath; and Cospatrick's sons could get on with administrating the remainder of the earldom to the best of their ability. And, to be sure, George and Beatrix happy in each other's company, and enjoying being parents of Patrick.

That infant throve.

The news from England was otherwise, and quite extraordinary. The fighting was still going on along the Welsh Marches, indeed intensifying, this largely because of a dramatic situation regarding that awkward man Hotspur, Earl of Northumberland. He had fallen out with King Henry, whom he had never actually supported, and now had gone so far as to renounce allegiance, declaring that John Mortimer, a direct descendant of Edward the Third, should have succeeded to the throne after Richard, and that Henry was a usurper. More than that, he had urged Mortimer to fight Henry, allying himself to Glendower; and warfare was proceeding on the Welsh borders with increasing violence. By an odd coincidence, Mortimer held the English title of Earl of March, this of the Welsh area, so that there were two Earls of March, and on opposite sides, in this struggle.

Hotspur was a bizarre and unaccountable character. But at least he was not presently assailing over the Scots border, although his brother had gained and was holding that Cocklaws Tower.

This last did not worry George overmuch, although some, the Homes in especial, considered that this ought to be righted, even though it was not Home territory and the occupation was part of a private feud between Percys and Cranstouns, a typical cross-border situation. Urges for him to take action did not have the Master drawing the sword meantime.

As it happened, he did not have to do so anyway, and this on account of a development, as so much else that year. George was astonished and taken aback that April of 1403 by a visit at Colbrandspath from, of all people, Robert Stewart, Duke of Albany.

He arrived one afternoon unannounced and at the head of quite a large force of the royal guard, to the alarm of the neighbourhood, George in especial. But despite his armed following, he did not come in evident enmity, whatever his attitude to the Earl Cospatrick; quite the reverse indeed. He came, scarcely in friendship but in professed amity, as far as such was possible for that dire character. He announced, curtly, that he had just taken Cocklaws Tower, dispossessed the Percy garrison, and now came to express goodwill.

All but startled, unbelieving, suspecting he knew not what, George stared.

"I have heard that you have scored a victory over the scoundrelly Percy of Northumberland," he said. "That is well. You are serving the kingdom rightly. Now – I require your aid, young man."

"My . . . *my* aid?"

"Yes. In two matters. One, over my son, the Lord Murdoch. He is held prisoner in England. This new Douglas to blame for that. He was with him at a raid over the border, and they were overwhelmed at the attack at Homildon Hill. Your father, who was there, is known to be close to Henry of England, however unsuitably. Indeed now fighting for him against the Welsh, and against this of Mortimer and Percy. If you will send to him, to the earl and have him use his influence with Henry to have my son released, I will reward him. And you. Forbye, I and King Robert could use him, your father's aid, here in Scotland at this pass. Against ill-minded forces. If he will return here, and use his power and men to the realm's weal – that, and renounce his foolish claims to the crown – I will have King Robert pardon his indiscretions and treasons, and assure him of my goodwill.''

George gulped, fingered his chin, and gazed. "You, you my lord Duke, seek my father's return? Not to . . . ? His *aid*? This is . . .'' He could not finish that, shaking his head. Was this a trap, to lure his sire into?

"I am willing to overlook past follies,'' he was told. "I require my son back. And seek stout support for the throne. Your father could serve the realm well in this. If he would. See you to it.''

"How, how am I to do that, my lord Duke?''

"Go see him. Or send him sure word. If he heeds, and acts, his forfeiture will be repealed, and he will serve himself well. *You* have done well, at that Nisbet Moor. Now prove yourself still more useful, Master of Dunbar.''

"How, my lord, can my father be sure that this is not just . . . some ruse? To get him back and into your power?'' That demanded some saying on George's part, to the realm's regent.

"Is my word not good enough for you, sirrah!''

The younger man inclined his head, unspeaking.

"See to it, then. And you will not suffer. Nor will he, your father.'' Albany turned on his heel and strode back to his horse, clearly with no intention of lingering longer at Colbrandspath.

Bemused indeed, George watched him and his long column go. He went in to tell Beatrix.

Would his father respond if he did send the word? As, almost certainly he must.

After due deliberation, it was decided that the matter must be put to the Earl Cospatrick. He, George, would not go himself, his place being here, to act the earl meantime. He would send his brother Colin with a letter. Then it was up to their father. Would he agree? Seek to gain this Murdoch's release? Give up his claim to the crown? Return to Scotland? This, when so many whom Albany saw as in his way had been assassinated? It was doubts all the way. Yet surely his own duty was clear. The word had to be sent. Beatrix agreed.

He rode to Johnscleuch to see Colin.

Reaction could not be speedy, of course, with that long way for Colin to go to the Welsh Marches, and for so vital a decision to be made, with all consequences considered. George, waiting, had a word with Sir William Hay on it all, and that man declared that his superior would probably be wise to accept Albany's proposals; at the same time taking all due precautions as to his personal safety from possible murder attempts. This last must ever be borne in mind. Not that the Earl of Dunbar and March would be easy to assassinate, warned. But Albany was known to be faced with serious problems at this present, many lords and magnates uniting against him, over the deaths of the queen, young Rothesay and now Drummond. He probably had decided that he needed Cospatrick's help, and would thus pay for it.

In fact, the tidings that reached Colbrandspath from the south thereafter, in the first instance, came not from his brother Colin, but from those famous retailers of tidings, the wandering friars, who were the news-bearers of the land. There had been a great battle at Shrewsbury, near the Welsh border, between Henry and Glendower's allies, Mortimer and Hotspur. The Percy had been slain, and the Welsh driven back into their own mountains once more. So that was the end of the Hotspur menace, glory be! Had Cospatrick and Gavin been present? Even Colin?

They had, and thankfully survived. Colin arrived back not long afterwards, safe and sound, with his report. Yes, their father would accept Albany's gesture, with due caution needless to say. He would do what he could to get the young Murdoch released, on as fair terms as was possible. And he would return to Scotland and his earldom, renouncing his claim to the throne, meantime at least, his forfeiture repealed. Whether he could indeed co-operate

161

with the regent remained to be seen, but he might well be able to help in controlling excesses and establishing some degree of peace and accord in Scotland, his known association with Henry of England aiding. Both kingdoms might benefit, especially with the Douglas power now being held in check. He would leave Gavin with Henry as a sort of token of continued alliance.

So George was going to see his father again, after so long an interval.

Cospatrick duly arrived back in Scotland in late August, a man wary, but by no means in any placatory frame of mind, indeed determined to make his presence felt and take a leading role again in the land. Having been so close to King Henry, and proved himself successful in warfare, and now being all but beseeched to come back, he probably had reason to be, if not exactly pleased with himself, at least confident of his position.

He was, of course, much upset at having to take up residence in Colbrandspath Tower instead of his castle of Dunbar, declaring that this must be put to rights, and swiftly, one of the first matters that he had to put to Albany, among sundry others. He was not going to trade any sort of support to that character cheaply.

Unfortunately he had been unable to bring back the son, Murdoch; this, as it happened, on that young man's own choice. He was anything but a guarded prisoner in England, all but an honoured guest, and a companion of the young James Stewart, Duke of Rothesay now, at the Tower of London and Windsor Castle, where Henry, in his absence on the Welsh Marches, had ordered these two young Scots cousins to be well treated. He saw them both as potentially useful hostages, but had no animosity towards either of them. So Murdoch, quite enjoying himself, better than he ever did in his father's company, indeed somewhat afraid of him, was in no hurry to return home, where he saw himself as little more than a symbol, an heir.

162

Cospatrick would have to explain this to Albany, with such tact as he could muster.

The earl was interested to see his first grandchild, Patrick, another ultimate heir, and congratulated Beatrix amiably. He would see the rest of his family soon, but first he must head off for Scone, to interview the regent.

George wondered over that interview, so significant for them all. His father obviously considered himself to be in a strong position, or he would not have been asked to return.

Cospatrick used one of the Dunbar ships to sail up to the Tay, and Scone, glad to have these at his disposal again; and also glad of the revenues which George and his brothers had gathered for him from the wool trade in the interim. Sailing out of the harbour and under the castle bridge, he shook a fist up at the battlements above him.

He was not gone for long, only four days, and came back apparently fairly well satisfied. Albany, more unpopular than ever before, and mistrusted throughout the land, needed someone like the Earl of Dunbar and March, with large manpower at his disposal, now that he could not rely on that of the Douglas. Albany had been disappointed at not getting his son back, but had to gloss over the fact that Murdoch was well content to remain in England with young Rothesay. As to the matter of Dunbar Castle, he had put forward a typically Albany-like solution for that problem. Apparently, some years before, he had handed over to Archibald the Grim parts of the Stewart's Carrick earldom, to ensure that earl's continued backing, this including Lochmaben Castle, the Bruce's former stronghold, and North Annandale. Now, he would take them back, as having been a personal favour, this as showing his displeasure over the capture of Murdoch at Homildon Hill, and instead transfer them to Cospatrick. The fact that that man had no desire for these faraway properties was of no matter. Douglas would desire them back, so close to his own lands; so he would certainly be prepared to exchange them for Dunbar Castle, which he probably did not greatly value. This could then return to its rightful lord.

163

George, for one, wondered at this convoluted device, but recognised that his father was dealing with a master of such strategies. But he did remark that they would have to be very much on their guard in case some similar artifice was contrived against themselves, sooner or later. Cospatrick declared himself well aware of the risks of supping with the devil, and was not going to be caught out, never fear.

And what did Albany require of him, George asked, in return? He was told that, so far, nothing specific. Just the fact that he was now seen to be co-operating with the regime, and more or less replacing Archibald the Grim. Cospatrick smiled as he conceded that. But it took two at least to co-operate effectively!

As to claims to the throne, this had not so much as been mentioned, save in that the earl had agreed to go fairly soon to Rothesay Castle, where King Robert lived almost as a hermit, to declare his resumed fealty.

George learned something which his father had not spoken of previously, that King Henry, in gratitude for the support given in the Welsh warfare, had presented Cospatrick with certain lands and manors in England, forfeited by the treacherous Hotspur and others. These were being put in Gavin's name meantime, who was remaining with Henry. The earldom was expanding.

The earl said that he had a journey to make westwards, not in a ship this time, although that would have been convenient, for it was to an island, Bute; but to sail right round Scotland, some seven hundred and fifty miles, with the hazards of the Pentland Firth and the Hebridean seas, this as against a ride of barely one hundred, with a short sail from the Ayrshire coast, did not make sense. He was to visit King Robert, to renew his renounced allegiance to the monarch in person, so that his forfeiture could be annulled. And there was this of the temporary transfer of the lands of the royal earldom of Carrick into his name before they could be exchanged for Dunbar to be dealt with. He declared that it was suitable that George should accompany him on this visit, as the heir to the earldom.

So, in a day or two, it was farewell to Beatrix and little Patrick, and the long riding commenced, by Edinburgh and the Calders to the Clyde at Motherwell, passing the night at a monastery at Allanbank; and on next day by East Kilbride, Newton Mearns, south of Glasgow, to Lochwinnoch and the Firth of Clyde at Largs, scene of the famous battle, which George was interested to examine. Scows made regular ferries across the six miles to the Isle of Bute from there.

Although Rothesay was a royal castle, it seemed a strange place for the King of Scots to reside, remote and isolated; but for Robert the Third, that strange occupant of the throne, it was a sort of sanctuary for a man retiring, timorous and yielding, although studious. He lived here as a recluse in this island hold, so different a man from his many brothers, Scotland had always required strong kings; here was the reverse.

The visitors had no difficulty in gaining audience, at least, and although not exactly welcomed they were nowise rebuffed. John Robert, still in a bed-robe at midday, sat at a table littered with books, parchments and manuscripts, a watery-eyed man of sixty-three years, and looking still older, a sorry figure, yet with something about him which George at least felt as meriting respect – not that much of this was shown to him by officials, who came in even while the Dunbars were with him, bringing papers to sign. This indeed was the monarch's one and continuing official activity for his realm, signing; signing the unending stream of documents that required the royal superscription and the privy seal to become effective: transfers of land, judgments, appointments, promotions, council decisions and acts, statutes and the like. Quill and ink-pot ever at his side, he signed all scrawlingly without so much as reading a word.

The issues that had brought them there aroused no real interest in the king, and were accepted with nodding and grey head-shaking, this as more papers were brought in for signing.

The visitors, not pressed to stay although not actually dismissed, recognised that the audience was not to be prolonged. Exchanging glances, they bowed themselves out.

They did receive some food and drink from the keeper of the castle, one of the many illegitimate Stewart brothers. They then returned to the quayside to board one of the ferry-scows.

It seemed a long way to have come for those few minutes of talk. But at least they had given their sad liege-lord some ease of mind over his surviving son.

And now, oddly, Cospatrick was, for the moment, lord of much of Annandale, in name at least. But, it was to be hoped, not for very long.

17

Back at Colbrandspath they had to wait for some weeks
while the process of informing Archibald Douglas, gaining
his agreement for the exchange of the properties and the
resulting vacation of Dunbar Castle took place, patience
being required. But at length it was all done, Douglas
apparently being well pleased to get Annandale back, and
with no real interest in Dunbar. The family assembled in
thankfulness to stage a notable and all but triumphant
return to their home, the folk of the town turning out to
celebrate the occasion with relief.

Much tidying and improvement had to follow within
the castle after its occupation by the Douglas garrison; but
there was plenty of help for this, and soon matters were put
to rights. The earl decided that some sort of demonstration
would be appropriate to mark the occasion, and his re-
sumption of powers and status. A great gathering was
staged, and all the vassals, lairds and major tenants were
invited, as well as friends.

This proved to be a joyful occasion, after so much of
threat, upset, concern and uncertainty. If all was not yet
right in the kingdom, at least their lord was back and in
command of his two large earldoms, with the regent
requiring his support and therefore unlikely to cause *them*
trouble meantime, whoever else he might afflict.

The announcement was made, during the proceedings,
that the Lady Janet, George's younger sister, was to wed
Sir John Seton, heir to the ageing senior vassal, this to
much acclaim. Her sister Elizabeth, who was to have
married the dead David of Rothesay, was still unwed,
but there were plans for her also.

In all this George and Beatrix took their part, and little Patrick came in for much admiration. They were always happy, however, to return to their own home at Colbrandspath.

Parliaments had been few and far between in Scotland these past years, Albany preferring to rule without them. But one was called now, a sign that the regent was aware of general criticism and his unpopularity. Ostensibly it was to deal with the matter of Donald of the Isles and the northwest situation, although this was nothing new. Cospatrick suspected that it was largely to demonstrate *his* new support of the regency. If so, he would be expected to play some prominent part in the proceedings. He thought that his heir probably ought to be present. Not that George could attend as a commissioner; but he could watch from the gallery of the great hall of Stirling Castle where the parliament was to be held. One day he would have to take part, so it would be an education for him.

It did prove to be an interesting occasion, however controversial it might be as to purpose. In actual truth it was not a parliament at all if the monarch himself was not present, only a convention, the King-in-Parliament; but the regent, as representative, was held to suffice.

The Lyon King of Arms, acting High Sennachie, introduced all, the high officers of state coming in procession first, the Marischal, the High Constable, the Lord Justiciar, the High Chamberlain and the High Treasurer. Then the earls, Cospatrick among them. Then the Chancellor, Bishop Gilbert de Greenlaw of Aberdeen, who conducted the proceedings. And finally Albany himself, to be led to the throne. He declared the session open.

There was a fair attendance of lords, commissioners of the shires, provosts of royal burghs, and bishops and mitred abbots, the Three Estates of the Realm. George saw Seton of that Ilk among the county commissioners, while his future brother-in-law, Sir John, sat beside him in the gallery along with the papal envoy, ambassadors, countesses and other wives.

168

It was all very formal, at first, with the Chancellor leading off, asking the Primate Bishop of St Andrews to pray and commend their deliberations to Almighty God. This over, he proposed the appointments to various state and national positions. This dealt with, he called on the various officers of state to give their accounts, the High Treasurer reporting on the national revenues, not cheerfully and indeed calling for increased taxation, which earned him growls from throughout the hall. The High Constable listed the new keepers of royal castles; the Lord Justiciar spoke on keeping the peace of the realm, with accusations at some of the lords there present. The Marischal detailed the state of the royal forces, such as they were. These last produced mutterings. Then the Chancellor turned to the throne, and invited Albany to address the assembly in the name of His Grace the King.

That man wasted no time in preliminaries. He declared flatly that Donald of the Isles, not present, as he should have been, was presently much disturbing the king's peace in the north-west areas, with attacks on certain clans, grasping of lands, threatening still greater offences, indeed claiming the succession to the earldom of Ross. He had even presumed to offer a peace treaty, over the Isle of Man, to King Henry of England, acting like an independent sovereign. This had to be dealt with, and promptly. He did not mention that the said Donald was his own cousin, his father, John of the Isles, having married one of Robert the Second's sisters.

There were some murmurs voiced at this from the company, but no great outcry. There was only a very small attendance of northern lords and chiefs, and the great majority present were not particularly interested in what went on in the Highlands and Isles, looking on these as far away and barbarous territories with folk speaking an outlandish tongue, and unworthy of concern by more responsible subjects.

Albany cut short such reaction by announcing that His Grace's *leal* northern subjects had to be protected from this Donald's shameful aggression. And moreover, the King of England shown that no subject of the King of Scots could be in any position to propose treaties with him on any matter thus assailing the realm's dignity and repute. Donald of the Isles must be taught no uncertain lesson.

He paused, and looked over at Cospatrick, on the earls' benches.

"We are fortunate," he went on, "in the recent return to Scotland of the Earl of Dunbar and March from the Welsh warfare. He is not only on friendly terms with King Henry of England, but is uncle to the young Earl of Moray, captured at the unfortunate affair of Homildon Hill, along with my own son, leaving only a child Master of Moray up in the north with his mother. So my lord of Dunbar is in an excellent position to represent His Grace and this parliament up in those difficult parts, and to bring Donald of the Isles to heel. This with the authority of parliament and the regency. Is it agreed?"

Cospatrick rose from his bench, bowed briefly to the throne, and resumed his seat. No opposition to this proposal was voiced.

Albany waved to the Chancellor, and sat back.

It was all as simple as that. Up in the gallery, George marvelled. Albany was seen to have the support of Cospatrick, which implied some sort of favourable stance with Henry of England, and his own authority emphasised. Here was statecraft indeed. Did his father see it as suitable and satisfactory? That brief bow seemed to indicate so.

There were other matters of administration and governance to be dealt with by the Chancellor and the members' votes. But clearly that had been the main business of this parliament, whatever the commissioners thought of it, many having come long distances to attend.

Presently Albany abruptly rose, and the session became thereby adjourned.

In their lodgings in Stirling town that night, the earl assured his son that he was well content with it all. In no way was he being seen as subservient to Albany, however valuable. On the contrary, after being all but a forfeited outlaw, he was now being seen as foremost among the earls. And this mission would give him opportunity to provide some help to his nephew Moray's wife and child up at Darnaway.

But what of Donald of the Isles? George wondered.

His father shrugged. That remained to be seen, he said. But his brother, the previous Moray, had been friendly with Donald's father. This might prove to be of some significance and help.

Instead of leading a large force up through the Highlands to Moray, as probably was expected, Cospatrick, and George with him, sailed comfortably northwards in one of their own vessels, heading for Inverness. There were more ways of opening an egg than smashing it with a hammer, the earl said.

It made quite a pleasant voyage, whatever they might find at the end of it, never out of sight of the land, up the picturesque coastlines of Fife and Angus and Kincardineshire – where his father pointed out to George the mighty castle of Dunnottar on its cliff, the seat of the Marischal – of Aberdeenshire and round its great northern headland into the approaches of the Moray Firth itself. Thereafter they could have turned in to one of the Moray havens nearer to Darnaway, into Burghead or Findhorn or even Nairn; but Cospatrick wanted to make enquiries at Inverness, which constituted the capital of all that eastern Highland area, and where he would be able to learn the state of affairs prevailing much more effectively than from the countess at Darnaway, he was fairly certain.

This was new territory for George.

Turning in to the mouth of the River Ness, their shipmaster was able to dock their vessel all but under the walls of the castle on its ridge in the midst of the town, not a dominant fortress like Edinburgh, Stirling or even Dunnottar, more an administrative centre. Its keeper should be a vassal of the Earl of Moray.

He proved to be a son of Brodie of that Ilk. He was very knowledgeable and helpful. And almost at once he was able to give them surprising information, that the Lord of the Isles would not have to be sought for among all the wild clan country to the west, as anticipated, for he was actually presently in residence comparatively nearby, at Dingwall, a mere dozen miles or so to the north, at the head of the Cromarty Firth, this the capital town of the earldom of Ross to which he was claiming heirship. He had been there for over a month, with his wife, the Lady Margaret, who was a sister of the ninth Earl of Ross. That earl, now dead, had married, as his second wife, the Lady Isabel Stewart, daughter of Albany, and had an only child, Euphemia, who was, strangely enough, at the age of twenty-two, insisting that, although she was Countess of Ross in her own right, she was going to devote her life to Almighty God and take the veil. If she did indeed do so, she would have to renounce her position as countess; and Donald was claiming the title in right of his wife. It was an involved situation.

So now they saw why Albany was so concerned that the Islesman should be put down. The young and godly countess was his own granddaughter, and so he himself might claim that great earldom, probably the largest in the kingdom as far as wide lands were concerned, if Donald's wife, who had the prior claim, was ruled out, which she could be, if she and her husband were condemned and got rid of for treason to the crown. Ross had long been a sought-after prize, even the Wolf of Badenoch having married, in name, the widow of the previous earl, although no children resulted.

George was quite lost in his understanding of the intricacies of this whole affair; but his father seemed to have a sufficient grasp of it. They would go and see Donald of the Isles at Dingwall.

But first, he decided, they must see his sister-in-law,

172

George's aunt, the Countess Marjory of Moray, and the child Master. She was related to all the principal actors in this convoluted drama, she the eldest daughter of that so prolific monarch, Robert the Second, therefore sister of Albany, the Wolf of Badenoch and Donald's own mother. King Robert had had no fewer than five legitimate daughters and five lawful sons, however lawless, with almost countless bastard offspring; so unravelling the relationships was all but a superhuman task.

They obtained horses from Brodie, and set off eastwards the twenty-five miles, by Culloden and Cawdor, to Darnaway, this just south of Forres, through excellent country, with the mountains blue in the distance.

Darnaway Castle, the main seat of the earldom, was a fine and large house, not particularly strongly sited, among extensive woodlands of ancient, gnarled pine trees. They found the Countess Marjory, whom of course they knew well, her usual kindly and attractive self, in her late fifties now, and welcoming. She was worried about her son, captive in England, but Cospatrick was able to reassure her that being held there, under the present regime of King Henry, was no dire fate, indeed possibly to be preferred in some respects to life in Scotland under her brother's rule for those in lofty places. He did not have to apologise over his judgment in this; she was not under any misconception as to Albany's ruthlessness and John/Robert's weakness, as of the Wolf's savageries. The Stewarts had not always been like this, she did claim however.

The boy Thomas, her grandson, was a cheerful youngster, and not at all interested in the serious situation in which he lived, only in his sports and private ventures.

On the subject of Donald of the Isles, her nephew, the countess was helpful. She said that she liked him, as she had done his father, and judged that his claim to the earldom of Ross, if indeed effected, would be for the good of all the north, if not for the realm at large. It was an extraordinary heritage, covering perhaps four thousand square if very upheaved miles, probably quite the largest in extent in the land, but divided very much into two distinct entities, Easter and Wester, and these so very different in character. Basically this eastern part, much smaller in area, was infinitely the richer as to land, fertility, prosperity and trade, and was always looked upon as their homeland by the earls. The west was vast, mountainous, the clan country, and these clans always at war and feud, accepting little authority save for that of their own chiefs, in a high world of heather and rock and peat-bog, lochs and torrents, islands and peninsulas, and with the great Lordship of the Isles always looming and threatening to the west further still, in the Sea of the Hebrides. If Donald did become Earl of Ross as well as master of that last, he almost certainly could control this sprawling, wild entity, and bring peace of a sort to its difficult people who so badly needed it, as no one else could do, certainly not her brother Albany, even if he had any concern so to do. So she favoured Donald's claim, as her dear husband would have done.

Cospatrick accepted that. But was Donald any threat to this adjacent Moray earldom?

She thought not. His father and her husband had been friends and had come to terms, and Donald had grown up all but in association with Moray. Moreover, if he won Ross he would have more than enough on his plate to satisfy even the most demanding appetite.

This seemed sound judgment. So, Dingwall then, and some arrangement with Donald which would satisfy parliament, if not Albany himself. Back to Inverness.

As the eagle flew it was only about thirteen miles to the town of Dingwall; but there were the Beauly and Cromarty Firths to be negotiated on the way. Cospatrick decided that it was best to go by ship.

They sailed up the coast of the Black Isle, past Rosemarkie, to turn into the narrow mouth of the Cromarty Firth, and up this for some twenty-five miles to Dingwall near its head, much longer travelling but simpler than by horseback. It proved to be quite a large town. They found room to dock amid more other vessels than they had expected to find, among which were five longships, dragon-prowed, of the Islesmen, the so-called greyhounds of the sea.

The castle, former seat of the Norse invaders, which gave name to the place Thing Vollr, meaning the meeting place of a council, was not on any rock or lofty site, but on levels near the waterside, surrounded by a double moat, fed by the tides. This was now the main seat of the Earls of Ross, the town stretching further along the shore.

The pair did not have to go seeking Donald there however, for, as they were disembarking, in behind them came one more dragonship, at great speed and flourish, to draw up all but alongside, its sixteen long sweeps, each pulled by three men, rising vertical in a proud and practised gesture. There could be no doubt as to authority here.

A youngish man climbed with agility on to the quay and, eyeing Cospatrick and his son, these well dressed and not in Highland fashion, inclined a quite handsome head, and spoke, but not peremptorily.

"We have visitors, I see. And from distant parts, no?"

"Visiting, yes. As are you, I think!" The earl was not to be bested by any stranger. He gestured at the longship. "Such does not belong to the earldom of Ross, I judge."

The other waved a hand. "Perhaps the earldom of Ross belongs to it, sir! I am Donald of the Isles."

"Ah. I deemed that it might be so. *I* am Cospatrick of Dunbar and March. And my son, the Master. And you it is whom we have come to see, my lord."

"Dunbar? And March? The earl himself! Then – you have come a long way."

"You could say so, yes. And of a purpose. You know of me, then?"

"Who does not in Scotland? And now in England also, I think! We are none so ignorant in the Isles, my lord."

"You may know why I have come, then?"

"At the behest of that Stewart who now calls himself Albany?"

"At the behest of the Scots parliament, my lord Donald. Which *you* did not attend."

"I have more to be doing, whatever, with my time than heeding Stewart summons! As, I would have thought, would have such as yourself!" He waved towards the castle. "But – come you. If you have travelled all this way to talk with me, we can do so the better over a goblet of wine, or of what we call the water of life."

He led the way to the two drawbridges over the castle moats, Cospatrick and his son exchanging glances. Some of the wild-looking Islesmen from the dragonship came along behind them.

At the castle they were introduced to the Lady Margaret, whose home this had been until she married Donald, a pleasant, comely woman; also to their two children, Alastair, or Alexander, and Mariot. She was prompt in offering them hospitality, and spoke kindly of Cospatrick's sister-in-law, Marjory of Moray. It all made a hopeful atmosphere for negotiations.

When, taken to a withdrawing-room off the lesser hall, the men sat down to talk, Cospatrick sought to maintain as friendly an attitude as was possible, considering his mission.

"Parliament, my lord, had it put to it that you were assailing and oppressing chiefs and clans in these parts, subjects of His Grace, and causing much . . . disharmony. Breaking the king's peace. Also were wrongfully claiming the earldom of Ross. It was not known that you were already here, in this principal Ross castle."

"My wife's former home, where she was reared," came the intervention.

"So I have learned. Parliament decided that this matter must be seen to, and I was appointed to come up to Ross to . . . assert the crown's authority."

"By parliament? Or by Albany?"

"Parliament agreed to it."

"But it was at Albany's direction, I swear!"

"Perhaps. As regent, he has his duties to maintain the peace of the realm."

"And uses them to advance his own interests! He would have me murdered, like so many others, if he could! For *he* would have the earldom of Ross."

"That may be so, my lord. But it was on this account, of the realm's peace, that I was sent north."

"What, then?"

"To discover the facts of the situation for parliament. The true position. And to learn what needs righting, and how to bring that about."

"All that needs righting here is that a strong hand should be empowered to control the unruly and feuding clans. Authority be established. And since most of it all takes place in this earldom of Ross, the earldom should be in the right and strong hands. Not in the hands of a young woman who dwells in a nunnery! And I, through my wife, claim this earldom. Moreover, the lawlessness here affects my own lordship. For all my territory is not in the Isles. I have much land in the mainland also. So I am the one most concerned."

Cospatrick was in no position to deny that. "You say that these chiefs and clans who complain of your attacks do so without due warrant, my lord?"

"They do so for their own ends, not for peace and general weal. See you – and why? Not the Camerons, the Mackintoshes, the Macphersons, the Shaws, the Macleans, the MacNeills, the MacDougalls, the MacGillivrays, the MacIntyres and the MacIans – save some of these against Alexander Stewart of Badenoch, the Wolf! And Campbell of Argyll is hot against myself. All these others see me as friend. It is the northern clans who seek to grasp lands further south who call me foe: Mackenzies, MacLeods, Mackays, even Sinclairs. And these Albany is using for his own ends, with the Campbell's assistance."

"You say that these many clan chiefs see you as their friend and protector? How can I assure, convince parliament as to that?"

"Go see the chiefs themselves, Mackintosh at Moy, none so far off. Cameron at Lochiel. Macpherson at Cluny,

Shaw at Tordarroch. These you can reach without over-much trouble. I will find you horses . . ."

It seemed sound guidance and fair suggesting, George, listening, judged. Donald seemed honest and reliable, and with the right on his side. He thought that his father was feeling the same way. This of going to see some of the chiefs would help to confirm their judgment.

Leaving it at that, they moved back to the lesser hall, and found the Lady Margaret expecting them to stay overnight in the castle, although Cospatrick said that they could go back to their cabin on the ship. This Donald would not hear of, and they settled in appreciatively.

There was really no more talk on what had brought the visitors north, but much of conditions in the south, especially in England, of King Henry and the Welsh wars. Donald informed that it was not a treaty that he had offered to the Plantagenet, but merely an assurance that, while he looked on the Isle of Man as traditionally part of the lordship of the Isles, he accepted that its proximity to the English coast called for an especial relationship and a trading understanding. This seemed fair enough.

Before bedding down that night, Cospatrick broached the intriguing subject of the Stone of Destiny, which was said to be in the keeping of the Lords of the Isles. Where was this precious symbol of Scottish pride and national heritage?

"That I may not tell you," Donald said, smiling. "It is hidden where only myself, my brother, and one or two others may know. It was handed over to my ancestor Angus Og of Islay and the Isles by Robert the Bruce on his death-bed. He was told to hold it secure until a worthy successor sat on his throne; this because Edward the Third of England, your Henry's ancestor, was still threatening Scotland, and would have grabbed the stone if he could, as his grandfather had tried to take it in 1296, seeing it as the symbol of Scotland's nationhood. He failed. It was prob-ably a Roman pagan altar, which St Columba adopted and

178

turned into a Christian shrine, as demonstrating his conversion of Alba and Dalriada to Christianity. Bruce, dying, was leaving only a five-year-old son, David the Second, as monarch. So this handing of the stone over was a wise precaution."

"And still you hold it, hidden?"

"Think you that the Stewarts are worthy successors? *You*, who by rights should be on the throne!"

"Ah, you know of that! If I was king, would you give it over to me?"

"If you swore to rule as the Bruce had done, yes."

"My line was and is a deal older than Bruce's! But, yes, he, with Wallace's aid, won Scotland's freedom. I would seek to be a worthy successor."

"What is the stone that the English hold in Westminster Abbey, then?" George wondered. "They call that the Coronation Stone."

"It is a lump of Scone sandstone, no more!" he was told. "This the Abbot of Scone, knowing that Edward was coming for the stone, had quarried and placed before the altar there to deceive the Hammer of the Scots, as he called himself, while he hid the true Stone of Destiny. Edward, later, realised that he had been duped, and came back to Scotland in two years' time, and pulled Scone Abbey apart, stone from stone, seeking the real one, but never finding it. Only when Bruce had secured the kingdom and freedom was established was it brought to light again. There is no comparison between the two stones. The Lia Fail, to give it its Gaelic name, is much larger, seat-height – as was needed for the monarchs to sit on at their coronation – whereas the London stone is only eleven inches high, so that the English had to make a chair over it. Moreover the Lia Fail is not of red sandstone, but dark, and like marble, highly carved and decorated, Scotland's Marble Chair as it has been called. We, in the Isles, hold it secure, as commanded."

Cospatrick turned to his son. "Heed you all this, lad," he said. "If by any miracle, or by God's will, *you* should

179

ever sit on the Scottish throne, demand you the stone! You would be its rightful custodian, not these MacDonalds!"

They left it at that, agreeably.

The next day, instead of accepting Donald's horses, but glad of the guide he provided, one Alastair mac Alastair, presumably another MacDonald, they sailed back to Inverness where, on Brodie's horses, the three of them headed almost due south a dozen miles, as directed, into the higher country of Strathdearn, the beginning of the mountains, to reach Loch Moy, on an island of which rose the castle of the Mackintosh. Their guide had no difficulty in getting co-operation from boatmen there, using Donald's name, to have them rowed out to the islet, where they found the chief entertaining MacGillivray of Strathnairn, head of a lesser clan of the great Clan Chattan federation, of which Mackintosh was the leader.

One of the greatest of the Highland chiefs, clad in tartan, this elderly man received them with a sort of proud condescension; but when he heard that they came from Donald of the Isles, he promptly became affable, and pressed whisky upon them. At this, they really had no need to ask for his feelings for the Islesman; and MacGillivray, a younger man, all but a giant, was loud in his praise, declaring that without Donald they would have the wretched Mackenzies, MacLeods and the rest down upon them from the north, and the Campbells and those Badenoch Stewarts from the south. They gathered that there was no need to seek Macpherson and Shaw assurances, for these were also part of the Clan Chattan, the Children of the Cat, whose slogan was "Touch not the Cat but a Glove!". Mackintosh could speak for them.

He did not speak for Cameron of Lochiel however, whose name, when mentioned, was received with tight lips. It was gathered that there was not exactly a feud with the Camerons, but no love lost.

They were offered hospitality for the night at Moy, but elected to move on for the Cameron country. But Lochiel appeared to be a good and rough fifty miles away, so it would take a long day's riding to reach it. But they ought to get as far as the head of long Loch Ness by nightfall, where there was a large Benedictine priory where they could put up for the night, Alastair mac Alastair assuring that he knew the place.

So it was the road for them again, westwards through the hills and by many lochs and crossing many river fords, by Farr and on to Dores, to reach the southern shore of Loch Ness, and into what was known as Glen Albyn, or the Great Glen of Alba, that vast cleavage of Highland Scotland, famous in story.

They were glad to reach the priory at the head of the loch that night, where the River Tarff entered it, and duly blessed Holy Church, as ever, for the kindly reception. What would travellers do without the monkish brothers?

They learned that Lochiel was still almost thirty miles away, down that lengthy glen, past Lochs Oich and Lochy and the mouths of the prominent valleys of Garry and Arkaig. The Cameron chief, they were told, could be at his houses on either Loch Arkaig or Loch Eil; so they would be wise to try Arkaig first, as much the nearest.

In the morning they did that, much impressed by the scenery of steep jagged mountains, dark, brooding lochs, yawning ravines and cascading torrents, all so very different from their own hilly country of the Lammermuirs and its waters. Small wonder, they said, that these Highland-men had the reputation of being wild.

Turning into Glen Arkaig, they were fortunate in finding the Cameron chief in his castle of Achnacarry, a man of middle years, with a lively family of youngsters, evidently a widower. He too spoke favourably of Donald, saying that he hoped that he would duly become the Earl of Ross, and keep the northeners in their places; for his own clan territory here was all too near that of the Mackenzies and MacLeods, or some of it, these ever a menace. The Islesmen themselves had used to be a danger, but since his father John's days, and Donald's, they had become their protectors in some measure. If Ross and the Isles were joined, then they could rest secure of a night.

They took their farewell of the Cameron and family, intent on getting back to that priory for the night. Then it would be up Loch Ness-side for Inverness in the morning, satisfied that they had fulfilled their mission as far as was possible. What Albany would think of it was another matter.

On the way up the twenty-three-mile-long loch next day, George at least was on the lookout for a possible sighting of the strange beast which St Columba had encountered on his way north to convert King Brude of the Picts to Christianity, and which was said to inhabit these waters, as did the one in Loch Morar, his father pooh-pooing. In this, sadly, he was disappointed.

At Inverness they said goodbye, with thanks, to Alastair mac Alastair, who had made a good travelling companion, telling him to assure his master that the clans they had visited had all thought well of Donald of the Isles; and that this information would be passed on to parliament in due course.

Then it was embarkation and the return voyage to Dunbar, their crew quite sorry to be leaving the apparent delights of the northern capital, especially its womenfolk.

18

For George it was joy to be back to Beatrix and little Patrick. But for his father it was less rewarding. He had to go and report on his mission. And, although in theory he had gone at the behest of parliament, that body met only occasionally and at the summons of the crown, that is the regent. So it was to Albany that Cospatrick had to report; and what he had to say was hardly likely to commend itself to that man, however hopeful for the peace of the Highlands.

He went off to Scone with no anticipation of favour.

However well content to be a family man again, George found himself faced with a problem only a day or two after returning home, one that could not be ignored, of this he was left in no doubt. Sir Thomas Home of that Ilk, chiefest of the Merse vassals, came to protest that his castle of Fast had been taken over by what he called an English pirate, named Holder, and this evil robber was making depredations in the neighbourhood therefrom, particularly into his own barony of Dunglass, this none so far from Colbrandspath; indeed, they were fortunate to have escaped assault here also. He, Home, was come to demand action from his earl.

This, needless to say, much concerned George. In his father's absence he felt bound to try to do something about it. Fast Castle, halfway down its great cliff, was one of the sights he had mentioned to Beatrix when he took her to visit St. Ebba's Head. His brother Patrick, who had been keeping Beatrix company during the Highland interlude, was loud in his declarations of affront to the family and the earldom. Fast was only some seven or eight miles from Colbrandspath. How dare this Englishman do this!

The three of them, with Home's escorting moss-troopers, rode off eastwards, then, to discover the situation.

By Siccar Point and the little chapel of St Helen's, they came to the mighty precipices, with the seas snarling white on the reefs and skerries below. A mile thereafter, along the winding and dizzy-making cliff-top track, and they came to see Fast Castle, perched on its isolated stack of rock part-way down the headland, no likely place for any castle, all but inaccessible to occupier or to foe. It had been built by one Stephen Pepdie, or Papedy, of the Dunglass family, and for no good purpose, that was sure, indeed to lure shipping on to the rocks below where, wrecked, in the ever savage seas, they could be plundered. Hence the name Fast, which was but a corruption of Faux, meaning False. Home had wed the heiress of the Pepdies, and along with their barony of Dunglass he had gained this grim hold. Now, it seemed, he had lost it to another, an English wrecker and robber.

No banners flew from its two towers, but smoke did rise from chimneys, to be blown away levelly, so it was occupied.

There was no way that horses could win their way down that cliff to reach the projecting stack; so the party had to dismount and leave their beasts with one of their men, and pick their way onwards, downwards, on careful feet. Home informed that access usually had to be gained from the sea. No large vessel could approach close enough, but there was a lofty cavern underneath the castle, this entered by the tides, and small boats could win into this. There was a shaft, bored through the solid rock of the cave roof, which led up into the hold, by which men and goods could be hoisted up, a strange and awkward ingress indeed, but all adding to the security.

Working their cautious way down, with the screaming seafowl eddying around and above them, they presently came to where a great fissure had split the rock-face, and this had to be worked round, precariously. Beyond, there was a brief, grassy and more level approach to a drawbridge spanning the gap between castle-stack and main cliff. But Home led them away from this, up another steep climb some way, to a point where they could look down on the stronghold, this because, he pointed out, arrows could be shot at unwelcome visitors from the guardhouse at the other end of the drawbridge – this bridge presently raised – and he was taking no chances with this Holder character, a notorious killer.

They were able to reach a position on the precipitous face directly above the castle, but just out of arrow-shot, he declared. And there they saw that they were indeed being watched by men on the two towers and in the small courtyards below. Fists were being shaken up at them. They saw more than that, from their viewpoint. Round a sharp bend in the headland, hidden before, was a sheltered inlet in which a quite large vessel was moored, sails furled.

Shouts came up at them, and then a couple of arrows. But these were sent as gestures rather than the targeting of the visitors, for although they did reach this height they had lost their thrust and fell harmlessly nearby. It would take good yew longbows, not the crossbows normally used, to be effective at this range.

Home, a man of later middle years, cupped his hands to his mouth, to shout.

"You rascally English robbers! Pirates! Wreckers!" he cried. "I am Home. This hold is mine. Dastards, you have taken it! Begone! Leave it. Leave it, I say. Or you will suffer, as you deserve. I will have it back. And hang you. Hang you all!"

No response came back to them. Probably his words, however angry, had not been heard above the screeching of the seabirds, for his voice was not notably strong.

He turned to one of his men to do the shouting instead; but Patrick Dunbar, who had a good pair of lungs and was assertively inclined, volunteered to yell. He bellowed roughly the same message.

Cries came faintly up to them, but the words were not to be known. More arrows followed, but no more effectively.

This confrontation was obviously futile.

More fist-shaking, on both sides, was as far as they could get. Home, shaking his greying head, led the difficult way back to their horses. Fast Castle was no easy nut to crack. It would be impossible, he declared, even to get siege-machinery, sows, battering-rams, mangonels, to assail it, placed as it was. How this Holder had gained it was not known. Home had not troubled to garrison it, seeing it as of little value to him. But now he wanted the interlopers out.

Back on the high ground again, he said that he would have some of his people, from Dunglass, keep an eye on the hold, and seek to assail the intruders if and when they moved out of it. That was all he could do. But did not the earl have ships at Dunbar? Could not these attack that Holder's vessel, and at least cut him off from supplies and put an end to his activities?

George pointed out that his father's vessels were trading-craft, not warships such as this English one was, no doubt. But he would see if aught could be done. His brother Patrick was eager to make the attempt, but George said that they must await their father's return from Scone before any such move was made.

So it was back to Colbrandspath and Dunbar.

The earl returned three days later, and in grim mood. He had had a dire interview with Albany, as feared admittedly, and that man, beyond being merely disappointed and critical had been actually threatening. He had declared that Cospatrick had been prejudiced from the first over Donald of the Isles, had believed his lies and had failed the crown and the realm. This was not acceptable, and the failure would not be forgotten. In vain Donald's non-hostile attitude towards the rest of the realm had been emphasised, and the Isle of Man situation explained. The regent remained inimical. And when that man was so, it behoved the other to watch his back!

George asked his father what he would do about it, then.

Would that murderous devil came after him? Send assassins?

Who could tell? But probably not, in this present situation. He would know well that much of the nation was against him, few lords supporting him, even the Douglas keeping his distance. He would not wish to have the large Dunbar and March earldom actively against him. But he, Cospatrick, would gang warily.

On the matter of the Fast Castle intrusion, the earl was angered, but was against his ships being used against this insolent invader. They were not equipped for fighting, and this Holder's craft almost certainly would be, if he was known as a pirate. The Dunbar seamen were not to be sacrificed, these on whom so much depended. They must think of other ways to get the creature out of Fast.

George saw it that way also.

Winter was almost upon them, and whatever the severities of the weather, the snows and ice and difficult conditions for travel, peace as far as strife was concerned, if not actual goodwill towards men, was apt to prevail.

George was a peace-lover, however otherwise his ancestry. Beatrix at least rejoiced at that.

Early 1406 brought significant tidings. The boy James Stewart, now become heir to the throne, precarious heir indeed, had been collected from his desparate father by the Sinclair Earl of Orkney and taken to, of all sanctuaries, the mighty Craig of Bass islanded at the mouth of the estuary, until a ship could be obtained to take him to security in France. Albany, learning of it, but unable to assail the Bass, had word sent to England that the ship should be intercepted, as abducting the young prince, who should be taken and held safe until such time as he, the regent of Scotland, should deem it wise to return him to his father.

Henry, off on his Welsh campaigning, could not be consulted, but his representatives at London did as suggested, and James Stewart never reached France, but was captured. The boy was taken to the Tower of London and

put in the care of the Constable; the Earl of Orkney, still
with him, left to find such quarters as he might.

The King of Scots, heartbroken, had died shortly thereafter, quietly, undramatically as he had lived. Probably few
would actually mourn him. But what now? His surviving
son and heir, James, was held in England. And the next in
line was Albany himself. George, for one, judged that the
youth was infinitely safer in London than he would have
been in Scotland.

A parliament had to be called to deal with the situation,
to assemble at Perth, convenient for Albany at Scone, this
however delayed for two months, just why was uncertain.
It would be a very significant occasion, in more respects
than one.

Meantime, Cospatrick recognised that he ought to try to
do something about Fast Castle – or seem to do so, for he
knew well that the place was all but impregnable. But
Home was pressing for action, and Patrick supporting him.
A demonstration, the earl said, was all that could be
mounted in the circumstances; but he had to make it a
fairly impressive one.

So quite a large force was mustered, on horse and foot, to
head eastwards for the cliff-tops. There, all along the
broken and twisting but lofty crest, the horsemen, over
one thousand of them, were sent to draw up in a lengthy
line far above the castle, but entirely visible therefrom.
These in place, with banners flying, the earl and his sons
and some senior vassals, including Home himself and Hay,
with perhaps a couple of hundred men on foot, most armed
with crossbows, commenced the awkward and cautious
descent on the steeps towards the hold's approaches, Cospatrick's own great standard well to the fore, however
difficult to carry down that crooked and slippery slope.
Necessarily all this took time.

When, at length, all reached the point within hailing
distance, and massed there as far as the uneven ground
would allow, a long trumpet flourish was sounded, and a
stentorian-voiced individual bawled that here were the

lord Earl of Dunbar and March, Sir Thomas Home and Sir William Hay come to demand the vacation and yielding up of this Home stronghold to its rightful owner, and this forthwith, or everyone therein would be for hanging. This demand was followed by a sustained clamour of shouting from the men around, and, despite the prevailing seabird screeching, this was heard by the cliff-top horsemen, and taken up all along that half-mile line.

No response came from the castle.

Patrick was for advancing to within arrow range. Undoubtedly they would much outnumber the defenders with their crossbows. But what was the point? George asked. The enemy were behind their stone walling, and few if any could be hit, while they would be in the open, unprotected, and would lose many. For what? Their father agreed. They would just bide where they were, in waiting threat, this until darkness. He did not see what else they could do to any effect. Even Home had to recognise this.

That they did, then, for a couple of hours, however exasperating it might be. At length, with the dusk, and beacons being lit on Fast's towers and walls to light the scene, the Dunbar force had to turn and make their way back over that challenging terrain, while they could still see to do so, the horsemen above seeing, and doing likewise. At least they had shown this Holder that he was being closely watched, and any inland assaults would now be vigorously dealt with.

No one was satisfied, but facts had to be faced.

George, in due course, again accompanied his father, by ship, to the Tay and Perth for the parliament, the gallery for him, of course. He was scarcely looking forward to the proceedings.

Albany took complete charge of all from the start, ignoring and superseding the Chancellor. Without any regrets voiced over his brother's sad demise, he announced that, while James, Duke of Rothesay had to be considered now to be King of Scots, he was a helpless captive of the

King of England, and likely to remain so, and therefore monarch in name only, quite ineffective as to the rule of the realm. He himself, the regent, was next in line for the crown, and must to all intents occupy the vacant throne. So he would no longer be styled regent but now governor of the Kingdom. None could say otherwise. And as such he would rule with a firm hand, let none mistake.

No cheers greeted that statement from the throne, even from his numerous brothers and nephews.

He made one or two further declarations as to general policy: peace as far as possible with England, alliance with France, the royal guard increased to be a standing army, the impoverished treasury to be supported by additional duties on imports, and the laws of the land more rigorously enforced by Justiciars and sheriffs. That said, he turned to glare at Cospatrick on the earls' benches.

"I have important business from the last parliament to deal with," he declared. "That session required that the unruly and insolent Donald of the Isles, who was terrorising much of the Highlands, as well as assuming the earldom of Ross, even making his own pacts with England, like some monarch, was to be given final and definite warning that his wickednesses must cease and he return to his own Isles. And the Earl of Dunbar and March was sent by parliament so to inform him and demand his withdrawal. In this duty that earl has failed parliament and the realm."

Cospatrick rose from his seat to reply, but was waved down.

"Not only did Dunbar not send the Islesman off, but he has actually returned commending Donald's claim to the Ross earldom, this quite insupportable and contrary to the will of parliament. I say that he, Dunbar, must be censured, and in no mere formal fashion. And from this throne, as governor of the Kingdom, I must ensure that!"

There were murmurs from all over the hall, but no sort of sustained acclaim.

Cospatrick rose again, and despite more wavings to sit, remained on his feet and spoke strongly.

"My lords and fellow-commissioners, I have a right to speak here, and to defend my name against these accusations by my lord Duke Robert. This is a parliament, not some petty court hearing. Is it not so?"

That did gain some cheering and general agreement, for all Albany's scowl.

"I did see the Lord of the Isles, and told him of parliament's concern. But previously I also saw the Countess of Moray, my lord Duke's own sister, who was in a good position to know, up at Darnaway, and she assured that this Donald was the benefactor of the Ross clans, and those of Moray, as was his father before him, keeping the land-hungry northerners, Mackenzies, MacLeods and Mackays at bay. No nun in a convent could hold that difficult earldom, and Donald had as much right to it as any. His wife was the sister of the last Earl of Ross. Who has got a better claim?" He looked at Albany. "If my lord Duke claims it, he has to go further back in the line—"

"Folly!" Albany interrupted. "Sit, you!"

"I have not finished my report to parliament!" Cospatrick remained on his feet. "My lord Chancellor will confirm my right!"

The so-far unheeded prelate, Bishop Greenlaw of Aberdeen, who in theory was presiding, nodded.

"With my son, the Master, I went to speak with the Ross clan chiefs, to hear if they would confirm Donald's word, after I had spoken with him at Dingwall Castle, the earldom's seat. These, Mackintosh, of the great Clan Chattan, MacGillivray, Cameron and the rest, all of them spoke well of him, Donald. Without the Islesman they would be constantly at war, they said, defending their lands against the northern aggressors. They all said that he should be Earl of Ross. If my lord Duke doubts this, he should go up to the north. He will learn that I speak the truth."

He sat down.

"That was ill done!" Albany declared. "The word of a man prejudiced. I counsel parliament to reject it."

Sir Alexander Stewart, an illegitimate son, one of many,

of the Wolf of Badenoch, jumped up. "If that is a motion, my lord governor, I second it. I do so."

"Address myself, the Chancellor," Bishop Greenlaw reminded him. "My lord Duke did not make any motion. The occupant of the throne does not so do. Sir Alexander, do *you* make it a motion?"

"If that is as it should be, I so do."

Half a dozen other Stewarts shouted their support, but few backed them.

"Is there any opposing motion?"

All over the hall men were on their feet, hands on high. There was no need for any counting.

The bishop turned towards the throne. "My lord regent. Or Governor. You will note the situation. No counting of votes necessary. The will of this parliament is sufficiently clear."

Albany however was not so easily put down. "As ruler of this kingdom, *I* am responsible for due governance, and for peace to be established, and the crown upheld. This in all parts of the realm, Highlands no less than elsewhere. Parliament must accept it. Now, I require that the Act passed in 1384, for the suppression of caterans and Highland plunderers, be renewed and reinforced. This gives authority for all leal men to seize such caterans and bring them before the nearest sheriff for judgment. And if they resist, may slay them, this without having to answer for this deed. Such is presently the more required. I give notice that this Act is hereby renewed, and this made known to all."

Men eyed each other. That Act, of over a score of years before, had probably been forgotten, if even known of at all, by most present. It certainly permitted drastic action by all and sundry who were not Highlanders. Yet to overturn and cancel it, an Act of Parliament, would be a major undertaking, demanding considerable debate and voting, and with the crown's approval. George wondered whether his father would try to oppose it.

No voices were actually raised, however.

192

Sundry administrative and routine matters had to be dealt with. Then Albany rose, without any address to the Chancellor as was normal, and that frustrated prelate only managed to declare this session of parliament adjourned before the new governor strode out. There was to be no doubt who ruled Scotland now, dominant enough as had been the regency hitherto.

On their way back to their ship, Cospatrick told his son that he feared greatly for the nation – and for much else. Donald of the Isles, although he probably could look after himself, must be informed of this situation, and the revival of that Act. But what of young James, who was now the king in name? Nothing was more certain than that Albany coveted the crown itself; and that man would stop at nothing to gain it. Would it be beyond him to have the youth assassinated, even in England? He judged not. James must be warned – or at least his guards must be. King Henry should be apprised of it all. No one was safe from Albany.

George, eyeing his father, put the obvious question. What of himself, the earl? The new governor's enmity towards him was clearly renewed, that had been made evident. How safe was *he* from assassination? He could not hole up in Dunbar Castle all the time.

Cospatrick was looking grim. "I think that I shall return to England, meantime. To Henry," he said. "He is my friend. I can aid him. And I can warn James's guardians in London. Albany will not reach me in Henry's court, I think! Informed of the danger to James, he will act."

"Yes. But think you that Albany might decide to slay *me*? As heir to your earldom."

"I think not. You have too many brothers – Gavin, Colin, Patrick, David, John. Even he cannot kill you all, even Albany. I have thought of that. I judge that you are safe enough. But take precautions. See you, a notion came to me, at that Fast Castle. It must be one of the safest holds in the kingdom. If that pirate who has taken it can be got rid of, *there* would be a secure refuge for you, if you

193

believed yourself threatened. Safer than Colbrandspath. But I doubt that it will be necessary."

"We would have to regain it, first . . ."

They sailed back to Dunbar.

19

Probably wisely, Cospatrick did not delay his return to England, in the circumstances. He went by sea, in one of the wool-ships making for Veere; and at the parting told George that he was as good as Earl of Dunbar and March now, and to act accordingly. And to use his brothers to aid him.

So George used another of their vessels to take him up to Inverness and Dingwall, to inform Donald of the Isles of the situation regarding Albany's continuing enmity, and of the Caterans Act renewal, this visit on Cospatrick's orders.

He found Donald absent from Dingwall, although his wife was still there, her husband apparently on a tour round various chieftains down Ness and on Speyside. She was expecting him back in a day or two, and judged that their visitor would be better to await his return rather than go seeking him over so wide a terrain. He accepted that, and settled in at the castle in comfort, the countess, as she now was being styled, proving an excellent and kindly hostess.

George went exploring over the Black Isle of Ross, this not really an island at all but a twenty-mile-long peninsula, and very much a lordship on its own, ending at the fair-sized town of Cromarty, all paying allegiance to the earl-dom of Ross, although it was the seat of the vassal Urquhart clan. He was particularly impressed by the strength of Holy Church here, there being two large priories, one of Celtic Church origin and dedicated to one of Columba's disciples, St Duthac, and no fewer than six chapels.

On the third day Donald arrived back. He was much interested to hear George's report, shaking his head over

Albany, but not appearing to be greatly worried over the threats. Smiling, when told that that man's hatred was dangerous indeed, he mentioned that he could raise ten thousand Highlandmen in one week to counter any activities against him by land; and a fleet of one hundred longships by sea. How many vessels could Albany produce? As for assassination, he did not think that there was much peril for him in the Gaelic-speaking world of the clans. And when George mentioned the Badenoch Stewarts, his host hooted with laughter.

Although the guest had quite enjoyed his visit, he wondered whether it had indeed been worth while, as he returned to Dunbar.

And there he learned of most surprising news. He had been gone only one week, but evidently sufficient for an unexpected assault to be staged on Fast Castle, of all places, this by his brother Patrick, that lively character. The bold and imaginative escapade was recounted to him at great length, with pride, all but glee.

Patrick had mounted his assault by night, sailing down the coast in one of the wool-ships which constantly voyaged to the Low Countries, this towing behind it four fishing-boats filled with armed men from Dunbar. Well out from the stronghold, and after midnight, the smaller craft had been untied, and left to row shorewards, Patrick leading the first one and heading for that cavern underneath the castle. At that time of night, and in darkness, he did not think that any guards on watch would spot them, if indeed any seawards watch was kept at all. Finding the cave entrance was not easy in the said darkness, and in silence, with no talk, no oar-splashing nor rowlock-creaking, although the noise of the waves had helped in this. Eventually they had come on it, and drawn inside.

It had proved to be a great L-shaped hollow; and once deep within they had felt fairly safe to light lanterns. These had shown them that a sort of shelf ran the length of it at one side, all but a little quay, and at the far end, a gaping hole in the high roof.

The problem, of course anticipated, had been how to get up into this shaft. There would be hoisting-gear, but this would almost certainly be kept up at the top in the castle itself. So Patrick had brought ladders, these both of wood and of rope, these last such as used for climbing up ships' sides. Three wooden ones, lashed together, had made a precarious mounting device, but he himself had risked the climb up into the mouth of the hole, dragging a rope-ladder behind him. And there, to his relief, he had found what he had suspected must be there for the garrison's own use in descending into the cave, an iron ladder attached to the shaft walling. So the rope-ladder was not here required.

His brother Colin had come up behind him with a lantern; and surveying the further ascent with this, they had seen that they could climb to a hatch-cover of wood, which no doubt represented the entrance to some part of the hold itself. The next question, then, had been could they open this from below? Was it likely to be locked in some way, or weighted down?

Creeping up the rungs of that ladder, rusty on his hands, he had reached the trapdoor, and cautiously tested it, Colin with the lamp just behind him. And it had moved, lifted a little. So – it was possible to gain access beyond.

Carefully the brothers had returned down to their men, explained and given instructions. Silence was essential. The most difficult part would be the climbing of those lashed-together wooden ladders, wobbling as they were. Only one man at a time should climb. This would mean that there would develop a cluster of them at the first iron rungs above. Somehow they would have to wait there, huddled together or clinging to a rope-ladder which Patrick said he would lower alongside, attached to the topmost iron rungs. A score of men, armed with crossbows and swords, and with a lamp or two, would not find this easy – but it was essential. And quiet, equally so.

Then he had climbed up again, with Colin, to that wooden cover, tested the weight of it further, and, as it opened, felt the cold draught of night air on his face. So it gave access not into some chamber but into the open, presumably one of the little courtyards. That had been good; but he had wondered whether there would be guards nearby. At this time of night, probably not. Why should they patrol around all night?

Cautiously he had lifted the lid on its hinges and gently laid it flat on the naked rock, before climbing higher. Peering, he had seen no sign of life, only the nearby masonry of a tower-foot. Heaving himself out, he had turned to help Colin do the same. Then, leaving his brother to bring out the men, he went to explore the situation.

No lights had shown in any of the castle windows, and there had been no sound of voices. Fast appeared to be fast asleep! There might be men on guard somewhere, possibly in the gatehouse, but none had been making his presence obvious.

Patrick had gone back to the shaft where half of his company were already out and waiting. Now for attack, lamps extinguished. The gatehouse first, where, if any were on guard, these must be disposed of so that others would not be disturbed. Half a dozen of them had crept from the little courtyard up a few steps in the rock to another similar, and then on towards the outer walling. After the pitch darkness of that cavern, they had been able to see reasonably well now. Approaching the gatehouse steps, they had actually heard snoring, an excellent sign.

The door had proved to be open, ajar, and quietly they had moved in. Two men had been lying on the floor, asleep. These sleepers died quickly, throats cut, no remorse felt by the killers, for these had been savage slayers themselves, rapers and ravishers.

After a careful survey of the rest of the outer premises, and finding nobody to assail, they had held a whispered consultation. There were two main towers, both probably occupied. How many of a garrison this Holder had they had not known. So, one tower at a time, one-third of their men standing ready at the foot in case screams and shouts wakened others. Patrick had led the main party up.

It had all proved remarkably simple, however bloody. Sleeping men had made easy targets and, on the whole, not noisy ones, although there had been some groans and cries. Whether one of the dead was Holder himself they had not known. But none had been able to fight back. It had been dagger-work, scarcely chivalrous.

Finished there, they had gone down to find no disturbance elsewhere. They calculated that they had slain about thirty men. Colin had led the party up into the second tower, where only eight more of the garrison were accounted for. They had found no more elsewhere, wondering whether there were others down in that ship hidden in the inlet, which they had not in fact seen on their approach. They still had to try to deal with that.

This proved to be a much easier and simpler task than dealing with the castle. Taking only about half of their number, Patrick had led these down the shaft again into the cavern, to board two of their boats. Then, pulling out, they had rowed round the little but steep headland, and there was the ship moored. No lights showed on it. A wary circuit of it had shown that they did not need their rope-ladders, for one already hung over the side, awaiting crewmen. So up this they climbed, silent again, to the deck. Patrick had judged that there would not be many left aboard, and that their quarters would be at the stern cabin. Making their way thither, they had found steps leading down and a shut door. Opening this with extreme caution just sufficiently to listen, they had heard deep, regular breathing, no snoring this time. There was no light here either.

They had brought a lantern with them. Closing the door again quietly, they lit this and drew their dirks. Then, at a sign, they had thrown the door wide, and Patrick, light held high, rushed in, the others close behind.

There were a dozen or so bunks lining the cabin walls, but only two were occupied. The sleepers, thus rudely wakened, had sat up, staring, rubbing eyes. But not for long. They had died almost before they could have realised that they were endangered, cold steel efficient.

A quick search of the vessel had shown that this pair had been the only men left aboard. The ship, like the castle, was taken. And a lot of men were dead – but none of their own.

Some of the party from Dunbar had been seamen, so Patrick had decided that this vessel should be sailed back there as a prize. No doubt they would be able to make good use of it. So leaving a group of their people to hold Fast – not that any attack on it was to be contemplated now – the others, with the small boats in tow, managed to steer the pirate vessel northwards to their own harbour, all hugely pleased with themselves. It had been a highly successful night, by any standards.

George was loud in his praises, although he doubted whether he could have stomached all that cold-blooded killing. Perhaps Patrick should have been the heir, not himself?

So now they had a secure refuge should Albany seek to carry out further attacks. They need not keep Fast garrisoned. Home could appoint a keeper and two or three men; that would be enough. All the earldom's vassals had been told to be constantly on the lookout for possible enemies and strangers, whether armed troops of possible would-be assassins.

George, with Beatrix and little Patrick, whom they were now calling Pate, remained meantime at Colbrandspath Tower, only a few miles from Fast if any quick move should be called for.

The news that came from the north thereafter was of the severity of governor Albany's rule, allegedly to maintain the peace of the realm. No word of assaults on Donald nor the earldom of Ross was reported however. But there were Stewart tidings, surprising, of a different sort.

Sir Alexander, he who had moved to support Albany at

that last parliament, a bastard of the Wolf, was distinguishing himself otherwise. An effective fighter, why he had been knighted, he had demonstrated his aggressive tendencies in a different respect. The earldom of Mar, in Aberdeenshire, held by an ancient line from earliest times, had run out of male heirs on the death of the thirteenth earl, and his sister Isabel had become countess in her own right. She had married Sir Malcolm Drummond, he whom Albany had had slain. Now Alexander Stewart coveted it. Not for him any mere wooing of the widow. Presumably assured of the governor's support, he had led a sizeable force of Badenoch caterans against Kildrummie Castle, a major stronghold in the skirts of the mountains, and seized it, and the Countess Isabel with it. And holding it and her both, had promptly thereafter gone through a ceremony of marriage, even prevailing upon a bishop to wed them, she willing or otherwise. And he was now calling himself Earl of Mar, in her right. There were no reports of Albany taking any steps to counter this.

George wondered what Donald would be thinking about this. For the Mar earldom reached well beyond Aberdeenshire, getting as far north and west almost to the upper Spey, where it bordered the Stewart earldom of Atholl on the one side, and the Badenoch lands of the Wolf's earldom of Buchan on the other, these in turn both neighbouring Moray and Ross. Trouble Donald could envisage, undoubtedly, and such possibly encouraged by the governor.

As well that there were no Stewarts east and south of Edinburgh, George decided. But they were an acquisitive line . . .

20

As it transpired, and unexpectedly, it was not Albany and
the Stewarts whom George had to worry about soon
thereafter, but the English – or at least some representatives thereof. Whether this had any connection with the
Fast Castle affair and the killings of the Englishmen there,
or not – this seemed unlikely, for the man Holder had been
a mere pirate and independent operator – England's Vice-
Admiral, Sir Robert Umfraville, led a fleet of ten warships
up into Scottish waters, and in no friendly fashion despite
the prevailing truce, bringing with him his fourteen-year-
old nephew, Gilbert, who was called the Earl of Angus in
England, no Scot as he was. There had indeed been a line
of Umfravilles, Lords of Redesdale and Harbottle in
Northumberland, one of whom, over a century before,
had married the Countess Matilda of Angus as her second
husband. From her first marriage to a Stewart she had
produced a son, Thomas, who succeeded as earl, but he
had died without issue, and Robert the Second, in his
fondness for the Douglases, had bestowed the title on that
other Thomas, a Douglas, who had become Cospatrick's
friend, who had had a son. But the Umfravilles claimed
that this was a misdirection of the title, and that *they*, as
descendants of the Countess Matilda's second husband,
were the true earls, even though English nationals. They
pointed out that Edward the Second of England had
actually appointed one of them Joint Guardian of Scotland
during the Wars of Independence, as indication of their
Scottish links. Bruce, of course, had forfeited this, but the
Umfravilles still claimed the style of Earls of Angus, in
England. Now they were showing their teeth.

The admiral's fleet made for the Firth of Forth, and, after passing Dunbar, no doubt taking note of the prominent Tantallon Castle on its cliff near North Berwick. The fact that he had not raided Dunbar harbour was probably because he knew that the Earl Cospatrick was a friend of his own monarch, Henry, still fighting the Welsh. But once in the Forth, Umfraville went to work with a vengeance, on both sides of the estuary, his warships putting in at all ports and larger havens, burning, ravaging, plundering, capturing Scots vessels and sinking such as they did not want. These captured craft they filled with booty, oddly enough particularly grain and meal, for it had been a notably wet summer in England and the harvest there disastrous. Whether Umfraville did not realise that partway up Forth on the south side the land was owned by Dunbar vassals, particularly Seton of that Ilk and Lindsay of Luffness, or just cared not, these properties did not go unscathed, to George's indignation, but there was nothing he could do about it.

As far as Leith and Queen Margaret's Ferry on the one side, and Inverkeithing on the other, the warships went, and met with practically no seaborne opposition, for there was no Scots war-fleet, however many defensive measures were taken against them ashore. Albany certainly could have done with Donald of the Isles' great squadrons of longships and birlinns.

It all made a strange interlude, for it seemed to be only that, the admiral turning back and sailing south again, and making no attempt to occupy any of the land he had raided. It was learned afterwards that in England he had earned the nickname of Robin Mendmarket, this on account of all the grain and foodstuffs he had brought back for his hungry compatriots.

Albany, to be sure, could not just ignore this breach of the treaty with England and France. He sent protests to Henry, on the Welsh Marches. While waiting for a response to them, however, all learned that Umfraville, not content with his naval gesture, had changed his role of admiral for that of mosstrooping Marchman, uncle of the Lord of Redesdale, and had led a sizeable force up that dale and over the border at Carter Bar, to descend upon Jedburgh, and there ravaged and plundered, and set alight to all that would burn in the town – and this on the autumn fair-day – before returning to Northumberland.

This was too much for Albany. He did not have a fleet, but he could raise large numbers of men. He mustered some twenty thousand at Stirling, and marched for the border, ordering Douglas to do the same over in the west.

George, hearing of this rally, expected to be commanded to contribute the earldom's forces to it. But no such message came; and although he ordered readiness from the vassals, his men were not called upon. Perhaps Albany just did not trust them? No doubt he had been informed that Dunbar had been spared the Umfravilles' attentions, and assumed that Cospatrick's people were pro-English. There were no complaints at Colbrandspath Tower, although brother Patrick was eager enough for action. George wondered whether the governor might, in due course, return northwards by the Merse and Dunbar areas, and seek to demonstrate his enmity. So his folk were to be on the watch, and himself ready for a move to Fast Castle.

In the event, no such precautions were necessary. Albany proved to be a less capable commander of armed men than he was a strategist in affairs of state. He had visited Jedburgh, and told its people that they would be avenged. Then he had proceeded on through the Cheviots for Redesdale, to cross the borderline at Carter Bar and the Catcleuch. And there his force, strung out for a mile and more, was ambushed by Umfraville, cut up and broken, however greater in numbers, demoralised without capable leadership. No major casualties resulted, but the army, scattered and lacking informed command, began to drift back whence it had come, an inglorious result which did the governor's reputation no good.

All learned later that Douglas had done considerably better, making a successful raid as far south as Penrith in

Cumberland, returning with booty – although this would not greatly concern Umfraville, *his* area unmolested.

There were mutterings and murmurings throughout the land.

Fast Castle remained unoccupied, save for its keeper.

George had been feeling that something should be done to celebrate Patrick's success in capturing Fast, this being talked about all over Lothian and the Borderland. He would have liked his brother to have Fast Castle itself, as his own, but it was a Home property, and Sir Thomas, grateful as he was for the regaining of it, did not want to lose it. So George decided that he would give Patrick, so far with no lands to his name, the lands of Beil, four miles to the south-east of Dunbar, with its small old tower-house set on a terrace above the Beil Water. He judged that their father would not object to this. Cospatrick had told him to act as earl during his absence, after all. So his brother became Dunbar of Beil, and that spirited young man promptly set about looking for a suitable and attractive young female to make mistress of his new home.

There was a further family development only a few weeks later, the arrival back in Scotland of brother Gavin, who had been distinguishing himself also, but with less renown, even if also bloodily. He had been sent by his father to look after the manors in Lincolnshire which Henry had given them, and there had got into a dispute about tithes to be rendered on the properties to the Dean of Lincoln. The rights and wrongs of this were complicated, but the dean's official, one John Bleswell, had come in authoritative fashion to demand satisfaction, and he and his men had taken by force what they claimed was the due contribution in grain and cattle. This had much angered Gavin, and with some of his local tenants, objecting also, he had waylaid the ecclesiastical graspers, and a violent scuffle had ensued, in which Beswell himself unfortunately died. This aroused great declamation from the dean and other representatives of Holy Church, with protests to the king. Henry had smoothed matters over, ordered Gavin to repay the disputed tithes, but pardoned him over the deaths. Nevertheless, he had indicated that it would be best for that young man to return to Scotland in the circumstances. So the brothers were all united again, even if their parent remained in England.

Gavin intimated that King Henry was become a sick man, passing on the leadership of the Welsh campaigns to his eldest son, known as Prince Hal. It was being suggested that his ailment was in fact the Finger of God upon him, as the phrase went, meaning leprosy, this on account of the death of King Richard while his prisoner. This situation was, needless to say, greatly worrying Cospatrick. If Henry died, his friend, not only would he suffer major loss, but conditions for himself in England might well deteriorate, for he did not get on so well with Prince Hal. So Gavin had been ordered to discover the situation in Scotland as regards Albany, his state and control of the land, and whether or not a return home for himself was likely to be practical, or only apt to result in assault and warfare.

George was unsure about this, but set afoot all enquiries he could from various sources, especially from one of his father's vassals, Haliburton of Dirleton, who held a position at court. The findings were that the governor was more unpopular than ever, his harsh rule ensuring that, together with his failure over the border venture. In the circumstances, it seemed improbable that he would risk any assault on the Earl of Dunbar and March and his people; but of course, assassination was always to be guarded against.

This word was sent to Cospatrick.

Gavin was somewhat jealous of his younger brother Patrick's fame over Fast, and his being presented with the lairdship of Beil; but George felt that he could not hand over another of the earldom's properties without their father's consent, especially as Gavin had been sent home not exactly in disgrace over the slaying of a churchman but under rather a cloud.

He did place his brother in charge of Dunbar Castle,

however, while he himself remained at Colbrandspath Tower, which had become his own and Beatrix's happy home.

Pate was now six years old, of an enquiring mind, and a joy to them both. Beatrix would have wished for a brother or sister for him, but so far none was forthcoming.

21

They were into the year 1409 when alarming news reached them from England. Whether or not his illness was affecting King Henry's judgment, he had taken the remarkable step of having Richard Scrope, Archbishop of York, along with Thomas Mowbray, Duke of Norfolk, executed, this for conspiring with Hotspur Percy's heir to raise rebellion in the north. Norfolk was the former Nottingham, the Marshal. The slaying of such was criticised; but the public execution of an archbishop was almost unheard of, and brought down the wrath and condemnation of Holy Church and the anathemas of the Pontiff.

England was in upheaval over this, needless to say. And, added to sick Henry's troubles was the collapse of the triple treaty of peace between England, France and Scotland. The French King Charles, presumably at papal urgings, sent troops and ships to aid Owen Glendower, self-styled Prince of Wales, who, however indeterminate his fighting, long-drawn-out, along the Marches, now more or less ruled all Wales, and had actually established an independent Welsh parliament. So now the fighting along the March grew still more fierce, and Henry, all but incapacitated by his sickness, had to leave it all to his son, the other Prince of Wales, another Henry or Hal. The monarchy's standing had become low, with the English parliament now denouncing the king's mismanagement, his offending of the Church, and the wasting of the realm's revenues.

In these circumstances it was that Cospatrick came back to Scotland. And, curiously, not to escape animosity over his friendship with Henry, but at the latter's own request, this to ensure renewal of the treaty with the northern kingdom, which in these conditions was now very important for England; and in view of the traditional Auld Alliance with France, could not be taken for granted.

So instead of deliberately avoiding Albany's vicinity, Cospatrick was actually to go to him as Henry's envoy, a most unlooked-for development.

George, glad to welcome his father home, was much worried over this mission to Scone. Would Albany take the opportunity to strike? Here was the earl delivering himself into his bloodstained hands. But Cospatrick judged not. He came as ambassador from the King of England, and his murder would be as good as a torch to set warfare alight. And Albany would not want war, that was almost certain, with his growing unpopularity with nobles and people. This peace treaty would be important for him. The earl believed himself to be safe, at least for the time being. Moreover, he had something on a different level to tell Albany, which could please. Henry had been carefully arranging continuing education for his two hostages, James, the young monarch, and Murdoch, Albany's son. They were being treated as honoured guests rather than captives, provided with tutors, and allowed all sporting activities.

To pave the way for so important and significant a visit to Scone, Cospatrick sent George to contact his courtier vassal, Sir Walter Haliburton of Dirleton, whose fine castle stood only some ten miles west from Dunbar. His position was that of Deputy Treasurer, assistant to the High Treasurer, William Lauder, Archdeacon of Lothian. It being Easter-tide, Haliburton was at home. Dirleton was an attractive village grouped round a large green, with the castle rising close by on a rocky knoll, famous as the stronghold that held out longest in 1298 against that fierce prelate, Bishop Anthony Beck, Edward the First's warlike ecclesiastic. Here George experienced further surprise, in that he discovered that Haliburton had just been married, and his wife was none other than Albany's elder daughter,

Isabel, formerly Countess of Ross and childless, widow of that young earl, she in whose name Albany had laid claim to that earldom against Donald's assumption of it. She proved to be a gentle, quiet and quite pleasing woman, coming from such a father, and was clearly in love with her new husband. The fact that the governor had allowed her to marry Haliburton, no great lord, indicated surely that he thought highly of the Deputy Treasurer's abilities and effectiveness, probably seeing him as a source of revenues hereafter.

George explained the reason for his visit, and his father's requirement to approach the governor as King Henry's representative. He did not have to go to any great lengths in reminding Haliburton of the situation as between the earl and Albany, and the need for something in the nature of a safe-conduct for his approach to Scone. The other understood, and promised to make due representations. Without actually saying so, he indicated that he thought that his new father-in-law would be in no frame of mind to resume his well-known and long-standing malevolence at this juncture. He would be desirous of peace with England, and certainly would not wish for any hostile encounter with the forces of Dunbar and March at this present.

George was well content with that. Haliburton would go and see Albany forthwith.

So soon thereafter Cospatrick set sail for the Tay and Scone, George with him.

Ushered into the governor's presence, that man eyed his visitors warily, as they did him. Albany was a handsome man, now into his seventy-first year – in fact almost the same age as was Cospatrick. The Stewarts were apt to be good-looking, even the Wolf was; but their eyes often tended to give a different impression. This one had his nephew, the new Earl of Mar, with him.

"My lord Duke!" Cospatrick said briefly.

The other nodded. "Yes," he said. "Haliburton has told me of your coming. And your present . . . concern. You are here in the name of Henry Plantagenet. Sent by him."

210

"That is the truth of it. Otherwise I would not be here. Would not have presumed to come."

"No? You do not honour this realm with your company frequently, my lord!"

"I have my reasons."

"So! But now you are come. Over this of the peace treaty with England. Even though that is not yet expired."

"No. But with this of France sending aid to the Welsh, King Henry deems it best and wise to make it the more assured. Strengthened. This for the benefit of both realms."

"For the benefit of *England*, I see it, yes. But of Scotland?"

"Yes. Much benefit. Henry would restrain such as Umfraville and the Percys. And overlook Douglas's attack on Cumberland. Also he considers the matter of Donald of the Isles. With that proud lord and his great numbers of Highlandmen, and his many ships-of-war, Scotland requires peace with England."

Albany did not deny any of that. "Henry is a sick man, I hear?"

"He is. Of body. But strong enough in his mind. And in his hold over his kingdom. And his son, Prince Henry, or Hal, is an able young man, as well as a notable fighter."

"So be it. Scotland and England should be at peace, yes. I do not gainsay it. So – to the point. You have brought the papers? For renewal of the treaty?"

"I have." Cospatrick turned to take from George the roll of parchment that he had been carrying. "Two copies of it, my lord Duke. For your signature. Already signed, sealed and witnessed by King Henry."

Albany took the documents, but did not open them, handing them over to Mar. "Take these to the clerks to scan," he ordered.

When his nephew had left the chamber, he turned back to the visitors. "I have a, a request to make," he said, stiffly. "Through you. To Henry. I desire the return of my son, the Lord Murdoch."

211

"M'mm. He is with King James."

"That may be so. But I want him back."

"But not . . . King James!"

"That is another matter. But, my son is my son."

"They, he and James, are well content. Treated well. Given much freedom. They have their attendants, even tutors. King Henry has them considered as honoured guests. They are vouchers for this treaty of peace. Symbols, as might be said."

"Perhaps. But James is sufficient for that. I desire Murdoch to be with me here. Tell you Henry so. And — use your influence, my lord."

Cospatrick inclined his greying head. "I will do what I can, my lord Duke. But . . . Henry has his own requirements."

"Even so. And there is another matter. Englishmen still occupy Roxburgh Castle, near the borderline. It is a royal property, where many of my predecessors have lodged." George noted that word predecessors, by which was meant Kings of Scots; Albany clearly thought of himself as such. "The invaders must be removed from Roxburgh. Demand it."

"I will so inform King Henry."

"Very well." He waved a hand. "Provender and refreshment will be given you. And, if the wording is acceptable, England's copy of the treaty. In due course. With my signature and seal." Without another word, and no sort of farewell, Albany turned on his heel and left them there.

Father and son eyed each other. Scotland's ruler was not deigning to eat with them, nor have further association. But they had got what they had come for. And could not consider themselves endangered. Was that long-standing threat removed? Or only postponed?

A servitor came to conduct them to a lesser hall of the abbey premises, where a table was spread. As they ate and drank, alone, Mar came back with the treaty parchment. He handed it over, making no comment, and retired, no more amiable than his uncle. Unrolling it, they saw Albany's signature duly in place, with the red royal seal attached.

So it was back to their ship at Perth, duty done. Was Cospatrick going to be safe in Scotland hereafter? That Murdoch perhaps might prove to be the surety. And this of Roxburgh . . . ?

22

The earl was not long in returning to England with the treaty and his messages, but declaring that he would not delay coming back to Dunbar. Not that he trusted Albany, and deemed himself to be reasonably safe. But so long as that Murdoch remained in England the governor would probably find himself useful. So he would not press Henry to have the young man sent home over-soon.

Meanwhile, however, Patrick Dunbar, ever the impatient one, was not going to wait. He had discovered the woman he wanted to make mistress of Beil, and this none other than George's own sister-in-law Alicia Hay. So there was to be a wedding at St Baithan's kirk of Yester, and quickly. The haste of it all had George wondering, perhaps unkindly, whether his so urgent brother had been anticipating wedded bliss somewhat prematurely?

The ceremony, however prompt, went well, both bride and groom obviously much pleased with each other, and Sir William proud to have two daughters wed to sons of his earl. Beatrix was glad to have her sister coming to live so near to her.

The matter of English-occupied Roxburgh Castle had been spoken of before Cospatrick left, and Patrick had declared that, compared with Fast, that hold ought not to be difficult to reduce and take. It rose all but on the edge of their own earldom's lands, where Tweed and Teviot joined. *He* would see to this, in due course, after he had settled his new wife into Beil Castle.

Gavin, now having rejoined the family, was proving distinctly jealous of his younger brother's fame, and his Beil lairdship. Now he announced to George that *he* would make an assault on Roxburgh. Why wait for Patrick's convenience? He, Gavin, had seen much of fighting in the Welsh campaigns, more than Patrick ever had experienced. Much better that he should gather some of the earldom's manpower and drive the English out, rather than have to get King Henry to order it. The Scots ought to be able to tidy their own backyard rather than appeal to the English monarch to do it for them. More suitable and worthy of their repute.

George did not disagree with that, although he supposed that he himself ought to be the one to lead in such effort. But he had no ambition to be a warrior, or seek to outshine his brothers in such. His wish was to be a good earl and landlord, look after his people, preserve the peace, increase their prosperity, foster trade and good relations, and bring up young Pate to be a happy and good successor. Was that feeble, spiritless? Beatrix did not think so.

He conceded that Gavin should make the attempt. Sir Thomas Home would give him men – he would be grateful for getting Fast back – and the Kerrs and Swintons, the Turnbulls and local Douglases would no doubt contribute to the company, *their* lands being nearer to Roxburgh, and all be glad to see the expulsion of these Englishmen. Gavin took his brother David with him, although he had no experience of warfare, all wishing them well. Roxburgh was some forty miles away as the crows flew, across the hills, but they would have to double that collecting their force.

While all awaited news from the south, then, it was tidings from the north that reached them, and challenging ones. Donald of the Isles was on the move.

It seemed that the new Earl of Mar, Alexander Stewart, had been causing trouble along the northern and western rims of that earldom, as had been more or less expected, and had encouraged his half-brothers, the others of the Wolf's large brood in Badenoch, to do the same, this to the hurt of the Grants, Mackintoshes, Macphersons, MacLeans and Shaws. These had called on Donald for aid, and he had not failed them. Gathering a large force of the clans and his own Islesmen, he had marched south into Mar, determined to show who ruled in the north, and was said to be approaching Aberdeen itself. What would Albany have to say to this?

The nation held its breath. Donald was said to have ten thousand men at his command. This would be major warfare, no mere raiding.

Brother David arrived back at Dunbar with alternative and somewhat more cheering information. Gavin had had some success at Roxburgh, not all that could have been wished, but at least progress, apparently with the especial help of Sir William Douglas of Drumlanrig, a son of the Earl of Douglas who had died at Otterburn. He and Gavin had attacked the town of Roxburgh, some distance from that castle, and had roused its cowed inhabitants to turn on the invaders who occupied the stronghold under Percy leadership, it being only perhaps ten miles from *their* border. Quite a proportion of these incomers preferred the comforts of the town and its womenfolk to the inevitable austerities of the castle. These had been driven out, with some casualties; but unfortunately the fortalice itself had not been taken, its defensive situation too strong, situated as it was at the junction of the two great rivers and occupying what amounted to a steep peninsula. The garrison remained defiant. They were not there on King Henry's orders, it being purely a Percy initiative, as a convenience for them in their border raiding, enabling them to cross back and forth into Northumberland by the hidden Bowmount Water valley through the Cheviot Hills.

But at least the township was now back in Scots hands, so the Dunbar credit was somewhat enhanced. And there were not likely to be any unfortunate repercussions on King Henry's part, in the circumstances.

George congratulated his brother, even though, according to Gavin, it was largely Drumlanrig who was responsible.

Cospatrick's arrival home shortly thereafter confirmed that. Henry was pleased over the peace treaty, and certainly not seeking any reaction over the wretched Percys and their friends, who had caused enough troubles as it was. On the matter of Albany's son, Murdoch had no desire for any speedy return to Scotland, and had in fact given his parole to remain close to James Stewart in return for freedom to go where he would in England. So the governor would have to be told this. It, of course, suited the earl well enough.

However, the word reaching Dunbar was that Albany was meantime otherwise preoccupied, no longer sitting at Scone but actually on battle bent, or more accurately, on backing Alexander of Mar's battling. Mar had marched north to challenge Donald, and his uncle was leading a large force up through Atholl to Speyside and Badenoch, to get behind the Islesmen. This news concerned them all at Dunbar. They did not want to see Donald wedged between two Stewart armies.

The sad tidings were delivered two days later. Donald, aware of his danger, was in retreat. There had been a battle with Mar at a place called Harlaw, some ten miles north of Aberdeen, and although it had not been any disaster, with no great casualties on either side, Donald, aware of Albany possibly assailing his rear, had turned back, so as not to be caught between uncle and nephew. Mar was claiming victory over the warrior Lord of the Isles, an extraordinary assertion for a bastard of the Wolf. Donald, of course, had all the north-western Highlands and his Isles to return to, and was in no danger of being overwhelmed; but it all represented a setback to his renown, and might mean the loss of the earldom of Ross.

This last was more or less confirmed presently, with the announcement that Albany had occupied Dingwall, and this almost without having to strike a blow.

That summer's tidings were both good and bad for Dunbar and Colbrandspath.

Gavin was rewarded for his little victory at Roxburgh by

being given the barony of Cranshaws in the Lammer-muirs, and told that if he and his brothers cared to accompany their father to Bolingbroke Castle, in due course, King Henry had said that he would be glad to confer the honour of knighthood on all of them, for friendship's sake, and recognition of worth, a most note-worthy gesture in itself. George at least felt it totally undeserved; but Beatrix declared that he must accept.

First, however, George was given the less than welcome task of going to inform Albany, now back at Scone, of the situation as regards Murdoch, Cospatrick recognising that it would come better from his son, and there be less likelihood of accusations. It occurred to them that it might well be worth while for George to take his brothers Gavin and Patrick with him, these two having won a sort of fame in getting rid of English invaders of the governor's realm, thus supporting George.

So the three of them sailed for the Tay, this a new experience for the younger two.

As ever a lengthy wait was necessary to gain audience with the governor. When they were eventually ushered into the presence, they were accorded no warm welcome, George at least expecting none. When he introduced his brothers, and mentioned their successes against the Auld Enemy, they were offered a nod only by way of congra-tulation; and without any delay the demand made as to the Lord Murdoch – that, and where was their father?

George had to convey his message as best he could, that the said Murdoch had given his parole to remain in England in exchange for much freedom. He could hardly say that that young man had no desire to return to his father, and that his life in England was proving much to be preferred to dwelling under his sire's harsh thumb in Scotland, and that all that he could suggest was that young King James needed him and that he felt it his duty to be there.

Albany's scowl was eloquent enough, as he declared that

218

he could scarcely believe that his son was fool enough to remain in England when he could be at home, and aiding in the rule of Scotland. He must be made aware of his true duty, which was to come back, parole or none. That was an order, a royal command. And he, the Master of Dunbar, was to deliver it, since his father, the earl, appeared to be so ineffective. Let him see to it, and forthwith.

With that they were dismissed, George not mentioning that they happened to be going south anyway, to be knighted by the English king.

The brothers expressed themselves vehemently thereafter on the inadequacies of Scotland's deplorable ruler.

Even without Albany's orders there would have been no great delay in heading for England thereafter. Cospatrick worried about his friend Henry, and was anxious to see him, for he feared that he would not be with them for much longer. They sailed south within days, father and all his six sons.

They reached the mouth of the Wash, and Boston, in two days and a night, weather reasonable. George reckoned that it was almost twenty years since he had been here, although his father and Gavin had visited Bolingbroke fairly frequently. Also it was near the Lincolnshire manors that they had been given. They all rode the sixteen miles northwards towards the Wolds, he at least thinking of how much had happened, both on a personal and a national scene, in the interim.

This preoccupation was reinforced when they reached their destination and were ushered into the presence of King Henry, so great was the difference in the man they had met as Earl of Hereford. Gaunt, bent and frail, he received them in a room which served as bedchamber and presence-chamber, court-room and study, and all but chapel – for, with his end nearing, he had become concerned with the hereafter, especially with the Finger of God allegedly laid upon him over the matter of Richard. From this room Henry ruled England.

However sorry a figure he made, he received his visitors

kindly, clad as he was in a bed-robe, clearly glad to see his friend and sons. Infirm and wasted he might be, physically, but his mind was nowise deteriorated, and his eyes keen and alive.

They were asked about Albany, and conditions in Scotland, his knowledge of affairs there evident. But it was not long before he rang a bell for an official, who was told to bring the sword necessary for the promised knighting of the younger Dunbars, and to inform the resident herald to come and witness the investiture, and to take details for the charters each was to receive.

When these officers appeared, with much bowing, Henry, still seated, had the herald bring the sword and hold it beside him, so that he could lay his hand on the hilt without actually having to bear its weight. Then, George first, was called over, to kneel before the monarch.

"George, Master of Dunbar, of the line of Cospatrick, I, Henry, by God's Grace king, do hereby name and create you knight," he said. The sword-blade was lifted, and tapped first on one bent shoulder, then on the other, the royal hand still resting on the haft. "Be thou a good and true knight until thy life's end, I charge you. Arise, Sir George!"

The new knight got to his feet and bowed, stepped back a pace, and bowed again, the while wondering. Wondering that this brief and simple act and a few words could change his status in the eyes of men, raising him to a higher level, as distinct from styles and titles, heir to an earldom as he was. Knighthood was . . . different. Yet it had been achieved so summarily, concisely. Like marriage, he recognised, just a word or two and a touch and gesture. But, it seemed, sufficient.

Gavin was called next, and the same process gone through. He arose, to bow, Sir Gavin. Then Patrick and Colin and David and John, all knighted.

Voice still fairly strong, however weak the body, the king looked over at Cospatrick. "My friend, the least that I can do to demonstrate my esteem and show the value I

220

place on our so worthy association," he said. "This is my salutation to you, my lord." And relinquishing his hold on the sword-hilt, he held out his hand to the other.

Cospatrick went forward, to kneel in turn, not for the accolade, for he was already long a knight, but to take that hand within his own two, and to kiss it.

"Henry!" was all that he said, voice hoarse. But it was enough. He rose and stepped back.

None present failed to feel the emotion of that significant occasion.

Afterwards, with the King obviously exhausted, the young Dunbars all bowed themselves out of the presence, as did the officials, leaving the earl with the monarch. In an anteroom they turned to stare at each other, six new knights, scarcely able yet to comprehend it, shaking heads, exclaiming, pointing, even jerking odd laughs, before referring to each other as *Sir* George, *Sir* Patrick and so on.

Their father rejoined them presently, saying that King Henry was now resting, but that he hoped to see them again after the evening meal.

They dined well, in the company of court officials, and saw their royal host again, briefly, before he retired for the night. Even Patrick was tongue-tied and diffident.

None of them delayed long in seeking their couches that night. George for one had an early start in the morning.

The plan was that he should go on, alone, to London, to see King James and Murdoch Stewart, this on horseback, while his father remained with King Henry, and the brothers went hunting and hawking among the nearby Wolds. Their ship would be coming back from Veere to pick them all up in a week's time, and it was hoped that George would have finished his task and rejoined them by that time for their return to Scotland.

So, with one of the court officials and two grooms as escort, he set off next day on his strange errand as Albany's envoy. They went by Boston and round the head of the Wash, and through the area seemingly known as Holland

221

and Soke, to Peterborough and Huntingdon, where they spent the night in a monastery. It did not fail to occur to George that here was the place where their King David had gained all the riches that enabled him to build the many great abbeys of Scotland – Melrose, Kelso, Dryburgh and the rest – for he had married the wealthiest heiress in all England, Matilda of Huntingdon. Then they went on through Cambridgeshire, by Shelford and Royston, and got as far as Hertford for the second night. George would have ridden further each day, but his guide and companion was otherwise minded. They were able to reach London-town by midday thereafter.

They made their way through the crowded streets for the Tower, dominant at the riverside. But there the Constable, Sir Thomas Rempton, fetched at the behest of Sir Richard Spice, King Henry's representative, informed them that the distinguished hostages were no longer lodged therein but at Westminster Palace, two miles further upriver, an interesting development, indicative of the monarch's goodwill.

Thither they proceeded, to find the monastic buildings of the old abbey, this replaced by the majestic minster, turned into a rather rambling royal residence. Here they were received by the Lord Grey of Codnor, High Chamberlain, in whose keeping were now the captives they sought.

The visitors were conducted to a secondary range where, in a sort of library they found two young men busy at their studies beside a long table, one fair of hair, well built and showing signs of Stewart handsomeness to come, the other dark, wiry and intense of manner. These looked up from their papers interestedly.

George bowed. "I am the Master of Dunbar come from Scotland, sent by the governor, the Duke of Albany," he said. "One of you is, I am assured, my liege-lord, His Grace James, King of Scots?"

"I am James Stewart," the fair one replied, rising.

"Then, Sire, I salute you warmly, and would pay you

222

my leal duty as your faithful subject." And stepping forward, George sank on one knee before the eighteen-year-old, took a royal hand in both of his, kissed it, and rose. James looked all but embarrassed at this unaccustomed demonstration of homage. "I . . . I thank you. Dunbar, you say? Master of Dunbar? Then the Earl of Dunbar and March, whom I have met, will be your father? You come, however, from the regent Albany? Seeking *me*?" He sounded incredulous.

"I do. And from King Henry at Bolingbroke Castle, and from my father the earl, yes. But . . . also to see the Lord Murdoch, Highness." He turned to the other young man, a year or two older, probably. "My lord," he said.

The dark one shook his head. "I am Griffith ap Owen Glendower," he declared. "Not Murdoch of Albany."

Surprised, George looked from one to the other. "I, I am sorry, sir. Glendower? Of Wales?"

"Son of the Prince of Wales, yes. Captured in battle."

"My good friend," King James added.

"Then I greet you kindly. I had not known of this. I looked for Murdoch, with His Grace . . ." George recollected his duties, turning. "This, Sire, is Sir Richard Spice, whom King Henry has told to bring me to you."

"I have met Sir Richard. At the Tower."

George hesitated. He could hardly say that, however privileged and proud he was to see his monarch, it was not really he whom he had come to speak with.

"We, we interrupt you at your . . . affairs, Highness," he got out. "You must forgive us." He looked at Spice. "Where will we find the Lord Murdoch? I assumed that he would be with Your Grace."

"He is . . . in the town. As often," James said, shrugging.

"In the town? Not here?"

"He bides here, yes. But is much . . . absent."

"Oh. I see."

"You say that it is Murdoch whom you have come to see, in fact, Master of Dunbar. Not myself. Sent by his father?" That was James. "I fear that you may have some time to wait, then. He prefers the town and, and its attractions. To this!" And he gestured towards the table and all its papers.

Sir Richard Spice spoke. "Your Majesty, we regret troubling you. We shall await the Lord Murdoch . . . elsewhere."

"We shall be eating shortly. You should join us at table, sirs. We shall be glad of your company. We meet few guests. No doubt the Lord Grey will see to your comfort, meantime."

"The Lord Murdoch enjoys the company of ladies," young Glendower observed as they moved away.

Spice, who had formerly been Lieutenant of the Tower, was well known as close to King Henry; and the High Chamberlain, Grey, accepted them readily, offering them refreshment, but agreeing when they said that King James suggested that they eat with him. He said that he would join them at the repast.

So, soon they were washed and refreshed from their riding, and sitting at table with the hostages and the Chamberlain. George had not known that Glendower's son had been captured in the warfare, and was now making a trio with James and Murdoch. He liked what he had seen of the young Welshman, who sounded a born enthusiast. It made a strangely assorted party for that meal, but all got on well enough, with little observance of royal protocol.

Thereafter they had quite a wait before they were favoured with the presence of Murdoch Stewart; and when he did arrive it was with no apologies nor amiable greetings, even any respectful gestures towards his cousin. He was tall, all but handsome but with a slackness about the mouth, foppishly clad, and some years older than James. When George explained his identity, and that he had been sent by his father, the governor, calling him Lord Murdoch, he interrupted to announce that he was the Earl of Fife and Menteith, and should be so addressed.

Misliking what he saw and heard, George did not seek to

224

delay further his errand, nor to put it other than firmly. "Your father, the Duke of Albany, has sent me, my lord, to require you to return to Scotland, renouncing your parole. And forthwith. And I have it from King Henry that *he* permits it."

"I have no desire to return to Scotland meantime, sirrah! I do sufficiently well here at this present."

"Nevertheless, it is your father's command. A *royal* command." George glanced over at James who, in fact, alone could give such royal command.

"Tell my father that I will return when it is my wish so to do."

"I fear that he will not accept that."

"He can do no other. I am here as companion and counsellor to King James, and so will remain until he comes of full age, that at least."

Again George looked at the king, who shook his head, tight-lipped.

"If that is so, my lord of Fife, you are here as such at the governor's appointment. If he recalls you, how can you refuse?"

"I can. And do."

"What, then, am I to tell him?" Once more, to James George turned. "You, Sire, what is your royal decree in this? Is it your wish and command that my lord stays?"

"I have *no* royal decree or command here. I am but a captive in England. Well treated, but with no powers. I will not seek to come between my cousin and my uncle, who governs my realm. It is not for me."

"What, then, am I to say to the duke?"

"I will give you a letter to my father," Murdoch said. "That will be sufficient."

George looked doubtful. But, without another word, Albany's son turned and left the room.

"He knows his own mind," James said. "I am not his keeper."

"Shall I say to the duke, Sire, that you would have him to stay?"

"No. Not that. That would not serve anything, I judge. My uncle desires no word from me. I am . . . but a distant hindrance to him. A stumbling-stone between him and the throne that he covets."

"I am sorry, Highness, sorry . . ."

"One day, perhaps . . ."

They had to leave it at that, sadly. Spice shook his head over them all.

Presently a servant brought a sealed letter from Murdoch addressed to Albany. That was all. George had come hundreds of miles for only that scrap of paper. With nothing to wait for now, he took his leave of his young liege-lord, to return whither he had come.

At Bolingbroke, he was in good time to catch their ship coming back from the Netherlands at least; and with his father saying farewell to King Henry, an even more sad occasion than the leaving of James, for almost certainly they would not see him again on this stage of life's journey. Cospatrick was so upset that the matter of Murdoch paled into insignificance.

Home, then – with a further journey to Scone in store for George, to which he looked not forward.

However, in the event it was none so grievous an interview. For, when he saw Albany, and declared that his son was still in London and had sent this letter, the other had taken the missive, glanced at the seal, and, turning, left without a word of comment, the paper unopened. Nor did George see him again thereafter, an official coming to escort him away. Albany did not choose to discuss his family affairs with lesser folk.

Thankfully George headed south for Beatrix and normal and better living.

23

It was a year before word of King Henry's death reached Dunbar, a year wherein much happened in Scotland, not all of it greatly affecting the Cospatrick family. Albany's reaction to Murdoch's refusal to return home was to appoint his second son, John, as Earl of Buchan, a title become vacant since the Wolf's death some years before and his legitimate sons conveniently forfeited for various crimes, this making John of importance, as a warning to his elder brother. Also he had him married to Elizabeth, daughter of the Earl of Douglas.

Donald of the Isles, despite his setback at Harlaw, did not relinquish his claim to the earldom of Ross, and his wife, countess in her own right, although Albany held Dingwall, retained many other strengths throughout that great inheritance. Albany sought to capitalise on Mar's victory by sending three separate forces into the Highlands against Donald, but none of these was very successful, and made little or no dent in the latter's power. Indeed he emphasised this by concluding a new treaty with Henry the Fifth.

That king was less concerned over peace with Scotland than had been his father, and made sundry threatening gestures. But he was presently much more interested in the French situation. He crossed the Channel in great force, and besieged and captured Marfleur at the mouth of the River Seine, and shortly thereafter won the major victory of Agincourt. This French reverse had the effect of King Charles requesting Scots help, under the terms of the Auld Alliance, so the three-party peace was over. Albany had to abandon his attempts to bring Donald to heel, and instead consider how to comply, in some measure, with the French call.

He sent the new Earl of Buchan, with seven thousand men, to France to aid Charles. This however was not enough for that strange monarch. What he required was an armed threat at Henry's back, this on to English soil. Faced with this demand, the governor managed to raise a quite sizeable force, with Douglas's help, to march south, himself leading. And he chose to assail Berwick-upon-Tweed, while Douglas was to attack Wark. This of Berwick, of course, involved passing through the Merse lands, and could not but involve Cospatrick in some degree. The enmity between himself and Albany had been allowed to become, as it were, quiescent meantime, but it was by no means over; and this of a national assault over the border, and passing through the earldom, could not be ignored. Some sort of gesture had to be forthcoming, but without if possible committing himself to anything major. So he sent his most warlike son, Patrick, with some fifteen hundred men, to join Albany's host, while *he* sought to look the other way, in Dunbar Castle. George took the opportunity to visit Fast, with Beatrix and Pate, where he was safely unapproachable – not very heroic, but advisable in the circumstances.

They waited, and in due course had a report from Patrick on the expedition, and a scornful one. It had been far from a success, Albany's abilities as a commander nowise improved, however much some of his supporters, including Patrick, urged different tactics. The governor had settled his host down to besiege Berwick Castle, an all but hopeless task as they told him, that strong fortress all but impregnable. He had occupied the town with his troops, and sat there comfortably, and this for long enough for English assistance to arrive, under the Dukes of Bedford and Exeter. Fortunately Patrick had his men out southwards in time not to hold up these seasoned fighters but to warn Albany. And he had promptly ended the siege and retired northwards, evacuating the town, with considerable booty. Admittedly there had been almost no

228

losses, and the English had not pursued them far into Scotland, but was all hardly a feather in Albany's cap, even though he was declaring that it was his suitable compliance with the French request.

Later, they heard that Douglas had done better, taking Wark Castle and ravaging much of the English Middle March.

So much for the Auld Alliance. Albany, of course, was getting old, almost the same age as was Cospatrick, in their late seventies; and he had always preferred to leave military matters to others.

Scotland awaited the return of victorious King Hal from France with some apprehension.

Oddly enough, that king's first demand, when it came, was not for the return of Wark Castle nor any compensation for the Douglas assaults, but for the handing over of the young Percy Earl of Northumberland. This was the famous Hotspur's grandson. His father had been the second earl, who had rebelled against his kinsman by marriage, Henry the Fourth, and being vanquished had fled into Scotland, unlike his two allies, Mowbray of Norfolk and Archbishop Scrope, executed, and had taken the child with him. There, held by Albany as a possibly useful hostage, he had died, and the young Percy, now Earl of Northumberland, had been put into the care of Bishop Wardlaw at St Andrews. Now King Hal wanted him back, for reasons unspecified.

Albany saw his opportunity, and declared that he would agree to an exchange of hostages, not King James but his own son Murdoch. Whether Henry would have considered James anyway was not to be known; but he evidently considered Murdoch no great loss, and whatever that man's own feelings, he was sent home. Albany had his heir back after all those years. What transpired between father and son was not reported, although there were rumours aplenty. Young Northumberland, in turn, became a hostage in the Tower of London, for the good behaviour of the Percys and their friends.

229

Murdoch was promptly married off to Isabel, daughter of the powerful Duncan, Earl of Lennox, of the ancient Celtic line, who had no male heir, a judicious match for the Stewarts. George, for one, sympathised with the lady, knowing her husband's attitude towards women.

An eventful 1417 ended with reports of the death of Owen Glendower. His son, Griffith, still being a hostage with King James, probably would ensure an end to the Welsh wars for independence.

That year George had celebrated his forty-seventh birthday, and the twenty-first anniversary of his marriage to Beatrix, this joyfully acclaimed. Pate was now a lively young man of fifteen. Father and son together drew up a plan to build on Albany's unpopularity, and gain a proportion of the nobility and magnates of Scotland to unite in trying to win the freedom and return to his realm of King James. Henry the Fifth's preoccupation with his French lands was clearly making Scotland of no great importance to him, save as a menace over the Auld Alliance. If James was to promise, if freed, to maintain peace with England, even send hostages to ensure it, and agree to send no aid to France, Henry might well accept his return, this also to overthrow Albany. So, enlisting his brothers' help, they all set off as emissaries up and down the land to seek to enroll the great ones in this endeavour, Cospatrick warning them, however, that when it got to the ears of the governor, as it would, he undoubtedly would revive his enmity into active opposition. George's answer was that if a sufficiency of the lords could be shown to favour this course, Albany would have to go warily indeed.

In the event, this initiative met with very considerable success. George himself undertook the most significant task of all, to visit Archibald, Earl of Douglas at Threave Castle in Galloway. He had heard that this great noble, so long like his predecessor Albany's powerful supporter, was now much disenchanted with the governor, and he being used to advance Albany's cause without any corresponding advantage accruing to himself. Moreover he was particularly scornful over the feeble Foul Raid, as it was being called, against Berwick. George took his own uncle, Douglas of Dalkeith with him, and on the way they picked up Sir William Douglas of Drumlanrig, descended from the Good Sir James, the Bruce's friend. With these valuable adherents, he approached the earl, and had little difficulty in gaining his agreement that it was to the realm's great benefit that its rightful monarch should return and assume the throne. Much heartened and emboldened by this notable backing, he came back by way of Kilmaurs, in Ayrshire, where he saw and persuaded Sir William Cunningham to join their cause, a useful adherent, who had married a niece of the Bruce. Then on to Eaglesham to see Sir John Montgomery of Eglinton, a brother-in-law of Dalkeith, he likewise supportive.

Greatly encouraged, George returned home, to find that his brothers had been almost equally successful, and that there was a great desire among the Scots nobility for King James to come and occupy his throne.

So what was the next stage? King Henry was still in France, so he could not be reached directly; but he had left his brother, the Duke of Bedford, in charge in England, he who, along with Exeter, had relieved Berwick and seen off Albany. If he could be reached?

George made up his mind to tackle this further effort for his liege lord, and with his brother Gavin, who had known Bedford in the Welsh campaigns, set sail in one of their Dunbar ships for London, as he had done so often before.

The brothers had no difficulty in seeing Bedford, this at Windsor, and found him reasonably sympathetic to their suggestions. He himself had not the authority to release James, but promised to inform his brother and recommend it, in the cause of peace with Scotland, which was as far as he could go.

He allowed them to visit James at Westminster palace, where they found an interesting situation indeed. James had fallen in love, and this with a semi-royal young woman, Joan Beaufort, daughter of John, Earl of Somerset, who was a bastard of the late Duke of Lancaster, John of Gaunt, and therefore a distant kinswoman of Henry and Bedford. This romance was apparently being smiled on by the latter, and if it came to anything could only advance King James's cause, and do no harm to Henry's, if she thus became Queen of Scotland.

Well pleased with his efforts, and thanked by James, the brothers returned home. How long would it be till they saw the fruits of this endeavour?

Part Three

24

It is to be feared that hopes for the return of King James were, sadly, much delayed, this on various accounts. Partly concerning affairs in England, but probably largely because of Albany's second son's activities in aiding the French, he proving to be a successful warrior, which much troubled King Henry, especially when his father reinforced him with more Scots troops, scarcely an aid for any peace process – although perhaps effective in helping to keep James a hostage, however much George thought that it should actually *help* in getting the king returned, in order to displace Albany. Another hindrance to the cause might well have been James's own blossoming romance, which had him in no hurry to leave Joan Beaufort, and no permission for them to wed coming from Henry. Also, the English parliament and lords were getting tired of the formerly so popular King Hal's continued preoccupation with warfare in France, which was costing the nation dear, and for what benefit? Bedford was having to hold the fort for his brother, and much harassed.

At any rate, the King of Scots remained outwith his kingdom.

The next year, 1419, George became worried as to his father's health. Cospatrick's eightieth birthday found him a sick and ailing man, more or less confined to Dunbar Castle, with George having to act the earl in all matters. Not that this last greatly worried him, for he had been getting used to it for some time; but to see his parent declining, and losing interest in life, was a great sorrow for him.

The nation at large was in a period of waiting also,

waiting not only for the king's return, but for what was going to happen in the rule and governance of the realm meantime. For Albany, too, was not in good health, in his eightieth year, and Murdoch, Earl of Fife, tending to take over. And *he* was not liked, either, whereas his brother John, now in France, was more admired. It looked as though there might well be a clash between these two. If John of Buchan came home before King James did, and Albany died, there might well be upheaval indeed, and on a national scale, for it was said that their cousin, the warlike Mar, victor at Harlaw, misliked Murdoch and approved of John.

So both kingdoms were in a state of unease, events very much in the balance. And all this could not but have its impact on George, with one of the northern realm's greatest earldoms to manage. But he was finding his son of great help and support, Pate now acting as Master of Dunbar.

A matter which they could have done without was the situation prevailing in those manors of Lincolnshire granted to the family by the late Henry. Unsettled conditions in England allowed land-hungry characters to seek to grasp where they could, and absentee landlords offered opportunity. So there were continual complaints from squires and tenants there, with no authoritative action being taken on their behalf. So it transpired that, early in 1420, George's next visit to the south was in connection, not with King James and national affairs, but with this of the Lincoln situation. He sometimes wished that they had never been given these properties. Yet he liked the manors, so different from anything at home, and, as it happened, great sheep country with the chalk downs of the Wolds, although both the sheep and the hills so unlike their own Lammermuir varieties. The villages were attractive and the people friendly, and to be sure, the lands brought in useful revenues. And they were easily reached by sea, from the Wash and Boston.

Their visit, he judged, was reasonably successful, he taking Pate and his own younger brother David with him, and leaving the latter there to act as his representative, and to organise resistance to acquisitive neighbours and aggressors, David quite happy so to do.

George returned in April to Dunbar, with Pate, to learn the dramatic news. Albany was dead.

Scotland was agog. The man who had ruled it for so long, and so powerfully and ruthlessly, was no more. Few, if any, mourned him, even his son, it was said. But all wondered, what now? Murdoch, not liked, seemed no strong figure; but he not only would now be Duke of Albany but nearest heir to the throne, as his sire had been. He promptly declared that he was now governor, and called a parliament to confirm it. What alternative was there? John of Buchan, his brother? Would he come back from France, where he was making a great name for himself? And *could* he displace Duke Murdoch?

Cospatrick was in no condition to attend any parliament, but emphasised that while he was alive George could not attend in his place. He should go to it, but only to watch, not to take any part, save in that he might have some influence on sundry of those with votes, some of those lords whom he had visited and got to support the errand for the release of James, even perhaps the Douglas.

Duke Murdoch's parliament was held at Stirling Castle, not Scone Abbey, and he appeared at it dressed like a monarch and flourishingly acting the part. He did not have the air of authority that his father had shown, but he adopted a royal manner, and assumed from the first that all accepted him as regent and governor.

And, to be sure, there was in fact small choice, however little he was esteemed. There were plenty of other highly placed Stewarts, legitimate or otherwise, but none could claim to be heirs to the throne. The parliament was really only a formality, however much routine business fell to be transacted after the ceremonial appointment to the governorship, this proposed by Bishop William Lauder of Glasgow, the Chancellor, and seconded by the Primate, Bishop Wardlaw of St Andrews, a somewhat significant clerical demonstration. There was no alternative nomination put forward by the so doubtful lords, however glum was the atmosphere prevailing in the Great Hall of Stirling Castle.

The matter of the return of King James was, of course, raised thereafter, the new governor looking supercilious and adding nothing on the subject, however vocal he was otherwise. George wished that he could have contributed to the discussion, but that was not possible from the watchers' gallery.

So the new regime commenced. How would it compare with the one just ended? And for how long would it last?

After the eventful and autocratic rule of the late Albany, his son's governorship was in fact something of a relief to the nation, for although he strutted and behaved obnoxiously, with arrogance and pomposity, this offending most who had to deal with him, he made little real impact on the realm at large, apparently not greatly interested in actual rule and matters of state as distinct from his own style and status, leaving such to others, largely his own Stewart kinsmen, he merely acting the monarch, which, however galling, did not greatly affect the majority of folk. But the lack of real leadership did permit considerable local turbulence and feud. Mar was the strongest figure on the scene, but even he did not pursue his warfare with Donald of the Isles, who was able to reign in the Highland West as all but an independent monarch.

The governor's principal activity to take the people's attention was his womanising, which was prodigious, even for the royal Stewarts, his duchess an all but forgotten figure hidden away in the royal castle of Dumbarton in her father's earldom. In this at least Murdoch would leave his mark on future generations.

George, therefore, was left in peace to get on with looking after his father's earldom, and sufficiently busy this kept him and Pate. There were no English attacks over the border meantime, other than the normal mosstrooping raiding, so the Merse part of his responsibilities caused him little worry.

It was early in the year 1421 that George, still living at Colbrandspath Tower, was summoned to Dunbar Castle by brother Gavin. Their father had been found dead in his bed that morning, a quiet end indeed for that great Cospatrick, at the age of eighty-two, and this coming so soon after Robert of Albany's demise. Gavin indeed wondered whether that pair were still at each other's throats in the place to which they had passed on? But George asserted that they were unlikely to find themselves in any position so to be; for Albany surely would be consigned to wherever murderers were sent in the hereafter, while their father, who had lived an honourable and worthy life, would presumably be safely in Paradise.

So now George himself was the Cospatrick, eleventh Earl of Dunbar and March, with all that this meant, Beatrix a countess and Pate the Master.

25

George did not find his new position very different from heretofore, since he had been acting the earl for years, and the vassals, tenants and ordinary folk had got used to him as such. But it did mean that he and Beatrix had to give up their long tenure of Colbrandspath Tower and move into Dunbar Castle. Brother David took over their old and favoured house.

Also the accession meant that he now had a seat in parliament, which he did value; no more watching from galleries. Otherwise, life was much as it had been, although he greatly missed his father.

Duke Murdoch was not greatly concerned with parliaments, so there was no call to attend for some time.

Beatrix set about improving the amenities of Dunbar Castle, a quite major task. Because it was built on rock-stacks projecting out into the sea, the various towers linked by covered bridges, while all but impregnable from attack by land or sea, as Black Agnes, George's ancestress had demonstrated so famously, it made an awkward home to run compared with the small and compact Colbrandspath. The furthest seaward tower was probably the most pleasing to occupy, with its dramatic situation above the waves, the wide vistas and the clouds of wheeling seafowl ever around it; but it was the most inconvenient to reach across those narrow bridges. The largest and most commodious building, all but a keep, was the landward one, with its gatehouse and small courtyard. Beatrix decided that it must be their main quarters, while Pate could take over the outmost one, where he could fish from his bedroom windows – provided he had a sufficiently long line. For years the castle had lacked a resident mistress, and in consequence much had to be done to enhance its comforts, George approving.

The fact that there was little or no news of any significance from the rest of Scotland was to be welcomed in the circumstances, unusual as it was; but there was no lack of tidings from further afield, from France in especial, and this having its effects in England. King Henry's warfare had long been fairly successful, but now was becoming less so, and, as it happened, largely on account of John Stewart, Earl of Buchan, who was proving to be a brilliant soldier – and he was fighting for the French. Henry had got so far as to capture Rouen and to force the Treaty of Troyes on the opposition, this between France, Burgundy and England; but Buchan was still undefeated and menacing Henry's extraordinary progress. If France had had a more able monarch than the all but mad and ailing Charles, Henry would never have got so far. He was now claiming, indeed, to be heir to the French throne, and regent, having married, as his second wife, Katherine, Charles's daughter – even though she had a lawful brother, Charles the Dauphin. All this would, in effect, make that nation a province of England. And this would by no means suit Scotland's interests. The Auld Alliance must survive, as the only way to keep aggressive England in its place. So Buchan's efforts were to be applauded.

Brother Patrick was even suggesting that he should take a force of the earldom's men, and others, across the Channel to aid Buchan. But, to be sure, George would have none of that.

The year was not far advanced when it was heard that John of Buchan, with the aid of the heir to Douglas, Archibald, styled Earl of Wigtown, had won another battle, the most important and significant yet, this at Beaugé. This much perturbed King Henry, who, unable to defeat Buchan, resorted to the device of taking King James over to France to join him, this indicating that his cousin, fighting on the other side, was in treason against his lawful sovereign, and therefore contrary to the peace treaty. What James thought of this was not reported; but probably he found the freedom and military action a welcome change after the many years of his hostageship, Henry knighting him. At any rate, he remained in France with the English army, and got as near to Paris as Meaux, only twenty-eight miles, when Henry fell ill with dysentery, a grievous ailment causing much pain and near prostration. There was nothing for it but for the king to return to England, taking James with him. He got home just in time to see his wife Katherine present him with a son, another Henry, before he died, aged only thirty-five years.

So, instead of a warrior monarch, England suddenly had an infant king, who, it was claimed, was also heir to the French throne. And only six weeks later the sickly Charles died; and his son, the Dauphin Charles, was crowned king in France, while baby Henry was proclaimed the same in England, a ridiculous and most ambiguous situation which obviously could not be maintained.

In Scotland, Murdoch did nothing about it, despite the Auld Alliance. Deaths seemed to dominate the scene these days, not only for George. The two brothers of the late Henry had to take over the rule in England, Bedford going to France to continue the warfare and hold Normandy, and Humphrey of Gloucester remaining in London to act for their little nephew.

In the circumstances, George saw it as an opportunity to try to hasten the return of King James and get rid of Murdoch as governor. He thought that there was no need to go round all the other lords who thought as he did, and had done previously, but judged it probably wise to have the backing of the Earl of Douglas, now ageing but still the most powerful noble in the kingdom, who was now also Duke of Touraine in France. So, with Gavin, he made the long ride across the width of Scotland to Threave, in Galloway, and there found the earl sick, indeed in bed, but agreeing with his objectives. He also found that the son

242

and heir, Archibald of Wigtown, had recently arrived back from France, where he had been acting as lieutenant to John of Buchan. He also deplored Murdoch's governorship, and indeed volunteered to accompany George on a visit to the Duke of Gloucester, to try to gain James's release. They might be able to make use of Buchan's position across the Channel to influence their cause.

He said that he would join George at Dunbar shortly, and they could go by ship to London. Those wool-vessels of the Dunbars were a blessing indeed when it came to travel.

In due course, then, the pair of them sailed, George getting on well with the Douglas, and hearing much about campaigning in France. Buchan was declared to be the most brilliant commander Scotland had produced since Robert the Bruce.

Up Thames, they had no difficulty in seeing Humphrey Plantagenet of Gloucester, based at the Tower of London, although the infant King Henry was apparently with his mother at Windsor. A very positive character of middle years, he received them well enough, and was not surprised at the purpose of their mission. He did not commit himself to any return of James to Scotland, but did not dismiss it either. However he quickly made it clear that this could only be considered in conjuction with his brother Bedford in France, and at a price, a heavy price. George and Douglas were somewhat surprised at the tradesmanlike approach to the subject, almost as though it were to be a commercial transaction. Money seemed to be the principal requirement, gold and silver, rather than statesmanlike arrangements between the nations. Admittedly the late Henry's wars had cost the English treasury dear, and the ongoing French situation was still proving expensive. But pounds and merks seemed hardly suitable terms for the release of a monarch. However, this was Gloucester's reaction. He said that he would confer with his brother, and send word to Scotland as to figures, if it was agreed, and securities therefore. At least he did not seem to be against the general notion of James's freedom, only concerned with the profit to be made out of it.

With that the envoys had to be content; but George did emphasise that, if and when the terms were sent, it should be to himself at Dunbar, not to the governor Murdoch, who would not desire the king's return, and would provide no moneys, that for sure.

They went to see James thereafter, at Westminster, and found him actually in no great hurry to go north to ascend his throne; this evidently because of his passion for Joan of Beaufort. He was desperate to have her as his wife, and she, it seemed, was almost equally in love with him. But she was a daughter of the Earl of Somerset, who was a brother of Henry the Fourth, and the Plantagenets were seeking a high price for any permission to wed, the same tune that the visitors had heard at the Tower. He, James, had no wealth, of course, and he did not judge that the Scots treasury would come to his rescue. So – how were the necessary moneys to be raised?

George and Douglas said that while certainly they could look for no help from Murdoch, it might be possible to obtain the necessary silver otherwise. Most of the Scots nobility were much in favour of the king's return, and many might contribute, they themselves leading in the matter. And Holy Church was rich, and would almost certainly make a sizeable donation, Bishop Wardlaw, the Primate, an able and worthy prelate.

It seemed strange to be thus concerned over money, like merchants, something new for royalty and nobility. But if that was the price to be paid, so be it. George was aware that he, probably, was one of the wealthiest lords, thanks to the Lammermuir wool-trade, and could well make some major offering. After all, was it not better so than producing men to die in the national causes, as so often?

They had to leave it at that and await Gloucester's terms. They took their leave of their love-lorn monarch. As a man much aware of the imperatives of love, George was sympathetic.

The pair had to fill in some time at London before their ship came back from Veere, but found that no hardship, that city a lively place, the folk friendly enough.

George had to wait almost a month before the word was brought from Gloucester by the Dean of Westminster. And it was challenging word indeed. He and his brother Bedford, in the name of young King Henry, would be prepared to release James Stewart, and allow him to marry the Lady Joan Beaufort in return for the sum of forty thousand pounds. This sum was arrived at by calculating the costs of keeping James and his servants over the years of his captivity, for the provision of tutors for his education, and the sporting activities allowed him, all carefully estimated.

To say that George was astonished at both the size of this demand and the reasons given for the imposition, was to put it mildly. Were they dealing with usurers and chandlers? he wondered. For the release of a king. Had the like ever before been heard? The dean went on to say that the payment could be spread over a period of four years; but in the interim several high-born hostages must be provided, twenty-one of these, it was suggested, and the costs of their maintenance in England to be met by themselves. Also, as in the nature of an afterthought, no further reinforcements should be sent from Scotland to the deplorable Earl of Buchan in France.

George, all but speechless, decided that he must go and see Wigtown over all this, for raising such moneys was going to be a problem indeed. But what alternative was there? If they were to win their king back, and get rid of Murdoch, this must be attempted, more than attempted, achieved.

So it was to Threave again, there to find that in the meantime the old Earl of Douglas had died, and that now Wigtown himself was Earl of Douglas and second Duke of Touraine. This at least meant that, as well as very powerful, he must have considerable wealth, and could be expected to produce a sizeable contribution to the fund.

However that man pointed out that large lands did not necessarily mean large siller, moneys. But he recognised that he must help to give a lead. What was George himself thinking of?

Most in Scotland reckoned in merks rather than in pounds, the merk being approximately two-thirds of one pound sterling. So sixty thousand merks were called for, an enormous sum by any standards; that is fifteen thousand for each year of the four. Some magnates might commit themselves to an initial payment; but when they had the monarch back, would they be prepared to go on paying for another three years? This was what the twenty-one hostages demand was for; otherwise it would be quite likely that many would say let the English come and collect the arrears – if they could!

George, with his great wool revenues from the Netherlands, which few could match, had decided that he could give one-tenth of the first year's payment, that is fifteen hundred merks, a very substantial contribution, enough perhaps more or less to shame others into dipping deep into their pouches.

Douglas, on hearing this, looked unhappy, shaking his head. *He* could not match such sum, nor anything like it. Lands and men he had in plenty, but not wealth in coin. Few would have, he judged. Five hundred merks was the most that he could offer, and that a serious drain. But he had been thinking on this, and wondered whether an offer of men, to aid the English in France, would be acceptable instead of siller? If, say, he promised two hundred mounted men, led by knights, and another two hundred mounted archers, with crossbows, might that not serve? It could have the effect of making Buchan reluctant to fight against his own countrymen, and so help to bring the French wars to an end. Buchan was in fact now gaining nothing for Scotland in his fighting there. If it helped to get King James back and on to his throne, then John

Stewart might well see the advantage of returning to Scotland.

George saw the point of this; but whether Gloucester would was another question. But the five hundred merks would be a help, yes. Two thousand between them would make a good start for the first year's fifteen thousand. They could make this offer of men – but England was not short of manpower, with ten times the population of Scotland; whereas they were short of money clearly. So that might not be an acceptable alternative.

It was back to Dunbar, then, and the sending out of the brothers, and Pate, up and down the land, to appeal to the lords and great ones, while he himself set out, by ship, for St Andrews in Fife, to see Bishop Wardlaw. That was, he judged, where the main wealth of the nation was to be found, at least in money. The Church had been acting in the production of riches for centuries, through industry, trade and marketing, tasks beneath the dignity of the lordly and knightly ones.

Sailing to St Andrews was a mere forty miles, compared with almost four times that by horse, even taking Queen Margaret's scow-ferry across Forth. The Primate proved not to be in his palace-castle there, but over at the St Mary's College of the new university, which he had established, superintending the lecturers, tutors and pre-lectors, and the allocation of students to each. It all being something new to Scotland, as distinct from priestly training centres in abbeys, much such guidance was necessary, it seemed, especially in non-religious subjects, for the teaching of which, philosophy, medicine, civil law and the liberal arts, foreign tutors had had to be brought in, largely from Paris, where the bishop himself had trained. The institution was now ten years old, but it had taken time to establish all twenty-one lectureships and seminaries.

George found the bishop, not in St Mary's College, which was reserved for ecclesiastical studies, but in a separate building called the Pedagogy, in the South Street of the town. He was a fine-looking man in his mid-fifties. He listened to the visitor's pleas with sympathy and understanding, declaring that he would have wished to subscribe handsomely to the ransom; for he had an especial interest in and fondness for James Stewart other than just loyalty to the crown: on David of Rothesay's murder by the late Albany his young brother had been put in his care by King Robert, here at St Andrews, as the safest place surely from that duke's possible further menace. He, the bishop, had acted tutor to the prince before he was sent off on his way to France, and captured. But, unfortunately, it was pointed out, the establishment of this university, and its growth and development, had cost the bishopric and primacy funds dear, and he could not give as he would have wished. But he would make what gesture he could, and urge his fellow bishops and all abbots and priors to contribute. Also seek to have Holy Church promise to guarantee the completion of the final total for each year, this of fifteen thousand merks. As token, however, he would give herewith one thousand merks, which was the most that he could afford. And he thought that Bishop Lauder of Glasgow, the Chancellor, head of the wealthiest diocese in the realm, would give as much. He would so advise.

George sailed back to Dunbar, well pleased. They had already three thousand of the required fifteen thousand merks promised.

Back home, he went to see his vassal Sir Walter Haliburton of Dirleton, now Treasurer, who owned lands also in the shires of Perth and Forfar. That man announced that the nation's treasury was empty, Duke Murdoch, his brother-in-law, very extravagant. But he would give one-half of his own annual increment to the appeal, this amounting to four hundred merks.

So the total mounted.

It took a long time for George's emissaries to travel round the land and interview and persuade the nobility, baronage, prelacy and senior clergy to make some donation. Meantime George was considering the parallel matter of the prominent hostages to be enlisted for the ransom payments. Gloucester had declared the specific number required, twenty-one – how he had arrived at that figure was not stated; but it meant much selecting and more persuasion was going to be needed, an unhappy business. And the said persons were going to have to pay their own expenses while in England, which would not make the duty any more popular. George had taken on an invidious and unpleasant task. But somebody had to do it if King James was to be freed and the governor displaced. Beatrix praised him for his dedication and resolve.

It was early 1424 before the total of fifteen thousand merks was not only promised but collected. George and Archibald Douglas were now faced with the duty of taking it all down to London, and finding out the hostage requirements, something that they did not look forward to. So far no volunteers had offered themselves, as was hardly to be expected.

They sailed for the Thames in the rough weather of January, with the sackfuls of coin, which was received at the Tower with most evident satisfaction, Gloucester himself presiding over the careful counting of it all. And in return, he gave them the long list of hostages.

They were astonished at the detailed identities of the men chosen, clearly drawn up with the aid of an adviser very knowledgeable about Scotland and its significant personalities. There must be spies working in high places there for the English. All twenty-one were actually named. George was much concerned to see his brother Patrick among them. Also his vassals Haliburton of Dirleton, Sir John Lindsay of the Byres and Luffness, and Sir Adam Hepburn of Hailes. There were two semi-royal Stewarts, Sir David, elder son of the Earl of Atholl, and Sir Robert of Lorn; even the husband of Murdoch of Albany's sister Marjory, Sir Duncan Campbell of Argyll. Douglas did not escape either, his uncle, Sir James

Douglas of Balveny nominated. Sir John Montgomery of Ardrossan was among the thirteen others, one of those who had supported George's two missions regarding King James. How had Gloucester obtained all these names? Somebody very close to the rule in Scotland must have been involved. Could it possibly be Murdoch himself? After all, he knew Gloucester well from his period in England with James, and might possibly see it as a means of getting rid temporarily of characters whom he might consider enemies.

It all made a grievous duty to take home with them; but they could not get King James back without its implementation.

For his part, Gloucester agreed that James could marry the Lady Joan; and, on the arrival of the hostages, could make his long-waited journey north. The said hostages, they were informed, would be allocated to the care of different lords throughout England until the full ransom was forthcoming. And some portion of the first year's payment would probably be remitted as a dowry for the new Queen of Scotland.

The visitors, pondering it all, went to see James at Westminster, and found him with his bride-to-be, joyous at the prospect of their forthcoming marriage, even more than of the return to Scotland. Admittedly he would be faced with a major and challenging task then, confronting Murdoch, taking over the rule of a land so long without a resident monarch and divided in allegiances, and with all the clan Stewart kinsfolk in high places to be dealt with, some possibly not eager to see him. Small wonder if James was somewhat doubtful. How long would it be, he wondered, before the long list of hostages could be assembled and sent south?

That his visitors could not tell him; but they would seek to have it done as swiftly as possible. All the understandable reluctance to be overcome, much of the land to be covered in the doing of it, a matter of months was envisaged.

The lovers exchanged glances at that, but had to accept it.

Back home for the envoys, then, with those busy and difficult months ahead of them.

26

The weeks that followed were testing, even worse than those previously spent in raising the ransom moneys. This of informing, and all but ordering, in the name of the monarch, the designated hostages, was a trial indeed. George decided it best to do it all himself, claiming the royal authority, and at least telling that he was sending his own brother and three of his earldom's senior vassals to form one-fifth of the company. None he saw was happy about the burden laid upon them, demanding to know why, because an English duke had picked on them, they must accept what amounted to a four-year exile? Explaining that the request he brought was in the king's name, not Gloucester's, in the nature of a royal command, helped, but did not make the prospect any more pleasing. George had to indicate that it was, in fact, something of an honour, and that James would show his gratitude, no doubt, hereafter, reward those who had thus served him so well, to their cost. Some of the men were less reluctant than others, seeing the stay in England as possibly of some interest, and, not exactly a vacation, but a respite from problems at home; others recognising that the monarch's return and the putting down of Murdoch and his regime was going to be a demanding and possibly dangerous time, which as hostages they would be spared. But none greeted the intimation with joy.

Fortunately nearly all the nominees were to be found south of the Highlands, although George did have to travel as far as Argyll and Atholl. It all took him almost two challenging months, and did not add to his popularity, Pate and others having to look after his earldom meantime.

At least he could offer the chosen ones conveyance south in two of his Dunbar ships, he himself going with them, also Douglas. Patrick was one of the least disgruntled of the company, he ever in search of new experiences.

On the Day of the Annunciation of Our Lady, then, at the end of March, the two vessels sailed with their high-born passengers. They all watched their native land receding with mixed feelings, yet some with a kind of anticipation. Few had ever been outwith Scotland previously.

At London, which had most of those arriving in much wonder at its size, the multitude of great buildings and the teeming population, they discovered that King James and Joan Beaufort were already married, having been wed in the Priory of St Mary Overy, Southwark, across Thames, and by the bride's own uncle, the Cardinal Beaufort, with great display and flourish, this on account of the bride being a Plantagenet rather than the fact that she was becoming wife to the King of Scots, even Gloucester present.

The arrival of the hostage company at Westminster Palace took on the nature of a celebration of the union rather than the start of a period of all but captivity, with Queen Joan thanking them all and James promising rewards in due course. The young woman's most notable good looks helped. Even Gloucester was welcoming, as he saw his project maturing as he had planned. He had arranged where each hostage was to be based, assuring all that they would be well treated. It all made a very unusual situation.

Two days of this, with quite notable hospitality – paid for, of course, by the vast ransom moneys – and it was farewells among them all. George said his goodbye to Patrick, who was to be sent into the keeping of the Prince-Bishop of Durham, almost the most northerly of the hostage places, Douglas seeing his uncle off to the seat of the Lord Cromwell. They themselves would return to Scotland in one of the ships; but the king and queen would

253

travel north through England, in some style, later in the month.

The culmination of so much labour, negotiation and persuasion, it had all made an occasion that would be spoken of for long, and George's part therein prominent. But it would be good to get back to Beatrix and Pate and a more normal life.

It was six weeks later that the great company set out, on horseback, at last to welcome the King of Scots back to his own realm. George had been very busy organising it, eager that it should be representative and illustrious. He had had little difficulty this time, for almost the entire nation had been looking forward to this event for so long, and, these last years, to an end to Murdoch's rule. He and Douglas led a party of six other earls, Angus, Crawford, Lennox, Moray, Orkney and Strathearn, with Hay the High Constable and Keith the Knight Marischal, also some of the younger and fitter prelates, plus unnumbered lords, barons and knights, over three hundred of them. Some had thought to come to greet the royal couple at the borderline itself; but George asserted that they should emphasise the international importance of the event, signalised by the Treaty of London as it was being called, which included a seven-year peace accord between the two kingdoms, by proceeding some distance down into England for the meeting. After all, the new Queen of Scotland was an Englishwoman. And since Patrick was now in the keeping of the Bishop of Durham, why not there? Use him, as one of the hostages, to symbolise it all. None objected to this.

The word was that James and Joan were making a notable progress of it up through the English shires, anything but speeding, from city to palace, castle to abbey; indeed, it turned out, calling at some of the places where other ransom hostages had been sent, to assure them of royal appreciation. So, as it transpired, the Scots welcoming company had quite a wait at Durham. However, the Prince-Bishop, one of the wealthiest prelates in England, as well as so evidently important, was in a position to provide adequate hospitality and entertainment, and did so with a fair grace, the cathedral town of Durham all but taken over by the visitors from the north.

It was good to see Patrick again, who appeared to be quite well pleased, thus far, with his situation, finding life in a religious house better than he had anticipated, with little that was actually monastic about it, indeed the feeding better than he had ever experienced, and ample activities round about, sporting and otherwise, even female company it seemed, to keep him lively.

When king and queen did arrive, it was with an entourage almost as large as that awaiting them, to tax further the bishop's resources, English knights and lords by the score. James was in excellent spirits, obviously enjoying his journey and the feeling of freedom after all the years of nominal restraint. He greeted George and Douglas warmly, as well he might, after all their efforts on his behalf.

Much of the English escort was to turn back hereabouts, on the edge of Northumberland, for here the Percy earl thereof was to take over, with, of all people, Sir Robert Umfraville, who had so distinguished himself against Scotland earlier. Also Sir William Heron and Sir Robert Ogle, Wardens of the East and Middle Marches of England, odd company for George and his like to associate with.

It seemed that James had decided to enter his kingdom not at Berwick but further west, this in order to halt at the abbey of Melrose in the Middle March of Scotland, especial in that the Bruce's heart was buried there, and it claiming to be the foremost shrine in the land, although not all ecclesiastics agreed with that. There he was going to give thanks to God for his delivery.

So they went north-westwards, by Derwent to the English Tyne, to reach and halt at the great St Andrew's Priory of Hexham, which was accepted as a worthy place to stay in, since St Andrew was the patron saint of Scotland. Next day it was up Redesdale, passing near the site of the

Battle of Otterburn, smilingly pointed out to James, with the Percy looking grim. When presently they crossed the borderline at Carter Bar, Umfraville and the two English wardens left them, duty done, but Northumberland still remaining with them. They progressed down to the Jed Water and to Jedburgh's town and abbey, for one more night's lodging, the townsfolk acclaiming their monarch tumultuously.

From there to Melrose was only a dozen miles or so. The mitred abbot there had a great assembly of the local magnates awaiting to salute them, some of them George's own vassals, including Home of Cowdenknowes and Swinton of that Ilk, all eager to hail their liege-lord and his lady. James went and paid his respects to the spot before the high altar where his famous ancestor's heart was interred; and then, in a ceremony of thanks and praise for his long-looked-for return, he swore, with a hand on the Bible, to fulfil the terms of the Treaty of London, maintain peace with England, and seek to rule his people right-eously, this witessed by the Percy, to report back to Gloucester.

From Melrose next day there was the forty-mile ride up Lauderdale and over the Lammermuir Hills by the heights of Soutra, passing the great hospice of the monks, estab-lished by James's ancestor, Malcolm the Fourth, the Maiden, which he pointed out to his Joan proudly, asking if they had the like in all England? And so down into the Lothian plain, with Edinburgh's Arthur's Seat and castle hill beckoning them on, and the blue waters of the Firth of Forth, with the coasts of Fife beyond, all highly pictur-esque, the queen enthralled.

Word of the royal arrival had been sent on ahead, and the streets of the city were thronged with cheering crowds to shout their joy that their monarch had finally entered his capital. They made for the Abbey of the Holy Rood, under Arthur's Seat, rather than the citadel-castle on its rock, as more comfortable for the queen than the accommodation of the bare fortress a mile away. Joan was greatly impressed by the mountain, as she called it, and all the other hills on which the capital was built, seven of them, she was told, the Athens of the North. Also all the tall stone buildings, even the common folks' tenements, which she was not used to.

And now James had to do more than wave acknowledgments to his welcoming subjects, and act the monarch. And the first such act was to send for the governor to come and deliver up to him the Great and Privy Seals of the kingdom, symbols of authority. Murdoch had made his seat of government Stirling Castle, not Edinburgh, nor his father's Scone, and may have expected the king to join him there; at any rate, he had not come to Edinburgh. So the Marischal and the High Constable were sent to Stirling, thirty-five miles to the north-west, to bring him into his liege-lord's presence.

James had been only a boy of eleven years when he left Scotland, and had seen but little of the country, even Edinburgh and the Lothians. With days to wait for Murdoch, he was able to explore, first the capital and its surroundings. Then, on the third day, George took him and the queen eastwards to Dunbar, to see the towns of Musselburgh, Travernent, Haddington, North Berwick and Dunbar itself, where the populations could display their loyal appreciation of the royal return, provosts make welcoming speeches, and landowners and lairds come to make obeisance.

Beatrix, presented, acted the competent and glad hostess, so much so that Joan there and then declared that she must become one of her extra ladies-in-waiting; and James made the gesture of knighting Pate, much to that young man's surprise and delight.

They spent two nights at Dunbar, and visited the dramatic coastal cliff scene to the south, including Fast. Murdoch might well have reached Edinburgh by this time, but he could wait. Then back to the city.

At Holyrood they learned that the governor, or *former* governor, had not yet arrived. It was decided that the fortress-castle itself was the place to receive him, as the royal seat. George, for one, was very interested to be present to see the meeting of these two cousins.

So it was up to the castle with them, there to inspect its mighty strengths and fortifications, the tourney-ground on the approach to it, fairly narrow as this was, the ancient chapel of St Margaret, and the sheer precipices on all sides but the east. Joan admitted that she preferred Holyrood.

Word from the Marischal and Constable arrived at the abbey that they, with Duke Murdoch, should reach Edinburgh by next day's noon. The latter had taken his time to obey the royal summons.

Joan did not accompany them back to the citadel next forenoon. At midday the reason for the ex-governor's delay became apparent: he had been assembling some of his close supporters to bring with him, these including Walter Stewart, the ageing Earl of Atholl, his uncle and James's; Alexander, Earl of Mar, the victor of Harlaw; Sir Robert Graham, kinsman of the Earl of Strathearn; Sir Robert Stewart, grandson of Atholl, whose father was one of the hostages in England; and sundry others. These, with Murdoch, were ushered into the presence of a tense King James, he backed by George and Douglas and the others of the escort.

This confrontation had been bound to be dramatic, these two cousins once so close as fellow-captives, but one freed and one not; and since their parting, the freed having assumed the rule of the other's kingdom. Now the king was stiff, tight of lips; his cousin not so, apparently anything but.

With all but a swagger Murdoch strode into the chamber, hand outstretched, smiling easily. "So, Cousin – here is a great occasion," he declared. "Our reunion. After . . . how many years? Eight is it? Or nine? I greet you warmly, I who have served you faithfully in the meantime, held your throne for you. All hail!"

He had to drop his arm, since James made no move to grasp that hand, but only inclined his head briefly.

"I welcome your . . . appearance, Murdoch," he said. "After so long. Your *belated* appearance! You did not come to meet me, as all these others did. After all the years!"

The duke waved the unshaken hand. "A realm to rule, James. Many duties, much labour. As you will discover. Unlike languishing at Westminster. I say that you will find that I have tended your kingdom well enough, and it no light task. With so much to see to. And so many difficult lords to keep an eye on!" And he glanced over at the ranks behind the monarch, brows raised.

"M'mm. You are relieved of all such now, then. I, I trust that I shall find reason to thank you hereafter." James paused. "Have you brought the seals and tokens?"

"To be sure. Sir John Hall here, my Chamberlain, has them." And he beckoned.

A stocky, youngish man stepped forward, with two red velvet pouches from which he extracted the Great and Privy Seals of Scotland, with the figure of King Robert the Third sitting on his throne on the obverse sides, and mounted on a horse and holding up a sceptre on the reverses. Bowing, he presented these to James, who took them, eyeing his father's crowned image with a sad shake of the head, and then turning to hand them to Hay of Erroll, the High Constable.

"That, my lord Duke, relieves you of any responsibility for the rule of this my realm, as governor," he said. "So be it." He drew a deep breath. "You all have my permission to retire." And he waved away his cousin, uncle, and those with them.

Taken by surprise, Murdoch opened his mouth to speak, probably protest, but thought better of it, looked at Atholl and the others behind him, and shrugged. Then he bowed, but not low, and turned, by no means backing away, his party following suit, to leave the chamber.

George, close behind the king, noticed that James's hands, held behind him, were trembling. That interview had taxed him, most evidently.

He spoke quietly. "You would be alone, Sire?" he asked.

James nodded, unspeaking.

His own party bowed themselves out of the apartment, George backing away and others doing the same, although perhaps this was premature, since the monarch was not yet crowned, the High Constable leaving those significant royal seals on a table.

James Stewart had indicated that he had taken over the rule of Scotland.

It was not very long before he rejoined his supporting company to return down to Holyrood, his composure recovered. There was no suggestion that Murdoch and his friends should accompany them there.

The necessary coronation ceremony was now foremost in the minds of all. This to be as soon as practically possible, at Scone Abbey, as was traditional. The lords and land-holders had to come from all parts to offer fealty, and time must be given for them to assemble. But there was a problem, in this instance, other than that of mere travel. The MacDuffs, Earls of Fife, were the hereditary Cor-oners, and had held that privilege of placing the crown on the head of each new monarch from time immemorial – or at least from the year 1056, when MacDuff, Thane of Fife, had, on the order of Malcolm Canmore, slain King Mac-Beth so that Malcolm could ascend the throne; and as reward had been given many privileges, including the right of this line to act the crowner. This had been done at each succession until Duncan, twelfth Earl of Fife, died, leaving only an heiress, she who had crowned the Bruce. She had wed four husbands without producing a child, until the fifth one did, and he was Robert Stewart, Earl of Menteith, son of Robert the Second. He therefore became Earl of Fife in her right, and was thereafter created Duke of Albany. Murdoch, his son, therefore held the earldom of Fife now, and so was hereditary Coroner, with the right to place the crown on James's head.

This unfortunate situation greatly concerned the king, needless to say. But none of his advisers could suggest any acceptable alternative. Someone had to do the crowning, and with the rightful individual available, former governor as he was, no one else could replace him. Murdoch had sons, lawful and otherwise, but it would serve nothing to use one of these in his place. James had no option but to accede to it. But he declared that, thereafter, he would demonstrate his feelings in the matter.

George suggested that it would be seen none so unsuitable by most, the final and irrevocable handing over of complete authority by the former ruler to his liege-lord, he who had made such a mockery of government.

James admitted that since he had re-entered his realm he had heard nothing but dire reports of the utter folly and misrule he had come back to, on the part of this man and his chosen associates, the licentiousness, the contempt for the law, the lack of control over the local tyrannies of many nobles, the extravagance and the plundering of the nation's resources. He shook a fist in the air, and exclaimed to his lieutenants, "Let God but grant me life, and there shall not be a place in my dominions where the key shall not keep the castle and the bracken bush the cow, although I myself shall live the life of a dog to accomplish it!"

Somewhat astonished at this outburst, his hearers recognised that Scotland was now to have a very different monarch than it had had since the death of the Bruce.

The coronation, however partial in acceptability it might be – for Donald of the Isles was refusing to return the Stone of Destiny from his Hebridean fastnesses where Bruce had told him to keep it until a worthy successor sat on his throne, this as indication of his disapproval of the entire Stewart regime – was set for the twenty-first day of May.

Meantime, George returned to Dunbar, to relieve Pate and Gavin who had been deputising for him in his duties as regards the earldom.

There, in a day or two, they heard that James had made a significant move in his attitude towards Murdoch, by having the latter's eldest son, Sir Walter Stewart, arrested.

That young man had been appointed by his father keeper of the royal castle of Dumbarton, at the mouth of the Clyde estuary; and he had distinguished himself by appropriating much of the dues to be paid to the customs on the import of sundry goods to Glasgow, the greatest port in the kingdom, and otherwise misbehaving. He was to await trial. No doubt Murdoch himself was intended to take note.

Since they could go as far as Perth by ship, George took his wife and Pate with him to witness the so important and momentous coronation. Beatrix was, after all, to be a lady-in-waiting on occasion. They found the king and queen lodging in the Blackfriars Monastery at Perth, and were warmly greeted. They were, indeed, able to spend the night in the same large establishment, at the royal command.

Next forenoon the procession set out on the three miles to Scone, a lengthy cavalcade, everyone much exercised over the day's proceedings, James himself looking all but grim, although his wife was in good spirits.

They processed first to the abbey-church, which they found already packed, and there had to be some ejecting in order to get the royal party within, Murdoch present, and clad in much greater splendour than was James. Here the Primate, Bishop Henry Wardlaw, the king's former tutor, with the abbot, held a preliminary and fairly brief religious service of dedication, and the king made his vows to serve Almighty God as his faithful servant, and to rule the nation entrusted to his care in as worthy fashion as his humble disciple was able. The anointing oil was blessed by the abbot, who then gave a general benediction, and led the great company out to head for the nearby Moot Hill for the crowning, escorted by a choir of singing boys and the rhythmic clash of cymbals.

This was a strange but ancient location for the installation of a monarch, a small, isolated hillock amid woodland, on the top of which the actual coronation always took place. There was something almost pagan about this, leaving a church for a hilltop; but then the Scots kingship itself dated from pagan times.

So up the side of this mound the king, queen, the bishop and abbot, Murdoch and certain of the officers of state, led now by the Lord Lyon King of Arms, had to climb.

George and the other earls and prelates and nobles remained on the low ground, backed by the huge watching crowd, among whom the majority of the company from the church had to stand, including Beatrix and Pate.

Up on the summit a throne-like chair was placed, with a lesser one beside it but slightly set back. The King of Arms, now acting High Sennachie, in charge of the arrangements, conducted James to the greater chair, saw him seated, bowed, and then had Joan seated on the second one. He positioned the officers of state, including the Knight Marischal and the High Constable, behind, these bearing the crown, on a cushion, the sword of state and the sceptre. The Primate was led to stand on the right side of the monarch, he now carrying the ampulla with the anointing oil, and Murdoch on the left.

This completed, the Lyon signed to his trumpeter, stationed half way down the hill, who blew a long blast for quiet.

"James, by the Grace of God, son of Robert the Third, King of Scots, dedicated and blessed, acknowledged by all the realm, is here to be anointed and crowned," he cried. He turned to the Primate. "My lord Bishop."

Henry Wardlaw moved round, to stand in front of the throne, raising the ampulla. "In the Name of the Father, the Son and the Holy Spirit, I hereby anoint you, James Stewart, as High King. May you reign and rule over this nation as viceroy of the Most High, in all justice, wisdom and power, until thy life's end." And pouring some of the holy oil on to his fingers, he stooped to make the sign of the cross with it on the brow of the monarch. "With this unction I thee anoint. Praise be to God!" And he stood back.

Brief as this was, there was silence throughout all that

263

gathering. It was thirty-four years since last this solemnity had been enacted, and few indeed present had ever seen and heard the like.

Lyon spoke again. "Murdoch, Earl of Fife and Duke of Albany, as is your right and privilege, I call upon you to place the crown of Scotland on the brow of His Grace James."

There were breaths drawn, not only James Stewart's, as Murdoch turned, picked up the golden crown from the cushion held out by the Marischal, and raising it high, with a flourish, paced round to stand before his cousin. For long moments he held it so, in a prideful stance, as the two men's eyes locked, before, carefully not bowing, he placed it on the royal head with something of a jerk. Then he stood back, and bowed, not to the king but to the great company, and moved to his former position on the left, with not a word said.

It had been a notable display.

James had sat through it set-faced, and remained so. Not for him, at this juncture, to raise voice.

Lyon did so, and loudly, forcefully. "God save the King!" he cried. "God save the King!"

All on and around and facing the Moot Hill took up the cry. "God save the King! God save the King! God save the King!" On and on it went, in a paean of praise, rejoicing and celebration. Scotland had a crowned monarch again, after eighteen years.

When the acclaim died away, Lyon announced the next stage. It was an important one also, as demonstrating the principle that the land was now the monarch's, all the land, whoever owned it having to acknowledge that they held it of the crown. This was to be demonstrated by each owner vowing fealty to the king on his own ground. But to save the monarch having to travel round every mile of his dominions to receive the oaths, an alternative had been devised, the simple symbol of every landholder bringing a pouchful of soil from his terrain to be spread on the ground in front of the throne at coronations, so that both king and lord could place a foot upon it before offering fealty. The legend was that, as reign succeeded reign, the Moot Hill in consequence had grown ever higher, although this was probably purely allegorical. Nevertheless a fair amount of earth did accumulate on each occasion, for there were a great many lords and lairds to perform their duty. So a very large attendance was demanded at the ceremony.

So the long process of oath-giving commenced. And, to be sure, since precedence and seniority was strictly adhered to, the first to do so on this occasion was Scotland's only duke, Murdoch, James having to accept this, along with so much else.

That man, with his customary self-esteem, came smiling, to fling down his couple of handfuls of soil at James's feet, and making an all but scornful show of it. Arms out, then, he bent on one knee, to reach for his cousin's hand to clasp between his own two palms, to declare the oath.

"I, Murdoch, my lord King, your governor and regent, first subject, cousin and *heir*, do offer you my loyal duty, as required." That word heir was emphasised, however inappropriate on such an occasion; but of course it was a fact, until the king himself produced a child, Murdoch being nearest in line to the throne of all the many Stewart cousins.

James withdrew his hand swiftly, glared, but did not speak, as the other rose and resumed his place beside the throne, casting a glance at the queen sitting close by and observing all keenly.

Then the other royal Stewarts, starting with the Earl of Atholl, climbed up to make their fealty, only Earl John of Buchan absent, in France, James looking with interest but no great favour on each of them. Most of these, although close relatives, he had never met. None of them made any great show of their oath-taking.

The royal kin's duty over, the other earls followed on. There had been some question as to precedence here, for Archibald Douglas was undoubtedly the most powerful noble in the kingdom, Donald of the Isles absenting himself as usual; but Dunbar and March was much the older earldom, especially if the original earldom of Northumbria was taken into account; and moreover, the Cospatricks were of the original Celtic royal line, which none others could boast. So Douglas insisted that George went up first – the first also to receive a smile from the tense monarch.

The long succession of earls, lords, barons, knight and lairds followed, a process which, however brief each contribution, took well over an hour, with a certain amount of dispute among those waiting as to rank and seniority, the monarch having to be patient indeed. Bishop Henry led Queen Joan off to the abbey, and some of those around the throne chatted among themselves. Murdoch of Albany strode off from the hill casually.

But at length it was over, and thankfully James rose. Lyon was signing to his trumpeter when the king spoke to him, telling him that he was to call a special sitting of parliament, while all the important folk were here, this at Perth in five days' time. Only the monarch himself could have so ordered, for normally forty days' notice was required for such an assembly. But this was a very special occasion, and the command had to be accepted.

The royal procession formed up at the hill-foot and return was made, first to the abbey, for hospitality, and then to the Blackfriars at Perth.

There was no sign of Murdoch now.

Five days allowed George to return to Dunbar, with Beatrix and Pate, in a twelve-hour sail, and so to spend a little time there looking after affairs, before getting back in time for the parliament.

27

That first and hastily called parliament of the new reign was very significant, especially in that, although it was in theory presided over by the Chancellor, Bishop Lauder of Glasgow, in fact James himself more or less conducted it all, so that it was very much the King in Parliament, as was the official name for the Scots legislative assembly. If the king was not present on any such occasion, it was not called a parliament, only a convention, and could not pass certain acts.

James was obviously determined to make it clear to all that he intended to put right all the misrule and wrong-doing of the long period of the Albanys, father and son, and to restore good government to Scotland. After all, he had had plenty of time to consider it in his captivity; and moreover had seen and taken note of the good and the less good of English rule to guide him. So this occasion was very much his, to be his means of letting the nation know his intentions and determination. Most of the speaking, therefore, emanated from the throne.

He started by declaring that there had been long years of grievous mismanagement, which must be rectified. But he did not actually mention the names of his uncle and cousin. None there doubted, however, that he was not absolving them.

His first detailed announcement was to say that he was going to revive the appointment of Lords of the Articles. This was a system of a specially appointed committee of selected authoritative individuals to carry out the decisions of parliaments on various aspects of rule. This had been abandoned by the two governors, who had preferred to order their own supporters to carry out their wishes; indeed parliaments themselves had been few and far between.

Then he emphasised that Holy Church was to take a much greater part in affairs of state than in the recent past, the Primate, bishops and mitred abbots to act with as much authority as earls, lords and barons, these often better representing the needs and wills of the common folk, his subjects.

Next, there was to be a proclamation issued against the prevailing feuding and private warfare that went on between much of the nobility – let all these take note. This behaviour had been tolerated for too long, not only among Highland clans. It must stop.

Needless to say, all rebellion against the crown was to cease, and anything such to be treated as treason and punished accordingly, this by the forfeiture of lands and goods, and, where advisable, execution.

The countryside, he had learned, had long been troubled by gangs of armed robbers and ruffians, who stole and ravaged. All lords in their own territories were to be held responsible to see that this ceased, and to commit such trespassers to the local sheriff or Justiciar for punishment.

Then there was the matter of customs and duties on imports from foreign lands, payable to officers at ports and havens. These had been appropriated frequently by lords, taken from the due collectors, to the loss of the realm's treasury, which was presently all but empty, he had discovered. Special officials were to be appointed to see that this was rectified.

Payments of the royal ransom moneys to England had fallen into arrears already, fifty thousand merks being presently due; and to raise these extra funds new taxes, however unpopular, had to be imposed, charges made on all lands and goods, cattle and sheep stocks, whether held by lords, lairds, tenants or farmers, the Church, burgesses and trade guilds. It was a charge on the nation, and all must contribute, however little liked. The royal lands them-selves would be the first to be so taxed.

Fishings were not to be exempt. Hitherto fishermen had paid no contribution to the realm's funding. In England and France it was otherwise. There must be some revenue gained from the labours of fisherfolk, as from others. The Lords of the Articles were to see to this.

Finally, Scotland had no standing army, as had other nations. The providing of something such was to be con-sidered and instituted, so that the realm was not dependent on the forces of its lords, all of whom might or might not be helpful. The other monarchs of Christendom could carry out their policies, and those of their parliaments, without having to plead with their nobles for assistance. Scotland must have the same. That, if it was to retain its independence and play its part under treaties and alliances. This would take some time to achieve, it was admitted, to muster and train. But meanwhile he, the king, was issuing a directive that weapon training must be made a general exercise, in particular the use of the longbow. This had never been much used in this realm, yet it was the most effective of weaponry in war. The Welsh were expert in the making and use of long yew bows. These were infinitely better than crossbows, with three times the range at least, crossbows fair for sport but less useful for war. This matter he would personally see to, having practised much longbow shooting in England. And in time all male subjects, from the age of twelve on, would have to make themselves proficient in the use of these weapons.

With that, King James handed over the conduct of the remaining routine business to the Chancellor, while the earls, lords, chiefs, commissioners of the shires and pro-vosts of the royal burghs all but reeled under the impact of it all, George not the least of them — for much thus announced would affect himself and his earldom greatly, with the sheep stocks, wool trade, imports of cloth and the fishing, in particular. And he found himself appointed as one of the Lords of the Articles.

269

They had a monarch again indeed, and one who knew his own mind and would see that his orders were carried out. Scotland was going to undergo changes indeed, it seemed.

The king, with many of his supporting lords and prelates, went back thereafter to Edinburgh, on horseback; but of course George and Pate had their ship on the Tay awaiting them, and would be home the sooner. They would have much to tell Beatrix. How much was the new reign going to cost them, in time as well as siller?

One point struck them as strange: the monarch had made no public mention of Albany. And that man had not been present at the parliament.

It was not news of Murdoch, however, wherever he was, that reached them at Dunbar shortly thereafter, but that man's brother, John of Buchan. He was dead, in France. And not only he, but Archibald Douglas's son and heir, the new Earl of Wigtown. There had been a great battle at Verneuil, against the English, in aid of King Charles, and this time Buchan had not won, although he was now Constable of France. Apparently the French wing of his army, under the Viscount of Narbonne, had failed the cause by attacking too soon, and alerting the English to the Constable's flanking assault, as it were springing the trap. There had been great slaughter, and many Scots had fallen with their leader, including Sir John Swinton of that Ilk, one of George's senior vassals, and one of the Home brothers. The realm had lost its foremost soldier.

George, much concerned over his own losses, had opportunity to condole with Douglas over the death of his eldest son quite shortly afterwards, for a meeting of the Lords of the Articles was called at Holyrood Abbey at which they both had to appear. There it was James himself who more or less instructed them all on their duties. There was no doubt who was King of Scots these days, unlike during the reigns of the two previous monarchs, Roberts Second and Third.

This Articles arrangement was in order that the various items decided on by parliaments should be fully considered and carried out effectively, such as taxation, the armed forces, law enforcement, the ransom-money collection, the fisheries valuation and so on, this by these commissioners, who would have to report to further parliaments on progress, a very practical system. Each of the chosen lords would preside over one or other subject of discussion and decision, and George's was that of taxation – which would scarcely make him more popular. Douglas, as was suitable, was to head the armed forces question, Hay the Constable the law, and so on.

All these items were considered in general there and then, and guidance given by the king on each. George promised carefully to look into this of taxation and its possibilities for advancement, well aware that his own position in this vital matter would be anything but enhanced. He would report at the next meeting of the Articlers.

It was after this session was over that James took George and Douglas aside, to speak with them privily.

"You two, my friends, cause me great embarrassment, I fear," he said, shaking his head. "To my sorrow. For I owe much to you both, and rely on you for the hereafter. Yet I must seem to show disfavour towards you. Forgive me, I pray. It is this of Verneuil, that sorry battle where my cousin John died. And your son, my lord of Douglas. You see, that warfare and battle, with the Scots involved, was in fact a breach of the treaty with England. My cousin was fighting for the *French* side against the English. And I, and Scotland, agreed to aid and support the King of England, and he ourselves. John of Buchan therefore was, and has been for long, fighting contrary to the terms of our treaty. You see it? And your son, my lord Archibald, and some of your people, my lord George, were fighting alongside my cousin, and died, the Earl of Wigtown and Sir John Swinton, and a Home laird, in especial. This is . . . unfortunate. In more than their deaths." He paused.

271

His two hearers wondered, eyeing him.

"This of the battle is known by all now," the king went on. "And as signatory to the Treaty of London, I have to do something in the matter. It could be claimed that you both are, in some degree, guilty of an offence, a kind of treason indeed, in that a son and a prominent supporter of yours were fighting against the English, and this had to be known to you. Do you see it?"

"Treason, Sire!" George exclaimed. "Treason! Because vassals of mine were fighting alongside Buchan? I scarcely knew of this. Many other such would be doing likewise. Are they all to be named traitors?"

"It was considered, Your Grace, that to fight for John of Buchan was to win spurs indeed," Douglas added. "He the greatest commander Scotland has produced for long. A sign of martial prowess to aid him, Scotland's warrior. All but a crusade. The English had invaded France, our partner in the Auld Alliance . . ."

"I know, I know it," James admitted. "But despite all that, it had become in breach of our peace treaty with Henry. And so, in effect, treasonable. And those who disfavour my cause know it. I have already been so informed. They will use anything against me that they can, close kin as they may be. They will be demanding some action from me."

Wagging their heads, his two earls looked unhappy – as indeed did James.

"So, I fear that I must make some move. Some token, that I will not allow breaches of our treaty to go unpunished. I have no option. I have thought on this, thought much. And what I propose is that I put you under arrest, in name. Both of you, my friends, however ill this seems to you, who have so greatly helped me. Arrest, as I say, in name only. Not in fact. You are free to do as you will, go where you wish – save out of this realm. But thought to be suffering royal displeasure over this matter. Do you understand? A king has to act for the nation, be seen to do so. Your son and your friend were acting against the terms of our treaty. A term of arrest, then, in some measure, you must seem to pay. Until I can declare it sufficient, and cancel it. Arrest in name only. How say you?"

George spread his hands. "This is . . . a wonder! Under arrest! For a form of treason! To you, Sire! Whom we both so honour and support. But, but if . . ."

"Even if it is only in name, Highness, and does not restrain us in any way, as you say, it must impair our names and repute," Douglas asserted.

"None so greatly, I judge, my good friends. It is only a gesture. I will soon release you from this of arrest. And show my regard for you, otherwise. I have already made you Lords of the Articles. This all will do you little hurt. But it will be seen as myself being fair, impartial in my rule. And not only to my enemies but to Henry of England, which is important. I must still critical tongues."

George bowed. "As you wish and command, Your Grace."

"It is not as I *will*, man! It is as I must! Can you not see it?"

"How do we act in it all, Sire?" Douglas asked.

"As you always do. As though there were nothing different. Act my friends. As you are. And I will lift the arrest as soon as I may. And pray for your understanding." James held out a royal hand to grasp each of those palms which had so recently made fealty to him. "Now, enough of this, my arrested friends. Let us go and drink to our friendship, good as it is. And eat. And ease my mind, as well as yours."

What more was to be said?

After the three of them dined, alone, George went home to tell Beatrix of this most extraordinary situation, a man bemused; that and to work at his sorry task of devising improved and increased taxation, which would cost him dear as well as others. What a man must put up with to be a loyal subject of a determined monarch!

28

Whoever it was intended to impress, this of nominal arrest did not in fact affect George's life to any degree. Indeed he more or less forgot about it, with nobody mentioning it to him, if it was generally known at all. And he was very busy, not only with the earldom's affairs but with this of taxation and duties. Why he had been chosen for the task was evident. His harbours of Dunbar and Eyemouth were among the busiest on the east coast because of the wool trade with the continent and the bringing in of cloth and woven goods, also the wines and tiles and other products that the wool-ships brought back in exchange. And these and many other havens were the bases of fisherfolk innumerable, his sheep stock in the Lammermuirs uncountable, cattle in the Merse lands a large source of income. All this was now to be taxed.

He consulted with his vassals and tenants, his shepherds and fishermen, and found all reasonably helpful – so long as the taxes were fairly modest. The earls had long had an understanding with the Dunbar fishers, who gave about a tithe of the fish caught as duty to their lords, and for the upkeep of the harbour walls against the storms, and their storehouses and ice-houses and other necessary facilities. Now George proposed that his half of this tenth should be allotted to the treasury, and a further twentieth of the catch's worth be given by the fishermen themselves, he explaining the need, especially over the king's ransom payments, this accepted without any great protests. Customs and dues were already paid at the ports, and these had to be upped, but not greatly. The sheep and cattle stocks had to be counted, roughly, and some calculation made as to value and contribution. The worth of the land itself, and its distribution as between lord and vassals, was the most troublesome of all, a headache indeed; but it had to be done. It all proved a very useful guidance for George to put before the Articlers, as advisable for the nation at large.

Pate helped in all this, and between them they managed to soothe the fears of most of their folk, lairds, tenants and fishers. But it all took a considerable time.

When he had completed the task as best he could, George sent his son to Edinburgh to enquire of the monarch when the next meeting of the Lords of the Articles was to take place. He was brought back the information that his own was actually the first to be ready, and that the others would be told to hasten up. Word would be sent when a date could be settled.

Meantime James indicated his appreciation of George's services, arrest or none, by appointing him Chief Warden of the Marches, an added responsibility that he could have done without, however suitable for an earl whose lands stretched along the East and Middle Marches.

George had family matters on his mind the while, also. Beatrix's aged father, Sir William Hay of Yester, was failing and was not expected to live much longer. And his son John was one of the hostages in England. The old man was desperate to see his heir before he departed this life, to pass on his instructions and desires for the family and the line, with responsibilities involved. His daughter was very worried for him, and besought George to try to gain an exchange for the hostage. She had two other brothers, David and Edmund, and both were prepared to change places with John, for their father's sake. Could this be arranged? George promised to speak to the king on the matter. He was uncertain as to how this hostage matter was decided, and had been settled. He thought that perhaps it was only heirs to titles and baronies who had been considered important enough for the role. She had pointed out that Patrick Dunbar had not been an heir; but he said that being an earl's son perhaps had sufficed.

275

So, instead of waiting for the next meeting of Articlers, he rode to Edinburgh to see the monarch.

James proved to be sympathetic. He pointed out that it had been Gloucester himself who had nominated the various hostages, just how and why was uncertain, it being strange that he had the necessary information to be able to choose names in the first place. Somebody must have been working for him in Scotland. Murdoch, perhaps? At any rate, he, James, would do what he could in the matter, send a letter to Gloucester urging this Hay exchange. Also informing him of the so-called arresting, if he did not know of it already, indicating that the treaty terms were being heedfully observed. This was the best that he could do.

He listened to George's account of the taxation issue, with approval, and said that the other Articlers ought to be ready with their findings in a week or ten days, for the meeting. He also informed that Queen Joan was expecting to give birth in about four months' time, when, God willing, he would have an heir to the throne, displacing the deplorable Murdoch. Then, they would see what could be done about that disgrace to the name of Stewart, he no longer able to claim heirship.

So that was why the king had delayed taking action against his cousin: this of heirship to the crown, which he presumably judged carried some immunity from assault. Murdoch, wherever he was, would be wise to watch his step.

The king had more than this to say to George. He was concerned about having a suitable home for the pregnant queen and for himself since he was going to start a family. Holyrood Abbey was a comfortable enough lodging, much better than the castle of Edinburgh, but it could not be any permanent dwelling-place. And the other royal houses, Stirling, Dumbarton, Rothesay and Edinburgh itself, were all strongholds, well enough for defence but making only grim homes for a family. Roxburgh, however, was different, down near the border. It had been the favoured house of many of his predecessors. David the First, William the Lion, Alexander the Second had been born there. But the English had taken it long since, so near their border, and despite treaties of peace it was still in English hands. He had asked Gloucester to deliver it up, but had been told that this was a matter for Bedford, the commander of the young Henry's forces, not himself, and nothing had been done about it. It was a fine place, by all accounts, strong but pleasingly situated in excellent country, no rock-top citadel. And it was on the edge of the Merse, was it not, George's earldom. Had not his brother, Sir Gavin, sought to take it some years before? Now, could Roxburgh be regained, and form a pleasing home for his queen?

That was why he had been made Chief Warden of the Marches, George now realised, Roxburgh very much in his Middle March. He was to prospect the situation there, and advise how best to bring the place back into the royal possession.

But first there was the meeting of the Lords of the Articles. This proved to be quite satisfactory for James, George's taxation suggestions already given to him. Douglas proposed that each senior landholder should commit himself to provide a certain number of armed and horsed men to the royal command, whatever his attitude towards the cause, and whether or not he was supporting it with his fuller strength, this obligatory. A survey of all who had taken the oath of fealty at the coronation should be made, in the name of the Articlers, and a specified figure for this decided upon, the extent of lands, the population thereof and availability noted. Douglas himself would commit himself to one thousand. These detachments should be required to meet at least once each year, with others, at convenient assembly places, to practise acting together as parts of a unified army, under chosen commanders, not necessarily their own lords, and give proof of their training and effectiveness in various warlike arts, not only this of required longbow use but all other weaponry, and the best formations for attack and defence in the field, horsed and afoot. These companies would provide the backbone and kernel of any nationally summoned host.

This was acclaimed by all to be an excellent plan.

The Earl of Crawford, who was himself Justiciar south of Forth, had co-operated with Hay of Errol, the High Constable, over the better enforcement of the law. The present Justiciarships were over-large, and at least four new ones should be instituted to promote better and fairer justice. These should oversee the sheriffdoms of their areas, and improve the standards of ability and training of such local judges, curtailing the present all too prevalent custom of lords appointing younger sons and family retainers to these positions, often with no qualifications therefore. The same to apply in the cities and royal burghs. Recognised and consistent punishments should be ordered for a range of crimes, not just the usual hangings, scourgings and imprisonment, with fines for lesser offences, these to be paid in cattle and sheep as well as moneys, and the revenues thus produced used to assist necessary expenditure.

Approval was expressed by the monarch again, and by the others.

Keith of Dunnottar, the Knight Marischal, had been given the problem of local feuding, fighting and land-grabbing, and he had kept in touch with the Constable and Douglas over this, since armed forces would be apt to be necessary to deal effectively with it; also Justiciars to be involved, an offender to account to them, however lofty of rank. But new laws against such major breaches of the peace should be promulgated by parliament, and earldoms and senior lordships made responsible for the carrying out of such, failure to do so being punishable, with the said magnates arraigned before the next parliament for censure and fining.

The Chancellor, Bishop Lauder of Glasgow, the only churchman among the Articlers, had, in consultation with the Primate and other senior clerics, drawn up a list of how the Church could further help in the better governance of the realm. The extension and increase in the number of parishes was to be advanced, new priests therefore forthcoming from the new University of St Andrews; this ought to aid in not only the spread of Christ's message of love throughout the land, but the greater respect for law and order, and therefore assist in worthy rule. All abbeys, priories and monasteries were to widen their activities in their localities, especially in matters of industry, crafts and trade, become less enclosed communities, working with the parish priests. Holy Church had all but a monopoly in certain trades and commodities, such as bee-keeping for the provision of candles and oils, the making of mead and honey wine; the evaporation of salt water to make salt for preserving meat and fish for export; the greater use of manure and sea-weeds for improvement of fertility on the land, this also aided by drainage; and the extraction of outcropping coal seams for fuel. All these activities, extended through the parishes, should assist in bringing prosperity to the people and so aiding in government.

James was very much in favour of this last, and said that he would welcome the Church's extension of its activities in the nation at large towards better living, in more respects than the spiritual. He then thanked all present for their so excellent and beneficial contributions. Their further help would be appreciated, and the next parliament to act on it all.

Before George departed, he was reminded about the Roxburgh situation.

So, soon thereafter, with Gavin, it was southwards for Kelso and the Tweed, some thirty-five miles through their own Merse country, then west another mile or so, across the bridge replacing that which Gavin himself had destroyed some fourteen years before in unavailing efforts to free the area of the English, to where Tweed was joined by the River Teviot. The river junctions formed a sort of narrow arrow-head, this providing a strong position for the royal castle. George knew it of old, of course, but had never examined the close surroundings in any detail.

At Kelso they found the situation unusual indeed. Here, nearby, was a castle occupied by the English, yet occasioning the townsfolk and monks no real trouble. Members of the invading garrison did not act as though inimical – for the two nations were at peace – and even came to purchase supplies now and then, posing no threat. Otherwise they apparently kept themselves very much to themselves, not seeking to dominate the surrounding area. Just why they continued to occupy the castle at all, nobody really knew; but it had been in English hands for years, a sort of toehold in Scotland, their own Northumbrian border within sight only a few miles away. It may well have been something to do with Percy pride, for the captain of the hold was a kinsman of the Earl of Northumberland. At any rate, no protests from the Scots authorities had been able to shift them. Indeed, so out of the way and comparatively remote was the place for those who had been ruling Scotland for long was it, that no real effort had been made to redeem it. Certainly the Albanys had never considered it to be worth going to war with England. But now King James wanted the castle back.

They did not venture too close to the castle, needless to say, but were able to perceive and recognise its strengths, weaknesses less easy to discern. The joining of the two rivers had created a wedge of rocky ridge, steep on either side and at its point, water flowing close, along the summit of which the elongated castle ran in a series of towers within high walls. No siege-machinery could reach up to there. The only approach was from the west, and there all necessary defensive measures had been taken, deep ditches excavated and outworks built, with drawbridges and gatehouses. No assailant would get near the main structures without first having to deal with these, and getting mangonels, battering-rams and sows to any effective position all but impossible.

They came to the conclusion that the only practicable

assault would have to be by boat, on the south, Teviot side, and possibly at night, with the steep bank scaled from there, using anchor-tipped rope-ladders and the like; only the garrison would be well aware of this, and had their own boats tied up there, and would not fail to be on the alert. Some distraction on the other northern and western sides, at the same time, just might be helpful. Otherwise, starving out the garrison seemed to be the only alternative; and with their own boats to go and collect provisions, by night, that would be a doubtful and slow process, they would have to tell the king.

George wondered about the village of Roxburgh itself, more than a mile away to the west. Could help be got from there? If any weaknesses at the castle were known, they would be apt to be learned there.

They rode on to the village, for it was more than any castleton, quite a community, the distance from the stronghold being accounted for by it not being considered suitable for other houses to be, as it were, on the royal doorstep. It had its own church, a couple of inns and a mill.

There they spoke with the parish priest, the miller and others. They found none of these at all hostile towards the Englishmen, even less so than the Kelso folk. The castle occupiers apparently caused them no trouble, some of them quite friendly indeed, especially towards the village women, and even apt to spend the night on occasion. None there professed to know of any weaknesses in the hold's defences, no suggestions as to assault forthcoming.

So, nowise encouraged by their inspection, the visitors returned to Kelso, and spend the night at the abbey and back to Dunbar next day. It was to be feared that King James would not be enheartened by George's report. It seemed that he should look for a house for his queen elsewhere. Surely there must be a sufficiency of alternatives?

29

George duly reported on the findings regarding Roxburgh to the king, who received them with disappointment, but declared that he was still determined to try to win back the castle. As to other royal houses than the mighty strongholds unsuitable for a queen about to become a mother, the wretched Murdoch and his brood were occupying Falkland in Fife, Doune in Perthshire. Rothesay on its island was remote and inaccessible. It was nearing Yuletide and no time for military action, but in the spring he would make the attempt. By then the queen should have been delivered of a child and heir for him, and he would feel free to deal with Murdoch.

So George found himself given a breathing-space, over this venture at least, and was able to spend Christmas and the festive season at Dunbar, thankfully. But 1425 would be a significant year for himself, as well as Scotland in general, he recognised.

He received notice, as did all concerned, that the second parliament of the reign would be held on 12th March at Perth, when much would be decided. But until then he had a blessed period of peace and normal living. Why had *he* been born the eldest of his father's sons? Any of the others, Patrick in especial, would have made a good, effective and spirited earl. Although Pate might do none so badly when it became *his* turn.

But the time did come for George to make for that so important parliament at Perth, and he took Pate and Gavin with him, the latter to advise the king regarding Roxburgh if that matter came to be discussed. St John's Town proved to be tight-packed for the occasion, and there was just no room for the Dunbar trio in the town, so they had to lodge in their ship in the Tay. The large numbers attending the assembly would have been anticipated; but they were swelled apparently by Duke Murdoch having rallied all possible supporters to be present, recognising that this meeting might well be a highly critical one for himself. Queen Joan had given birth to a daughter, Margaret, only a week or so before.

George and Gavin presented themselves at the Blackfriars monastery the evening before the parliament met, and found James much exhilarated over becoming a father and, if somewhat disappointed that he did not yet have a son, did not show it. At least he had an heiress and she could succeed, so now Murdoch was no longer heir-presumptive, and could be dealt with as he deserved – this, no doubt, why that man had come, as it were, in force.

The king questioned Gavin closely on Roxburgh, and said that in a month or so, all being well, he would see what could be done about it.

At the parliament opening next day, the hall was more crowded than George had ever seen it. James, making a striding entrance, greeted all, and asked the Primate to pray for God's guidance on their deliberations, for much of importance would be dealt with. Their business would undoubtedly take them a number of days to consider and decide upon. Then he handed over to the Chancellor, unlike the previous occasion, and sat. All others could therefore do the like.

Bishop Lauder said that they had first to deal with the proposals and decisions of the parliament of nine months before. These had been considered fully and worked upon by the appointed Lords of the Articles. He would now ask these to present their findings. He himself had been given the matter of the Church's better contribution to the realm's weal to advise upon. This he would now offer them all.

That took a considerable time, and not all there were greatly interested, so that more than once the Chancellor

283

had to bang his gavel for quiet. There were cheers however when he announced that Holy Church would give a greater contribution to the national treasury than heretofore, under the new taxation proposals.

Then it was George's turn to stand, and speak on taxation, which *did* concern all present to be sure, and won him little indeed in the way of applause. He kept it all as brief as possible, but had to raise his voice frequently against the murmurings and objections, the Chancellor with his gavel coming to his aid. He did end by pointing out, ruefully, that he himself would be one of the largest sufferers in this respect, which at least produced some ribald cheers.

Douglas came next with the armed forces subject, and he was better received, although there was considerable debate as to numbers demanded from different lords for this of permanent contributions of armed men to form the nucleus of a national army. Lengthy discussion on this ended the first day's debating.

The second day, the Knight Marischal led off on the subject of feuding and private wars, and received little more acclaim than had George on taxation. But it was agreed that something had to be done about it, and none could suggest better than proposed.

Crawford and the High Constable dealt with the law, crime and punishment. This was not well received either, although the establishment of fines for certain offences, instead of the customary hangings and scourgings, did commend itself to not a few, who probably saw some of the fining moneys adhering to sticky fingers on occasion.

So it went on, the king sitting through it all looking grim-faced most of the time. Ensuring the reform of rule and governance was not easy.

Attendances on the various days varied, and no doubt much debating went on in lodgings and taverns of an evening.

There was also much routine business for parliament to attend to, other than this of the Articles and improvement

284

of rule; and the sixth day was a Sunday when there was no sitting. So it was not until the eighth day that they came to what George, and so many others, had been waiting for, the matter of past misgovernment and crimes committed in the names of the absent monarch. And now it was for James himself to take over.

He did it in no gentle nor hesitant fashion. He said that for eighteen years there had been shameful mismanagement of the realm while he was a child and a prisoner in England, abuse of power, corruption, murder — his own elder brother among the victims — oppression of the people, failure to enforce the laws, and other evils. That was all now to cease. But what of the perpetrators of this wicked state of affairs? Sadly, members of his own family of Stewart had grievously failed the nation. His uncle, Robert, Duke of Albany, had now gone to face a higher court than Scotland's; but his son Murdoch, until the birth of the Princess Margaret his heir to the throne, had disgraced the Stewart name likewise, members of his family with him, and these supported by some who should have known better, such as Walter Stewart, Earl of Atholl, his uncle, and others. He, Duke Murdoch, and these, would now have to account for their sins and failures, as was right and just . . .

At this stage, Murdoch rose from the front of the earls' benches and strode from the hall, followed by the elderly Walter of Atholl.

James, set-faced, declared, "None may leave a parliament while the monarch is still present. This is the King in Parliament. Those who have just done so will be arrested." He turned to the Lyon King of Arms. "See to it, my Lord Lyon." Evenly, he went on. "All offenders in my realm will answer for their deeds. But must be given a fair trial. Therefore I hereby appoint certain loyal and able subjects of high degree to form a jury, and to judge these high-born prisoners. And who better than these who have already proved themselves as the Lords of the Articles? These I, James, appoint to try Duke Murdoch and his sons Walter

285

of Fife, Alexander and James; also Duncan, Earl of Lennox, goodsire of the said Murdoch. This trial to be held at Stirling as soon as possible. As well as the said Lords of the Articles, I shall appoint others to the jury. This by my royal decree."

James had waited nine months for this. Now there was to be no more delay. And he made it clear that, if the accused were found guilty, the death penalty was to be imposed.

So George found himself one of the judges of Murdoch and his kin; and however much he deplored their sins, he would not enjoy condemning the sinners to death.

It took twelve days for this momentous and unparalleled trial to be held, to allow for all necessary details and proofs to be assembled. Meanwhile the prisoners were sent to be held in various safe places, not together, to ensure safety from possible rescuers: Murdoch at Caerlaverock Castle in Dumfries-shire, Walter in the Primate's castle of St Andrews in Fife, Alexander to the Bass Rock in the Forth estuary, their brother James managing to escape to the Highlands oddly enough. George had Lennox sent to his own castle of Dunbar. And there was an interesting development. The uncle of both James and Murdoch, Walter, Earl of Atholl, who had been one of the principal sinners, apparently suddenly changed his stance to pronounced loyalty to the throne, and was prepared to give evidence against Murdoch, and so was to be pardoned to assist in the prosecution, this raising eyebrows.

The trial, however dramatic, was in fact very brief. Other jurors, to make a total of twenty-one, had been added, and the king, although not presiding, was present. No great number of witnesses was required, for all the nation knew well of the offences committed; but Walter of Atholl did earn his remittance by giving evidence against the accused. The defence was merely formal, an overall denial of wrongdoing and any misdoing, in the cause of government and national security. Murdoch and his two sons Walter and Alexander, together with Duncan of

Lennox, were found guilty, also the missing son James, and were condemned to be beheaded next day at the Heading Hill of Stirling.

James had won his grim battle.

George did not attend that dire event, although Gavin did.

The return to Dunbar thereafter was made thankfully, this sorry affair over at last. Before they left, James said that the Roxburgh assault would go ahead shortly. He, the king, would accompany the attackers, but it was to be done in the name of the Chief Warden of the Marches, and by men of the March earldom, not the new royal armed force, this to ensure that it could not be claimed by the English to be a royal contravention of the Treaty of London. So George would supply the manpower.

James was not a Stewart for nothing.

30

In fact it was some time before the king, with so many other matters of rule to see to that summer, arrived at Dunbar for the descent upon Roxburgh, September indeed. He announced that the decapitated offenders had been buried at the Blackfriars church in Stirling. Also that he had appointed the turncoat Walter, Earl of Atholl, to be High Justiciar, this in the hope of keeping him from further ill-doing, and of giving other such Murdoch supporters the notion of changing sides, for reward. Not that he trusted his uncle one inch.

George had long had all prepared, as far as he was able, for the Roxburgh venture, less than hopeful as he was for any success thereat. The Homes, Swintons, Kerrs, Turnbulls and other borderers had been readied for weeks to provide the necessary force – not that large numbers were of the essence, save as a demonstration, for it was not judged that reinforcements would be forthcoming from Northumberland to the aid of the castle's garrison, in view of the treaty. And the stronghold's situation was such that it could not be attacked in force; and siegery called for no great host.

So Beatrix acted hostess to their royal guest for a couple of days while the Mersemen were being mustered.

They rode to meet the gathering at Swinton, and found some three hundred assembled, all much impressed to be in the company of the King of Scots.

From there all proceeded south-west down the Leet Water, to Leetholm and Eccles, reaching Home Castle, where they spent the night. And on in the morning to Kelso, another eight miles.

Leaving the force there, so as not to arouse alarm at their target, George and Gavin took the king, with Home and the new Swinton of that Ilk, to survey discreetly the castle and its immediate surroundings.

James was not long in perceiving the problems involved in assailing this strength. As George and Gavin had reported, any siege-machinery could not be got up into position to reach the walling, while the narrow western approach was protected by ditches, drawbridges and guardhouses. The only possibility of an attack was by night, when men could climb up the steep banks, hopefully unseen, with rope-ladders and scaling devices, this having to be done also from boats on the Teviot side. And if this was not successful, then there would be nothing for it but siege.

George and Gavin went on to the village of Roxburgh to arrange for boats to be brought downriver after dark, and a watch instituted that no warning of it all was sent by possible sympathisers with the garrison, this while James and the other two went back to Kelso to prepare the company for a night assault, and to order more boats to be assembled.

Being September they had to wait until quite late before it was dark enough to proceed. They divided the company into three groups of one hundred each: one to sail up by boat from Kelso; one to go on to Roxburgh community by a round-about route to get more boats there; and the third to march by land to the northern or Tweed side of the castle, there to attempt the scaling process. One hour from midnight the venture commenced.

George and Gavin, with the king, went with the land-based party. They went on foot, for there was only a mile or so to go, once across the bridge over Tweed, and horses would be of no help, and apt to be heard. Silence, or as nearly so as was possible, was ordered. It was to be hoped that the Roxburgh village party had not aroused any notice by watchers of the garrison on their way thither.

At any rate, no beacons nor wallhead lanterns were to be

seen as they approached the castle. If the Percy keeper and his people were unsuspecting of attack, not many guards would be apt to be parading the wallhead of a night, it was judged. After all, the castle had been occupied by the English for years, and few attacks made on them. George, Gavin and the king went forward alone to prospect once more.

They saw no sign of life nor movement at the castle, midnight now. They decided that the attempt should be made forthwith. Their worry was that the boat parties did not attack too soon, and rouse the sleeping garrison. Scouts had been sent westwards and to the Tweed banks to seek to prevent this, from Roxburgh at least. The Kelso boats could not be so guided.

So the men with the scaling-ropes and ladders were moved quietly forward to the bank-foot, on this north side. The castle extended along the ridge for fully one hundred and fifty yards, so there was scope for not a few climbing ventures, fully a dozen, to be attempted. The rope-ladders and strong hempen cords each had anchor-like hooks attached to them, and these had to be flung up so that they went over the parapet, and there, hopefully, caught on the stonework behind and anchored the ladders, enabling men to climb up. Inevitably not all would so hook at the first throw, and they would be apt to clatter as they fell, and this was the hazard, for the noise could arouse the guards on duty, how many such being awake unknown. Therefore the throwing up had to be carefully timed, all together as far as was possible, so that little preliminary noise was made. Even so, some of the hooks would almost certainly not grip, however able the throwers, and the hurling would have to be repeated.

Gavin went along the line of men placing ladders and ropes, these latter knotted at one-foot intervals to allow climbers to hoist themselves up from knot to knot. Satisfied that all was in order, he would give a single shout to commence.

As about to shout, he cursed instead. All there did. For

sudden noise erupted, and not from their own waiting men but from further off, from the south side of the castle, clatter and yelling and hubbub. Attack had started on that flank. It could only be the Kelso group striking first, in error.

Angered the land party might be, but they had to act, and at once, all recognised. Without waiting for Gavin's order, the rope-throwers promptly commenced their efforts. The actual throwing was not so difficult, for the walling was only a score of feet in height, and heavy as the anchors might be it took no great strength to hurl them up and over the parapet on to the wall-walk. It was making the hooks catch firmly on the masonry thereof that was the task. This was best done by jerking and dragging the ropes this way and that in order to snag against and adhere to some projection in the stonework or the walk's flagstones. There was something of an art in this, the parapet walling itself helping, and some men were better at it than others. And the catching had to be firm if the hooks were to hold sufficiently for men's weight to be borne as they ascended. Guards up there, of course, would heave the ladders and anchors back down; but in a surprise attack like this there were unlikely to be many on duty at midnight. And any there were would be apt to be now at the other side dealing with the Kelso assault. Once the sleeping garrison was aroused, of course . . .

Four of the dozen throwers did catch their ropes at the first attempt, and quickly men went clambering up, swords and daggers drawn, while repeated casts were made on either side. The parapet and wall-walk were gained by these, and such had, as their first duty, the firm anchoring of other ladders and ropes – this if they were not to be fighting for their lives with defenders. If such was not the case they were to wait until a sufficiency of their comrades got up to join them, for individuals to set off on their own would be suicidal. The sleeping garrison would have been quickly awakened by the noise, and come to defend their premises.

Only one man at a time could, of course, climb each swaying rope, so it took minutes for any sizeable numbers to gather at the wall-walk; and by then the alarm would have aroused all in the various castle towers. Quickly indeed defenders came running along the walk, with spears and axes, yelling, while the majority of the attacking force was still down at ground level, waiting their turn to climb, and could do nothing about it.

Bodies, dead, wounded or just thrown over, came crashing down to them, enemy as well as friend, with most of the ladders being cast down also, so little or no aid could be offered to those up there fighting. It became chaos and a hopeless situation; and those of the Scots up there who were able and could find a rope came slithering down fast.

The attack at this side, therefore, had been a failure. What of the other, south, side? It was to be feared . . .

Soon there was increased shouting and jeers from above, more bodies being thrown over, and now some crossbow arrows shot down at the waiting group – not that these were apt to find targets in the darkness. This seemed to indicate that the garrison was in full command of the situation.

James Stewart shook his fair head, grievously disappointed at the collapse of this his first military venture.

There was nothing for it but to retire, and with little hope of any success elsewhere now that the defenders were fully aroused and ready, the Roxburgh group stalled from any attempt.

Siege, then. All their manpower was to be grouped round the castle, or as nearly so as the situation of it made possible, with those rivers so much hampering this. The Teviot, although the lesser stream, was actually the wider here, if shallower; and this, it was recognised, was going to be a major handicap in the investment of the stronghold, in particular keeping food supplies from reaching the garrison by boat, at night, especially with the English border so close at hand. Watch would be maintained to seek to prevent this, of course; but with miles of river upstream and down to launch boats from, it would be all but impossible to keep the odd boat-load from reaching the defenders; and quite a lot of food, meat and meal, could be stowed in even a small river-craft, to enable the English to survive, water no problem.

Well aware of all this, the three hundred were placed into the best possible enclosing positions, and so en-camped.

Siegery was, inevitably, almost as unsuccessful an experi-ence for the would-be attackers as for the defenders, it was soon recognised. Prolonged idleness soon palls on active men, and, with nothing they could do now in the way of assault, they had just to wait. Morale soon sank. One or two boat-loads of food destined for the garrison were captured, some found being carried by Roxburgh village sympathisers; but almost certainly others won through, for the defenders had their own boats moored alongside the walls on the Teviot side, and this bank could not be attacked effectively now that the castle was alerted.

King James and the other leaders could find occasional respite and comfort at Kelso Abbey when desired, but the rank and file could not. Boredom soon developed among the besiegers. After all, they were ordinary working men, farmers, shepherds, cowherds, fishermen, millers and the like, only mustered for this effort by their masters, all with their own livings to earn and families to support. Sitting idle quickly had them discontented, objecting, quarrelling among themselves. Some had to go prospecting for their own food supplies, which by no means made them ap-proved of locally; but by and large it was apathy and the desire to be elsewhere.

This applied to the leadership also, in some degree, King James in particular. After all, he had a realm to rule, and an adored wife pregnant again. With no signs of yielding from the besieged, and envoys under white flags going daily to demand submission and being scornfully rejected, the monarch began to consider returning to

Edinburgh, for a visit at least, and coming back again if possible. George and the others felt the same way.

Then word reached them of a new situation that had developed on the national front. The French had sent a delegation under the Archbishop of Rheims and the Stewart Lord of Aubigny to seek to negotiate a marriage between Louis the Dauphin and the infant Princess Margaret, in due course, this to cement the Auld Alliance, Treaty of London or none – and this was being expressly recommended by the Pope. James had to pay heed to the suggestion. It was therefore a prompt return to his capital for the monarch.

George, as Chief Warden of the Marches, was left in command of the Roxburgh situation, little as he and Gavin saw any success in it as likely. No resumed attacks were practicable in darkness, for fires were now being lit nightly on the walls; and by day approach within arrow-shot would be costly indeed. And feeding the three hundred grumbling men was becoming ever more of a problem. In their opinion, Roxburgh Castle was going to continue to be unassailable, as indeed it had been for years.

A few days after the king had left them, they decided that enough was enough. George had his earldom's affairs to attend to, as well as the monarch had his nation's. And his men were getting restive indeed. There seemed to be no profit in remaining. The order was given to pack up and go. A messenger was sent to inform James of the fact.

Beatrix and Pate would be glad to see them home.

31

There were no recriminations from the king over the retiral from Roxburgh, he well enough aware of the position. What they did hear was that, impressed by the papal authority, he had tentatively agreed to the possibility of an eventual marriage for the child Margaret with the Dauphin of France, and he was sending Bishop Leighton of Aberdeen and the Archdeacon of Lothian, the Chancellor's brother, to negotiate on the matter with Sir Patrick Ogilvy, he suggesting that a betrothal of, say, at least five years might be agreed before any sending of the princess to France. The bishop thereafter to go on to Rome to inform, and to discuss the situation regarding England with the Pontiff, for of course this aspect of it was of much concern, with the very real possibility that it would arouse claims that the Treaty of London was being breached.

This situation produced a command for George to go to Edinburgh to see the king, this to his apprehension. There he learned that he was to proceed to London once more, as envoy, to inform Gloucester that no departure from the treaty's terms was envisaged, and that peace with England was still a priority. Also that the French marital alliance in the future did not mean any sort of military assistance – this the more urgent to ensure in that Archibald of Douglas had meantime, while they were at Roxburgh, departed for France with quite a large force to aid in the Auld Alliance, this without consulting James. The monarch was much perturbed. So George was to go forthwith, and while in London to tell Gloucester that the assault on Roxburgh was not intended to be in any way an anti-English gesture, but merely seeking to regain a royal palace for his own and his English wife's use. And if possible to obtain a Percy retirement therefrom.

George, then, had to take ship again to sail for the Thames, October now upon them.

Gloucester proved to be at Windsor with young King Henry, so the extra journey was called for, by barge upriver. He did find the duke concerned about the Scottish-French situation, his brother Bedford angered by the Douglas support for the enemy, and this of a marriage proposal seeming to amplify Scotland's French leanings. George assured him that this of Douglas had been done without the royal authority, and that King James was still committed to the terms of the London treaty. He made a point of introducing the Pope's approval of the French marriage, and the papal concern for France – for England was, no less than the other nations of Christendom, under the Vatican's spiritual sway. This did have a helpful influence on the discussion, Gloucester having to concede that no English offence was to be offered to the Holy See. He declared that he was heartened by George's assurances of Scotland's adherence to the peace treaty, and that he would expect this to be demonstrated hereafter in no uncertain fashion.

On the matter of Roxburgh, however, the duke was less amenable. He had had complaints from Northumberland over the attack and siege, and did consider this an unsuitable act. Admittedly Roxburgh was over the border and into Scotland; but its castle had been in English hands for long, and its occupiers doing no harm to the area. The Percy Earls of Northumberland saw it as a means of helping to ensure a diminution of Scottish mosstrooping raiding over the border, at least in the Middle March, and as such well worth maintaining. He, Gloucester, was not going to order an evacuation of the castle, in the circumstances, for anything that deterred this long-continuing cross-border raiding was of value. He hoped that King James would see it so, likewise. The King of Scots must have numerous other palaces for his occupation?

George could not deny that, but indicated that see-mingly Queen Joan Beaufort had a preference for this one, so near her native English soil, and in pleasing country. He had to leave it at that.

It was back to London, there to await the return of his ship from the Low Countries.

The subsequent report to James was received with modified appreciation.

It was too early to learn anything of the French and papal situation. But he did hear that the king had now taken over all the properties that had been occupied by Murdoch and his sons and supporters, save those of Atholl and the Grahams. These included the old dowery-house of Linlithgow, which one of Murdoch's many mistresses had been occupying, and which had been badly damaged by fire quite recently. This, only some eighteen miles from Edinburgh, had been seen by Queen Joan on the way to a visit to Stirling, and she had been greatly taken with its site on the edge of a loch and in pleasing country, with ancient town so close by attractive also, and this conveniently near the capital. So, in place of Roxburgh she had chosen this; and rebuilding and renewal after the fire was now being put in hand. It was no strongly defensive fortified place, but now that the Albany regime was disposed of there ought to be no need for defensive monarchial residence, he judged. He, the king, was quite happy about this. It might take some time to repair fully; but one wing of it was undamaged, and the royal couple, with their child, would spend Yuletide there instead of in Holyrood Abbey.

So George was able to pass his own Christmas, and welcome in 1426, at home, and be thankful to do so.

He often thought of his brother Patrick, like all the other hostages, lingering in England; but Gloucester had assured that they were being well treated, on his orders, and paying guests rather than any sort of captives, so that was a comfort. The new taxation arrangements had ensured that the ransom payments for the monarch's release were not in arrears, so half the period of the hostageship was now over.

This was some comfort also. The Hays had found an acceptable substitute for Beatrix's brother, and Sir John was back at Yester, acting head of the family.

With spring weather improving sea travel, James now demonstrated his initiative in an unexpected measure, indeed two of such, for one was to be announced and endorsed by a parliament to be held, of all places, at Inverness, this in April. The reason for choosing this faraway location for most delegates, was the death, just before Christmas, of Donald, Lord of the Isles, this and his succession by a young son, Alexander. The island lordship, so long a thorn in the side of Scotland's monarchs, might now be brought into a better relationship with the crown; and a demonstration of power and authority at Inverness, capital of Moray and principal town of the north, was judged to be the place to emphasise it, with an assembly of all the great ones of the kingdom there, in an area long dominated by the Islesmen. Not that all the said Lowland lords and magnates welcomed this choice of venue, and having to travel that lengthy road through the mountains to get there. George, however, could go by ship, and was able to offer transport to a number of his friends and neighbours.

Actually his vessel, moored in the harbour at the mouth of the River Ness, was not without significance for the main reason for this parliament. For here James announced his new plan for the nation's advance, well-being, prestige and trade. He intended to institute a further chapter in Scotland's story, this aimed eastwards. He was going to forge links with Norway, Sweden and Denmark, kingdoms hitherto but little known to Scots save by repute, and indeed ill repute, as the lands of the former Vikings. These days were long past, but those Scandinavian realms could now make good and useful friends, and partners in trade and commerce, as well as national influence. They were, in fact, Scotland's nearest neighbours, apart from England, only some three hundred miles of the Norse Sea separating them. Shipping would be necessary, but the Norsemen themselves were expert at building ships. And Scotland was not without its own vessels – and the king glanced over at George on the earls' benches in Inverness Castle's hall.

James elaborated. These countries were rich in timber of various sorts, iron-ore, copper, the useful oil of whales, amber for use in making paints, but above all this of shipbuilding, grown from their Viking longships. And ships Scotland much needed. The Bruce had considered seeking to establish relations with these lands in his later years, but had died before anything much was done about it. Now he, his descendant, would take up the challenge.

Not all the lords present were greatly interested, nor indeed in this of commerce in general; but the churchmen present certainly were. And of course George was, with his wool and his ships. Some of his own predecessors had had dealings with Norway, although his father and he himself had not.

James declared that he would send an embassage over the sea to test out the possibilities; and he proposed that this should be led by his Chamberlain, the Lord Crichton, and the Prior of Bothwell, his Almoner. No doubt the Earl of Dunbar and March would supply a suitable vessel to take them. On their report much would depend.

A further announcement was the safe delivery to Queen Joan of a second daughter, Isobel, joy somewhat muted that it was not the long-awaited son and heir to the throne. Other business included dealing with the new Lord of the Isles, Alexander, youthful and inexperienced, and much more hopeful to bring to order than had been his warlike father. This gathering of the realm's great ones near his mainland territories ought to make its mark upon him. And if he was offered a yearly payment or pension, payable out of the taxation, as could be also proposed for the Isle of Man, which he claimed as overlord, this might well make him an amenable subject; and this of Man could commend itself to the English, near whose coasts that island lay, and which its unruly inhabitants frequently threatened.

This all was accepted.

After the parliament was adjourned, George had a word with the monarch, saying that he would be happy to provide a ship for the embassage. And could he send with it a representative of his own, possibly his brother David, to find out the possibilities for his Lammermuir wool, James agreeing.

Brief visits to Darnaway and Dingwall, both of which had been important to ancestors of his own, and then it was back to Dunbar.

32

In June the Scandinavian mission set off, brother David going with it, George judging that it would be good if new markets were found for the wool, and relieve his dependency on the Low countries buying, with each year's price given him decided by the Burgomaster of Veere, the Staple, a monopoly that could be unfavourable. An alternative could be helpful.

He was finding his duties as Chief Warden of the Marches distinctly burdensome, with so much else on his mind. Yet, with his own lands on the East and Middle Marches, it was useful to have some oversight in that troublesome area where raiding and reiving were almost an accepted way of life, and not only across the borderline. So he besought the king to replace him by someone not unconnected with the earldom, possibly Gavin. His brother had got on well with James at the Roxburgh affair, so Gavin was duly appointed, a major step up for him.

George awaited the other brother's return from Scandinavia with interest. It was seven weeks before David and the embassage won back from across the Norse Sea, he and all the others much impressed by the Norsemen – as they referred to all the folk of the three kingdoms over there – and able to encourage King James in his hopes of association, exchange and trade. They had met with a good reception, and had brought back with them a trio of representatives to discuss matters with the king, the Danish one an expert on shipbuilding, well pleased to advance dealing with the Scots, and prepared to send over shipwrights to instruct, as well as providing the best sorts of timber. George's own builders could no doubt learn profitably from such. It was the Norwegian envoy, however, who was most interested in the wool, that land being less than ideal sheep country. He was able to offer better prices than was the average from the Netherlands; and this would be a help not only in the moneys earned but in using this new trade to enhance the prices set at Veere, by the competition.

George was thankful for his liege-lord's initiative, and David's efforts.

He was less pleased, however, when, in September, he was summoned to Linlithgow to be informed that he himself had another journey to make, and not to London this time but further afield, to France. Gloucester was making admonitive and warning noises, and declaring that the peace treaty was being breached, in a much greater way than that of Roxburgh. Apparently his brother Bedford, in France, was complaining that the Earl of Douglas was causing much trouble, with his thousands of Scots soldiery aiding the French. This must stop, or there would have to be retaliatory measures taken, continuation of the treaty endangered. And since the release of the King of Scots had been gained not only by the ransom moneys but by this Treaty of London, the hostages therefor could be held for further than the four years arranged, that and possibly treated less generously.

This all was greatly worrying James, and he desired George to go to France and see to the matter. He was known to be a friend of Douglas, and so the best to undertake this task, to urge that man to return to Scotland with his force. He had gone there without the royal authority in the first place, and now was endangering the peace.

George pointed out that his friend was second Duke of Touraine as well as Earl of Douglas, and no doubt, as such, he owed a duty towards the King of France. His father, the fourth earl, married to His Grace's sister Margaret, had been given the duchy those years before by the French monarch for his great help; and indeed he and his successors had been honoured with the style of Lieutenant-General of the armed forces. So his son's support for the present regime there was not to be wondered at.

James said that he was aware of all this. But Douglas's first duty was to Scotland, not to France, he the most powerful noble of the realm. And his present activities imperilling the peace. So he and his men must return, George to employ his every effort to convince him of his duty.

Not happy about this, George could not disobey the royal command, nor deny that he was probably the obvious one to undertake the mission, and with a ship to get him to none so far from Touraine, in central France. He had to bow to the inevitable.

He was somewhat cheered, back at Dunbar, when Beatrix announced that she would wish to accompany him on this errand. She did not enjoy being always left alone on her husband's many travels. She had always wished to see France. And she got on well with Archibald Douglas, and might help to persuade him.

Leaving Pate in charge then, they embarked on the *Lammerlaw* for quite a lengthy voyage, with the prospects of not getting home for some weeks. They had to sail down the English coast all the way to La Manche, as the French called it, and then westwards along the Channel's nearly three hundred miles until they could round the great Brest peninsula to be able to turn southwards. Then down the west coast of France to enter the Bay of Biscay, one hundred and twenty more miles, eventually to reach the mouth of the River Loire estuary at St Nazaire. Tours, the capital of Touraine, was on this long river, far up into central France; but fortunately it was possible to get their ship up as far as Nantes, capital of Brittany, where Loire began to narrow in, another forty or so miles. So by Nantes they had covered not far off nine hundred miles. Here they had to hire horses. Beatrix was a better French-speaker than was George, which was a help. And she was a good horsewoman.

A day's riding through pleasant and fertile country, with picturesque villages, brought them into Touraine. Douglas might not be there, they recognised, but off fighting somewhere to the north. In which case George would have to leave his wife at Tours, where he understood Douglas had his chateau, and go in search of him, this no task for any woman. Presumably he would be able to find one of the chateau keeper's men to guide him.

They came to Tours, a handsome city on the banks of the Loire, clustered round three great buildings: the ancient abbey of St Martin, famed as where that notable missionary had guided St Ninian to bring Christianity to Scotland a thousand years before; the great cathedral dedicated to St Cratien, another early evangelist; and the palace-castle of Chateauneuf, this the ducal seat. And at this last they were thankful indeed to find Archibald Douglas in residence; and not only him but the distinctly feeble King Charles the Seventh of France, taking refuge here, a sad figure.

To say that their friend was surprised to see the couple is to put it mildly. But he welcomed them warmly, even when he heard of the reason for their visit – which did not commend itself to him. There were disadvantages in being the subject of two monarchs.

But learning of what amounted to a royal command to return home with his force, Douglas had to admit that he was a Scot and no Frenchman, accepted that he must obey, especially when Beatrix added that she and they all had missed him in Scotland, and that his great earldom was none the better for his absence.

He pointed out that making the move back was not to be accomplished speedily. His troops were scattered with three different French armies, and reaching and reassembling them would take time. He had in fact been going to set off northwards in a couple of days to join one of the companies – so it was as well that they had arrived when they did. They would have to tell King James that he would return, as commanded, as soon as was practicable, and could arrange the shipping for his men. It might take months. And winter was not far off, with seas unfavourable for travel for large numbers. So it could well be the spring before he reached Scotland.

George recognised this, and said that he would explain it to the king.

They were handsomely provided for that night at the chateau.

Next day Douglas took them to see the basilica tomb of St Martin, and heard how Ninian, a British young man, son of a Galloway chieftain, in the search for true religion went to Rome in the later fourth century, and on his way home called at this Tours where Martin was making his base to Christianise Gaul, and had become its first bishop. Learning much from this vehement saint, in 397 he reached Galloway again, and founded his chapel, known as Candida Casa, the White House, at Whithorn, a southern most extremity of that land. From there he sought to convert the Gaelic-speaking Britons, and, working northwards, preached to the southern Picts of what became Lothian, even King Loth's first wife, King Arthur's sister, becoming a Christian, and she the grandmother of Kentigern or Mungo who founded Glasgow. Sadly, this first endeavour largely lapsed, Loth also reverting to paganism, the druidical sun-worship triumphing; and it was not until a century and a half later that Columba came over from Ireland to more northerly parts, and from Iona succeeded in converting first the Irish-Scots of Dalriada and then all Pictish Alba.

From the abbey they went to the cathedral of St Gratien, a much later cleric of the early twelfth century, who compiled the innumerable texts for the teaching of canon law of Church discipline. Here was buried their Archibald's father, the fourth Earl of Douglas, killed in warfare, first Duke of Touraine. The son's guests had not realised that their friend was thus concerned over matters religious, thinking of him, also, as more of a warrior.

The following morning they took their leave of him,

with added respect, and rode off down Loire again for Nantes and their *Lammerlaw*, mission completed; although whether James Stewart would be satisfied with it remained to be seen.

They made rather better time of it on their nine-hun-dred-mile voyage home, with the winds south-westerly aiding them and less tacking required. Even so, it took them almost a week's sailing; and it was the beginning of October before George was able to get to Linlithgow to report to the king on his prolonged errand.

James was appreciative of the efforts involved, but disappointed at the delay in Douglas's return, this of months before he was likely to appear. Why could he not have come back with George, and left his lieutenants to bring on the troops? This delay of months would not please Gloucester and Bedford. Matters were not going well for the English in France, and they were anxious for swift action, and using the Scots treaty situation to aid them. George pointed out that the Douglas force was apparently divided into contingents with three French armies, and reuniting them could only be done by the earl-duke himself, and would take time; and that the shipping assembly would also do so. Could His Grace not send to Gloucester and say that the desired Scottish involvement on the French side was over, and although the return to Scotland might be somewhat delayed, the situa-tion was as requested, and in process?

James, shrugging, said that all this would scarcely be apparent to that Plantagenet duke; and since it must be explained to him, the obvious explainer was George him-self. So he should go forthwith down to London again, and make the matter clear there. It was still only October and sea travel not yet difficult. He could be there in a few days' time, and the issue effectively dealt with.

This was hardly a welcome further mandate and call on his time and responsibilities; but George did see that it was the manifest and expedient way of coping with the situa-tion. He glumly bowed his assent.

James, actually patting his shoulder, declared that he recognised that he was asking much of his good friend. But he promised that hereafter he would seek to limit his demands.

So, with the *Lammerlaw* now laden with wool for Veere, four days later the weary envoy was on his way south again, Beatrix sympathising. She did not suggest accompanying him on this occasion however.

In the event, this mission was none so difficult. He found Gloucester settled for the winter at the Tower of London, and actually more concerned over further uprisings in Wales than over the Scottish situation. He accepted George's explanation of the need for Douglas's marshalling of his divided soldiery and the consequent delay in leaving France, content that he could send word to his brother that the Scots were no longer acting against English interests there, and the treaty provisions restored.

All that four-hundred-mile extra journey for a mere half-hour's interview.

George had to spend most of a week thereafter in London town awaiting his ship's return from the Netherlands, not as a guest in the Tower, but lodging in a riverside tavern nearby among shipmasters. But he quite liked that city and its friendly folk, and found little difficulty in filling in his time. He made no demonstration of the fact that he was a Scots earl, and indeed quite enjoyed being all but anonymous. He realised well that he was a fairly simple character at heart.

Then, in due course, home to Dunbar, and then to Linlithgow to report. He hoped that his liege-lord would not forget his promise to spare him in duties on the realm's behalf for some time to come.

33

James Stewart was as good as his word, and, with Gavin acting Warden of the Marches, George was able to devote himself to the tasks that he preferred, the management of his earldoms as well-ordered, peaceful and prosperous fiefs and polities, his folk looked after and his own circumstances comfortable.

He was particularly interested in the development of the wool trade with Scandinavia and the Baltic states, and increasing his sheep stocks, not only in the Lammermuirs but all over his lands, encouraging his vassal lairds to do the same, to their own advantage. Also he learned of a new source of trade – that of salted herrings. Apparently the Baltic Sea was very lacking in salt, all but fresh water, inland as it was, and because of this its fish stocks were very moderate and different from those of the Norse Sea and the Atlantic. The herrings there were very small and thin, and salt-water herrings much favoured. So here was one more opportunity for his fishermen and the salt-pans folk. If all this was scarcely a great noble's accepted role, he was unconcerned.

It was weeks before he saw his monarch again, and then it was he who made the move, not James. For he learned that Douglas and his men had indeed returned to Scotland in May, and Douglas had been promptly summoned to Linlithgow and there accused of having endangered the peace treaty, and arrested, this time not just in name but in fact, and was now confined in Edinburgh Castle. Much distressed by this, George went and sought audience with their monarch.

James received him kindly, and listened to his pleas and

what amounted to remonstrances with patience – and he was not a notably patient man. George claimed that Douglas did not deserve imprisonment. That he had done what the king demanded, at cost to himself over the duchy of Touraine. And that he was George's friend, and that friendship had been used to help bring about the return to Scotland. Now that man was being punished, and might well consider that he had been cheated and betrayed. He besought His Grace graciously to release him.

James asserted that Douglas deserved this. He had taken a force to France without the royal authority, and must have realised that he was infringing the terms of the Treaty of London. It was not for any subject to go against the policy of the monarchy. The Auld Alliance was a tradition, not any continuing treaty or compact. And England, with whom they *were* in treaty, was at war with France. So Douglas's was a treasonable act, and must be shown to be so by some demonstration of the royal disfavour. Open arrest would not do on this occasion, for Gloucester and Bedford had to be shown that due action was being taken. Once the four years were up, the ransom fully paid and the hostages released, it would be different. But that was a year ahead still, so this imprisonment was called for. Douglas had to be held for a month or two before release.

George was not convinced, but could not actually argue with his monarch. He asked that he might be permitted to go and see his friend, and explain.

James had no objection to that; and said that he could tell Douglas that he would be free in a couple of months.

So it was up to Edinburgh Castle, where he found his friend living in no real discomfort, however frustrated.

"Here I am, confined here like some felon!" he declared. "This for having obeyed the Stewart's request, which you brought me! I should never have trusted any of that brood! And, I think, I could unseat him from his throne! I have the men – more than James could ever muster. When I get out of this hold . . . !"

"See you, Archie, that is no way to look at it," he was

309

told. "It is unfair, wrong, that you should be imprisoned, yes. But it will not be for long – James said to tell you that. Only a month or two. But he does this for his realm's weal. He has to convince the English that the terms of the peace are not being broken, not with his consent. He has to act the king in this respect, as in others. *You* are a hostage of a sort, here. All those other hostages in England depend for their release, in one more year, on the treaty being maintained. The king understands that you are Duke of Touraine, and owe some sort of allegiance to the King of France for your duchy. But your first duty, surely, is to himself, whom you swore to serve and sustain at his coronation, you the greatest lord in his kingdom. This of your detention here is but a sign, an indication, that the treaty stands, the treaty by which he was released to mount his throne. A king has to act in such fashion, on occasion."

"*You* agree that I should be cooped up here!"

"No-o-o. But open arrest, as we both were given before, would not serve, it seems. What else could James do to show the Plantagenets that he is concerned that his subjects must keep the peace with England?"

"He will find me a doubtful subject and supporter hereafter!"

"Put yourself in *his* place, man! He was a prisoner for eighteen years. And twenty-one of his prominent subjects are now hostages for him in England, including your Douglas one. And he is responsible to them, as well as the weal of the nation."

Douglas had to nod his acceptance.

A thought then occurred to George. Would the king possibly consider allowing his friend to change his place of confinement? From Edinburgh Castle to Dunbar Castle? It might not seem so ill an arrangement, even to Gloucester. That Plantagenet knew George, and had accepted him as the King of Scots' envoy. It would seem none so strange, if he got to hear of it. He put the notion to Douglas who, needless to say, was very much in favour – if it could be contrived.

310

George stayed that night in the fortress, with the governor's agreement, sharing Douglas's room. In the morning he rode back to Linlithgow, where he did not have to work hard to persuade James to allow this change of detention premises, he being assured that the captive would be as secure there as at Edinburgh, George's word given on that.

So the two friends were able to remain in each other's company, and headed for Dunbar for Beatrix to have a guest to entertain for a couple of months, captive only in name now. It all made a very pleasant interlude, Archibald Douglas admitting that, as imprisonment went, it was more than bearable.

In mid-September the royal permission came for Douglas's freedom, and he was able to depart for Threave, from which its lord had been absent for well over a year.

Soon thereafter they learned that the king was having to turn his attentions to affairs in the north. The late Donald of the Isles had had a son, Alexander, now the lord, and evidently a headstrong young man determined to reassert the Islesmen's supremacy over the West Highland mainland, and indeed further east into Easter Ross and parts of Moray – after all, his mother was Countess of Ross in her own right. Mar, the victor of Harlaw and the rest of the late Wolf of Badenoch's many descendants, had been dominating the area since; now they were calling for royal aid. James had no great fondness for these, but recognised that the Islesmen, with their great fleets of longships and huge numbers of caterans, could be the greater challenge, and decided that these northern parts must be pacified and put under control, *his* control. And he chose to do this in an unusual and notably clever way. While assembling a large force, and calling on all the northern lords and chiefs to flock to his banner, he also announced that he was going to hold a parliament in Inverness, and demanded a full turnout of all entitled to attend. This meant that practically all Scotland's magnates who were not either too

311

young or too old to travel, and all the senior churchmen, had to make the lengthy, arduous journey up through the mountains, however unwillingly, and heedful to bring their armed guards with them into these lawless and, in general opinion, barbarous parts, vastly adding to the king's mustered strength.

So George had to go likewise. But at least he did not have to march there through the hills and over the passes, for he could go comfortably by ship. One or two others availed themselves of this facility.

They arrived to find a huge assembly of men crowding out the northern capital. And Alexander of the Isles and his mother were none so far off, with their teeming host, a mere dozen miles indeed, at Dingwall, capital of Easter Ross, a dramatic situation, as all were very well aware.

James sent to summon Alexander to appear at the parliament.

The young Lord of the Isles answered, not by attending but by moving his army southwards to the head of the Beauly Firth, even nearer to Inverness, a very strategic position.

King and Islesman called on all Highland chiefs and their clansmen to rally to their standards. The tension in the air was all but feverish.

When the Mackintosh, high chief of all Clan Chattan, arrived at Inverness, to bow before the king, there were sighs of relief, even though most of the Lowland lords looked on him and his like as little more than savages, speaking an incomprehensible language and clad in tartans. But if Clan Chattan, the People of the Cat, a huge federation, backed the monarch, then many others would do likewise, or at least, not support Alexander. It made a good augury.

The parliament was held in this atmosphere of excitement and anticipation. It is to be feared that its deliberations were scarcely calm, well-reasoned and constructive; but James had his way in it all. The business was distinctly unimportant anyhow; the whole reason for this parliament being held at Inverness was to confront the Islesman. The only really vital matter arose when the king announced that Alexander of the Isles should have attended the assembly, as was his duty, and had not, however, near at hand he was. The meeting would adjourn until the morrow, and meantime word sent to the island lord, summoning him to attend. And if he still did not come, he would be outlawed, and all their strength would be moved against him in battle.

This was accepted, with acclaim.

James, shrewdly, sent Mackintosh of Mackintosh with other envoys to Beauly to command Alexander, and to emphasise that the head of powerful Clan Chattan, as well as other chieftains, was not supporting him but the crown. He was to declare that, if that lord duly appeared at the parliament next day, he would be spared the punishment he had earned by assembling armed force against the monarchy, and only some token made as a gesture against him. And if he refused to come, all the mustered might of the royal host would be hurled against him. And, just to indicate something of what this meant, a quite large company of steel-clad knights and cavalry, such as the Islesman could nowise compete with, should accompany the messengers to within sight of the other's people, but remaining this side of the neck of the Beauly Firth, to be seen as warning, telling tactics.

So parliament stood down till the day following, all wondering what that day would bring forth.

In the event, James's strategy was proved effective and successful. The Mackintosh and the others came back from Beauly that night, to say that Alexander had recognised the facts of the situation, his mother at his side. He would attend parliament on the morrow, and make his peace with the king.

George was not alone in sighing with relief that night.

The reassembled parliament had to wait for over an hour next forenoon, with nothing particular to discuss, before the Lord of the Isles arrived at Inverness Castle, and brought his mother with him. She was, of course, Countess of Ross, and he could claim that it was in her right that he was presently occupying much of Easter Ross. He was a good-looking and personable young man in his early twenties, holding himself proudly; and when the Lord Lyon King of Arms ushered him into the hall, his mother at his back, he showed no sign of being there in fear or any sort of penitence. Presented to the monarch, he bowed, but not in any way subserviently. The countess, of middle years and confident bearing, herself looked anything but diffident.

All there waited in tense silence.

James spoke levelly. "My lord Alexander, and the lady countess, I greet you this day. You attend parliament, as you have not done ere this and as you should have done, when one is called, as do others of my responsible subjects. But now you are here, and I, James, welcome you, that we may come to some agreement over the position of your island lordship in my realm, to the benefit of all. How say you?"

The younger man inclined his head but did not speak.

"Your father rose in arms against my realm," the king went on. "He paid his price. And now you have assembled a host hereabouts, far from your isles. Why?"

"The earldom of Ross is mine," the only woman in that hall announced. "We are here of right." That was short.

"You and your son, yes, lady. But not the thousands come in arms with you!"

"Some of the chiefs and clans can be . . . unruly," Alexander said. "They can require controlling."

"As do you, my lord, I judge!"

Silence.

"However, you *have* come, at my call, today. Which is well. Are you prepared to offer me your simple duty, and fealty as your liege-lord? As all others have done?"

The curt nod of a proud head.

"You are less than . . . eloquent in your fealty, my lord!"

"I speak a different tongue from you, King James!"

314

"Ah, yes, to be sure. The Erse. But I think that you understand my tongue well enough! So, heed it. My royal commands for you are these. You are hereby declared to be under open arrest. And will remain so until I say otherwise. If you disperse your forces, and order all to keep my peace while you and your lady mother remain here at Inverness, the arrest will be short, and your lordship of the Isles and this earldom of Ross will be entered into a better and worthier bond with the crown, to the weal of all. You understand?"

"Arrest!" That was all but a bark.

"*Open* arrest, yes. That is a form of custody which allows freedom of movement within certain bounds. So long as you abide by those bounds you suffer little constraint. In your case these bounds are this Inverness and your lady mother's Dingwall. If these are not held to, then *close* arrest follows. You have it? This is my royal decree. And the will of parliament." James turned to look over at the great assembly.

Loud cheering greeted that, leaving no doubt as to the monarch's support in the matter.

The countess spoke. "And am *I* under this so-called arrest?" she demanded. "I would not believe it possible!"

"Yes, you are, lady. Not that it will greatly hamper you. Have you not the freedom of your own house of Dingwall? And this of Inverness. I could well be less . . . generous." The king turned again. "My Lord Lyon, show his lordship and lady out from this parliament." He all but smiled. "Unless my lord wishes to attend it further?"

Without any bowing, Alexander swung on his heel to head for the dais door before Lyon could beckon to him, his mother following.

Much talk and comment rose from the assembly.

So that was that. A simple and effective expedient, supreme authority demonstrated.

There was in fact no further business for that parliament to consider. The Chancellor brought the proceedings to a formal close, and the monarch left the hall.

George, like many another, shook head in wonder over it all. James was proving to be a crafty and skilful as well as a strong monarch, and demonstrating that all Stewarts were not weaklings or scoundrels. This of open arrest could be a serviceable device. It had not been heard of in Scotland before James used it; presumably he had learned of it in England. It occurred to George to wonder whether he himself, or Douglas, had in fact ever been officially freed from their own arrest? He had rather forgotten that he had ever undergone this constraint.

When, later, he congratulated the king on the day's developments, and offered him a quicker and more convenient return south by ship than the long riding involved – and had this declined because it was desirable to demonstrate his presence to sundry folk on the way – he did ask about his own arrest. He was smilingly told that, by not officially cancelling it, he could be kept in order if he ever considered transgressing! James added that it had been noticeable that the Earl of Douglas had not attended this parliament. George had not failed to perceive it.

Part Four

34

So passed 1427, and into 1428, without further calls for royal service from the Earl of Dunbar and March, for which George was thankful. He liked and admired James, but was by no means eager to act courtier, emissary or armed champion. And was now in his fifty-eighth year, not feeling in any way aged but more content than ever to confine his activities to the demands of his earldoms, which were many, although Pate was able to act for him ever more considerably.

He had been thinking for some time that it might well be worth his while to visit Scandinavia himself and, more importantly, the Baltic states and the Hanseatic League base at Lübeck. From what he had heard, the trade opportunities there were great, and hitherto untapped as far as Scotland was concerned. Who knew what advantages might accrue for his folk, himself and for the realm in general, from some enquiries and contacts there, if the Hansa confederation was as wealthy, influential and powerful as reported. Sending one or more of his ship-masters there to enquire was a possibility; but to go himself, one of the major lords of Scotland, might gain more than mere information, establish profitable links with what amounted to almost a new world, and a prosperous one. It might well seem merchanting to most of his fellow-nobles, but that did not worry him overmuch. Perhaps he *was* a merchant at heart? When he spoke of it to Beatrix she was prompt in declaring in favour – but only if she was to accompany him again. She had much enjoyed the visit to Touraine. This would be still more intriguing.

The more stimulated by her enthusiasm and having her good company in the enterprise, he decided to tell the king of it and its possibilities, for Scotland as well as for Dunbar and March.

With May upon them and the voyaging season started, in fact he did not have to go to Linlithgow, for word of another parliament had come, at Perth. James was very much in favour of parliaments clearly, and there had never been so many held in any previous reign, he seemingly finding them beneficial for his rule and the nation's well-being. And as still one of the Lords of the Articles, George had to appear.

He was able to speak to the king before the assembly began, and found James interested and in favour of this of the Hansa investigation. And the information that George was intending to go himself to the Baltic brought forth a project of the monarch's own. He had long resented this of paying tribute to the Kings of Norway, he said, and when George confessed that he had not known of anything such, had it explained to him that back in the reign of Alexander the Third, before the Wars of Independence, the Hebrides, hitherto dominated by the Norsemen, had been handed over to the Scots crown, but in payment of a sum of one hundred merks annually, in perpetuity. This was still being paid, through the churchmen, and he, James, saw it as unsuitable and undignified, as from one monarch to another. Now he was considering how to end it in acceptable fashion. If George, going over to Scandinavia, was able to negotiate some arrangement . . . ?

George thought it highly possible. It was known, he said, that the present king of all three nations, Norway, Sweden and Denmark, Erik, was permanently in debt to the Hansa merchants, an extravagant man. As indeed were many other rulers, part of the reason for the league's power. And if a fairly substantial sum was offered to him, in lieu of further annual payments, the chances were that he would be only too glad to agree.

Encouraged by this, James said that if he offered, say,

two thousand merks, from the new taxation, twenty years' payment, would King Erik be likely to accept? George thought that less would serve, perhaps fifteen hundred? Erik would possibly look on it as a godsend!

The king said that he would put it to the parliament.

He did so, and there being no opposition voiced, George found himself being entrusted with this sizeable sum of money to take to Norway, with power to negotiate, on his way to the Baltic.

The main business of this parliament was dealing with the Isles lordship and the Ross earldom, together with a closer relationship with the Highland chiefs, especially those, like the Mackintosh, who had chosen to support the crown at Inverness. Many of the lords present were somewhat scornful of anything such, but the matter was passed.

George returned home with royal blessings on his forth-coming journey eastwards.

Two weeks later, at the beginning of June, leaving Pate and Gavin in charge of Dunbar, the Merse and along the border Marches, George and Beatrix set sail in *Lammer-law*. They might well be gone for some considerable time.

The weather was good, and the voyaging pleasant, although easterly breezes at first did not help as to speed. In consequence it took them eight days to reach the Skagerrak and the coast of Norway and to head south there, round the northern tip of Denmark into the Katte-gat, to approach Gothenburg, the greatest port hereabouts. This was in Sweden, not Norway, but King Erik might be in any of the three realms, and a call here might save much time in searching for him.

Rob Kerr, their shipmaster, had been here a number of times, and had no difficulty in finding his way up the Gota River's estuary and obtaining a suitable berth in the large harbour, full of shipping, Beatrix, a keen sightseer, eager for new experiences. The city behind the dockland looked impressive.

None of them spoke Swedish, and the English tongue was little known here, but French served for their enquiries. They learned that King Erik was thought to be in Denmark presently; at least, he was not here in Sweden, and it would have been heard if he had gone to Norway. So it was a return to the Kattegat and southwards again, for almost another three hundred miles, to reach Copenhagen, the Danish capital; although Erik might well be at his summer palace at Helsingors, or Elsinore, at the northern tip of Zealand, one of the six major islands that made up Denmark, slightly nearer at hand. They should call there on their way.

They sailed down between the Swedish and Danish coasts, avoiding sundry small islands, for another one hundred and fifty miles, to where all suddenly narrowed in to what amounted to a mere channel, where the great island of Zealand gave the impression of being all but a detached portion of Sweden. Yet there, apparently, was where Denmark's capital, Copenhagen, was situated, not on the infinitely greater island of Jutland to the west. And at the very narrowest point of this channel, on a steep spur of hill, soared the Kronborg Slot, the royal castle, all towers and battlements, overlooking the Swedish coast, a strange place to position the Danish monarchy's summer residence. Although part of the reason for it being here, perhaps, the voyagers quickly discovered; for the narrows were patrolled by armed longships, these halting all, and demanding a toll payment for passage. It was not a very large charge, in merks, but enough to have George calculating how he might deduct this from the payment he had come to offer.

It was evening by the time they reached this far, and probably as good a time as any to find the monarch available, if he was in fact in residence here. Disembarking, George, with Beatrix and Rob Kerr, unhindered by guards although eyed interestedly, the woman at least, climbed the hill to the castle, this extensive and notably different in design from their own holds. They had left the sack of merks in the ship meantime.

322

There was no actual gatehouse, only a vaulted passage-way under one of the main wings of the establishment, and here the trio were duly challenged, but had no difficulty in convincing the guards that they were entitled to enter, despite the language problem. George got the impression that it was Beatrix's presence that got them in, comely as she was, and smiling.

At an inner courtyard they did not have to seek instructions as to where to go next, the noise emanating from one of the flanking buildings indicating entertainment at least, music, singing, shouting. Eyeing each other, the three of them made for that doorway.

No one was on guard here, and they went in, to mount the stair to where the riotous sounds were coming from. George began to wonder whether this was any place to bring his wife, even though there were high feminine voices and squeals discernible in the din; and indeed whether King Erik could possibly be here in such conditions. They passed servitors carrying platters, jugs and flagons on the stairway, but no attention was paid to them.

A great hall opened on the first-floor landing, and, gazing within, they saw a scene of all but bedlam and chaos. Long tables stretched up the hall, with a crosswise one at the far end. All was crowded, by no means all the occupants sitting at the said tables, some actually dancing and caverting on the table-tops among the flagons and dishes. Bodies were lying on the flooring, some obviously drunken, some in fact coupling. Many of the women present were half naked, some on the table-tops with skirts hitched up round their waists, white thighs gleaming, some bare-breasted. Instrumentalists up in a gallery provided the music of a sort. And at the top table the revelry was by no means toned down, in the centre seat a big bearded man, with one arm round a woman bare to the middle, while with the other hand he beat a slopping wine-flagon on the board, to the time of the music.

Staring, George turned to Beatrix and shook his head. To what had he brought his dear wife?

They stood for a few moments, none paying them any heed. Then he signed to Beatrix to wait there with Rob Kerr while he went forward to try to discover the situation. He had never seen the like in all his days.

Picking his way over and between bodies, and avoiding reeling characters, he perceived one man sitting in normal fashion, sipping from a goblet and considering all with a sort of patient resignation. Him George approached. In his halting French, and necessarily loudly, he asked what was to do, and who was in charge, if anyone was?

His informant shrugged and pointed to the top table. King Erik, he said. That was all.

George stood there for further moments, undecided what to do. If this was indeed the monarch whom he had come to see, was this the occasion to announce himself? Or should they just retire to their ship, and come again in the morning?

He decided that, having come this far, he might as well introduce himself; it could hardly be called craving an audience. He went on forward.

Reaching the crosswise table, he bowed before the man in the central seat beating the time and fondling the breast of the woman. He was eyed with no especial interest.

He bowed again, and said, again in his French, such as it was, that he was come from Scotland with orders from the King of Scots to see His Majesty. He had to shout it to be heard above the din. Was he speaking to King Erik?

The other at least picked up the word Scotland, for he repeated that enquiringly, still handling the woman, but setting down his tankard on the table.

George repeated what he had tried to convey, and added that he was the Earl of Dunbar and March, then remembered that here they used the word jarl, not earl. It might register.

It did. A Scottish jarl! That made an impression apparently. And the King of Denmark, Norway and Sweden thrust the half-full tankard of liquor at the visitor, in a gesture of welcome.

Bowing once more, George duly sipped, and handed the tankard back. He asked whether he might return from his ship on the morrow, to speak with His Majesty?

The king waved towards the laden platters of meats, fowl, fish and sweetmeats, offering refreshment. But, gesturing backwards, the visitor declared that his wife was awaiting him. And with His Majesty's permission, he would retire.

Permission casually nodded, he turned, to pick his way through the noisy and abandoned crowd to the waiting pair, to point back to the stairway.

Descending to the courtyard and out, they exchanged wondering and rather incoherent comments on what they had experienced. Was all this some especial occasion or celebration? Or was it the way evenings were apt to be spent at Kronborg Slot?

Back to the ship and sanity.

In the morning, they waited until well into the forenoon before climbing that hill again, to give King Erik time to recover. But when George and Beatrix were ushered into the royal presence all seemed normal, with no signs of inertia nor heavy reaction. Erik, seeing them alone, was a large bear of a man, seemingly in good spirits, laughing heartily and very lustily appreciative towards Beatrix, a typical Viking descendant perhaps. No explanation nor reason for the night before was offered.

George had thought well on how best to announce his mission to this monarch, without seeming to lack respect or to imply debts or monetary needs; although, if last night was any indication of Erik's extravagance, such could well be understood. When he could come to the point, he decided that this man was one for straight talking, a minimum of dissembling called for. But the problem of language complicated the issue. He would need Beatrix's help.

"Majesty," he said haltingly, "His Grace, King James, believes that the payment, the yearly payment to Norway, over the Scottish Hebrides, should come to an end." At least, that is what he intended to say, whether his French conveyed it or not. "This of one hundred merks, paid now for some one hundred and fifty years. It should end, should it not? Time, no? So His Grace sends me." He shook his head. "My wife, Majesty, speaks the better French. She will say it."

Erik, tugging at his ample beard, looked at Beatrix.

Well primed, she spoke, and persuasively. "Highness, our king's suggestion is this. Instead of paying one hundred merks each year, one final payment might be acceptable to you? This of the Isles of Scotland is now no concern of Norway's, you will agree? It is one hundred and fifty years since this of payment commenced. So – one final payment, and it is ended."

"I had forgotten that such was still being paid, lady," the large monarch admitted. "One hundred merks, you say? You bring me that, for the last time?"

Beatrix looked at her husband. "More than that, I think, Highness."

George, noting reactions, was thinking quickly. "His Grace James . . . would, would do this in royal style. So make the last payment greater. If Your Highness will have it so?"

"Ha!" Erik said. "Greater? How much greater?"

"To end it all with, with dignity, shall we say . . . ten times that sum?" He was taking a chance. "And we had to pay toll to your longships, to reach you here," he reminded.

"Ten times? Ten! One thousand of your merks? You would pay that?" Eric looked anything but disappointed.

"Yes, Majesty. One thousand merks. To finish all."

"Good! that is good. Yes, I will be glad to end this matter so. Your king will send me that money?"

"We have it in the ship, Majesty. Will you have your men to come down for it?"

"One thousand merks! Yes, yes. They shall go for it. With . . . my thanks."

It was as simple as that. Erik's treasury would be empty,

and one thousand silver pieces would mean a lot to him. And they were hereby saving King James an equal amount, who had been prepared to pay two thousand.

"Then, Majesty, that is our mission over."

"Tell your King James that I salute him. And no more payments."

"We shall tell him. Have we Your Majesty's permission to retire?"

"You will remain here at Kronborg? My guests?"

"No, Highness. We have to go on. To Lübeck. To the Hansa Association. On the matter of trade."

"Ah! The Germans! You would trade with them?"

"That is the intention, yes."

"Then you will require to be strong, my friends! Strong. For they are hard men, the Hansas. Men of iron!"

"Then we shall be . . . careful. We may *not* find them good to trade with. But we shall see."

"What can you offer them?"

"Much, perhaps. Wool, that in especial. Hides. Leather, tanned leather. Salted meats and fish. Salmon. Whisky. That is aqua vitae, strong spirits. Like schnapps or vodka. But stronger, no? Hempen sailcloth and ropes. Fish-netting."

"We could do with the like here, Jarl. But we are not strong traders."

"I shall remember that, yes, Highness . . ."

All this discussion had taken a considerable time because of the language problem. Erik offered them a midday meal, but they declined. After last night's example of the royal hospitality, they judged this wise. But they both quite liked this bear of a man, however unkingly by their notions, yet holder of three monarchies.

He proved helpful. He said that he would provide a pilot shipman to guide them down to Lübeck, through difficult waters. They accepted this gratefully.

Erik came downstairs with them as far as the castle entrance to bid them farewell, and to order guards to go down to collect the silver, quite a heavy weight as it would be. Also to inform a shipmaster at the harbour of the royal orders to act pilot. He said good wishes, this with a bellow of laughter, to King James and themselves.

Some counting and setting aside of merks would have to be done on the *Lammerlaw*.

Rob Kerr was glad of the guidance of a local skipper on the way to Lübeck. Apparently it was almost due south another two hundred and fifty miles, at the foot of the great peninsula that made up German Schleswig-Holstein and Danish Jutland, to be reached through shallow, isle-dotted seas.

Setting sail soon after midday, they quickly became very much aware of what shallow seas meant, for, leaving the Malmo channel between Zealand and Sweden, they entered the Baltic. This cold, land-locked sea lacked depth as well as salty water, and as a result its waves were much steeper, lacking the long, underlying swells of the Norse Sea. So when these, shorter but more abrupt, met the strong tides coming down from the Kattegat and the Skagerrak, the resultant turbulence was notable, and ships pitched and heaved almost alarmingly on the agitated waters. Kerr had warned them of this.

They had to pass the large islands of Mön, Falster and Lolland, as well as many smaller ones, somewhat similar to their own Hebrides, although lacking the white cockleshell sands, water reflections and colourful seaweeds, it all demanding much navigation, they being very glad of the pilot. They all had to hang on securely to supports because of the jerking, tossing and heeling. As well that the two passengers did not suffer from seasickness.

After Lolland they were into German waters, and had only another seventy miles to go. They hove to for the night in the lee of the island of Fenmarn, night-sailing in such waters, and the ever-increasing numbers of ships in them, making this advisable.

In the morning they were at the mouth of the great bay

of Lübecker Bucht, or bight, not unlike England's Wash but larger.

Never had the Scots seen so much shipping as herein, many of the vessels larger than their own, coming and going. The bight was wide, perhaps thirty miles across, and, sailing on the west side, they saw towns dotting that coast, with their harbours. That this was a busy and prosperous land was very evident.

At the head of the huge bay they came to an estuary, which their pilot told them was the mouth of the Traive River. Into this they sailed, and to join something like a queue of vessels, the sea traffic all but continuous. The scale of it all had George wondering whether, in fact, they could make any impact here, so clearly extensive was the trade established? Could Scotland really offer anything not already in exchange? Beatrix was more interested in the land they passed itself. This was where so much of England's and Lowland Scotland's far-back ancestors had come from – Angles, Jutes, Saxons.

They now had to sail up the narrowing estuary for about ten miles, still close behind other vessels, with more passing them outward-bound, flying flags of many different sorts. When they asked the pilot, named Jan, what nations these represented, he spread his hands. A great canal had been constructed thirty years before, to link Lübeck with Hamburg to the south, so shipping could now come up from Saxony, Bohemia, Silesia, Thuringia, the Rhineland, Poland, Slovakia, even Hungary. And as well as Norway, Sweden and Denmark, to the north were Lithuania, Latvia, Finland and all the Russias.

This was a new world for the travellers.

They slowly approached Lübeck itself, built on a low hill, all towers and steeples. The pilot said that there were two great outer harbours on the estuary coast and no fewer than nine in the river mouth, this the largest port in the Baltic. Which were they wishing to reach? All but dizzy with it, George said that probably the closest in to the city

329

itself the better. It was talk with the rulers here that they had come for, after all.

Actually, the nearer they got to the densely built-up area, the easier it was for their helmsman, for they were leaving behind most of the ship traffic now, that mainly concerned with all those harbours and docksides and their seemingly endless lines of warehouses, stores and granaries. Now ahead of them were taller buildings, the skyline dominated by spires, steeples and towers, three of these lofty and impressive indeed which, they were told were the cathedral, the Mariankirche, the Petrikirche, the last only recently completed. The Rathaus, or town hall, and the Diet Haus, seat of the league, were prominent also.

Somewhat overawed, and asked by Jan where they wished to be landed, George said that probably near the town hall to begin with, to introduce themselves to the burgomaster, and from there seek to reach the league officers.

With less shipping hereabouts, they found a berth beside tall gabled houses painted in bright colours, brick and wood not stone. Here they disembarked, no one paying them any attention although the streets were crowded. Jan said that he knew the Rathaus and would take them there.

Threading narrow streets, not unlike those of London, they came to a vast central square, this filled with neat lines of market stalls, everything giving the impression of order and discipline. A large and handsome towered building was pointed out as the town hall.

It was late afternoon, and it was hoped that they might see the burgomaster, and from him seek introduction to some senior representative of the Hansa League.

They had no difficulty with this official when their pilot introduced them, in the name of King Erik, as a jarl from Scotland. He was a little wizened man, keen-eyed and brisk, but respectfully so. George explained that they had come here over the matter of trade with Scotland, sent by the king thereof, and wishful to speak with whoever of the Hansa members might be likely to be interested. The

330

burgomaster declared that he would himself take them to see Herr Georg Mueller, who was probably the man they wanted. George hoped that he, having the same Christian name as himself, would present a good augury.

With the small man all but trotting alongside, they were conducted across the wide square, threading their way past all the busy stalls, to a magnificent building which they were informed was the Diet Haus, diet in this case meaning the Assembly House, almost a parliament, of the league. It was as well, they realised as they entered this, that they had the burgomaster as introducer, for the place was a positive warren of rooms and chambers and closets, on three floors, surrounding a fine central hall, and all busy with serious-looking men with papers and quills, bustling in and out of their offices. Anything less like the Kronborg Slot at Helsingors would be hard to imagine, all here seemingly dedicated to their work and immediate concerns – although not a few did glance surprisedly on seeing a woman in this ant-hill of activity.

They were led to a series of more handsome apartments on the first floor, with names and styles painted on the doors; and at one of these they were left standing, while the burgomaster went within.

George said to Beatrix, "Let us hope that this representative we are to see can speak more than German!"

They did not have long to wait before the door opened again and another man stood there with the burgomaster, quite handsome, richly clad but in sober fashion, of middle years and an assured bearing.

"Herr Georg Mueller. Und Jarl Georg von Schottland!" It was announced.

"Schottland! I know of Scotland." That was said in reasonably good English.

With sighs of relief George held out his hand to shake. "Herr Mueller, greetings!" he said. "I rejoice that you speak in our tongue. That is good, for I fear that we speak no German. Here is my wife, the Countess Beatrix."

"Lady, your servant. And yours, Earl Georg. My speaking is not of perfection, no? But I have some of your tongue. How can I you aid, Earl?"

The burgomaster bowed, and retired.

"We come on the matter of trade with Scotland," George said. "This hoped for. James, King of Scots, would increase his realm's trading and wealth. And he is advised that the Hansa League is, shall we say, the great trading empire of Christendom."

"We are merchants, yes. Trade our, our concern, is it? Come you, lady – sit."

Led within, George thought it suitable to introduce their pilot, still with them, as Jan, sent with them from King Erik from Denmark.

Beatrix said that they had heard much of the Hansa League. And were greatly privileged to meet one of its representatives.

Seated at a table littered with papers, they quickly got down to details and facts, if not figures, this Mueller soon wanting to know what particular goods Scotland had to offer, and to which preferred destinations. He seemed to be especially interested in the wool, which pleased George, asking about the qualities of the fibres, fine and coarse, and its usefulness for different types of clothing, blanketing, hangings and the like. Salt and salted meat and fish also appeared to be very marketable to the Baltic states, where salt was lacking, for it seemed that the Scandinavian countries, despite their Norse Sea coasts, did not go in for salt-making and evaporating-pans in any large way. Was Holy Church not so industrious here as at home?

As to whisky, Mueller was very enquiring. How did it differ from mead, schnapps, vodka and other strong liquors? George was no expert on this, but thought that it was probably stronger, more potent. It was much favoured in Scotland, of course; but visitors from England and other lands found it much to their taste usually. The other said that he would be interested to sample this. He was told that there was some back in their ship, and they would have some sent up.

Fish-netting might well be an acceptable import for the Baltic states, it was thought.

All in all, George was encouraged by the reception of his proposals, the more especially when Georg Mueller offered them lodgings in a large guest-house of the League nearby. He sent them off to see these premises, in the care of an underling; and they were much taken with the accommodation provided. Not only that, but he said that they must come and dine with him and his wife that evening. He would send someone to fetch them. He lived none so far off.

The visitors were well pleased with the Hanseatic League if this Mueller was representative.

That impression was confirmed in the evening when, taken to what amounted to a mansion, richly furnished, they were presented to Frau Hilde Mueller and a son and daughter. Also to another guest, who proved to be a colleague in the league hierarchy, one Johann Klarbach, who it seemed was much concerned with Russian trade. He also had some English.

George learned a lot that evening. It seemed that the league was influential in more than just trade and merchanting. It had instituted its own law code, over the years, known as the Laws of Lübeck, and these were applied to over one hundred cities and towns over a huge area of north eastern Europe where Hansa was in economic control. The league necessarily had a large fleet of ships, and its own shipbuilding yards, here at Lübeck but also at Hamburg and Bremen. The Viking ability to build their fast and renowned longships had been utilised to great advantage. Indeed it was largely due to the league that the Viking menace throughout Europe had eventually been put down, and a more peaceful and reputable regime established on the Scandinavians. Hansa had assembled a large army, back in 1370, and had defeated the Danish King Valdemir the Fourth, who had sought to appropriate their wealth and influence. They had put down piracy on the seas, ensured safe navigation, trained pilots, and largely

ended the prevalence of plunder and robbery and spolia-
tion on land likewise.

Altogether it made a highly interesting and instructive
evening.

The next day the visitors were taken round to see various
departments of the league's activities, and were left in no
doubts as to the opportunities for Scotland in Hansa trade.
The whisky sent up from their ship was much appreciated;
and it was judged that there would be quite a noteworthy
demand for *this* import at least.

So, mission accomplished, and new friends made, the
following morning they said their farewells and set sail for
home. Beatrix had made quite an impact, women not being
normally much in evidence in matters of trade and commerce.

They dropped their pilot Jan at Helsingors, but did not
linger there, other than to pay brief respects to King Erik,
where Beatrix received a comprehensive hugging and
smacking kisses.

35

They arrived back to find Scotland rejoicing. The hostages in England had been freed and returned home, the ransom payments all paid, the four years up. Patrick had arrived back at Dunbar, and great was the satisfaction and celebration.

George duly reported to the king on his Baltic enterprise, and James expressed himself as much encouraged over it all. They must use this opportunity for trade increase to the full. A detailed survey of what the Hansa people would be prepared to import must be carried out; and of course what best could be brought back from there, to their advantage. Would he, George, be prepared to lead such a further undertaking?

That man was very positive in declining the suggestion, since it was not a royal command. He pointed out that he had two earldoms to manage, and they had been somewhat neglected of late with his various missions on the realm's behalf. Perhaps his brother Patrick might be prepared to go in his stead, however, duly informed as to the situation there. After four years of detention and restraint as hostage, he might well find such journeying and activity to his taste.

James conceded that he had perhaps used his friend's services overmuch these past four years; and if his brother would go, well and good, provided with all the relevant information. But it came to him that a churchman should also go. All this of commerce and producing goods for trading was very much the clerics' concern, rather than that of lords and barons. Such could talk of costs and prices to be charged, and their ability to produce the quantities of

335

the various items. Was this not so? He suggested sending Master John Cameron, his own secretary, Provost of Lincluden Abbey, and bishop-elect of Glasgow.

George was all in favour of this. He would, of course, provide the necessary ship. He went home hoping that he might be spared more royal-inspired duties for some time. He had missed one more parliament, but knowing his liege-lord he did not think that it would be long before there was another – and these always seemed to result in tasks for such as himself.

It was almost November now and this not the best time to sail to the Baltic countries where, apparently, they had more severe winters than here in Scotland. Patrick declared that he was quite happy to take on this mission, and hoped that he would get on with the chosen cleric.

So, waiting for spring, the family passed Christmas and Yule together, enjoying it. They faced 1429.

The anticipated parliament, again at Perth, was duly called for late March, by which time Patrick and the provost Cameron were on their way across the Norse Sea. George found the king's flair for the improvement of his realm nowise abated, despite all his previous legislation, and at least one of the matters to be raised and dealt with was with his strong approval, this the problem of wolves. For some time he had been concerned at the increasing losses among his sheep stocks in the Lammermuirs, attributed to wolves, and his shepherds had been doing their best to hunt down the predators. Apparently the trouble was by no means confined to his lands, the creatures on the increase almost everywhere. So parliament accepted James's proposals for dealing with this. Every barony, lordship and Church property was to initiate wolf-hunts at least four times per year, and make a point of seeking out lairs and breeding-dens, where the whelps were to be destroyed. A payment of two pence was to be given to every man who brought in the ears of such creatures, this to be met from the nation's treasury, through the baronies; and fines laid upon such as failed to take up these measures.

Another serious problem was the alarming increase of leprosy in the land. It had long been a scourge, but recently the disease had become more prevalent. There was a chivalric order, the Knights of St Lazarus of Jerusalem, which specialised in the treatment and care of lepers, despite Holy Church's attitude to them as outcasts, with the Finger of God upon them, and dead already in matters spiritual; the wife of a leper could rank as a widow and marry again, for instance. And the members of the Order of St Lazarus were pressing for nationwide steps to improve the sufferers' lot, as well as to counter the disease itself, and to win the Church's attitude over to a more caring one. Now the monarch was recommending various decrees. No individuals with the disease were to be allowed to live in any town nor city, their dwellings to be in the order's hospices, and none of these was to be in populated areas. Lepers were only to be allowed within town gates for a very short distance, as far as special stalls placed there, where food was to be available for them, entry permitted only three days in each week, and never on market days. The Church was to be urged to assist in this, and remove their anathema.

Then the matter of some tradesmen overcharging for their services was considered. Many complaints were being made over this, craftsmen such as masons, smiths, tailors, weavers and the like reported from some parts as demanding greatly increased payment for work. The trade guilds were to take action on this, and to appoint wardens to fix suitable prices and to see that these were held to throughout the land, with offenders to be expelled from the guilds and associations, and forbidden to carry on their trades, and if they continued to do so secretly, to be imprisoned by the magistrates.

Another complaint was that wildfowl were often being slaughtered out of season, ducks, geese, partridges, plovers, blackcock and muirfowl. This was greatly reducing

337

numbers of a valuable source of food, and damaging lawful sport. It was therefore forbidden now to slay, by crossbow, net or snare, between Lent and August, this under penalty of fining.

James himself introduced the issue of increasing trade, and told of the Earl of Dunbar and March's visit to the Hansa merchants. He declared that here was great opportunity to benefit the nation. Another mission was on its way to the Baltic Sea to seek the entry of Scots goods to that large market, far greater than was generally realised. Each earl, lord, baron and laird was instructed to seek to improve production of goods that would be welcome there and elsewhere overseas. Shipping it all would be something of a problem, although as all knew, shipbuilding was on the increase. But the law that Scots goods were only to be carried in Scots ships should be repealed. And, to be sure, Baltic craft bringing desirable imports here could carry back our own merchandise.

The parliament should congratulate and thank the Earl George for this major service. George rose and bowed.

It had all made a busy session, reflecting the monarch's determination to improve conditions in his realm.

Soon after his return to Dunbar, George heard of an extraordinary development in France, the which was much upsetting the English armies still fighting there. A young peasant woman, only of sixteen years, had arisen, and not in France at all but in the duchy of Bar, lying between France and the Germanic states. This girl, Joan by name, claimed that since the age of thirteen she had been hearing the voice of Almighty God, and now had been given divine orders for the French to rise in fullest force to banish the English invaders from that land; and that she was appointed to lead them. This scarcely believable happening was proving to be very effective for the French. She had somehow made her way to one of the French armies, and although rejected with scorn by the commander, had returned home and then been further instructed by the Creator to renew her demands, this reinforced by visions of Saints Michael, Catherine and Margaret, patron saints of her country, this from the village of Domremy in Arc, of Bar-le-Duc. She had managed to impress the Duc d'Alençon, a kinsman of the Dauphin Charles, not yet crowned King of France; and riding at the head of French troops, clad in armour, she had won one battle after another. Bedford's forces were in retreat.

All marvelled.

At home, George's shepherds and tenants began to make good money out of wolves, something they certainly never had anticipated.

Military matters in France, however, heavenly guided or otherwise, were soon overshadowed, in Scots minds at least, by ones nearer at home. An older kinsman of Alexander of the Isles, still under open arrest, one Donald Balloch, set about proving that the Islesmen were still a force to be reckoned with. He did not march eastwards towards Inverness, as Donald and his son had done, but sailed southwards with a fleet of birlinns and longships to the Morvern area, landwards of the Isle of Mull, north of Argyll country dominated by the Campbells, ancient enemies of the MacDonalds of the Isles, devastating that district and making his base on the holy island of Lismore, this none so far from sacred Iona, burial-place of Scottish kings. Greatly angered over this, the Campbells had appealed to the monarch, they long-time supporters of the crown. James, short of sending an army to counter this Donald Balloch, had released young Alexander and sent him to regain authority over his lordship. This gesture proving ineffective, the Earl of Mar, victor of Red Harlaw, and the Stewart Earl of Caithness had been despatched to Morvern to punish this Donald.

George was thankful that he was not asked to contribute men to this venture.

In the event, Mar and Caithness were themselves taught a lesson. Used to battling in the Highlands as they were, they had never campaigned on the western seaboard with its innumerable lochs, peninsulas, sounds and islands, and their horsed soldiery were at a notable disadvantage against water-borne forces. Donald's longships could outpace and encircle them, isolate and cut them off, using the sea lochs as roads and the passes between for ambushes. Trapped eventually between two hosts of Islesmen, a ferocious battle had been fought, and great losses inflicted on the Lowlanders, Caithness himself being slain with sixteen of his knightly supporters, and Mar only escaping by precipitate flight – a dire humiliation for that son of the Wolf of Badenoch.

The Stewarts would not forget that day.

There was nothing for it but for James to seek to exert his authority. But he did not want to seem to go to war against some of his own subjects, especially with Alexander sent to regain control of the Isles. So instead he decided on a demonstration of his royal power, a progress into the north-west, to which he summoned all the greater magnates of his realm, each to come, not with an armed force, but with a company of knights and vassals. This to assemble at Perth.

George, of course, had to comply.

At Perth, not exactly another parliament was held but what was called a council of state, this to emphasise the unity of the kingdom. Also to deal with a newly arrived request from the Duke of Gloucester, in the name of King Henry, he concerned over the English reverses caused by this Joan of Arc's odd influence on the French, and the danger that the Scots saw it all as a cause for the increased support of the Auld Alliance. They, Gloucester and King Henry, wanted the peace with Scotland to be strengthened and made more evident. And they had sent the Lord Scrope, one of the English Wardens of the Marches, to offer the return of the castles of Roxburgh and Berwick-upon-Tweed to Scotland as inducement.

This of Roxburgh in especial appealed to James, and he indicated to the council his approval of a renewal of the peace treaty. Not that the one known as of London had expired; but some token of its continuing relevance might well be advantageous. He proposed that envoys should be sent to Gloucester to confirm this, and receive the surrender of the English garrisons of Roxburgh and Berwick.

Strangely, this was not exactly contested but questioned, and by some of the clergy in especial. It was over this of that Joan woman. If she was indeed being directed by the word of God, and by visions of the saints, and her efforts on the French behalf so successful, then could it not mean that their Creator was concerned in heaven that the French cause should triumph and flourish, and therefore that Scotland's support should be devoted to France, not England? That this woman was not even French herself made it a most remarkable situation, and must be taken heed of. This attitude provoked much discussion, and not a little of scorn from many, most there seeing this female curiosity as a mere temporary oddity and aberration, all but a folly indeed, and not any true intervention by the Almighty. At any rate, the decision to renew the treaty with England was passed, James glancing over at George significantly. That man saw himself as having one more embassage to make.

The council over, a move was made by the large gathering, not northwards but westwards, heading for the Campbell country. It was noticeable to George, and very much to his monarch, that the Earl of Douglas had not responded to this summons to Perth, along with some of the south-western barons who tended to be under his influence, this including the powerful Lord Kennedy. The king announced that these missing magnates were to ward themselves in Stirling Castle, as sign of his disapproval.

The great cavalcade rode off by Methven, where the Bruce had suffered his initial defeat, by Crieff and Loch Earn and up Glen Ogle to Glen Dochart, into the mountains now, to reach Crianlarich, none so far from the head of Loch Lomond, halting at monasteries at St Fillans and Auchlyne on the way, for such a large company did not ride fast. These hospices were not commodious enough to house more than a very small number of the entourage, so most had to camp overnight as best they might. They were heading, apparently, for the royal castle of Dunstaffnage on the Argyll coast north of the Oban, where Kenneth mac Alpin had brought the Stone of Destiny from Iona, before it was eventually taken on to Scone, this to save it from the Viking depredations. Dunstaffnage had had hereditary Campbell keepers since Bruce's time. Alexander of the Isles had been summoned to meet them there, with his chieftains, these to include the errant Donald Balloch.

They proceeded on up Strathfillan to Tyndrum, and so over the high pass beyond, after which it was really all downhill, with soon all the magnificent and breathtaking panorama of the Sea of the Hebrides, with its unnumbered islands, great and small, its lochs and peninsulas, seemingly reaching to all infinity. George recognised how these Lords of the Isles saw themselves as ruling a different realm from the rest of Scotland.

Down Glen Lochy and Glen Orchy to the foot of long Loch Awe, they skirted the foot of mighty Ben Cruachan, which the Campbells had made their war-cry, and through the dangerous Pass of Brander, they reached Loch Etive, where they saw longships out on the water, and took due note. A dozen miles along the shore of this and they came to the turbulent narrows of the Falls of Lora, where salt water fought fiercely with fresh; yet they realised that those longships must have threaded these falls to get where they were. And round a small headland, there ahead of them on a rocky projection, with the open sea behind, soared the three great towers and high curtain walls of Dunstaffnage Castle, their destination. All around the promontory on which it stood longships and birlinns were moored. Alexander of the Isles had arrived before them. He had had a much simpler and shorter journey, of course.

The royal company had to work its way round quite a lengthy inlet to reach the stronghold. There they found the Islesmen either in their vessels or camped on the approaches, Alexander himself occupying the ancient chapel nearby, for the Campbell keeper would by no means allow such inside the castle, the MacDonald – Campbell feud very much continuing, drawbridge over the moat ditch raised. However, the arrival of the monarchial party changed that, and the Lord of the Isles and some of his chiefs, a fierce-looking crew, were able to enter at least the courtyard within the sixty-foot-high curtain walling with King James.

Donald Balloch, it turned out, was not with Alexander. He had fled to Ireland.

Thereafter no great events took place at Dunstaffnage, other than the Islesmen voicing homage and service to the king. They made the announcement that some three hundred of Donald Balloch's caterans, who had terrorised Morvern after their victory, had already been executed. But the very fact of the monarch coming all this way to the Western Highland seaboard, with his principal nobles and churchmen, was a sufficient indication of his strength and determination. The journey had been well worth the making.

It was late October, and with that lengthy and difficult road back to cover, snow already beginning to cap the higher mountain-tops, and with nothing to be gained by remaining, the start of the return was not delayed; although it did seem something of an anticlimax to withdraw so soon, only one day after arriving. But James was satisfied, and few there had any desire to linger. So the move was made, Alexander and his fleet departing northwards in style, while the rest of them retraced their steps eastwards.

It had been a strange interlude; but George for one had been interested to visit this hitherto unknown and spectacular region of the kingdom.

He arrived home eventually to find Patrick just back from the Baltic, before winter storms could set in, and with much and helpful information as to trading possibilities and requirements and destinations. Quite a number of Scotland's products would be welcomed by the Hansa merchants, with, it appeared, whisky by no means the least of them.

It looked as though 1430 could be a rewarding year, in commercial as well as state affairs, King James confident.

36

Sadly, satisfaction with peace and prosperity was distinctly impaired thereafter by a grievous and nationwide outbreak of pestilence, this resulting in large numbers of deaths. It had been a particularly severe winter, the cold so intense that cattle herds were decimated, and many of the elderly and poorer folk died of cold, this also weakening resistance to the plague. The latter started in Edinburgh in February and quickly spread throughout the kingdom. Thankfully, it did not reach Dunbar, although it got as near as Haddington; but the snow and ice did seriously affect the sheep stocks in the hills.

These calamities had the effect of delaying the mission to London which James had desired George to make, after the Lord Scrope's visit to Scotland with the offer of the evacuation of Roxburgh and Berwick Castles in return for what amounted to a permanent peace treaty. But in March he set off – by ship, of course, roads anyway being impassable with snow and flooding – and accompanied by the churchman-secretary, Cameron, Provost of Lincluden, who had been helpful on the Hansa visit with Patrick. He also took son Pate with him, for his education in state affairs.

Actually the voyage was none so ill, for the weather conditions which had produced so much cold on land seemed to have spared storms at sea. They made good time of it.

They found Gloucester, at the Tower, in somewhat less co-operative mood than had been anticipated, critical of the delay in answer to his proposals. But it was more than that. The situation in France had much improved, Bedford being no longer defeated, the woman Joan's ridiculous successes thankfully finished; in fact she had been betrayed by the Burgundians and actually sold to the English. She had been brought to trial before a Church court, under a bishop, condemned as a heretic and a sorceress, and burned to death. So Scottish friendship was not so urgent for England, especially with Douglas no longer aiding the French. Gloucester still wanted the treaty extended, but was less willing to pay the proffered price. The Roxburgh garrison would be withdrawn, yes, but not that at Berwick Castle. It had never been intended, he declared, that the port and town of Berwick-upon-Tweed should be handed over, this being of much value to northern Northumberland; and its people had been much distressed by the prospect of the castle, which overlooked the town, being in Scottish occupation. So that was now not to be considered.

George did his best to change this English stance, but without success, and had to return home disappointed.

James was, to be sure, unhappy about it all, but he had other matters foremost on his mind at this juncture, with the plague still raging and the land all but untillable, floods everywhere following the melting snows, and the outlook for seed-time and harvest grim indeed. The nation was disheartened, and after all his efforts at improvement. But at least Roxburgh Castle was back for his use. And Queen Joan, pregnant again, was soon to be delivered, and who knew, might bear him a son as heir to his throne.

George himself returned to a dire lambing season, with the Lammermuirs still blocked with snow, and much of the low ground under water. The year 1430 was not going to be remembered kindly after all.

The next word George had from the king was surprising in more ways than one. Not only had his Joan produced for him a son and heir, but two of them – only, sadly, one had died almost immediately after birth. But the second, to be another James, was healthy. And George was invited to come and be his sponsor.

Quite overwhelmed at this honour and token of favour, he learned that the other godparent was to be John Cameron, his colleague on the London mission, who had now become Bishop of Glasgow, and was being nominated as the next Chancellor; so he would no longer be able to act the king's secretary.

George rode to Linlithgow, where he found joy prevailing, although tinged with sadness over the death of the newly born twin. But now they had a son and heir to the throne; hitherto Walter, Earl of Atholl, James's uncle and a son of the older Albany, had been heir-presumptive, this unless the Princess Margaret could have been accepted to succeed, which was doubtful, for Scotland had never had a Queen-regnant actually on the throne; moreover she was betrothed to the young Dauphin of France.

Queen Joan appeared to have recovered well from her difficult childbearing; and the two young princesses, Margaret and Isobel, were much excited at having a brother.

Henry Wardlaw, Bishop of St Andrews and Primate, despite his years, had come to christen the infant; and in the private chapel of the palace. The occasion was celebrated with much ceremony. It was a notable development indeed for George to be godfather to the new monarch-to-be, and a very clear acknowledgment of appreciation for all his efforts on the king's behalf.

Afterwards James told him that he was concerned that still there was no word of the English garrison retiring from Roxburgh, despite Gloucester's promise. Sir Gavin Dunbar, as Warden of the Marches, was to go there and urge immediate withdrawal.

The king also informed that Archibald Douglas had remarried. His wife Matilda, daughter of the Lindsay Earl of Crawford, had died while he was away in France. Now he had wed again, and into kin of the royal house, the Lady Euphemia Graham, daughter of Sir Patrick Graham and Euphemia, Countess of Strathearn in her own right, through whom this Patrick was claiming that earldom, to James's disapproval, for it was a royal fief, she a Stewart, granddaughter of Robert the Second. This match of Douglas's perturbed James. He was not happy about the Grahams' loyalty. The most powerful noble of his realm marrying into that family was somewhat worrying. Douglas was quite strong enough, without that.

George sought to reassure. His friend Archibald was to be trusted, he was sure – even though he had not come to join the royal progress to Argyll and Dunstaffnage.

James remained doubtful.

It occurred to George, on his way home, that he might be able to serve both of his friends, James and Archibald, by paying Douglas a visit and seeking to bridge the gap which obviously continued to separate them. A journey, not by ship this time, but across all Lowland Scotland to Galloway, then?

Beatrix, when she heard of this proposal, insisted that she should accompany her husband. She much preferred going off with George on his expeditions than being left alone at Dunbar – for nowadays Pate was occupying Colbrandspath Tower, as the Master, with his own life to live. And far from trying to dissuade her, although he did point out that it was now early November and riding conditions could be rough, crossing through all the hills, George was glad of her good company, for she remained young at heart, and their love for each other remained as strong as ever, however much acquaintances shook their heads over them.

It made, to be sure, a lengthy ride south by west, fully one hundred and fifty upheaved miles, by Cranshaws and Polwarth, Ersildoune and Melrose, Selkirk and Moffat, and so over Annandale and into Galloway. They continued by Moniaive and St John's Town of Dalry to long Loch Ken, and so down to Threave Castle. But there were abbeys and priories and monasteries all the way to offer them comfortable quarters for the nights, thanks to King David the First. They did the journey in three days,

348

without any great problems or delays, although flooding did still occasion some diversions. They were aware, however, of the sorry state of the land and its people, after all the miseries of plague, dire weather and bad harvests, even the churchmen feeling the pinch.

They found that Galloway, at least, had been largely spared the pestilence, although it had suffered in other respects, it being great cattle country.

Douglas and his new wife, however surprised at this visit, were delighted to see them, no question as to their welcome, the two women, despite differences in ages, quickly approving of each other. Beatrix was fascinated by Threave Castle on its islet in the River Dee.

It was unsuitable, of course, for George to indicate, in the countess's presence, that the king was concerned over Douglas allying himself with the Strathearn Grahams, of whom he was suspicious. He had to wait until he could get his friend alone to introduce the matter, although he did indicate that James was disappointed that no Black Douglas support had materialised for the demonstration against the Islesmen, when the *Red* Douglas, Angus, had been there. Also that he had failed to ward himself in Stirling Castle in consequence. This was waved aside.

But later, in private, when the subject of the marriage could be broached, Archibald assured that there was nothing significant as regards his attitude towards the king in this match. He had met Euphemia at Dunure, in the house of the Lord Kennedy, with her brother, the Earl of Strathearn, and their uncle, and he had been much attracted to the young woman. She had not spurned his advances. Now they were very happy together. It was all nothing to do with the throne.

George pointed out that it was the Strathearn link with Walter of Atholl that was the trouble. He was known to be reviving the old canard that Robert the Second's first marriage to Elizabeth Mure was unlawful, invalid because of cousinship, and therefore their son, Robert the Third, was in fact illegitimate, and should not have succeeded to the throne. But that the sons of the second marriage, Albany and then himself, were the true heirs, not James's father. Strathearn and his and Euphemia's uncle, known as the Tutor of Strathearn, were agreeing with this. What a family was the Stewart one!

Archibald agreed with all this, but declared that he had no sympathy with this attitude. His non-attendance at the Dunstaffnage affair was merely because he had been otherwise engaged — in fact, getting married. And this of voluntarily warding himself in Stirling Castle was too absurd to be considered.

George sympathised, but asked his friend if he could go and assure King James that Douglas, with his great power in armed men, was entirely loyal to the monarchy as at present constituted, and could be relied upon to come to the aid of the crown in any major need? This was agreed, if scarcely enthusiastically. The pair of them could return to the ladies.

George and Beatrix remained at Threave for three days, and were taken to visit places of interest a-many, other castles and houses of the earldom, the quite large town of Kirkcudbright, the abbeys of Dundrennan and Sweetheart, the ancient Celtic Christian cross at Anwoth, and much else, this before it was recognised that the weather was not improving, and a return home was advisable.

They parted in friendly fashion, George feeling that some good had been achieved. Whether James would so judge remained to be seen.

In fact, the king proved to be less than satisfied. Even if not so intended, married to one of the Grahams, Douglas could be edged towards their wrongous, indeed treasonable cause. He, James, was crowned and anointed monarch, after all; and any move to dethrone him would be treason. That sort of talk could lead to action. The Strathearn earldom was a royal fief. He was going to reclaim it for the crown. Give the Grahams the lesser earldom of Menteith, a lesser lordship, and hope that they would be warned. Warn his uncle of Atholl also. His grandfather's first marriage had been declared lawful by papal precept, only in the fourth degree of cousinship. So there was no substance to their claims.

George said that Douglas was not contesting it, and would not. His marriage was out of affection and esteem, not policy.

He recognised that the Stewarts had never loved the Douglases. Was he wasting his time over this? Even though thanked for his efforts.

James told him that at least, however, the Donald Balloch problem was now solved. That Islesman's severed head had been sent to him by an Irish princeling.

37

The year that followed was one of gradual recovery for the nation after its trials, confidence and thankfulness beginning to replace depression and resentment. Like Douglas's, George's earldoms had not suffered as much as many; but he was enheartened nevertheless.

His next duty for his liege-lord was, of all things, occasioned by that thorn in James's side, Roxburgh Castle. It still had not been evacuated by its English garrison, and the monarch was wrath indeed. He declared it humiliating that he could not take it, his own house on his own ground and land, but it was impregnable, at least in his present circumstances. If only he had these new weapons of war that they all had heard of – none so new indeed, since English Edward the Third had used them at the Battle of Crecy in 1346, eighty-five years ago. And they were said to have been much developed and improved since then: cannon. Siege-machinery other than battering-rams and catapults and the like, of iron or bronze, using a powder which when lit exploded to hurl balls of stone or iron with great force over quite some distance, to smash down walls and towers. None such had ever been seen in Scotland, but it was said that Bedford had used them in France. Roxburgh could fall to such as those.

George wondered. He pointed out that the same difficulties that prevented sows and mangonels from breaching the walls would apply to these cannons, or so he judged: the steep, high banks and the riversides. Would it be possible to fire the balls up at such an angle? He did not know much about such things; but he would have thought that the castle's height above the closest to which they could get these weapons would prevent effective aiming and striking.

James said that the improvements carried out on them would, he believed, include length of range, just as long-bows had improved on crossbows. And if the cannon were able to be placed further back from the castle, the angle of fire would be much reduced, and the barrels, not having to be raised so high, able to aim lower. They might even be able to fire from across the river, and still hit the walls.

At any rate, he wanted George to go back to Gloucester at London and demand the promised evacuation of Roxburgh, and promptly. Why he had delayed this, God knew! Better that his royal castle should be spared damage by cannon-fire. But, if not yielded up, then cannon could be the answer. George was to try to find out all he could about these weapons while in the south. There must be men in England who knew about them, if Edward Plantagenet had used them eighty-five years before. And Bedford still did, it seemed. Even if Gloucester did have Roxburgh returned to him, it would be to Scotland's advantage to possess artillery. So – south again for his friend.

George could have asked why it was always himself who was sent on these errands. But he recognised that it was largely the availability of his shipping, going regularly to the Low Countries, that singled him out, this being quite the quickest and simplest way of getting the four hundred miles to London, and indeed elsewhere; and none of the other Scots lords could provide the like, less merchant-like than himself as they would declare. He must not grumble.

He decided that this would be a good occasion for Beatrix to go with him. On their return from London they could pay a visit to their Lincolnshire manor, which she had never seen. She was, needless to say, well pleased at this.

The *Lammerlaw* was at this time off to the Baltic with wool, nets and salt, so they had to travel in a smaller vessel, the *Deuchrie*, with slightly less comfortable quarters, but none so ill for a short voyage. But at least this craft would not have to go on to the Netherlands from London, and so they would not have to fill in time waiting for its return. Beatrix would be interested to compare London-town with those other cities she had visited.

In the event they had to go up-Thames to Windsor to see Gloucester, who was with young King Henry, now aged ten, a less than confident youngster. This additional journey, by barge, did intrigue Beatrix further, she finding the great palace-castle there so very different from all the other strongholds she knew. George wondered now how it would withstand an assault by cannon.

He left his wife with the young king at his studies while he had his discussion with the duke. That man was not exactly apologetic over the Roxburgh situation, but clearly embarrassed. He had to admit that the Northumberland Percys were something of a law unto themselves, and had presumably ignored his orders to vacate the Scots castle, which they had held for so many years; just why they were so determined to hold on to it was uncertain. George guessed that it was because it was placed so near to the upper Bowmont Water, the valley of which led through the Cheviot Hills into mid-Northumberland, as it were by the back door, and so could make swift and secure raids into Scotland, in typical cross-border fashion. However, he did not say so. At any rate, Gloucester agreed to send another order to vacate, in King Henry's name – but did not sound particularly confident as to obedience.

In the circumstances, George did not think it suitable to ask about artillery there and then. He would make his enquiries elsewhere.

So it was back to London with them, heading for the Tower, probably the best place to learn what he wanted. George was known there, and guessed that the Constable, whoever had now succeeded Sir Richard Spice, would be as hopeful a character to ask as any on cannons; and if he did not know much, could direct him to someone more expert. And coming there from

Gloucester and the king at Windsor, his questionings were not likely to be rejected.

As it turned out, Sir Ralph Howard, the new Constable, was himself quite well informed on the subject of artillery, and even took George and Beatrix to see a row of four large cannon based on a parapet-walk of the Tower itself, facing the Thames-side, as protection against possible attack from the river, unlikely as this might seem. They were heavy, clumsy-looking objects, long barrels made of iron bars bound together, set on solid mounts, each barrel with a deep cavity or hollow at its rear for the powder, this to be exploded by a lit fuse-cord, the which projected the ball, pushed down from the muzzle. Neat heaps of these stone balls stood beside each piece. Sir Ralph admitted that, as far as he knew, these weapons had never been fired, no cause arising; although, to mark special occasions, the powder in the breeches had been set off, with no ball, to make resounding bangs, which could be heard all over the city. He understood that newer pieces were now made of bronze, and superior to these, such as the Duke of Bedford was using in France.

He provided further information as to artillery in general. He said that he understood that the weaponry had originated in Italy, and indeed the most renowned canno-neer was an Italian condottiere named Bartolemeo Colleoni, who was supplying Bedford with bombards. There were, of course, various kinds and sizes of cannon, such as ballisters, scorpions and springels, with different sizes of shot and ranges. He was told that a new kind of shot was now available, called case-shot, which consisted of a round and hollow ball of leather, filled with small pellet-like pieces which, when the powder exploded and sent the ball up the barrel, burst, and sent a shower of these fragments in a spreading fan of small missiles, these no use against walls and masonry but deadly against soldiery, mounted or otherwise.

George asked about the powder needed, and was told that this was one of the problems about the new artillery.

Powder, it seemed, consisted of saltpetre, charcoal and sulphur or nitre, and had to be very heedfully made, there being variations in quality and power, and had to be tested always. And it could be dangerous for more than the enemy, for it was by no means unknown for the cannoneers themselves to be slain by their own powder, the explosions bursting upwards out of the fuse cavity instead of driving the ball along the barrel. So loaders had to be very careful, and the fuses long enough to allow the men to run back before the discharge, out of danger.

George noted all, especially the name of this Colleoni individual in Italy. He thanked their informant. He now had what James required of him.

Returning to the *Deuchrie* they set sail northwards for the Wash.

Docking at Boston again, they had to hire horses to take them up the Witham into the Wold country, which Beatrix found pleasing and picturesque. She blessed the late Henry Bolingbroke for giving this property to the Cospatricks, little as they had ever made of it. She said that they must come for spells, on occasion – by ship it was no difficult nor lengthy journey. It would make a notable change from Dunbar and the Borderland.

They stayed in the manor-house for a few days, exploring the vicinity and liking what they saw. The local folk accepted them in fairly friendly fashion, interested to see their absentee but nowise demanding landlord.

Then it was for home, after no long absence. As missions went, it had been an easy one.

James was very interested, in due course, to hear about the cannon, their varieties, uses – and dangers. He would send to this Italian expert for advice, and possible supply. He might find these case-shot pieces of value in dealing with any uprisings. But he hoped that it would not be necessary to send for heavy bombards for use against Roxburgh. It would be a sorrow to smash down the walls of his own house, so long denied to him.

38

Some three years of comparative peace and quiet followed for George, and indeed for the nation at large, with no royal demands made on his time. The weather was, on the whole, good, and the land, recovering, yielded its fruits, flocks and herds grew again, harvests were ample, and the people were able to live more contentedly. Pate was ever more taking over many of the earldoms' duties, which was a great help; and his father and mother could spend much more time doing the things that they enjoyed: fishing for flounders from small boats, angling for salmon, riding the hills, visiting the Craig of Bass and the Isle of May to watch the seafowl, especially the myriad of gannets at their extraordinary diving for fish, exploring in detail the dramatic coastline of the Merse from Fast Castle, and the like. Beatrix declared that it all was overdue. It had all been there for them to do, but George had always allowed duties to occupy his time, local and national. Now he sometimes felt somewhat guilty. But the woman held that life was surely meant to be enjoyed as well as ordered.

Presumably James Stewart enjoyed the prevailing conditions also, with his family, at Linlithgow, Rothesay and Falkland – although still not at Roxburgh. The Percys remained there, whatever Gloucester had said. And so far no artillery had arrived, from Italy or elsewhere.

There was, however, trouble over the crown's reclaiming of the earldom of Strathearn from the Grahams, that of Menteith being by no means accepted as a worthy replacement. There were mutterings from Walter of Atholl and others. But there were no calls upon George, save to attend another two parliaments at Perth, the second James's fifteenth according to his reckoning. Archibald Douglas did attend the first, and ended by being arrested and consigned to Edinburgh Castle. George did not exactly protest, but he did intercede for his friend, and was assured this it was only a gesture, taken because Douglas had been ordered to immure himself in the citadel previously, and had not done so. He would be released in a month or so, and would suffer no discomforts while there.

It was noticeable, however, that although freed by then, he did not attend the second of these parliaments. But then, quite a number of other senior nobles and magnates also found James's fondness for parliaments not to their taste, and were apt to absent themselves, however sound a policy for national well-being they represented.

A happening at the commencement of the year 1435, without actually disturbing the peace, did disconcert many of the nobility and raised eyebrows all over the land, not adding to the king's popularity. This arose out of the sudden death of the Earl of Mar, victor of Harlaw, who had become one of the foremost commanders of the nation. While his departure was a loss, it was not so much that which concerned the great ones of the realm but the fact that James promptly declared that, since he was illegiti-mate – he was a bastard of the Wolf of Badenoch – his earldom, although gained by marriage to Isobel of Mar, fell to the crown, this although the heir by birth was Isobel's nephew, the Lord Erskine. This, after the royal assumption of the earldom of Strathearn from the Gra-hams, set alarm bells ringing in many noble heads. The king now held the earldoms of Carrick, Buchan, Fife, Lennox, Caithness, Strathearn and Mar, and the duke-doms of Rothesay and Albany. How safe were any of their titles and lands? That the king was supreme, once crowned, was accepted; but the earldoms were the ac-knowledged successors of the ancient *ri*, the lesser kings who had elected the Ard Righ, the High King. Was this traditional and renowned order becoming endangered by the present monarch?

At Dunbar, hearing of it all, George judged that James was being unwise in this instance.

Soon thereafter there came about a development long anticipated, although its consequences were not. The Princess Margaret had been betrothed to the Dauphin Louis of France for years. Now, both at the age of thirteen, it was decided that the time had come for the nuptials to be celebrated. An illustrious embassage duly arrived from France, consisting of the ducal Archbishop of Rheims, the Constable, John Stewart of Darnley, King Charles's secretary, the famous poet Alain Chantier, and many other lofty personages. They were given a great welcome, whatever the girl-bride's feelings on the matter; and a suitable Scots escort assembled to conduct her to the kingdom of which she was one day to be queen. A fleet, consisting of three large vessels and six lesser ones was gathered, to which George contributed the *Lammerlaw*, although he did not volunteer to accompany the bridal retinue himself, sending brother David. William, Earl of Orkney, nowise one of the endangered earldoms, was put in charge, supported by John, Bishop of Brechin, the Treasurer Sir Walter Ogilvy, and other barons and knights. These, with the French ship, set sail from Leith with much ceremonial, this in August 1436.

The Auld Alliance was being emphasised.

It took only a week or two to demonstrate that the English recognised the fact and strongly disapproved. Gloucester, in King Henry's name, despatched a fleet to block the narrows of the Channel to prevent the Scots ships taking their princess to her new country.

Presumably King Charles and his advisers had been apprised of some such move, for precautions were taken, odd ones indeed, but which carefully did not amount to any outright act of war. A group of Flemish merchant-ships, laden with wine, was sent to get involved with the English vessels, making no secret of their cargoes and, if assailed, limpingly to flee from these. This temptation proved effective in dispersing somewhat the Channel-

359

blockers temporarily; and while these wine-ships were being pillaged, over quite a wide area, a fleet of Spanish warships, hired for the occasion, arrived on the scene, and was able to threaten the distracted English without actually doing battle. In the confusion, the Scots convoy slipped through, and thereafter was able to get safely round the Brest peninsula and into the Bay of Biscay, and thence on to La Rochelle. From there the bride's party had proceeded on to Tours, where the King and Queen of France awaited them, and the significant marriage, so long planned, was solemnised, with glee as well as pomp.

England had suffered an odd reverse indeed.

When word of all this reached Scotland there was much amusement throughout the land. But James was wrath. His daughter might well have been captured, as he himself had been all those years before on *his* way to France, by those piratical English; and this surely a dire contravention of the Treaty of London. He certainly could not ignore it.

But what to do?

It so happened that at this time more foreign shipping entered the scene, Italian on this occasion, bringing the much-awaited cannonry from that Colleoni, no very great armory but a selection of small bombards, sakers and falconets. James, eager as he was to try them out, and to demonstrate his anger at the offence offered to his daughter, decided that Roxburgh Castle was the obvious testing-ground.

Another expedition to the Borderland, then.

Gavin, as Chief Warden of the Marches, had to be present again. And George, involved in this of the artillery search, felt that he had to be there also.

So it was back to the junction of Tweed and Teviot once more, that troublesome spot on the very edge of the kingdom so important to the monarch.

George and Gavin were there before James arrived with the cannon, for these had to be slowly drawn by oxen. With a fair company of men they halted well back from the castle on the Tweed meadow, no reaction evident from the garrison. Quite a cavalcade in time arrived, for there had to be carts laden with balls and sacks of powder as well as the weapons themselves. Much interest was aroused, needless to say, in the ordnance – whatever the Englishmen in the castle thought and could see. There were three each of bombards, sakers and falcons, and no great supply of the necessary balls to fire from them.

The trouble was, of course, that nobody was trained in how to operate it all. George found himself being looked upon as the most knowledgeable, which was far from the fact, his information being solely what the Tower Constable, Howard, had told him, and that was elementary. Yet James seemed to be relying on him.

He declared to the little group round the king what he remembered as to details, emphasising the dangers of upwards and outwards explosions, the need for fairly lengthy fuses to enable the lighters thereof to get away to a safe distance before powder in the cavity was ignited; the fact that the explosion tended to jerk back the cannon at the same time as propelling the ball up the barrel, and so must not be stood behind closely. The heat generated by the detonation on the iron must be remembered, and care taken not to put in more powder too soon, any more than burning the hands. As to the ranges of the various pieces he knew not, and however near to the target stonework the bombards had to be placed to be effective. Even just how much powder to put into those holes. They must learn by trial and error – only to be careful indeed in their attempts at finding out.

James was all impatience to make a start. They would begin with the bombards, presumably the most effective for what they wanted, to smash down masonry, their name indicating so. There were four sacks of powder, but whether they differed in contents, or for use in different weapons, they knew not. The king himself insisted on trying his hand at the business first, to give a lead, however much George sought to dissuade him. At this stage, of course, they were well back from the castle banking and walls, well out of bow-shot, fully four hundred yards.

Selecting a piece, James poured a cupful of powder from one of the sacks into the breech cavity, so as not quite to fill it, in the cause of safety. Then he uncoiled a length of fuse, a ribbon-like cord which had been soaked in saltpetre. How long to make it? With flint, steel and tinder he lit a sample short length of it, and found it to burn quite fast, with sparks and crackle. They did not have an endless supply of this fuse, so must not waste it. But they reckoned that a yard of it as trial would serve. No ball down the barrel at this stage.

So, bedding an end of the fuse cord in the powder hole, the king stood back and lit the other end, dropping the burning line and hastening further away. Actually the burning took longer than they had anticipated, so there need not be so long a fuse used.

The explosion when it came, with a great flash, was certainly loud and strong enough to all but deafen those present, and to envelop them in clouds of black smoke. Whether or not it would have driven a ball along the barrel or burst upwards they could not tell. They went to examine the used bombard, which had indeed jerked backwards, and found the barrel red-hot, which seemed to be a good sign. They would not risk putting more powder in this one meantime, therefore.

They had learned that a much shorter fuse was required, and probably not so much powder. But all were cheered by their first trial.

Choosing another bombard, James tried again, this time seeking to find a stone ball that fitted the barrel, these varying in size. With a rod they rammed this as far down as it would go. Then the lighting of a considerably shorter fuse, and with less powder in the pan, but standing as far back thereafter.

This time the bang seemed almost as loud but there was rather less smoke – but enough to prevent them seeing whether or not the ball had been hurled. How to tell? They could not see down the barrel. But the mouth of it was hot, so the probability was that it had gone.

James sent watchers right and left some short distance, to be able to see the fall of shot not observable because of the smoke. He tried again, using the same amounts of fuse and powder.

This time the observers did report progress. A fountain of soil had been tossed up none so far from the banking of the castle-mound.

So far, so good. They must move that bombard closer, obviously. But it was working.

The company advanced with the weaponry. But quickly arrows began to come at them from the castle. The garrison must have longbows therefore; this was beyond any crossbow range. But it did mean that they could not risk much closer approach, unfortunately. Was it worth trying a little more powder to increase their own range?

They did so, and the result was a very loud crash and a blast of hot air, with some fragments in the faces of the watchers, although the ball was reported to be making an impact at the foot of the castle-bank.

They were learning. A slight overdose of powder.

But the lesson had its gloomy side. The shot was reaching the bank, yes – but the foot thereof, not the top and its walling. They were not getting the necessary height. This all along had been George's fear. The bombard barrels could not be elevated. So what? It was suggested that if they dug a little mound of earth in front of the weapon, and ran it up the side of this, it might serve to send the shot higher.

This was done, and the bombard pushed up at a slant. This, fired, produced a worse blast from the breech, the powder evidently, being thus canted, tending to explode outwards rather than forward.

James had the mound of soil reduced, so that the angle was less steep. The result was that the ball was reported as striking some way up the high bank, but not far enough to reach the masonry.

Frustrated, they debated. They were using up their powder and modest supply of balls, and to no effect.

Any nearer approach and they could suffer serious casualties from the defending bowmen. The bombard's range was just insufficient.

It was decided to try one of the sakers, a smaller piece with a narrower barrel firing lesser balls and using less powder. This, tipped up and fired, did send a missile to make a slight spurt of dust from the castle walling, but not sufficient to do any real damage.

They were balked, for the falconets were still smaller.

It was Gavin who suggested boats, on the Teviot. Would it be possible to load the bombards on boats, and tipping them up to fire effectively from that side?

Doubts were expressed. What would be the effect of the detonation on a small boat? And the men in it? They would be too close to the cannon. They could be struck by the recoil. The craft itself damaged, possibly capsized. They could try it, but . . .

All this had taken a considerable time. It was decided to camp for the night. At least they were besieging the wretched castle. The king and his close supporters would pass the night at Kelso, and arrange for boats to be sailed upriver in the morning.

Thoughts of this of firing from craft occupied their minds, none very hopeful. Gavin now proposed two boats together, with the use of a much longer fuse, which would give time for the lighter to leave the one with the bombard, get into the other, and be pulled away out of danger. Again doubts expressed, but it could be tried.

In the morning, this experiment took time and effort. First the bombard that was to test it had to be drawn back to Kelso, and with difficulty lifted on to the largest boat they could find, the weight of it a major problem, and the setting of it thereafter on a platform of planking based on the oarsmen's seats, this the only solution. The tipping up of the barrel therefrom was anything but easy, however necessary. And there was little room left for the fuse-lighter aboard. This would have to be done from the second boat, and the lighted fuse tossed over to the other as they pulled away.

Gavin gallantly volunteered to be the lighter on this occasion, since it all was his idea.

It was midday before the two craft could set off, with head-shakings but good wishes, the one towing the other, with the bombard already loaded, The king and George and the others rode off along Teviotside, to watch.

The oarsmen and Gavin took shields with them, for on the river they would be within easy range of the English bowmen, this an additional hazard.

Level with the castle, the two boats were laid side by side. Gavin climbed over into the one with the cannon, checked that all was in order as far as it could be, cramped as it had to be. Arrows promptly came winging over to them, these striking against the wall of shields the oarsmen erected, although one nearly struck the unprotected Gavin. He climbed back to comparative safety, lit the fuse and tossed it over to the other boat. The rowers pulled away hastily.

They had considered the river's current, but it proved to be stronger than they had anticipated, and the unmanned craft swung round and came drifting after the escaping one, causing the oarsmen to pull the more urgently.

When the explosion came, amidst the inevitable smoke, the watchers on the horses at the riverbank saw the result before the boatmen did. And it was disaster. The cannon, hurled backwards with great force, smashed through the timbers of the boat and plunged over into the river, the craft itself heeling over and beginning to sink. Where the ball went there was no knowing. Fortunately the men in the other boat escaped injury.

Roxburgh Castle was safe from cannon-fire from the river. And Gavin was crestfallen, however commended for his efforts.

So there was nothing for it but normal siegery, nobody coming up with any further suggestions as to better artillery strategy.

*　　*　　*

They remained camped around the castle for a few days, James loth to leave it, however much the nation's affairs demanded his presence elsewhere. The Roxburgh garrison showed no signs of yielding. At least the besiegers' leaders could spend comfortable nights in Kelso Abbey.

Then, surprisingly, the situation changed for the monarch, and this by the arrival of none other than his wife, Queen Joan. She came in agitation and urgency. A plot had been reported, and more than a plot. This to unseat James from the throne, a dire threat. It was the Grahams and their friends again, with Uncle Walter of Atholl in the background. Sir Robert Graham had actually sent a letter to James renouncing his allegiance to him as king, and demanding a parliament to be called to declare the monarch an impostor on account of his father's bastardy. He had scorned the gift of the Menteith earldom as an empty title, and passed it on to his nephew, Malise, son of Sir Patrick Graham of Kincardine, who was a mere youth presently resident in England. Walter of Atholl should be on the throne, as brother of the late Albany, both sons of the second and lawful marriage of King Robert the Second, the first marriage being invalid. Graham was being backed, he said, in this demand for a parliamentary decision by largely unspecified magnates, mainly Stewarts it appeared, even including Sir Robert Stewart, the High Chamberlain, a close associate of the king.

This grim and intolerable word emanated from the Highlands, where Robert Graham was presently hiding himself, and said to be seeking the support of Alexander of the Isles in his efforts; and from where he declared that a renowned Highland seer had predicted that Walter of Atholl would be wearing the crown before the year was out, and that his successor should be Sir Robert Stewart, Chamberlain, his son.

Needless to say the queen's tidings had James in a ferment of hot indignation. This must be dealt with immediately and with the greatest severity. Roxburgh would have to wait. He would call a parliament, yes –

but it would be *his* parliament. Meantime, his force here would disperse, but be ready to marshal to his standard, if required, in fullest strength and at short notice.

Astonished and scarcely able to believe it all, George and Gavin, with their men, saw the king and queen on their way northwards, before swinging off for Dunbar.

There they did not have long to wait before news reached them. A parliament was indeed called by the monarch, at Edinburgh, not Perth, this for 22nd October, all loyal commissioners to be present. And meantime a large sum in gold was offered for the apprehension of the traitorous Graham.

That parliament, considering the momentous reason behind its calling, was deliberately normal as to order and arrangement, the Chancellor instructed to have it so. James, after scanning the quite large attendance present, and noting that neither Atholl nor any of the Grahams, nor even the realm's Chamberlain, were there, announced briefly in level voice that there had been some shameful and traitorous ongoings reported to him concerning some who ought to know better; but that these would be taken care of; and all this parliament was called on to do, at this stage, was to indicate its faithful support for the crown, this before proceeding on to the important business of the session.

There were the required expressions of loyal duty in murmurs and exclamations and some cheering. Then the king handed over to the Chancellor, Bishop Cameron of Glasgow.

The motions and resolutions that followed were such as most of the lords, at least, found boring, although the representatives of cities and royal burghs less so, also the churchmen – and George, of course, much concerned. The matters were almost all connected with trade and industry, and the consequent effect on the realm's prosperity, this also to help the national treasury through duties on exports and imports. First, there had been a large increase in the import of English cloths and clothing, as a result of improved trade, and this was damaging commerce with the Low Countries, France and the Germanic states, to the displeasure of the Hanseatic League. This must be halted, by fines being imposed. Also shipbuilding was not being undertaken as much as was desirable, and this was limiting their exports. The towns and harbours of Lothian, Fife, Angus, Aberdeen and Moray were urged to improve on this. There was no lack of timber available; and the churchmen, in especial, could play a greater part in this important matter. The national money situation fell to be regulated, especially over silver for the coinage. This was tending to vary in value according to trading demands, which was not desirable. The worth of silver metal should be stabilised, so that all could rely on it for security, in the value of lands, employment and industrial production. Silver should hereafter be valued by weight.

And so on. The Lords of the Articles were to see that these decisions were carried out effectively.

Archibald Douglas was present on this occasion, but kept a low profile. He and George had a discussion later over this Graham threat to the throne. They came to the conclusion that, while it was shameful indeed, it was not likely seriously to endanger the monarch, few probably supporting it, even though there was perturbation among the nobility over James's policy of repossessing and acquiring earldoms.

Douglas had not forgiven the monarch for his internment in this Edinburgh Castle, however comfortable his quarters had been. It rankled when he reminded himself that he had a manpower sufficient to unseat the king, if so he pleased, even though these Grahams and Atholl had not.

George returned home wondering what James was going to do about this of Sir Robert Graham renouncing fealty and allegiance. It could not just be left and ignored as the behaviour of a resentful and foolish individual. So far there was no word of others following his lead. The king had clearly made a point of belittling it in his opening address to the parliament. But something was called for, surely. Would anyone choose to try to win that golden reward for delivering up Graham to his rejected liege-lord? Who *could* – other than perhaps Alexander of the Isles, with his hordes of Highlandmen?

39

George and his son and brothers Gavin and David, like so many others of high position in the realm, were called by the king to attend a very especial Christmas and Yuletide celebration at the turn of the year, at Perth. This was mainly to welcome the papal legate to Scotland, Aeneas Silvius Piccolomini, who was expected to be the next Pontiff.

They arrived from Dunbar to find the town even fuller than at parliament times, and therefore were thankful to have their quarters on the *Deuchrie* to sleep in, instead of having to search for accommodation in the crowded town and its environs. The king and royal family were, as usual, in residence in the Blackfriars monastery.

George was distinctly surprised to see Walter, Earl of Atholl present, despite his name being so linked with that of the Grahams; but of course he was the king's uncle, and his son, Sir Robert Stewart, the High Chamberlain and therefore close to James. Atholl appeared to be lodging at Scone, three miles away, and did not make his presence very evident.

Great were the festivities. The legate Piccolomini was a most notable character in more than his position in Holy Church, a famous poet and writer, who had been acting for the Vatican all over Christendom. James was delighted to welcome him to his realm; it seemed that he had used it to make some sort of pilgrimage to the White Kirk of Tyninghame, this none so far from Dunbar, where George's ancestress Black Agnes had been cured of some ailment by water from a holy well there, which had thereafter become renowned for its healing properties. That the legate should have known of this was extraordinary. He now amusedly complained that since it seemed such pilgrimage should be made barefooted, in their Scottish winter conditions he might well require some holy water bathing on his way back, to salve his damaged feet! He proved a congenial guest, and congratulations over Scotland's support of France the main reason for the visit.

The celebrations went on well beyond Yuletide, and presently George decided that he had had a sufficiency, and wanted to get back to Beatrix. So he left his brother David as his representative, took leave of James, and sailed back to Dunbar with Gavin whose duties as Warden of the Marches called him.

It was early February when the utterly appalling news reached them. King James was dead. He had been assassinated, at Perth, and this by Graham, come down from the Highlands to join his fellow-conspirators – and these had included the Chamberlain, Sir Robert Stewart, Atholl's son, whose closeness to the monarch had enabled the murderers to reach James when he and his wife were preparing for bed in the Blackfriars monastery. And George's own brother David was seriously wounded in seeking to defend the king.

George sailed for Perth, in stunned and major distress, to bring David back from the monastery where the monks were caring for him.

From them, and his brother, he learned the grim details, or some of them. The monarch's armed attackers, allowed into the royal quarters by the Chamberlain, had met with resistance from David and other loyal defenders, and in the resultant noise and clash of weapons, James had become warned to some extent and sought to bar the door. But the door-bar had been removed. The clamour at an outer door indicated courtiers attacked, this when brother David slew one and disabled another before himself being sorely wounded. James had recognised his great danger. He hid himself in an underground cellar, actually a drainage passage reached by a trapdoor in the bedroom flooring, ordering the room door somehow to be barred. The queen and her two ladies-in-waiting, both Douglases as it happened, Catherine and a younger Elizabeth, could find nothing to be used as bar to slot into the four great iron hook-like staples in stonework and door timbers. Gallantly Catherine had used her arm instead as a drawbar. But the invaders, hurling themselves at the door, smashed it open, breaking the young woman's arm in the process, six of them, led by Robert Graham, plunging in. Finding the monarch missing, and demanding his whereabouts and not being told, they struck the queen, and dragging her away, discovered the trapdoor on which she had been standing. Daggers drawn, they opened this and jumped down upon the unarmed and indeed unclothed king, to stab and stab, Graham himself finishing the dreadful business. So James, King of Scots, passed from one kingdom to a better one.

Apparently thereafter, in all the ferment and confusion, Queen Joan had been spirited out of the monastery by loyal servants and the monks, and carried, with her children, the young James, now king-to-be, and his sisters, to Stirling Castle, where they were now in the care of Sir Alexander Livingstone, the keeper. At least they should be safe meantime in that impregnable royal citadel.

Devastated, mind in a whirl with all this, George began to wonder as to his own position now, as of other of King James's and his queen's friends. What was expected of them? Atholl, now next heir to the throne after the six-year-old boy, would be in supreme command of the realm, with his evil Grahams and other supporters. Almost certainly he would seek to get rid of his grand-nephew if he could. And possibly, the late monarch's friends also, himself included? What to do about it all, he who was no warrior? Douglas – probably he was the man to consult. A visit to Threave, then?

He did not have to do that, however, for who should arrive at Dunbar Castle a few days later but James Douglas of Balvenie, uncle of Archibald, a huge bear of a man, sent by the earl. And with a grim message. Archibald was ill, it seemed, or he would have come himself; indeed this uncle was much concerned for his health. But that was not why he had come. He had been sent to warn George. He, Douglas, had learned that Atholl and the Grahams were determined to weed out the murdered king's friends, just as George had begun to fear, those who might actively support the queen and young James; and the Earl of Dunbar and March was seen as one such, and had been specifically named as to be disposed of. Douglas himself was probably in no great danger, for he had been known often to be at odds with the king, even imprisoned by him. Also his large manpower and remote Galloway base would protect him. But he was concerned for his friend. These assassins were utterly unscrupulous and determined. Did George want to see his earldoms turned into what would amount to an armed camp, and to keep them that way? And would even such precautions be effective? If they could find means to kill the king himself, would such as George be safe?

Balvenie had come, therefore, to advise his friend to leave the kingdom for a while. The menace was very much there. His earldoms had been declared forfeited to the crown, on the pretext that his father, Cospatrick, had been declared traitor and paid allegiance to the King of England, so that the son was holding his patrimony unlawfully. Also his brother David had taken arms against Atholl's cause, and slain one of his important allies. And the other brother Gavin had promptly been dismissed as Chief Warden of the Marches – Balvenie himself was West March Warden – and another, Patrick, was known to be a very dangerous man. So a departure out of Scotland, for a period, would be wise for the family. They had lands in England, did they not, given by Bolingbroke? A spell there, in the meantime, until it was seen how matters went under this new and shameful regime. Atholl was an elderly man, and might not live very long, if he was not unseated anyway. There could, before too long, be a nationwide rising to support the young James. This was Douglas's advice and urging for his friend.

George found himself at something of a loss, needless to say. But Beatrix, desperately worried, pleaded with him to pay heed to this warning. His life could depend on it. Let them go down to the Lincolnshire manor and be secure, until Scotland was safe for them again.

Pate, at Colbrandspath, was more in favour of raising men and fighting it out.

Gavin arrived next day from the Borderland, angry, and alarmed also. He had been dismissed like some scullion, and threatened. It was intolerable, and dangerous.

George sent for the remaining brothers, Colin, John and Patrick.

Presently they were all sitting round a table in Dunbar Castle, with Beatrix and Pate, to consider every aspect of the situation, David also there, recovering from his wound. The discussion went back and forward, for long. Patrick strongly supported Pate over making a fight for it, on their own ground. Gavin tended to agree with them, but was concerned with precautions. Colin and John, the least assertive of the brothers, favoured the move south, and of course Beatrix was not silent on the issue, the safety of her beloved her prime essential. But it was the injured David who really swayed them to decision. He had been closest to the dire events, knew the temper, abilities and utter ruthlessness of the enemy. He opted for a departure for Lincolnshire, at least for the time being.

George clinched it by reminding them all of his vassals, the Hays, the Setons, the Lindsays, the Homes, the Swintons and the Kerrs and others. Were all these to be sacrificed to warfare with the present rulers of the land? With their common folk? Did he not owe them his protection? And not only in their safety from oppression, but in their well-being and prosperity? This of trade and wealth of the earldom had its own great importance. It could be maintained, he felt fairly sure, from England. Their ships could link Dunbar and Boston, on the Wash. He and his would not sit idle on their Nanneby property. Commerce could continue with the Low Countries and the Baltic. And they could develop sheep-rearing more intensively in the Wolds. He, George, was reasonably friendly with the Duke of Gloucester. They should have no trouble there, his father's links with the Plantagenets at least being an advantage in this respect. It was all none so grievous a prospect. And it might not need to last for so very long.

The matter was decided. They would go south, and very shortly, in case of any swift descent upon them here. But some of them would keep coming back to Scotland, to remain in touch with their various properties and people. They would not act tame exiles. They were, after all, the Cospatricks.

George wondered whether, perhaps, the very fact that they *were* the Cospatricks lay behind Atholl's and the others' hatred and fears, since they could claim to be the true heirs to the Scots crown. The end of the line, indeed.

EPILOGUE

The settling in on the extensive Nanneby property in Lincolnshire took time, of course, but the brothers were well pleased with it all, seeing the countryside as favourable and the Wolds in especial to their taste, Pate also. Fortunately there were lesser manor-houses and farmeries dotted about the estate to provide quarters for them all to occupy and make use of, so that Beatrix did not have them all to put up in their own establishment. There were no reactions from London.

Months passed as they awaited news from Scotland. The first they heard, of any consequence, was that, in some unexplained fashion, the keepership of Stirling Castle, and therefore the custody of Queen Joan and the young King James the Second, with his sisters, had been transferred from Sir Alexander Livingstone to Sir William Crichton of that Ilk, who had been Master of the Household to the late monarch, and who ought to prove a suitable guardian for the royal family meantime. This information came to them by means of a letter brought by a mendicant friar from Archibald Douglas. He declared in it that he was ailing still, but was seeking to do what he could to stir up the lords, magnates and senior churchmen of the realm to bring to justice the assassins of the late king, and have the new child-monarch crowned. This was good news.

The next they heard was still better. Douglas and his allies had succeeded in toppling Atholl, who had adopted the style of regent of Scotland, and he and his son, Sir Robert Stewart, had in fact been beheaded. Douglas himself was declared Lieutenant General of the Kingdom at a parliament held at Holyrood in Edinburgh, although that man was too sick to attend, and plans were being made for the boy's crowning, but not at Scone Abbey, the traditional coronation place, for Perth and the north were still in the hands of the Grahams and their friends. So there were fears for the future of the monarchy still. And Douglas, however active of mind, was now confined to Threave.

Rejoicing over the end of Atholl and the former Chamberlain, the Cospatrick family debated as to what they should do now. It was decided that Gavin and David should sail north – for their ships continued to make calls into the Wash now and again on their way to and from the Netherlands – to discover whether or not it was safe for a return to be made to Scotland. Gavin would test out south of the Forth and Clyde, and seek to contact Douglas; while David, who had the property of Kilconquhar in Fife, would learn what he could of the more hostile north.

It was a month before Gavin got back, and with a report very mixed as to its reception. Douglas was bed-bound, his son, the Earl of Wigtown, fearing that *he* would be the Duke of Touraine any day now. The Grahams, now calling themselves Earls of Strathearn and Menteith, and their allies, dominated all, including the earldoms of Mar, Atholl and Buchan. And an extraordinary situation had developed in the Lowlands. The two hitherto comparatively minor barons, Livingstone and Crichton, had become rivals in their grip on the young king, who had been hastily crowned, and was being held alternately in the citadels of Edinburgh and Stirling, depending on which happened to be his keeper; and so in fact these two were seeking to rule the land meantime in the royal name, however much they were known to hate each other, a state of affairs which clearly could not last. Queen Joan was no longer with her son, having sought the help of various loyal Stewarts against these two upstarts, and was said to be at present actually in the south-western Highlands in the care of Sir John Stewart of Lorn, known as the Black Knight.

This upheaval and confusion in their homeland had George and Beatrix all but bewildered, and thankful for the peace of their Lincolnshire Wolds.

377

David returned in due course, with the word that Archibald Douglas was dead, and that the new earl-duke had gone to France. Conditions in Scotland were all but chaotic. Hepburn was holding Dunbar Castle still, however, but strongly advised against any return there of its master and mistress until some sort of order and stability was effected in the land, guidance accepted by George, even though his brothers regarded it less favourably.

David was going back, he hoped permanently, to occupy his Kilconquhar barony. And he said that the Moray earldom was now in the hands of a youthful kinsman, who needed guidance and support. He judged that his brothers might well go and establish themselves up there, where Black Agnes had come from, and might do well for themselves as well as for the young earl, in an area not involved in the turbulence elsewhere. For Alexander of the Isles had regained a firm grip on the Great Glen, Inverness and Ross, and the Grahams were anxious not to offend him, while Livingstone and Crichton had no least interest in such faraway parts.

The other brothers agreed with this suggestion, and said that George also might be reasonably secure up there. But that man was otherwise minded, with his wife's strong support. They were very well content here at Nanneby, finding life pleasant, without stress, and with no urge to become active in Scots affairs again, whether or not the earldoms of Dunbar and March still existed after their official forfeiture. Also here, from nearby Boston, George was able to supervise the commerce and trade on which his Dunbar folk so much depended. This he certainly could not do from Moray. He would remain. Pate could do what he thought best, but this was the place for his parents. It might be the end of the line for the Cospatrick earls – but that suited himself and Beatrix Hay.

And it was so. These two never returned to Scotland. There had been eleven earls of Dunbar and March. There would never be a twelfth. Scotland must do without them, if it could.